Strange Adventures

Strange Adventures

by
Mark R. Sneller

Published by Fresh Air Press

Visit Mark's website at
marksneller.com

This edition was prepared for publication by
Ghost River Images
5350 East Fourth Street
Tucson, Arizona 85711
www.ghostriverimages.com

ISBN 978-1-7368917-0-4

Library of Congress Control Number: 2021905184

Printed in the United States of America
April 2021

Other books Mark R. Sneller:

A Breath of Fresh Air

Greener Cleaner Indoor Air–a Guide to Healthier Living – 2nd Edition

Toxic Exposure

Dying to Read

The Mars Virus

The City Beneath The Earth

Contents

AUTHOR'S NOTE

As a teenager, I fell in love with stories about great scientists and doctors who discovered germs and defined the germ theory of disease. I also became captivated by science fiction and years later, managed to meld the two in many of my writings. When I look over those stories and novels, with the exception of *The Mars Virus* novel, I find that many of them have a common theme: the betterment of the human condition. This betterment comes about through accidental good fortune mixed in with tossing rocks into still waters. There is also the occasion when I chide the human race for our preoccupation with sniping at one another, when in reality, as a species, we can be a whole lot of fun.

Admittedly, there is a certain amount of extremism in some of the stories. To my thinking, that represents the ultimate in idealism. A few of the the stories in this volume are based on personal experience (e.g. *The Incubator, The fight at the Poker Game*).

Another (*Entity*) evolved from a single sentence that grabbed me when I read Stephen Crane's short story *The Open Boat*. Others followed the question: What would happen if? *(Time Zone, The Magical Powers of Laszlo Pearce, Telepathy School)* and still others are just silliness *(Soap Opera, The Floozy)*. Finally, I included a collection of Jeffrey Shenero short stories, in keeping with my Shenero novels *Toxic Exposure* and *Dying to Read*. These stories include: *The Incubator, The Mushroom Caves of Palau, Arena Games,* and *When the Devil Went to College.*

As always, I hope the reader enjoys this varied assortment of tales as much as I enjoyed writing them.

THE INCUBATOR

I refuse to die with freaking black bread mold growing on my skin and inside my organs and brain in a humidity chamber, as if I were a loaf of bread in a sealed package.

We were holed up in a home on the outskirts of Lawton Oklahoma, about an hour's drive from Oklahoma City, southwest along U.S. Highway 44, and slightly less if you're coming from the University of Oklahoma in Norman.

Let's keep it simple: A very unpleasant death appeared to be the singular option because of its utter grossness.

We were entombed in a life-sized culture dish, or, death-sized, if you will, solidly trapped in a warm room with mold growing at our feet and which was beginning to grow on and in our bodies. Only one uncertainty remained: the manner of our death: Would it be a slow respiratory strangulation or would it occur by some unknown and probably hitherto undescribed affliction?

Unquestionably, none of us would have any desire to die in the manner in which I envisioned and which reality dictated, but I did not tell the others about reality and, by definition, the certainty of reality.

A cloudless sky greeted me in the cool morning air as I left Norman, Oklahoma, and drove to Lawton. My schedule was such that I had no lab sections or classes to teach on Fridays, effectively giving me three full days a week off. When you're married to a university, you're never really off, but it was close enough. Carmen, my secretary/office manager would answer calls and send out billings generated from my private consulting firm.

My GPS easily located the street in question, this time not spinning me in circles, which it enjoys doing on occasion. I took in the upscale homes in the neighborhood and the quality of the late model vehicles parked in the drives. No cars up on blocks around here. A number of lots were vacant and several had homes under various stages of construction. The housing business appeared to be good in north Lawton.

The Thomas' residence was located in a cul-de-sac off a quiet neighborhood. The two-story red brick house sat upon a good rise, with a view of a small lake to the south. A similar style home stood next to it to the west. Vacant lots occupied the remaining portion of the immediate area with dogwood and elm trees predominating the local vegetation. An occasional towering pine made its point.

Pulling into the large drive of the hillside home with my SUV, I parked behind one of two pickup trucks already in the drive. One of them was a clean white Ford 150. Lettering on the door read: "Ted's A/C and Heating, Lawton OK," with a phone number beneath the lettering. I looked upward and saw two men on the roof working on the air conditioning units. Presumably the units belonged to the upper and the lower portions of the home. Music blared from a small radio near where the men worked.

The second truck, the one I parked behind, was a beat-up old Toyota with some dents on the driver's side. The rear bumper had been displaced. On the door were the words "Ken's Restorations—We serve all of Oklahoma," painted in red. Smaller letters presented a phone number.

I moaned. From riches to rags. From cheery sunlight to darkness in a flash. Please, not that Ken. Jeff, bail out now or enter the twilight zone.

Indeed, to reinforce my bad decision to see what could go wrong, to ensure Murphy's Law had not vacated the premises, my old nemesis, Mister Crew Cut Ken Bradley, stepped out of his truck to greet me. Apparently, an insurance company had made a terrible mistake and hired Ken's Restorations to conduct the repairs. Notice I didn't say, "Complete the repairs."

"Junk people drive junk cars," somebody had once told me. While that didn't apply to most professional people with whom I associated, but in

Ken's case, it couldn't be a truer statement.

Nose-and-Tongue Ring Ronnie, his six-month-pregnant well-tattooed bimbo assistant stepped out of the passenger side wearing cutoffs and sneakers. Her pink butch haircut was an added perk to her dress ensemble.

I suspected that Ken had already trained Ronnie in other matters. No doubt his former wives would agree. The rumor was that he'd already had three divorces and was making child support payments for five children. The expenses were killing him. After the first two, he swore off women and got married again with the understanding there would be no babies. His latest divorcee assured him that she was fixed and there was no way she would have any children. Triplets. Then came the divorce. Couldn't have happened to a more upstanding citizen. Now Ronnie had entered the picture.

She was not without her own issues. She'd moved from company to company because of a modest background in her father's construction business. She was fired each time for various violations related to "consorting issues." Obviously, Ken's Restoration found that she possessed the necessary skills to be an important adjunct to his business. This suggested that she'd worked for him close to three months, plus or minus, given the state of her pregnancy.

When the call came to my office, Carmen, my wife and office manager, was told that the homeowners, Thomas by name, would be gone for the day.

Both wife and husband were attorneys. She worked in Lawton. He worked in Oklahoma City. Carmen told me to get the key from the man next door to the south. We scheduled the time that I would inspect the area of the home that had the problem. Nobody told me that Mister Wonderful would be there.

In this particular case, a water supply line to the upstairs bath had broken thanks to city pressure testing. A retired neighbor who watched homes for the neighborhood had discovered the water loss soon after it occurred and had called a plumber to prevent further damage after checking with one of the Thomas's. The hour when the pressure testing had occurred was unknown. The city wasn't talking. It never does.

I can formulate a number of reasons why we do things against our better judgment. These reasons might include desire to please, desire for a better outcome than the first or second time, bucking heads with fate because you were in the mood to do so, a poor perspective on the problem at hand, and so forth.

Therefore, despite my better judgment based on hard lessons, common sense, and a screaming voice in my head to run away, I agreed to permit both Ken and Ronnie to accompany me, and thusly, had permitted bad luck to be my partner for the job. In a word, it all fell on my head.

Neither of us even thought about shaking hands when we met that day. Our shared experiences go back years when somebody had to fix his messes.

Why he remained in business was beyond the cognizance of this feeble mind.

As if he had been called by name, the neighbor came out of his house with the key and introduced himself as Walter Fitzgerald. Walter appeared to be somewhere in his seventies with most of his faculties. Everybody in the neighborhood relied on him to look after their home in their absence, according to him. Walter shook hands with Ken and said, "Say, we met a few days ago. Right? You too," he said to Ronnie.

"She was here with you?" I asked Ken.

"She needs the experience," he replied.

Walter and I shook hands. The top two buttons of his shirt were undone and I could see a lengthy well-healed scar beginning from the top of the breast bone and dropping down beyond sight; a sure indication of open heart surgery.

Walter led us to the front door, inserted the key and bade us enter the domicile. "Can I see what you've done so far?" he asked to nobody in particular.

"Sorry, Walter, we don't like non-work personnel to enter a contained area."

"Oh, it isn't contained," responded Ken. "There was no need to."

"Then I can go in," Walter said, enthusiastically.

"Sure," responded Ken.

"No, you can't," I stated flatly. "It's against regulations."

Walter looked at Ken who just shrugged. If that

was an emotion from Ken, it might be the first one ever observed. Walter waited an instant and saw that I remained resolute, so he returned to his house. The three of us entered through the unlocked front door and Ken led us up about fifteen steps to a balcony area with a railing that overlooked the great room. The home was well appointed. The homeowners had good taste in artwork and furnishings.

Ken led us down the hall to the bathroom at the end of the hall on the right. The door was only partially closed, not contained in heavy-gauge plastic, and wasn't taped shut. An air return register was set in the ceiling outside the bathroom.

Before the bath we passed one bedroom and across the hall lay two more. Ken told me that his company had removed the upper layer of flooring from the water damage and needed an inspection and clearance test to determine if there was any mold present. I was reluctant to permit a pregnant woman to be on-site under conditions where the unknown prevailed, but Ken assured me that we would be in and out of the bad area within five or six minutes. Also, he wanted her to gain more experience.

Ken pushed on the swollen oak door and it refused to be moved. Then he placed his steroid-fed right shoulder against the door and pushed. The door opened, albeit reluctantly. "Tell you what," he said, proudly, "What's inside sure stays inside."

I entered the room and hauled along a collapsible tripod, a cosmetic case containing air pump, collection cassettes, and other accouterments necessary for air and surface testing. Ronnie and Ken followed me. As I opened my mouth to caution him, Ken leaned his hulking shoulder against the door and slammed it shut.

Once inside, I flipped on the light switch and five one-hundred watt bulbs were reflected off the vanity mirror. The bathroom was simple with a single-sink vanity and a step-in shower; no tub. The door to the shower was open and I could see the shower surround consisted of a single piece of wrap-around plastic. A small window was located above the surround. *Pretty cheap for a custom built home, I thought*. At the same time I saw that the floor was completely black. Taking it for glue-down mastic, I asked Ken about it because the place reeked terribly with eye and throat-burning pungency. "There is no mastic. This is just the layer between the upper and lower portion of the sub-flooring. We cut the floor in a jiffy and that was that," he retorted matter-of-factually.

No, that was not that. My mental alarm bells went off and I immediately took out a quick sticky tape surface sampler and touched it to the black floor we were standing on. My portable microscope didn't lie and neither did my nose. This could only bespeak of formaldehyde, octanol, along with a score of petrochemicals produced by actively growing mold.

Looking up from the microscope, I provided the male portion of my audience with the bad news trying to hide the quaver in my voice, yet smiling all the while. Trust me, the smile was not for fun, it was out of great fear. "Did the thought ever cross your mind that whatever you do, you do it wrong? We are standing on what looks like a pure culture of *Aspergillus niger*. This mold loves to grow on damp structural materials. To the human, it is invasive and does very nicely in persons with a lowered immune response, such as guys like you."

Ronnie looked frightened. Holding her belly, she asked, "Is that as bad as the black mold?"

"It is black," interjected the gym rat, proudly exhibiting his vast knowledge about colors. "That makes it black mold."

It's worse than that, folks. My armpits were beginning to sweat. I said, "No, actually this is the same kind that grows inside your bag of bread." This particular species produced ten thousand times the number of spores than did the reputed famous black mold known as *Stachybotrys*. "Just about any microbe can be harmful under the right circumstances. We have the perfect circumstances right here. You locked the three of us in a trap, Ken. If it grows on wood and petroleum-based glue-downs and bread, and fruit and dust, and soil, why the hell shouldn't it grow on a person's flimsy body?"

I hadn't meant to be so gruff, but Ken is one of those people who knows how to push your buttons. And under these circumstances, there was no reason to skirt the issue. Everybody needed to know the facts so we could all make decisions. "Why do you think your eyes are burning right now?" I threw in as a closer.

"My eyes aren't burning," Ken responded.

"Then those must be tears of joy," I commented. "I estimate that the level of toxic gases is a good hundred times the normal indoor concentration. Face it, if the spores don't get you, the poisons in the air will."

"Then we need to get out of here," Ronnie screeched.

"Exactly," I commented.

"Okay, then, let's go," shrugged Ken, as easily as if he were pumping another set of barbells—dumb-bells in his case—and probably wondering what all the fuss was about. He made a move to grab the door handle.

This was getting tedious. "In case you didn't notice, the upstairs air return register is located in the hallway just outside this bathroom, in the 'OFF' cycle when we came in. Now it's 'ON', and if we open the door, the register will suck in spores from this room and send them throughout the home. Then the home will have to be cleaned."

"The filter will take care of that," contributed Ken, smartly, digging deep into his vast warehouse of memorized facts. I wanted to slap him. "And don't talk to me what to do or what to notice," he concluded.

"Somebody has to since your mother isn't here." I tried to push the bastard to the limit, adding, "Were you born stupid or did you take advanced classes?"

My mouth owned me, not the other way around. "First, why didn't you get this vanity out of here?

The commode, as well. You damn well know the mold is going to grow on the particle board of the counter and grow beneath the unit.

"Number two: The filters that are here will not handle spores this small. Basically, whatever is harmful goes in one side of the filter and goes out the other side."

"You're just full of knowledge, doctor. It must be nice to have a career where you get to run people down." We were both seated and were facing eye-to-eye.

"That wasn't the bad news, bubba. That was the good news. The really bad shit will come later," I whispered such that only he could hear it. "You know, when this shit starts to grow out of your nose and mouth. And you made it all happen. Lucky us."

Which probably won't happen until after we were all dead, but I wasn't going to tell him that part. Let the prick think about it.

"I have to pee," whined Ronnie.

"Tie it in a knot," sneered Ken.

I so dearly wanted to throw down with the guy. The kid might be promiscuous, but she was pregnant and had to deal with that while stuck in this bathroom along with the two of arguing.

The man stood six-two and weighed two-thirty. He carried too much belly fat, but one couldn't deny that he possessed a lot of arm and shoulder strength. My bet was that his balls were the size of BBs thanks to years of steroid usage, but they must have been working all right when he entertained

Ronnie. He'd been a bully all his life. It was time for the bullying and life as he knew it to come to an end. As things stood, it could also apply to all of us. (Thankfully, Walter had not been trapped in this room with us when Ken had slammed the door shut. The nightmare could have been a screaming death for all of us.)

In contrast, I stood five-eleven, weighed fifty pounds less and ran a lot. My old college years as a water polo player and karate guy gave me endless memories of the old days. Today, my temperament and drive remain to motivate me every single day.

Ken and I were both in our early forties. I could still hit as hard as ever whenever the seductive temptress of opportunity smiled my way. Right now she was giving me a side-wise, yet encouraging glance, which bespoke the words: "Just a straight shot to the point of the chin." I shoved out further thoughts that are best left unspoken."

Instead, I put my actions into words. If you can't strike while the iron is hot, use a different hot iron. Besides, a good fighting philosophy is this: If you defeat your opponent physically, he can come back to hurt you. If you defeat him in spirit, the victory is permanent. Now, if you defeat him physically and in spirit, it's a fair guess you won the battle.

"Shut up, Ken. You're the one who didn't fix this place properly. You didn't set up a proper dehumidifier; you didn't set up proper protection outside this room. And what were you thinking when you removed the top flooring? You knew there was going to be water retention between the layers of particle board. Boy, are you a royal screw up."

I began to disturb myself. I had become unscientific and too pissed off. Okay, it felt good to become belligerent with this monkey, although that didn't help the cause of self-preservation, especially because the path down the future road frightened the hell out of me. Literally rotting away in a jail cell for hurting this guy held no attraction to me. Neither did trading my life for his. I'd rather rot away in the comfort of my own home with a bottle of quality Russian vodka in my hand than be comfortably ensconced in a jail cell.

My immediate problem had become Ken, as if he were an object, an end goal. On second thought, my immediate problem was my thinking process. Habitually, I face a problem head-on, not avoid it. For some reason, I feel secure doing that. Let the shrinks work that out. Now, I found myself out of character, deflecting, not trying to solve the problem of escape. Instead, I made Ken into the problem, which made absolutely no sense unless my thinking process was becoming warped. There was only one reason for that.

Ken knew I had struck home when I laid into him about his job performance, but the humanoid said nothing. This was a great surprise, because one of his many nicknames is "Ken—my dick is bigger than your dick—Bradley." Normally he would have a retort whenever somebody espoused real knowledge and he'd try to modify your knowledge based on the narrow range of his own life experiences.

I couldn't stop my mouth. If my previous comments didn't hit him in the BBs, maybe the next salvo would do it. My thoughts carried me to the extreme. I teetered between rage and professional behavior, legal versus wanton destruction of another human, yet not concentrating on finding a way out of this mess. My throat was getting sore from the chemicals in the air and from talking so much in this alien environment. "Not only that, Ken, but you screwed up that hospital job last month. You allowed the containment barrier to fall down and you exposed the cancer patients to a high concentration of mold spores that killed two people. Oh, I'm sorry, didn't you follow the cases? I had access to the autopsy reports."

"Hey, don't tell me how to do my job. I've been doing this stuff since I was seventeen," Ken puffed himself up. "How long have you been lording it everybody you meet? I mean, when the word got out you would be on this job, I just tingled with excitement."

"Oh, you got me there, Ken. My parents made me go to school so I could learn to read and write and add and maybe gain a few social skills. So you've been unprofessional a lot longer than I've been professional. The only thing that's going to tingle with you from now on is the loose change in your pocket because that's all that you're going to own. Don't you even care that the same mold spores I identified were the same ones that killed two people?"

"Bullshit, Shenero. They were dying anyway. And nobody can prove that your mold killed them."

My mold? "Wrong again, Bradley. Watch for the coroner's report and make plans for another life. It's called either second or third degree murder. Probably second because your negligence caused the deaths."

Ronnie jumped on the band wagon. "Yeah, Bradley. You're a screw up. That's all you ever do, isn't it? Screw things, up!" Her hands flew to her belly. Another rumor had it that Ronnie always called men by their last name, even in bed.

"Hey," Ken responded defensively, almost flippantly, as the great ape postured. "I hired a bad worker. It can happen to anyone."

"No matter what, you're responsible and you're the bad worker," inserted Ronnie. "I was there. Remember? You told me a whole different story from what the doc here says and I believe him. So, you think this is bad, wait until we get into court. We'll see what I can get for child support. You lied to me, Bradley."

Gee, Ronnie, why beat around the bush? And what did he lie to her about? Did he say he loved her or that he'd make her a partner or that he would give her money or take care of the baby? Knowing Ken, my guess is that he dug himself a hole in which he is presently standing and is proceeding to pull in the dirt behind himself.

The man stared at me as though he had been watching TV for twelve hours straight. But the sub-human refused to give up the fight. From no-where he brought forth a bellow: "Sure, Ronnie, you've got two others you're collecting free money on. What's one more?"

"Back at you," she volleyed, spittle flying from her lips.

Ronnie began to rub her temples. I felt the same way. It wasn't like smelling a little musty dirt. Here, the odors would soon go away, an indication that the chemicals were deadening the sense of smell—a defense mechanism. It could happen with perfume and it could happen with poison. Then our brains would want for oxygen thanks to bad chemicals dissolved in the blood. Our thinking would cloud and things could go very wrong after that. Correction: Our thinking is already clouded.

True as all this might be for the sake of science, we were trapped in a damned bathroom with no obvious way out. "All right, guys. How about we hop onto the vanity so we don't disturb the spores on the floor," I said, doing an about face from my thoughts and deflecting the conversation back to the problem at hand, a good deflection from endless accusation. Generally I use people like Ken as a measuring stick. If one does exactly the opposite of what they suggest, you're bound to be right almost all the time. If the idea had come from him I might have thought there would be something wrong with it and would be tempted to stay where I was.

Parts of the floor puffed up with spores as we moved. Other parts were so wet and slimy that we chanced slipping and falling, if we weren't careful. I knew we were already covered with the tiny life forms and once on the skin or on clothing, each of the millions and billions of tiny three micron-size spores would be sending forth a germ tube, just like a bean projecting a sprout in order to begin growth into an adult that will mature into another plant with countless seeds of its own. There was one major difference: Beans didn't digest fabric, flesh, lungs or brain tissue. If you get enough bad guys overrunning the stockade, your defenses won't matter anymore.

My progressively worsening thought sequences drove me to cold sweats. Dying didn't bother me. Dying under these circumstances along with these two scared the hell out of me. What would we do when the end came? Would we hold hands and sing or forgive each his own trespasses?

I gently hopped onto the vanity, with Big Ken next to the door, me sitting in the middle and Ronnie sitting on the far edge with her feet resting on the commode and her back to me. The shower was directly in front of her. My seat was uncomfortable because the sink was under me with the faucet poking me in the back. I had about three inches on the edge to work with.

"What other complaints do you have," Ken sniped with considerable venom. His day-to-day mood swings were well known, but today under pressure, the man appeared to be on the fringe of being out of control. We all were.

Then Ronnie attacked, pivoting around so she

was facing the same direction as we were and looked sharply to her left so she could eye Ken. "Complaints, Ken? How about the fact that you should be cleaning toilets for a living; although you'd find a way to screw that up too, and since you're a steroid using junkie, I've got a better use for your spare money.

"Here's the drama. Yes, the baby is yours and I'll prove it when the time comes. That'll be when I file a lawsuit against you for this mess right here."

Unless I miss my guess, Ronnie had decided that she didn't like her latest employer. The woman was sharp and must have had some kind of education. The part about the lawsuit was sweet music to my ears. That meant I would get to testify in detail about Ken's incompetence. If I lived, that is.

If Ken felt dejected, he didn't show it. Instead, he wouldn't let it go. "What's the matter, Ronnie? Don't you love me anymore? You sure loved me once."

"I was drunk and nearly asleep, Ken. Is that your definition of love? Do you remember when I said, 'No'?"

Ken laughed. "You saying 'no'? That's a laugh." The man ran a hand through his crew cut—a nervous reaction.

"Okay, little man. You give your version to the judge, and the baby and I will give ours," she sneered.

Good point, Ronnie.

Ken shrugged. Nothing affected this guy.

At that moment the power went off. In true Einsteinian fashion, a physicist might say that it was a folding back of the space-time continuum where two disparate crises meet at the same time and in the same place. Others like me might say, "Oh, shit, what now?"

The power outage was undoubtedly due to the workmen servicing the air handlers on the roof. We weren't in total blackness because a small window above the shower permitted a little of the early morning light to enter the room, albeit the window faced the north.

"This is good," said Ken. "Now there is no suction outside from the air return to spread the spores through the house so we can get out of here."

"You mean like you probably did the first time you worked on this room? Then go for it," I suggested, knowing what would happen; actually awaiting the outcome of his antics in a diabolical manner, expecting comedy relief.

From his seated position on the vanity next to the door, Ken pulled on the door handle, silently at first, then with entertaining noises. The brute grunted and stained as hard as he could. The door had swollen into place, as if had been welded to the door frame, thanks to Ken's initial shove against the entire door to slam it shut. His meager efforts were a cheap comedy show, with only our lives on the line.

Ronnie and I did an eyeball exchange and that triggered a laughing attack that only stopped when we both began to cough and gag from the spores and

the stink in our lungs. Every time either of us began to talk the laughter began anew. Finally, with
a hoarse and raspy voice, I managed to utter, "Uh,
Ronnie, I wonder how the door got closed so tightly."

Through her own tears, Ronnie directed her attention to her former bed partner. "Now what, big
shot?"

The employee had just fired the employer. The
woman was not ignorant. She did have her little pec-
cadilloes, like having unprotected sex and not learning from her mistakes. Like everybody, she had her
own hornet's nest to deal with. But she had a wit
and might have turned out all right in another life.
Who knows, she might, yet. Before Ken could give
a rejoinder, she added with a plaintiff cry, "I really
have to pee."

"Go ahead and use the shower drain, if you need
to," I said. "We won't watch." At least Ronnie had a
door to close to cover her actions.

If Ken had spoken a single word during these
moments, my right fist would have spoken for me,
but we didn't need a writhing bleeding body on the
ground to cause the release of more spores. Hopefully, my time with Ken would come, just him and
me—no witnesses.

Shifting from my uncomfortable position, I
stretched out my legs. I felt as though I was on one
of those old fashioned stocks to sit in public for days
on a wooden board with a thin ledge going across
your ass with your arms bound onto some other de-

vice. The only thing missing here was people throwing stones or rotten fruit at you.

So far, we had accomplished nothing. The jerk was being a jerk; he and I were coming to blows; Ronnie had to pee; and there was no serious creative thinking. So be it. Would it be necessary to tell them what will happen if we don't get out? It's coming to that. Right now, we needed to play the hand we were dealt.

What were the spores doing on my skin? That was the first thing I had to know, like a bubble forming way beneath the surface that finally rises to the top of the muck.

My work equipment lay in the bag at my feet, so I hooked one of the straps on my nylon tote bag with my foot and pulled up the bag to where I could reach inside. In the dim light, I pulled the portable microscope from its small case that measured about five inches on each side. I retrieved a microscope slide from the bag and scraped my exposed arm skin with one edge and along my face with another edge, followed this with the placement of a cover slip over the cells that had been scraped off. Then I placed the slide beneath the self-lighting scope. The view was quite spectacular. Countless small black spherical spores were sending down a tiny strand of mycelium into my skin. The cold sweat of fear ran from my forehead down the back of my spine and mingled with the stench of the petrochemicals in the humid air. I repacked the instrument and set the bag back down on the floor.

Her own task completed, Ronnie returned to her perch and offered, "An idea," she held up one finger. "How about if we all fit into the shower. Can't we wash this stuff off of us?"

"Theoretically . . ." I began to explain the plusses and minuses of her suggestion, until Ken chimed in.

"It won't work," he said. "Before we cut out the sub-floor, I turned off the water to both floors at the manifold in the utility room."

Ronnie began to cough and then scratch her neck.

Somebody once thanked me for giving them moral support for their project. In Ken's case it would be safe to call it immoral support. I don't know how it works. All I know is that whatever some people touch or try to do turns out wrong almost all the time. Is it tied to the thinking process or something below that; some, as yet, undefined truth to the universe?

This bastard needed a "real larnin'," as country folk like to say. If we survive this, I'll take care of Ken, trust me on that. I'm like a dog latched on to a pants cuff. Except for one minor addition: I go for the jugular. This guy had a bad reputation. He paid off plumbers to obtain referral on water-damaged homes, strictly against industry policy. He gouged the homeowners whenever he or his small staff of employees did the work. Since the insurance industry paid him directly, Ken felt he could charge whatever he wanted. So far, he'd gotten away with it. However, if I should survive this day, Ken will become my new pet project. He had no business in this business. How many times I didn't know about had he endangered the lives of others? How many people had actually gotten ill or died as a result of his incompetence?

Why was I so flagrantly hostile to this man? Incompetent people are a dime a dozen. Is it because of the many lives he has negatively affected? Maybe because people like him give the industry a bad name? No, that's too thin. Perhaps there existed some underlying factor where I saw myself in him, in some regards? There must be a psychiatrist somewhere who would be willing to put the blame on me because of my intense distrust and dislike of another person. The shrink might say, "What the hell's the manner with you, Shenero? How dare you dislike a man who tries so hard to make an honest dollar and raise a family? Or two? Or three?

No. Ken was just plain unlikable from the first day we'd met years before, and if he had any positive qualities they were well hidden. You could look into his eyes and they were always the same: stone cold, humorless, emotionless—a shell filled with a cluster of mistakes and bad luck events waiting to happen. Now the bells were ringing to toll our deaths together. Hopefully, it would be in mortal combat. Guaranteed it would not be in loving embrace.

I shook my head. The chemicals were taking over. The violence could start with me.

Ronnie sat next to the role of toilet paper, so I asked her to tear off several squares for us to hold over our mouths and noses to breathe through.

I didn't want to give one to Ken. I wanted him to breathe in the spores and become a case study for the medical literature. But I did anyway. At least the paper would keep out the spores, but not smell of chemicals. The bathroom stunk like a toxic waste dump. In fact, by the EPA's definition, this room actually did qualify as an undesignated storage facility for toxic and hazardous substances. Certainly, the formaldehyde produced by the mold was at least equal to the amount found in any new manufactured home. At least builders are required to post a warning in the home for that issue. How many homes provided to the New Orleans' victims were unsuitable for habitation just because of one problem alone? Tears ran from my burning eyes. I tried not to look at the floor; black in its entirety.

"Doctor Shenero, maybe you could bang on the ceiling with your tripod and somebody could hear us," Ronnie offered, with limited enthusiasm.

Ken scoffed at the idea, but I tried it for several minutes to no avail. Apparently the pounding wasn't loud enough to overcome the music coming from a radio on the roof.

"Here's another idea," I said, and pulled out my cell phone. "Ken, we're going to call your company and instruct them as to how to set up a critical containment barrier outside this room with a change of clothing for all of us including themselves and for them to force the door open with whatever means so we can get out."

Four people's lives were at stake here including

the baby and all were in the hands of Ken. Scary thought. His motto should be: *If you can't do it wrong, then don't do it at all.* For years, I'd taught this stuff at the university and now I was here; hopefully not making history.

"It'll take them two hours to get here to do all that," Ken said, his voice objective.

"You on a schedule?" I queried, noting that he was most likely to be the first to be infected thanks to his poor immune response, in turn thanks to his steroid usage. I got Ken's office number from him since it is not part of my Contact's list, hit SPEAKER on the phone, and punched in the number. All I got was NO SERVICE on the screen.

"Let's try your phone," I demanded, rather than suggested.

Resignedly, he gave it to me and I got the same response. "I could have told you there is no phone service out here," Ken contributed, smugly. I should have guessed. A nasty storm that blew through here the previous week had probably taken out the cell phone towers.

I gently lowered myself from the counter and stepped into the shower stall. I tried the same number with each of the cell phones with the same non response. Then I tried 911 to no avail. Then I reached out the window and hit redial, quickly pulled in the phone and checked the screen to read No Service.

My mind's eye could picture the spores beginning to grow in our lungs and black fuzzy mold covering all of our bodies while being poisoned by the mold's chemical byproducts. I saw newspaper headlines: *Trio found dead in bathroom covered with black masses of mold. Workers gag and several hospitalized. Experts fear contagion that may spread. Lawton Health Department calls CDC to investigate.*

I began to scratch and cough. The itching that Ronnie exhibited had become real for both me and Ken. We also scratched various exposed places on our body and coughed. I desperately wanted to relate to him in lurid detail about how we were now lower on the food chain than the spores which were utilizing our bodies as substrates for their survival and, concomitantly, for our demise. If Ronnie had been absent, no problem.

How long would it take for someone to figure out we were here? They couldn't reach us and we couldn't reach them.

"So what's going to happen to us?" Ronnie stared at me almost pleadingly, coughing as she spoke.

"We're all going to need medical attention. We're going to need to watch for symptoms of persistent coughing after we leave here and tell our doctor what happened. He might want to follow our lung function and run some blood tests."

Clinically speaking, of course. The last thing she needed to hear was the truth about what was happening inside her body and on her skin. Ken tried to give the appearance that he cared less about any of it. Hey, when you're a man, you're a man. Right Ken?

At that Ronnie declared. "Screw this and screw you both. I'm calling for help." She jumped down from the vanity to go for the window and hit a slick spot on the floor. She fell hard onto her back with one leg crumpled beneath her striking the vanity with her head. A dark cloud of mold spores billowed up from the floor as though someone had taken a fan to a quantity of gunpowder. The spores quickly melded with the rest of the air space and settled onto our bodies.

Ken looked on as if it were a TV commercial or a boring game show as I gently stepped down and slowly straightened her leg. Only semi-conscious, Ronnie cried out in anguish. I reached into my tote kit and pulled out a couple of small packets of alcohol wipes which I tore open and applied to an oozing area of blood on the back of her head.

Coughing, almost without control, I seated her onto the commode while she held her head in both hands. I said, "Look, how about if we just kick out a section of sheetrock between this room and the next. There's space between the commode and the vanity to do that. Then we can tear out enough to kick out the wall in the next room. Ronnie is the smallest one of us and can escape through the hole and go for help or call for help on the home phone."

The wall we were facing while seated on the vanity was an exterior wall. So was the distant portion of the shower surround. The door to the hallway was firmly swollen shut.

"You better check for studs first," Ken advised.

I knocked on the wall between the commode and the vanity, a space of only fourteen inches. I hit a solid sound in the middle and hollow sounds on either side of that.

We all heard the vibrations and echoes and knew what they meant. I had hit a solid two-by-four wooden stud right in the middle. No escape there. Or could there be. Those studs are only attached at either end with nails. A few good kicks may do the trick to loosen at least one of them to aid in its removals. That was one plan. Were there any others?

"Okay, guys," I said, digging deep to sound confident. I felt as if we were on the right track. "Let's deal with the area above the commode. Now I can get up onto..."

"Forget it," contributed Ken. "That is, unless your pocket knife can cut through water pipes."

"No, but we can bang on them. I have a lot of metal objects in my kit. Even my knife will make noise."

"Except that these are all plastic pipes," contributed Mister Positive.

I refused to die like a loaf of bread in a sealed package. What would the headlines read after we were found and would my students say that I deserved it, that it was the perfect way for Dr. Shenero to die?

My thoughts about my classroom took me to the stories I told about archaeologists who had found various tombs where mold grew on the mummies and who subsequently died because of the "curse of the mummy." They too had inhaled countless spores in a short period of time. Was this room to be our mummy's tomb?

"*What's inside sure stays inside*," Ken had said.

I muttered some curse words and began to cut out the sheetrock in the wall above and behind Ronnie, who sat bent over to make room for me, massaging her head with one hand and scratching various areas of her body with the other. She reminded me of a monkey.

At that very instant, the power came back on and our senses were blasted with a thousand watts of brightness just as our eyes were dark-adapting. Footsteps could be heard on the roof. The workmen were leaving. It also meant one man was already on the ground and had thrown the breaker switch. That was when their work truck started up.

"Ken, get to the window and yell for help," I demanded.

"Why me?" was the response.

"Because you're the dumbest one here and you're also the tallest and have the best chance of yelling through the window. That's why."

"What am I supposed to say?" asked Ken, in full denial of the present circumstances that had befallen us.

"Hey, tell them you want to order a large pizza," Ronnie contributed, sarcastically.

The window faced the wrong direction anyway. There really wasn't much chance for the men to hear anybody yell. They didn't. The truck drove off back to Lawton.

I had another idea. "Okay, big shot, let's see some of that steroid strength of yours. Grab the commode and rip it off the bolts that are holding it to the floor."

Ken saw I was serious when I took Ronnie by the arm led her into the shower to give him room to work. As if he does this sort of thing before breakfast every morning, the beast wrapped one arm around the tank and one around the base of the commode he began to yank and pull and rock it. Within sixty seconds the toilet lay on the floor and we had a good three-foot by five-foot hunk of drywall to work with. Ken and I started kicking. When we made holes, we grabbed the sheetrock and pulled it loose. We kicked out a couple of vertical studs and then kicked out the adjoining wall in the adjacent bedroom. All three of us made it through the opening to freedom.

The good news was that, from our end, the entire home would not be expected to be contaminated because we had avoided opening the door to the bath and didn't have to expose the air return to the spores. A professional might request an entire air testing of the home for a variety of reason related to this event. That professional would be me.

I took my work equipment with me to the car sucking in deep breaths to try and clear my lungs. I went to the trunk and grabbed my gym bag and walked back to utility room. I found the water control valves, turned on the one for the downstairs, left the one off for the upstairs, and took a long soapy shower in the master bath, coughing and blowing up as much muck as possible. I changed into my gym clothes, packed my khaki slacks, work shirt and shoes in the bag and returned it to the car. The other two were stood next to the truck a few feet away arguing heatedly. I checked my watch. It read almost eight thirty. Less than a half-hour had elapsed for the entire episode. So much for Ronnie's five minute exposure time.

I must have cut a great figure; a big yellow flower, standing there in sneakers, yellow jogging shorts and yellow Tee-shirt for visibility during street running. When I motioned for Ken to come over, he grinned and followed my beckoning wave like an obedient little doggie. I led him around the rear of the house, away from the prying eyes of Walter, as well as from Ronnie's view, should anybody ask her later about the incident.

A few moments later, I returned alone, gave Ronnie a slight wave, to which she gave me a Texas' Hook 'em Horns sign with her fingers. Then this bedraggled scientist climbed into his SUV and headed back to Norman.

Ken was going to have to deal with the insurance company that hired him along with their bills for damages he incurred regarding his negligence on this job, my formal report, lawsuits, various doctor's bills from my physician and Ronnie's, and his, if he had one. Then he had to deal with the state health department and possibly the Feds for the hospital incident, an assortment of lawyers including the homeowners' claims for damages, major dental surgery, and Ronnie. Of course, there was always the unexpected. It wasn't going to be pretty, I mused.

I congratulated myself on making up the story about the deaths in the hospital. It might have happened, if the air currents hadn't carried the spores in the other direction. I figured the jerk would sweat plenty thinking about murder charges until it was time to sweat reality. I only hoped the reality wouldn't include illness or worse to Ronnie or me.

As it turned out, Ronnie and the baby were fine. It took her a couple of weeks for the cough to go away, but I have every faith she'll be healthy. I heard she moved in with her parents.

Not so, Ken. His cough got worse by the day. He didn't develop what we call Farmer's Lung from breathing in a lot of spores from mold growing on hay or grain. He developed a classic case of disseminated aspergillosis, in other words, with no immune system to control the little beasties, the spores spread throughout his entire body and his brain. In a month he was dead.

Sometimes mold spores do what they want. That's the part that will continue to bother me for the rest of my life.

THE FIGHT AT THE POKER GAME

Sometimes people make a hard rule for themselves because they got handed a lesson. But occasionally, a person can get away with breaking the rule and not get caught for a while. Then they get bitten hard enough to remember why they created the rule in the first place.

To this day, fifty years later, I'm not sure whether the fight was caused by soldiers, myself, or the liquor. In retrospect, it started (and ended) because of a misunderstanding among five drunks. And, of course, because I broke one of my new rules.

This story begins after my two year Peace Corps Volunteer (PCV) stint in India had ended. Floating in (on) the Dead Sea, I began to reminisce. A little more than two years ago, my mission statement from the Peace Corps amounted to the following: "*You and your partner will replace two volunteers who began this program. You will occupy a large building, house, and feed groups of approximately*

ten Indian high school science teachers at a time for
a period of 10 days. The state will direct them to you.
They will be educated and unaccustomed to working
with their hands. During that time you will design
scientific equipment and instruct them on how to
construct the equipment from scrap materials. You
will purchase the materials from 'local' suppliers.''

That was then. This is now. To get to this place, I
had hitchhiked my way to Kashmir, Kathmandu, and
through the Middle-East (back then you could do
those things). My visits included Amsterdam, Damascus, Baalbek, Istanbul, Ankara, Athens, Mykonos, and Beirut, including parts in-between, with adventures in each. In most of those cities, the future
would not smile happily upon. In Damascus, I had
met a couple of young business gentlemen who sold
me various inexpensive goods and promised to send
them home to my grandmother. She received them.
I often wonder what had happened to these men of
honor; indeed, what had happened to honor itself.

Certainly, every PCV had his or her share of
tales. One that stands out in my memory was told
by Roger, who served four years in Columbia, South
America. He belonged to the Columbia 1 group, the
first of many to work in the country. He was a former
college gymnast who did well in the NCAAs. He
majored in agriculture, applied for the Peace Corps,
was approved, and got sent to a small village two
days hike out of Bogota.

Unfortunately for Roger, he had to pass through
a number of villages every couple of months when

he needed some personal supplies. Each time he walked to and from the big city, Roger would have to endure the chants of "Yankee go home," and, " How's your mother?"

At five-six Roger wasn't tall and had enough self-discipline to ignore the catcalls.

Under his direction, his village's productivity tripled, thanks to better irrigation methods and crop rotation. He visited other more outlying villages to assist them in the same manner and became a friend to everyone. Aided by a kick-start in Peace Corps training, His Spanish quickly became excellent. Locals loved him and pleaded for him to stay longer. So he did.

At last, after four years, on his way into the big city to catch the flight home to the States, Roger heard the all too familiar catcalls. Enough was enough. He walked across street to the porch in front of one bar where a number of locals had been harassing him, dropped his backpack and said a number of words to the leader, then grabbed him by the shirt collar, lifted him off the ground and slammed him against the side of the building. He said a few more personal words to the man that the others couldn't hear then let him down.

Of a sudden, Roger became a hero, a man among men who had finally shown his grit. Everyone invited him in to have a few beers and stick around for yet another two years, but Roger had a plane to catch.

The moral of the story is that one has to find a

way to relate to the local populace, even if it takes outer strength to do it.

There is the short and sweet story about Jerry who joined a program fresh out of college. Jerry was a world-class mountain climber and a go getum kind of guy. Very popular, he did well in his classes because he really wanted Peace Corps until Cheryl joined the program a month late. It turns out that Jerry and Cheryl knew each other in another life and had carried on a torrid affair, so they picked up from where they left off. They began to miss classes and were warned. A prospective volunteer is always paranoid about getting cut during training.

Jerry and Cheryl get married right before leaving for their tour overseas. He made it through and had a lot of potential for success, not so Cheryl, but they slid her through because of the marriage. Shortly after arriving to the country, Cheryl gots sick and stayed sick and both of the left to go back to the States. They were divorced shortly after returning. Cheryl thought she wanted the Peace Corps, but wanted Jerry more. Jerry wanted the Peace Corps and got cut off at the knees. Jerry went back to mountain climbing while Cheryl went back to waitressing.

Now, Burt was gregarious, personable, and inquisitive—the perfect man to determine the population of an island chain in Polynesia. The way he told it, he couldn't come up with a good number because each time he would row to another nearby island, the islanders would celebrate his arrival with a grand party, after which time he would spend some time recovering and row off to another island. Two years later he reported how many people were on each of the islands under his jurisdiction and not a single person could dispute his claims.

As for me, the short version is this: teaching science teachers how to construct scientific equipment from scrap materials, traveling some 20,000 kilometers on third class unreserved trains and buses, going through the rabies series of vaccinations, getting drunk with fishermen on Jack Daniels they had bootlegged from a ship, studying six languages simultaneously, visiting houses of ill repute in Bombay (Mumbai) while pretending to be a Russian, befriending a wealthy one-legged beggar in Madras who spoke many European languages, witnessing unspeakable cruelty to children about which I could do absolutely nothing, hobnobbing with the poorest of the poor and the extreme intellectuals, getting accepted to graduate school, trading fighting skills with knowledgeable Indians, not trading my camera for a loin cloth, going to the village cock fights as a guest of the constable, looking so haggard that a beggar tried to give me money, enrolling in a hospital for a few days to get away from it all where I came down with food poisoning, getting stoned on hashish in Nepal with the Himalayas in front of me, nearly running head-on into a spider the size of a hairless tarantula that hung in the middle of a web that spanned two trees 20 feet apart, trapping a monster scorpion beneath a pail in my bedroom only to find it to be gone in the morning, sleeping under mosquito netting, trading my rupees for their dollars with merchant seamen, and trying to stay out of trouble. I saw myself as lump of clay thrown into the hands of life to be pounded, carved, and sculpted into *something*—a work in progress.

In order to get to where I presently floated, (salt content 34%, ten times saltier than normal sea water) I had to catch a ride from Damascus from a young couple and got dropped off at a large six-by-eight-foot sign written in both Arabic and English. A left arrow pointed to the Dead Sea; a straight-ahead arrow pointed to Jerusalem, and a right arrow pointed to Jericho.

I got out and headed left toward the Dead Sea, the lowest land-based point on the face of the earth, and which bragged the highest salt content of any body of water. Salt-tolerate microbial life refutes the claims that nothing can live in that drying body. Belief in the sea's curative effects still remains.

Tired of being scorched by sun and, for that matter, tired of reflecting, I got back to living for the moment. Changing into traveling garb, I walked the short distance back to the main highway, where I caught a bus to Jerusalem. My evening and night were spent at a drunken fest thrown by some large eclectic tourist group which I managed to join without notice. In the morning, I declared to the gods of sanity that I would swear off alcohol forevermore.

Leaving Jerusalem with Tel Aviv as my goal, my

thumb soon attracted an ordinary car whose driver purported himself to be a freelance cab driver. No meter adorned the dash. After we negotiated a price, I found myself in a rattling car on a dusty on a very hot ride over a myriad of potholes into Tel Aviv. Loud, yet mysteriously captivating, Middle-Eastern music played on the car's radio. My jovial and bearded driver deposited me at a very economical hotel with blessings of The Almighty. Initially, he refused my first offer of a tip, but, just as politely, accepted my insistence on him taking the money.

In truth my residence for the night turned out to be a low-rent flop-house two stories in height situated only a couple of streets behind the most popular, rocking nightclub in the city. According to my driver's inside information, patrons from the club frequented my temporary residence, *so please be wary of loose women.*

I was tired, hungover, unshaven, dressed in old 501 shrink-to-fit blue jeans and wore a sweat-stained and India-monsoon-washed red Oklahoma Sooners Football cap along with a ragged Hang Ten Hawaii surfing tee shirt. My sneakers were well worn but comfortable. My socks could stand a washing, with backup socks in my pack.

I checked in for the night with an overweight, balding middle-age man who sported a serious comb-over. The clerk took one look at me and must have thought I was pretty much on a par with his other clientele—possibly even overdressed.

My weary five-ten 180-pound body lumbered

up a seemingly endless number of rickety wooden stairs to my room situated several steps to the right of the landing. I wasn't sure which was shakier, my tired legs or the wobbling balustrade to my right that threatened to send me to my death at any instant should I lean against its rotted wood.

The steps creaked as I climbed. My sixth sense perceived that the left wall of the staircase contained psychic emissions. These were tales of both loves and loneliness that had been absorbed by the wall over decades of episodic events; certainly more than I was ready to listen to at that time; yet soon enough, would contain my own tale for another person more willing to listen.

My simple intent was to call it quits for another hot day and to read myself to sleep. Proud of my courageous decision to swear off alcohol, I struck the landing and lumbered right toward my room. Unlocking the door, I gratuitously deposited my backpack onto the floor next to a sagging bed in a dank room—a room I most definitely did not want to hear any stories about.

My pack was heavy with Volume Two of Lord of the Rings, which I had traded for Plato's The Republic some days earlier. I exited the dankness, closed the door behind me, and walked several steps to hit the communal water closet half-way down the long landing, passing two other units on my right, one of which projected sounds of a whip cracking. I briefly and reflexively considered going out to close the bars and, okay, pick up a babe, despite the deafening mental klaxon that blared, "Warning! Danger of overload!" However, being a person of great inner strength, I decided that it was never a good idea to ignore this alarm and quickly manned up to cast sinful thoughts aside.

Ambling out of the WC and zipping up my fly, I heard raucous laughter to my right. Never one to ignore such an entreaty, I turned toward the sounds. In a few wary steps, I passed another two units and came upon an open door. Stopping at the entrance, I saw a room filled with smoke. Within the haze sat four men wearing military fatigues playing cards at a round table. A small fan atop a small corner dresser ensured that the smoke would be evenly distributed. A quick look around provided me with crucial information: playing-cards and chips on the table, one or more liquor bottles on the old wooden floor next to each player, one of the four wearing a black beret with his back to me, and all men of European or Middle East persuasion. (How you persuade a person to be of a certain ethnicity, I never could understand.)

A shortwave radio played Prokofiev. The piece concluded and the broadcaster announced the station to be Radio Moscow and Liszt's Les Preludes would be played next. He made the pronouncement first in Russian, then in French, then in English.

Holy shit, I thought, Radio Moscow is going to play *Les Preludes*, theme of the old Flash Gordon TV series. Next, they'll be playing Rossini's *William Tell Overture*, theme of The Lone Ranger.

This gave me an at-home feeling. I'd frequently listened to that station while in India in lieu of its competitor, Voice of America, if only for the presence of classical music rather than the boring middle-of-the-road non-descriptive stuff played by VOA. At that time, VOA would not play Elvis Presley, even when everybody else on planet Earth was playing him, including Radio Moscow. The short wave radio didn't lie.

Mr. Beret turned toward me, following a head nod from one of the others. A smaller man at the left asked me something, which I took to mean, "And who might you be?" in some foreign tongue that had a definite trace of Slavic. Perhaps they had taken me to be a derelict who had just risen from a park bench with only a newspaper missing from his face. Perhaps they might not be far from the truth.

I responded by saying that I was a lost American Peace Corps Volunteer who was still looking for India after two years traveling around the world and could anyone point me in the right direction? It quickly became obvious that none there spoke English, let alone understood American humor.

I did note they understood the word American because their ears perked, but little other response. They looked at one another with drawn eyebrows, so I tried Spanish, German, and Hindi, and a trace of other languages, which I had studied on my own while in India, and had listened to on shortwave. For grins, I threw a little Telugu and Swahili at them. Finally, I realized that my mainstay, French, was lying in wait. The language had been recently tried and tested by me in Pondicherry, an old French colony in southern India.

"Yes!" proclaimed Mr. Beret, in French. "I speak French."

I repeated my earlier introductory statement. He laughed, then translated to the others who laughed long and hard with me; or at me, I couldn't tell which. They engaged in conversation amongst themselves for a few moments. Then the man seated across from Mr. Beret mumbled something in French about a no-breed American.

The French speaker stated, "We are UN Forces stationed in Cypress and we are here on time off."

According to him, this was their third night in Tel Aviv and the poor suffering foursome was resting up from nightclubbing, and all the attendant perks. He spoke to the others in another tongue, which I now picked up as Greek with occasional Arabic words thrown in.

I knew those tongues because I had spent my college years as a biologist learning countless Greek, Latin, and Arabic words used for scientific descriptions. Unfortunately, I didn't understand jack in those particular languages when it came verbs and adverbs in conversation, although I could fake my way through a written test fairly well.

I also knew a little Russian, because I grew up with my Russian grandparents. Unfortunately, they insisted on speaking only English as they raised me, except for when they got into shouting matches at each other, a not infrequent occurrence when the Russian came out. The bad words and insults is what I mostly became familiar with growing up, although a few decent non-descriptive words might have been buried among them.

Mr. Beret was a larger version of a fireplug. Grizzled, he had the appearance of one who had served in serious military combat operations. I logged the information. As I did so, I also noted the soft knuckles of the man across from, and to the right of him.

Not so the man to his left. His knuckles were very large and deformed. They looked like two-by-four inch rectangles of concrete. As a rough guess, I say he didn't get those hands by hitting them into cotton pillows. More than a few battered women might have remembered those hands.

My greeter pronounced himself as Arnaud and introduced the small wiry man to his left, the man with the knuckles, as a Greek named Prometheus. The dark handsome well-groomed mustached man across from him, whom I initially thought might be Israeli, turned out to be a Lebanese named Rony. To Arnaud's right sat a large man, perhaps six feet at 200 pounds, a gap-toothed Bulgarian with a jovial countenance on a pale fleshy face named Vladimir. He couldn't have been over nineteen, five years my junior.

I took all men to be fit, wary, and definitely willing and able and make an opponent unfit, unwilling, and disabled.

After Arnaud's introductions, I strategically explained in French that my ancestors had come from Russia and mayhaps some from Hungary. This statement served to elevate me to the status of a brother. This is with the exception of the Lebanese man who had made the nasty comment.

This no-breed comment had served up some raucous laughter. The insult was aimed at the backbone of my country and pissed me off because that was precisely what my country consisted of—a people of all ethnic backgrounds who coexisted one hell of lot better than ethnicities in most other countries. In fact, our ethnicities were not physically fighting to become dominant, but strategically and economically trying to become equal with one another. Not to mention their out-of-control militias, terrorists by the score, and drug lords running amok. I let it go for the moment. With the good graces of time and planning, I would return the favor.

Arnaud made the pronouncement that, since I was an American, I must know how to play poker. At my nod, he asked if I might teach them the game. The sly looks they gave each other did not escape my attention; nor did the poker chips already on the table. I knew that chips might be used in the popular Middle-Eastern gambling game of Shush Kush, otherwise known as backgammon, but hand-held cards were not used. Something was awry.

I gave a simple reply. I'd just hitch-hiked through a half-dozen countries, got the moisture sucked out of me in the Dead Sea and was seriously hung-over from just last evening in Jerusalem, and what the hell, I'd love to show them how to play. My fatigue left me in an instant and Arnaud found another chair for me to sit between him and Vladimir.

Through Arnaud, I explained in French the basics of poker. They all caught on too fast. Meanwhile, I kept an interested eye on every skull and crossbones that I could see on the floor next to the men. These included *Russia Vodka, Jack Daniels,* Scotch, Gin, Hornitos and Patron Tequilas, and liquorish-flavored ouzos. I saw no Tennessee or Oklahoma moonshine. Too bad. They didn't know what they were missing. Obviously, the men permitted no water to taint their digestive tracts.

For the sake of better international relations, I struggled with the decision to put my abstinence on hold, then decided to socialize for only a couple of drinks. To my credit, I did remain almost a non-smoker. We'll count the smoke in the room equivalent to a couple of packs of cigarettes.

I walked around the table, looking at each hand, advising, and faithfully fulfilling my role as an inebriated American instructor of poker who was teaching the game with slurred tongue in a foreign language to inebriated foreigners who were trying to listen with slurred ears.

God, I loved these men who protected the world from the bad guys, who probably drank more than they did, although, on second thought, this might be up to question.

Before long, the conversation turned to warfare and their physical training. Lest they get any funny ideas about rolling Mister No Breed, I let slip a brief note that I had once studied karate and offered to show them a few moves. My statement stopped the conversation and my comrades became interested in pretending to learn from the American. I explained that it would be hard to teach them if they insisted of holding a smoke in one hand and a bottle in the other.

Reluctantly, they all set down their raison d'etre; drinking. The table and chairs were put aside and for a period of time I taught them basics such as non-telegraphing of a movement, sphere of influence, lax eyes versus penetrating eyes, how to fold a proper fist, and when, how, and where to use elbows and knees. Not surprisingly, Arnaud, the strongest, proved to be the most adept with wiry Prometheus a close second, especially when it came to in-fighting. The small man with the knuckles could flow and was very quick, which helped push me.

Ultimately, I ensured that each of them got a few dings. How does the saying go? It's not really a bruise that hurts, it's the subsequent hits on top of the first one that result in much greater and more long-lasting pain.

Understand that as a long-time Black Belt with the Japan Karate Association, I had gone into full-contact for a short while during my college years spending many an hour practicing defense against simultaneous attackers.

At that moment it was crucial for me to gain a little respect as an American, but I left out any multiple defense aspect. Call it an insurance policy; and, as a little note, I hadn't remained completely fallow in my practicing or teaching of the arts during the previous two years, and had taught fighting skills to a number of Indians, and had picked up a few skills in return.

The training lesson concluded, my beleaguered comrades and I required a serious fluid intake to replace the liquor we had lost during the exercise once we had returned to playing poker. The hour was still early. The nightclubs hadn't opened yet. Once again, the languages flowed. My French became nearly fluent, at least to my ears. We taught each other initial swear words in different languages, laughed, and slapped each other on the back.

I was bleeding precious money. The room, already heady with cigar and cigarette smoke, became a cauldron of steaming, hot sweating men who drank hard liquor and who told raucous stories. We used the universal language of hand signals; that is, once we all understood the necessary ingredients for telling the basics of sexually explicit stories: women, men, various sexual acts, loving, cheating, and lying. On occasion, one of us would take a WC break.

I phoned in and spoke in English to order several pizzas. Everybody blinked when the pizza delivery person showed up—a knock-down gorgeous blue-eyed creature from heaven. She stood maybe five-four with really nice medium-size boobs and short coal-black hair with blemish-free skin—not white, not brown, just Middle Eastern. She wore tan slacks and a tan button-down blouse. Along with the three large pizzas in her hands, she wore a sidearm, probably a 9 mm Beretta, not an unusual sight in Israel. Her belt contained pockets for extra magazines. No handcuffs. Before us stood a true goddess about whom I could easily entertain numerous fantasies.

She looked each of us directly in the eye, as though gathering information for later processing. Her eyes sparkled, but her full lips were tight and unsmiling. Our own eyes locked for a moment and my heart stopped. I ensured she received a very generous tip.

After she departed, it was natural for the five of us to discuss her relative merits, such as, did she have a boyfriend and who gave a shit if she did? Did she take her gun to bed with her, and if so, what might she do with it? And so forth.

During one of my pee breaks, I inventoried my losses and slapped myself. How can I be so stupid? These guys are UN forces and poker is a common game among soldiers. They're playing me like the dummy I look like.

At least I never mentioned a word about a crucial aspect of poker; that of reading tells. I had ignored that myself, all the while being plied with alcohol and being robbed. What was it my father had once told me? Be very wary of bad friends.

Once that realization struck, I girded my loins and got serious. Soon I began to get my money back and then began to take theirs, despite their increased grumbling. Sometime later I checked my watch and found it to be four a.m.

Almost all the chips were stacked in front of me. My lungs ached, as though I had jogged in a smog-filled city. My head split and the world began to appear off-kilter.

Vladimir went to take a leak and missed the chair when he returned. It took sympathetic hands and several attempts to reseat the large man. Even Arnaud began to fade.

I told them one more round and I was done. When the round finished, I stood on jelly legs, placed a hand on the table for support, and was reminded to take my share of the cash which was inside a box on the floor to the left of Arnaud. I honestly declined, backed up, and attempted to explain that they should split it between them, because I had held the unfair advantage of experience; however, my ability to communicate had declined significantly.

At that point the mood became somber. There was some tough talk around the table, even as Arnaud unconsciously rubbed his right shoulder socket where I had previously, accidentally, punched him during our practice session, while others had been occasionally rubbing their forearms, sternums and shins, where they, too, had been accidentally dinged.

The obvious became manifest: The soldiers would sacrifice their bodies to the twin gods of righteousness and indignation, in order to stand fast, and to enter the lion's den occupied by principle.

The four agreed that I take the money and there was no "or else." Verstehen Sie? Katalavaineis? Jafhamu? Novisse? Accipere? Tu entiendes? That is to say, do you get the drift, Mister Whatever-got-under-the-fence to make you American?

Appropriately, Tchaikovsky's Marche Slave began to play, my all-time favorite classical piece ending with a dynamic crescendo.

The way I saw things at that moment, it would be eight, not four, assailants. Fortunately, Vladimir chose that moment to slide down onto the floor, where he began to snore. That left six. Then Rony went to the WC to throw up. That left only two—Arnaud and Prometheus, along with their doppelgangers. What concerned me now was the political aspect: Might I spend my vacation in a foreign jail courted by bad lovers?

Not casting aside the innate sense of self-preservation and the alpha male concept, sometimes it's just good common sense to get out of a fight. Refrain from violent behavior, right?

So, to my mind, it would be to the satisfaction of Arnaud and Prometheus—my own included—to take the money. I spoke some words out loud to myself in Russian— something stoic and simplistic like: "Gosh darn. I guess I'll just have to take the money and thanks for the great fun," and took an unsteady step forward to collect the winnings.

The Russian language does not flow like French, with smooth and usually soft liaisons connecting the words. It's more abrupt. It's full of wicked south Slavic consonant clusters and gutturals. I mean, you could say in Russian, "Could I please have a drink of water?" or "It's nice to meet you and go ahead, take my first born" but if you're not smiling, somebody might think you just told them their parents were monkeys. Apparently, the soldiers thought I just swore and that I was moving toward them in aggression.

Fully prepared to give my remaining hosts a weak salute and an unsteady bow and return to my room, I now faced military men bent on combat. Doubtless, they had side-arms and rifles stashed somewhere within easy reach. I couldn't let anyone get into another room for whatever reason. I was also confident that, in terms of self defense, nothing I had taught them would stick.

Prometheus was the first up and in a full charge, hardened fists flailing. The man had innate talent, but I already knew him and his moves. I had my choice of targets. Using my fully rotated eight-inch reach advantage, I waited until he reached the very outer perimeter of my zone and ran a vertical punch straight down the chute. I wanted to hit him in the solar plexus just beneath the sternum, where my fist would fit in nicely, but I swayed and missed. My punch went wide of the center, but I think I caught him in one or two ribs before losing my balance. Arnaud, the heavy weight, followed a half-second after Prometheus' charge. The man was no dummy. Seeing what his protégé had not accomplished and seeing me nearly fall, he attacked. To my credit, I went on auto-pilot. Suspecting he would fake to the face and come in low to my left shin with his booted right leg, I stepped to the right, parried the kick with my left fist hard into his lower calf muscle just above the ankle, then pivoted back with a hard punch with the right fist to his lower left rib cage; enough to seriously damage the floating ribs. I followed up with a solid left to his cheek bone, big knuckles leading. Enough of this crap. I needed to stop him. You do not want to go a second round with your opponents and you do not want to shoot a bear with a .22.

Just when I thought the fight was over and feeling the urge to puke, Rony, returning from the WC, charged at me from behind. I didn't need the last guy to take me out. It wouldn't read well on my obituary. So I dropped him solid with a back thrusting kick square in the sternum with my left leg and lost my balance again. I fell forward and caught myself from hitting my face into the edge of the table. Rony dropped like a sack of potatoes and rolled around clutching his rattled ribcage. I think I loosened it. He won't be laughing anytime soon. It was a little gift from his half-breed American friend.

Remembering the money, I found my way to the box on the floor and it grabbed all in a big wad, then left, closing the door behind me. I slid my left shoulder against the left wall down the hallway bumping into a few doorways until I met my room—to this day grateful I had befriended the wall opposite the stairwell.

Somehow, I found the door knob to my room, stumbled in and fell upon my bed face down, grunting as I did so, gasping for breath and feeling worse than I could remember ever feeling. The room spun uncontrollably. I became violently ill and deposited my innards onto a floor mat beside my bed. The combination pizza was the last to exit.

With head splitting and breathing my own breath, bad enough to make a cat lift its tail and turn away had one been present, I managed to pick up the mat and take it into the water closet where I washed it off and had enough sanity to soak my head, drink pleanty of water, rinse out my mouth and piss like a racehorse on a flat rock. I returned the mat to its original position, swallowed a couple of aspirin tablets and opened the windows to air out the room, as well as myself.

Next, I locked the door and tried to sleep in a world all aswirl. Visions assailed me of four very pissed-off soldiers who were riddling my room with bullets. Did they know which room was mine? Did they even know if I was staying at this hotel? I decided not to wait to find out.

The sun would be up shortly. Sleep or no sleep, it was time to clear out. Dreaded overload warning alarms blared again. Not taking time to brush my teeth, I ensured my water bottle was full, divided my money into two pockets, changed shirts, threw a couple of sticks of peppermint gum in my mouth, resoaked my head and quickly reorganized backpack. I needed to get back to the basics of tourism. At the moment, running for my life fit in there somewhere

With Jerusalem in my mind's eye, only thirty-six

miles away, I began the trek by leaning heavily against the psychic message wall of the stairway. I survived the descent, and exited the hotel, looking around to get my bearings, and headed out. Affixing my sunglasses to reduce the glare of stray light, I walked, moving quite slowly with the memories of the previous hours presenting themselves as a randomized collage of flashing images. I dreaded the rise of the intense sun which promised to add to my woes. I vowed once again to never touch another drop of alcohol. What came to me then were memories of what had happened after meeting a Japanese ship captain in the Chinese restaurant back in India, and more recently, the altercation I got into in Bobby's Bar on the Grecian Island of Mykonos.

I lumbered onto the open road with an occasional vehicle passing in either direction. Some indeterminate time later, the sun rose and I heard the gravel crunch as a car pulled next to me.

"I thought it might be you. Do you want a ride?" I heard a woman's voice say. It came out as, "Doo you vant a dride?"

I took off my sunglasses and looked over to see the blue eyes of the pizza girl who was leaning forward to look at me out the window, with a smile as broad as beauty can make it, complete with pink full lips.

This time she was even hotter than the first time I had seen her. In fact, now there were two of her. They both wore blue jeans and a plain white Tee-shirt. The great boobs were still there.

I regained my focus and managed, "Uh, yes, thank you. I could use a ride," It seemed like an acceptable and polite thing to say; not overly intellectual, and most definitely, something that shouldn't get me into any more trouble.

I had to wait for a moment to get in, while she moved an Uzi submachine gun from the passenger seat and placed it between us. Setting my backpack on the floor between my feet, I chanced a glance at the back seat where I saw a set of folded camos and a red beret—the signature hat of a paratrooper with the IDF, or Israeli Defense Forces. I wouldsoon to find out that she was an instructor. A rare and tough breed.

I closed the door. Thankfully, all the windows were open.

"Where are you going?" she asked, with eyes sparkling in the morning sun. She still wore the sidearm. She glanced at the knuckles on both my hands, which were either bloody or swollen. My face was unmarked.

"Yerushalayim," I answered, staring at her in disbelief and wonderment.

"I heard what happened back there," she offered, nodding her head backward toward Tel Aviv.

"How . . . " I began, bewildered.

"My partner had another delivery at the hotel this morning and he told me about it when he saw the ambulances and talked to the drivers. Some drunk from that room had called for them. Your story will grow," she laughed. Her perfect teeth gleamed. "You will become a legend."

The legend part I didn't care about, but I did feel considerable relief from the paranoia that had gripped me, knowing that my friends from the night before wouldn't be coming after me, at least not for a while.

"Don't you live back in Tel Aviv?" I asked, stupidly—a question that had nothing to do with anything.

"Yes, but I'm going back home to visit my parents," she replied, checking her mirror and pulling back onto the road.

Then she asked, "Where are you staying?"

"I have absolutely no idea." That was the honest truth.

"Do you have money?" she asked.

"Yes, a fair amount." That was also an honest answer.

She suggested a place. After I assented, she said, "I'll take you there," and stepped on the gas. Traffic picked up, coming in our direction, as people headed for work in Tel Aviv.

I set my head back on the seat and closed my eyes for a couple of minutes, letting the cool morning air of the desert try to blow the smoke and liquor from my brain. I must have stunk.

"You seem like an interesting person. Do you want to go out with me tonight?" she asked a couple of minutes later.

I opened my eyes and swiveled my reclined head in her direction. Who was this creature? Obviously, she preferred the direct approach. Adrenaline began to dissolve away the fatigue. "That would be really nice. I'd like that, although I wouldn't mind a little sleep first."

"Good, I'll pick you up at ten. That's when the night life starts."

"What's your name?" I asked.

She told me hers and I told her mine.

"It will be fun to party with you and to know more about you. Maybe have a drink. A woman likes to feel safe."

A drink? Her feel safe? I thought, as I looked at the firepower in the car. "Well, maybe just one drink," I answered. We began to talk.

I will admit that night, exactly fifty years ago, turned out to be very interesting.

My wife and I still laugh about it today.

NEW COLONY

Almost as though it were scripted, Patel heard the blip override the monitor's background noise as he was leaving his apartment for work at 9:30 p.m. He closed the door and turned to the screen. His large dark eyes stared at a sharp peak as it slowly moved across from left to right. Something wasn't right.

Berkeley was a distant place from his birthplace in a fishing village on the Bay of Bengal in India, and is exactly where he wanted to be. At an even six feet in height, the dark-skinned Indian's passions were in radio-astronomy and intergalactic astrophysics.

Reclusive by nature, Patel was quite secure in the knowledge that he was destined to be a loner and wasn't invited to many parties unless they were program-related or were held in Roswell, New Mexico. He did enjoy attending both.

This blip was different than most, but similar to one he had observed shortly after arriving at the facility some six months prior when his supervisor,

Jerry Harwick, dismissed the peak as a spurious event. Those things will occur on occasion. Harwick remembered two others occurring prior to Patel's arrival.

Now it was on-screen again. Patel wrote the time onto a slip of paper and put it in his pocket.

Puzzled, Patel retraced the signal and played it again and again. On closer examination he found a short peak immediately following the larger spike on an otherwise nearly flat line disturbed only slightly by background noise.

Patel wanted to slow down the peak and examine its components, which would require heavy equipment. Dressed in his usual blue jeans, Tee-shirt and wearing a light jacket suitable for a Northern California summer, Patel locked his apartment and drove to his workplace, rich in electronic equipment and where actual work spaces had been inserted almost as an afterthought.

Patel went to his desk, threw down his lunch bag and hung his jacket over his chair's back. He checked the paper in this pocket, glanced at the wall clock wall and reversed the monitor recording to the proper time. He watched it closely until the spike appeared. He slowed its movement until bumps made their appearance along the peak's edges. He integrated audio and could discern individual sounds with breaks between them. A lot of information seemed to be compressed into a short burst of energy. This was no ordinary peak on a graph.

Intrigued, he checked the signal's height and ran

a computer search for similar peaks. Three others were identified, all within a two year time period; none before. They possessed similar properties; a sharp peak followed by a short spike.

Now, Patel's curiosity morphed into excitement. At 1:00 a.m. Patel called Jerry Harwick.

Harwick was a bearded elderly man with a pronounced pate. Slightly overweight, he always dressed immaculately even though half his life was working mathematical equations which pertained to various eclectic jobs his profession required. He enjoyed two things in life more than any others: golf and looking for aliens. Many men and women had spent their entire professional lives looking for outsiders and jumped at any opportunity

Although he was accustomed being called during his hours off regarding spurious events, Harwick's curiosity became aroused based on details given him by Patel. He arrived within a half-hour, dressed in a fresh white shirt and pressed denims, to review the last peak his understudy laid out for him.

"Let's look at the other three," Harwick said.

With Harwick peering over his shoulder, Patel punched in keys.

"Damnation, looks like they're six months apart," Harwick declared. "First we've got pulsars rotating at hundreds of times a second, now we've got this business showing up twice a year down to the microsecond. What next?"

Patel slid his chair back and stood, looking down at the screen, deep in thought. "Wherever these noises are coming from, the object would have to be in line-of-sight. Equipment glitches don't do that, do they?"

"Not to my knowledge," said Harwick, pulling lightly on his short beard. "Hell, man, could be the moon, a satellite, another planet, a star; it won't be a weather balloon. They send their signals continuously.

"I have a funny feeling about this. Let's send out a request to a dozen or so affiliates and see what they've got—usual places; Arecibo, Atacama, Moscow, Goddard, your home institute in Bangalore. We don't need everyone. A number in both hemispheres will do for now. But let's not send a gang message. Send them out individually. I want to keep this as low key as possible for now."

Patel sent requests for information, a common event in the field, while Harwick replayed the recording. Most replies occurred within a few hours. Some had recorded spikes while others had no record of the occurrences. Those with the recordings were found to be in line-of-sight of the moon and had reported their data in microseconds.

Patel checked his own spikes and also noted the microseconds. This was important to them because it meant that if the pulses were coming from the moon, they would take longer to reach more distant observatories than closer ones.

"Let's triangulate, if we can," said Harwick. He walked over to his desk computer and punched in numbers. Patel stood close to his side.

"Looks like it's a particular area we need to look at," said the supervisor. "It's still dark out, but the moon itself is bright enough and I want to have eyes on before daylight obscures our vision. Let's see if we can find an available scope over there."

Patel signed on to an available telescope and activated the coordinates. The men settled down to view a large television screen to view the moon in close-up, as telescoping images slowly scanned the area in question.

The pair scanned for over an hour. Harwick suddenly stopped the scope's movement. The vague shape appeared on the northeastern edge of the lunar surface. It was difficult to see because it blended almost perfectly with the soil color beneath it, similar to a horned toad in desert sand.

"Don't say nothin' to nobody right now." Harwick actually whispered.

"I don't believe it. It looks like a spaceship," proclaimed Patel, also in whisper mode, his large eyes seeming to bulge out of his head.

"Exactly, it *looks* like a spaceship," said his mentor. "One thing you have to learn about science in general and astronomy in particular is that strange and unexpected things occur that we don't understand or refuse to understand.

"This is probably before your time, but several years ago a face was captured by satellite on the surface of Mars. Books were written by noteworthy persons about how aliens created the face as a message. Space alien buffs were disappointed when further investigation found that shadows were cast by a big rock to make the single rock look like a face. "So, let's take this slowly."

Both men's hearts were pounding. Even a false lead can be exciting until it fizzles out.

Harwick punched numbers into a phone on his desk. "I'm calling Dana Altman. You know her."

"Professor Altman, the linguist?" Patel said, puzzled. "Why a language expert?"

Harwick didn't answer. He had already picked up the phone.

Dana Altman served as full Professor of Linguistics at Berkeley, whom Harwick first met forty years earlier while he was a Rhodes Scholar at the Institute of Astronomy at Cambridge University. While studying at Cambridge, they met when she was a graduate student in linguists. Each held a deep interest in the other's specialty and they developed a solid friendship sparked by a brief fling they'd enjoyed.

Harwick had been hired by Berkeley to teach astronomy and to work with the SETI program when he could. He had maintained contact with Altman. Several years later she was hired by the same university and sought to continue with her interest in astronomy. Both were delighted to regain their friendship while she visited the facility on occasion.

British by birth, Altman stood a thin five-six with well-kept coiffed gray hair and friendly blue eyes. She always wore clothing or jewelry with blue in it and maintained her British accent with a sense of pride.

While Harwick was married and divorced, multi-lingual Altman soon married an older man, a wealthy yachtsman, spending her vacations on the open water perusing the skies as they traveled between continents.

Altman arrived at the lab shortly after being called wearing blue cotton slacks, and a tan pullover. Harwick explained the rcordings to her in more detail. He didn't want to tell her about the ship on the moon and had cautioned Patel not to say anything about it. This had to be taken one slow step at a time.

Harwick turned to the computer and varied the audio speed to match the bumps on the peak.

"It's a speech pattern," Altman declared, not certain what to make of it.

"How so?" Harwick asked.

"Look, guys, close your eyes and listen to breaks at the end of word strings. Listen to the rise and fall of intonations. Some end abruptly and some endings are softer.

"Let's hear the others," she requested. "I'm guessing they'll have the same attributes."

Now knowing what to listen for, Harwick and Patel could understand what she meant.

"I'm going to download a software program in linguistics and dig a little deeper," Altman declared, taking charge.

Once Altman downloaded the program, it became clear that visual and auditory patterns were not Chinese or Asian or numerous other languages built into the program. She confirmed this by painstakingly overlaying sound patterns of the other languages on top of the one they were examining, sliding them back and forth and found only an occasional and co-incidental similarity, but no real matches.

"Jerry, can you record these sound patterns onto paper for me?" Altman requested.

Harwick entered dates and times into the computer and hit the print button. In minutes they found less than one page of notes for the first recording and several pages for each of the other three, especially the last page which was the lengthiest and appeared to have numerous repeated symbols.

Eager to get to the prize, Harwick could wait no longer. "Patel. You have the honors."

Patel turned on the screen. A split screen showed the moon on the left and the spaceship on the right, melding into the moon's dust.

"You would have thought I was crazy if I'd told you over the phone, so I bit my tongue and waited for your analysis," Harwick said, softly. He stood next to her with Patel on the other side.

Altman gasped and looked from one man to the next. Harwick raised his eyebrows and gave a brief smile while Patel merely shrugged.

The three found themselves treading a fine line between excitement and caution. The first pulsar that was found had rocked the boat until it was discovered to be a spinning neutron star emitting regular beams of electromagnetic radiation and not messages from star people.

Still, before them lay evidence strong enough to

require follow-up. The three stood as statues. They were of the same mind: This was no hoax. From all sounds and appearances, Earth was under observation by aliens who were sending information. Were they sending it to Earth, or elsewhere? If so, where?

Approximately 40 Earth years later and thousands of light years away, thirteen members of the Supreme War Council sat in attendance and Admiral Trak stood before them.

Six members were seated to the right of Braken, Commander of the Armies. These were experienced in one or more world-conquering campaigns. To Braken's left sat six newer members who were fresh out of military school to replace retired or recently deceased members or who were recently appointed thanks to their prowess in command of continuous social uprisings at home.

None of the new group was familiar with the procedures regarding the conquest of other worlds. None were clothed and hair covered their bodies.

Braken addressed the being standing alone in front of the long semicircular council table. "Admiral, when you returned with seven other warships, you told us the remainder of the fleet would not be coming home. Is that correct?"

Trak felt disoriented and angry. Trappings garnered from many worlds gave great splendor to the palace council chamber. The trappings changed color as the dual suns shifted their position.

"Yes, sir," was all he replied, holding his anger

in check.

Braken nodded at the prisoner's response. "And you stated you believed a single human caused that occurrence. Is that also correct?"

"Correct—along with bad luck." Trak responded.

Braken exploded, "How could a single Earthling destroy our space fleet?"

Admiral Trak hung his head in obeisance as he bit his tongue, yet his emotions roiled. He wasn't certain where to begin. He had recently come out of hibernation and his mind was still racked with emotions, typical withdrawal symptoms. The journey to Earth and back lasted some 20 years each and the Kurlian mind refused to adapt to sleeping so long.

Kurlians did not believe in enslavement or re-training of sentient and dominant species. They did fervently believe in their wholesale elimination which meant that, as their empire grew in size, its fleet grew in number and absorbed what it could. This included oxygen-rich planets with temperate climates, especially those capable of providing food and ores for the establishment of colonies. There were other planets lacking life, yet could still be mined.

No natural resources remained on Kurl. New resources were obtained from the worlds they engulfed. These barely helped sustain its own citizens. Infrastructure repairs were shoddy. Their war fleet was getting old and breakdowns were not uncommon.

Trak felt the need to lick his sweating hair away

from his eyes. The hair required brushing.

Braken forced himself to put his own emotions in check and leaned back in his seat folding his hands behind his head. "Now please tell us your tale of woe. How a single man causes the downing of our fleet and perhaps bring an end to a galactic empire."

Under direction by Altman, the team returned their attention to the auditory signals which were fed into a computer. It found similar words throughout the four texts and thus began the job of trying to order them.

Harwick called an emergency meeting with SETI's Board of Trustees and Altman reported to her department chairman. Within only a few days, several decisions were made by the President of the United States under advisement by the Pentagon: Get to the moon and onto that alien vessel and, if possible, find out where the hell those signals were being sent to.

Initial U.S. governmental response was to maintain a veil of secrecy, but this became too big to hide. A compromise was reached. Hide it as long as possible, but quietly prepare a press release in the meantime.

Several factors mitigated against use of the Vostochny Cosmodrome, the new Russian spaceport in Eastern Siberia for purpose of a moon launch: projected weather at the date necessary for launch, the unreliability of Soviet rockets for moon launches, and the essence of time.

Three months after Patel had discovered the signal, an American-made Saturn V moon rocket left Cape Canaveral in Florida. In the Lunar Excursion Module were two men who were designated to make the moon landing. In the Command module, one man would remain in orbit to await the other's return.

Three days after liftoff, the LEM landed within two hundred meters of the alien spacecraft and two men walked the distance. Each man carried a laser rifle simply operated by a large pushbutton suitable for use by men in bulky spacesuits.

As originally observed, they found the large chameleon-like spaceship to be about the size of a small cruise ship. It possessed the same color and texture as the moon surface with no visible points of entry. From their vantage point, the ship's upper portion was transparent and star fields were visible through it.

Braken tried desperately to compose himself. Fluttering his eyelids, he spoke soothingly, teasingly. "I chose you to command the fleet because your successes on previous colonization operations were beyond reproach. Am I correct, most honored guest of our house?"

Trak had conquered so many worlds that a feeling of guilt had worked its way into his conscious thinking. He was hoping to make Earth his last mission. It didn't matter anymore.

"Uh, to be perfectly honest . . . I can be honest, can't I?"

"By all means," said Braken, dripping with sarcasm, "Don't mind us."

Trak stood as straight as he could. He didn't need this. He had spent a good portion of this life on-board spaceships, and virtually all of the time in hibernation.

"If it makes you feel any better, it wasn't an accident. I'll upgrade my statement and call it a lucky shot."

"A lucky shot. Now I feel relieved," replied his interrogator, as he checked the dirt beneath his talons.

"Are you okay with a lucky shot, members of the council?" Braken looked to both sides.

The others either nodded or shook their heads, not knowing how to respond.

Braken held up a hand. "I don't want to waste Admiral Trak's time. I know he has a busy schedule. Perhaps he can help us understand the difference between luck and accident. So, what does a lucky shot mean? What did he shoot? A laser, a hand weapon?"

"A shot from a rock fired by a sling," responded Trak.

Thirteen Kurl warriors looked at looked each other, clearly not understanding what they were being told.

Braken said, "I don't get it. A stupid alien man slings a rock and we lose out on an entire planet and over forty warships?"

Trak retorted, not without a certain sense of satisfaction, "As an added note of correction, it wasn't a stupid alien man who shot the rock, it was a stupid little alien girl."

One of the council members spoke. "Last time I checked, the words for girl and man are synonymous. It is a human, is it not?"

"Yes, sir. But it was a female child."

"A fucking child!" screamed Braken, jumping to his feet.

He knew where his own rage came from and it wasn't just from Trak's screw-up. It came from the fact that twenty-five billion Kurl were crowded together and despite their magnificent cities they wouldn't stop reproducing or fighting, two curses of longevity. It came from the fact that despite all their endless conquests and their plunder and return of wealth, these only served to make his own people more satisfied and reproduce at an even faster rate.

Indeed, he realized, all their conquests were for nothing if their own world were to sink simply because of its own affluence. Government incentives stopped working at the ten billion population mark. Logistically, it was not possible to enforce any rules; practically, mass killings could backlash. Besides, those were to be directed toward aliens, not their own people. There was such a thing as common decency. Even sterilization clinics resulted in only a one percent decrease in population, which was overcome quickly.

Braken said, "Admiral Trak, you have finally given us good news. You say, only a single Earth girl-child destroyed everything by an act of bad luck or accident or whatever you want to call it?"

"Correct." Trak omitted 'sir'.

Braken decided not to acknowledge Trak's disrespect for the moment. "I feel so much better now. No telling what might have happened if the attacker were a fully grown man with any skill at all."

The others guffawed at their commander's comment and felt relieved they weren't the target of his wrath.

Braken's feelings were mixed. He had dearly wanted to go on this mission. Earth would have been a special prize, a planet with fabulous riches which might be offered as incentives for his beloved Kurl, somehow as trade to reduce their rate of reproduction. Perhaps there might even be a little something in it for himself.

He had profound doubts about leaving home to command the enterprise. He didn't want to leave for a prolonged period and come back to a home that had reverted to the Stone Age. Yet, if stayed home he might have been witness to such a reversion.

In the end he made the decision to stay home, do what he could and trust the fleet to Trak. Although there were many under his command who could send out military vehicles to trouble spots on Kurl, if he, himself, were gone during the planet-wide uprisings, the matter could become totally inflamed and uncontrollable. With great misgivings, he made the decision to stay because of his status in the public eye. As a result, the latest surge in uprisings diminished in frequency and intensity. Now, only hours before, a total of eight warships return, all with the orignal stores and colonists they initially left with.

Braken looked long and hard at the Kurl standing in front of him. They were out of promises to give to their people.

Patel sat transfixed as he watched events unfold on the moon. A disquieting thought came to him. If the ship were rigged to blow upon entry, it was ballgame over. Perhaps the aliens never had a chance to set the trap. If it did blow, it probably wouldn't matter where they parked the lander for it and the men to be destroyed. Then what?

One of the astronauts found a lever inset on either side of what they surmised to be the ship's front. After receiving instructions, the men made a full circuit around the vessel, touching it on occasion and reported a vibration from within. Seeing no entry point, one man pulled a level downward. A moment later mechanisms were activated in the soundless environment. A stairway descended and lights suddenly shone from within.

So much for parking your vehicle in a vacant neighborhood, thought Patel, as he closely watched the spacemen's actions via cameras affixed to the astronauts' helmets. He might as well have been watching television at home or in a public place. Everyone else on Earth was.

One man climbed the steps to enter the vessel and directed the second man aboard a few minutes later.

What they found were six dead aliens and a small

meteorite hole that ran at a forty-five degree angle from top to bottom. The creatures were covered with hair of medium length with short hair on the head. They possessed remarkably similar features to humans with opposable thumbs, three fingers and three toes, and a single nostril. They wore no clothing.

The men also found a cargo hold with three smaller ships and a port which could be opened for exit or arrival of the shuttles. Each shuttle contained food, water and a sleep chamber for two creatures. The power mechanisms for any vessel could only be guessed at.

They also found what appeared to be an operation manual within the smaller crafts and a number of operation manuals for the larger vessel. These manuals were printed on both sides of the pages onto extremely thin tough metallic wrinkle-free sheets. They digitally photographed each page.

The images were electronically sent back to Earth for analysis. This effort was done as a backup, lest they didn't make it back home for some reason. For now, it would provide scientists with a head start in trying to decode the manuals.

The astronauts found two creatures at a control center, three were found lying on simple beds without covers, and a single creature lay close to a shuttle craft. They identified a small galley and six pods laying side-by-side with injection ports, possibly for purposes of long-term sleep.

Could this larger ship be flown? It appeared to operational and only lacked breathing gas. Could it be oxygen? Would it even be needed? There was no doubt this spacecraft might traverse the moon-to-Earth distance, not in three days, but in hours or even minutes.

Back at Berkeley, Harwick and Altman, and now other linguists, desperately tried to translate the foreign symbols. It was no use. Without a Rosetta Stone, a parallel text written in a familiar language that matched the unknown, there could be no translation.

Or could there be? Perhaps they didn't need one. They did have parallel text in a manner of speaking in the form of auditory signals. Historically, these were never available to earlier translators of mysterious languages.

As were other experts, Altman was purview to the scanned pages from the manuals. She ordered the computer to list the most commonly used words in order of frequency. These were usually the same in most languages.

Daylight appeared through the cracks. With lot of cross-the-fingers guesswork, pieces were beginning to come together.

Braken took a deep breath. He believed the time had come to educate his newer recruits seated on his left. They who were inexperienced in extra-Kurlian operations, especially this particular one.

"Colonization takes a huge bite out of virtually all our available resources and channels them into a single operation. We reinvest in ourselves and it has always paid off. This is basic business policy. On worlds we appropriate we typically send nearly fifty ships. Each one is loaded with 1000 citizens we believe will best adapt to this new world. In this case we added several old freighters because we expected a bounteous first haul. Each ship also carries some 250 of our finest soldiers. These are seasoned commanders and veteran fighters. Some are even retired pilots.

"In addition, we typically send along materials necessary for taking what we can from the planet itself and to begin rebuilding a city or two for our people. The basic fact is that aliens and their cities mean nothing. We want their resources."

Braken paused as others nodded. Nothing complicated here.

He continued. "The nice thing about Earth, and which separated it from other worlds we have appropriated is that, after a little clean-up, only simple move-in would be necessary—another financial plus.

"They have enough oxygen in their atmosphere for us to thrive, endless amounts of free and running water, toilets, no changes in doorway size needed, no leveling of cities to rebuild from scratch. Even their transportation systems fit us perfectly. They have endless amounts of food in homes, stores, warehouses, and fields. It was all there waiting for us. Add a little biodegradable poison gas to quickly kill all indigenous animal life and we have a planet ready to be repopulated. Like the saying goes,

'Proper sterilization eliminates unexpected consequences'.

"The ores are a story unto themselves. Earth has riches such as we have never seen nor are likely to see again.

"We learned something important many thousands of years ago. Trying to negotiate with alien governments always caused us later grief. The same holds true for taking what we wanted and still permitting them to survive. The bastards just don't want to quit. This is some kind of universal constant.

"Okay, so far?"

The others nodded. They were learning from the expert.

Braken continued, "So what we do is to scout our target and if they have a moon, we'll cloak our scout ship and park it there or park in orbit and observe. Typically, we receive regular transmissions via supra-light wave. Their language isn't important. To our advantage we have a single one. This permits us to quickly recruit soldiers and experts from anywhere on Kurl. Primitive races have many. That's their problem.

"If everything looks good, our scout sends a final go-ahead and we proceed. In this case, twenty years later our battleships appear in Earth's skies after all our passengers awaken from a little time-out sleep in suspended animation. Simply put, we own some new real estate; prime property in this case."

Trak forced himself to wait patiently for a pause in Braken's monologue. There was none, so he said,

"That could have been one problem."

"What could have been a problem?" queried Braken.

Trak said, "The compressed messages. They're spoken and the words are sent by supra-light carrier wave."

"So? That's how information is sent," responded Braken, looking curiously at Trak.

"And received," said Trak. Evidentally, nobody got this, so he quickly moved on, not without a sharp bite to his words. "When we returned, home, you separated me from the others, placed all captains under interrogation, and neglected the fact that we had just come out of two consecutive sixty-year sleeps."

Trak knew better than most about effects of post-hibernation on both body and mind. Many years before, when hibernation techniques became practical enough to greatly expand the empire, emotional swings were always a serious problem among colonists and crew. Mood swings began immediately and took time to dissipate.

Over numerous voyages of varying length it was determined that releasing colonists too early after hibernation onto a new planet was counterproductive. Supplies were lost, injuries and deaths occurred.

A four-to-six week recovery period was required before anybody could leave the ship after a hibernation. Not so this trip to Earth. Nobody had recovered because nobody had ever undergone two long sleeps of close to 20 years each for the captains and crews of eight remaining ships who went there and returned.

Braken continued. "Now, do you recall the fanfare surrounding your departure? According to rumor, you were supposed to bring back enough food to feed everyone for a long time. Obviously, that was utter nonsense, but we permitted the public to believe it. Then your flagship appears along with a few others.

"I don't think any story will work now. Revolutionaries across the world are fomenting insurrection. You knew that before you left. It has always been that way, but now it's beyond repair. Have you ever seen billions who turn on their government; a government that is trying to protect them?"

"Yes, I have," said Trak. "In the old days on other worlds before we developed poison gas . . . "

"I'm not talking about that. I'm talking about here and now. Much of it is centered in this city. Now you return with nothing to show for it. Once the public learns of your failure, we will all be marked for extinction."

Braken took a breath and gave more facts to his audience. "In this case, the scout ship's hull was penetrated by a freak meteorite. Our brave Kurl commander had only a few moments to send home a last message prior to their deaths and told us the planet was ready for colonization, at which time he sent all the finalized coordinates for the landing sites.

"Thanks to you, former Admiral Trak, our powerful space fleet is now comprised of eight warships, a bunch of weaponless transports here at home, a few decrepit freight haulers, police craft, and military vehicles. We even called in every ship from all other sectors to provide you with as much loading capacity as we could find. And you lost it all.

"That's a far cry from an armada of space ships cruising at low altitude in our own skies and blocking out our sun's brightness. That vision used to be imposing and could quell an uprising unto itself, if you can remember the good old days. Instead of rejoicing that our entire fleet is home all loaded with captured food and materials, we have a net loss."

Trak knew better. Food only lasted so long. Kurl could have the food. Braken wanted materials. "Actually, another option would have been to send a second scout to find out if our first one was still there once they reported their own death," Trak said.

"We know what happened to the first one," Braken roared.

"No, you don't," Trak roared back. "You didn't know if it was there or gone. Another scout would have found that out," Trak said. "With that known, you might not have sent the fleet."

"I did consider that," Braken said, furious that the witness was second guessing his authority, which required him to defend his decisions before the council.

Braken stated, "My decision to follow procedure and use gas would not be affected by the scout's presence or absence. It's a moot point and that's why I am Commander of the Armies."

Trak reset himself, swinging his emotional pendulum back again. He strongly suspected his own death might be imminent after his challenging statements. yet would not be denied his tale. "Sirs, when we arrived, humans were ready for us. At first, even from their moon, our images showed us cities on fire. There were some lights in small communities and some minor to moderate skirmishes, but no significant movement of vehicles could be discerned planet-wide. Only a few million might be living. Only basic power could be detected. That's a fairly typical scenario for a post-apocalyptic event. So why is that my fault?"

Braken pondered. *Once the meteorite penetrated the scout and it lost all its air, did the cloaking device die? He'd have to check on that with his engineers.*

Beyond losing the scout, w*hat actually happened? How did we lose so many warships?*

A frustrated Braken bared his small fangs and with nostril flared, he said, "To start with, you are leaving something out. How did a single solitary alien girl kick our kenk within hours of your landing?"

Trak's temper rose again. He declared emphatically, "I'm trying to tell you. We detected only relatively few human enclaves when moved ourselves into our designated locations. I thought to conserve our bombs and gas in terms of expediency. Why kill something that is already dead? I mean, close to eight billion humans were missing. We have encountered such an event before on one or two other developing worlds, so I based my decision to not poison the atmosphere on this fact. This would permit us to land immediately rather than waiting weeks for the poison to do its job and dissipate.

"Commander, you were with me on one such occasion and you suggested we land and save weeks so we could begin mining operations. It worked then. I merely followed your example. We knew the humans were nuclear with planes and armies and possessed an endless number of small arms. Long ago, we'd faced this before the advent of our gas when we used our own atomics and lasers to subdue them. In this case, I followed standard procedure along with experience I gained serving directly under you," Trak reinterated.

Attempts to recover the scout ship resulted in the loss of lives being lost, after repeated and expensive lunar voyages. At last, the alien vessel was finally piloted back to Earth where it underwent critical examination along with the shuttles and the aliens themselves. (The choice of landing site and methods of decontamination were heavily debated.)

The direct flight home had been ordered. Nobody wanted to lose any of the alien spaceships for an exploratory mission throughout the solar system or beyond, especially if the light drive was somehow employed.

The many investigators learned that the sets of mathematical numbers embedded in the last message represented longitude and latitude coordinates down to the minute and second which corresponded to airport locations of some fifty large cities world-wide. A big problem presented itself: Nobody could figure out when to expect the visitors.

Researchers concentrated on the numerous diagrams related to a central double star with lines going outward, seemingly in three dimensions. The marvelous charts depicted relevant stars with their respective color and size—almost a GPS for space. Each line contained a symbol initially taken to mean light years distance, but later taken to mean years of time.

But what was a year? It could be travel time or distance or both, but they all ended at a different star. Several lines were dashed, one of which was directed toward a world believed to be Earth since the chart depicted five planets outside this world and two were inside. The nearest star to this solar system was a binary, one yellow and one orange. A red third star circled them both creating a three sun system. This matched Alpha Centauri system, closest star to the sun.

Quint, accountant for war fleets and seated to Braken's immediate right, sought to deflect the attack against Braken. Quint wasn't interested in logistics, only money. "Do you have any idea about what it costs to build and maintain a single warship?" he asked.

Trak knew, but wasn't telling. "Probably a lot."

Quint glanced at Braken for permission to continue and received a nod. "Very astute. Which computes to thousands of our own troops lost and four times that number of colonists. That's a lot of Kurl for an operation as simple as this one was supposed to be. After all, we're after spoils of war and don't give a damn about the indigenous population. Do you?"

"Well. . . "

"It's about expanding our empire, is it not?"

"Yes."

Quint's voice began to rise in volume. "It's about providing for our own people. Is it not?"

"Yes, it is."

"We lost our best crews that we've used over many years for exactly these kinds of operations whom we could have used here at home right now." Quint concluded.

"Permit me to intervene," said Braken turning his attention back to the council members.

"This was a mission of war. Forget old freighters and ore miners and assorted others. Each ship carries flaming jelly, poison gas, hydrogen bombs, Nova-class lasers, and conventional armament. They contain a hundred tons of food and crop seeds, a wide array of communications equipment and the best computers and galactic maps in three dimensions. Add to that a second cargo hold with compressed gas.

"Our heavy ships carry city-building machinery when it is called for, equipment for mining and ore smelting, individual and group modes of transportation, temporary sleeping pods for our people, numerous emergency shuttle craft, each with its own armament and food and light speed drives."

The newer council members knew nothing of this and glanced at each other in amazement at the incredible carrying capacity of the monstrous war-ships.

For Trak's part, he stopped caring. Once an ideal-ist, he had slowly evolved into a pragmatist. He saw no hope anywhere. Even a good intercontinental war that might decimate perhaps a billion or two would account for only a five or ten percent of the popula-tion. They needed a reduction in population of fifty percent or more to have a chance to survive.

Now he needed to finish and would not be drawn away from his goal. "We landed at predetermined airports belonging to major population centers to give us proximity to their respective cities. We chose only those cities with airports large enough to accommodate the size of our ships. We made our usual preparations regarding varying amounts light and temperatures around the globe for simultaneous disembarkation.

"At that time we were not attacked in any way."

Trak halted his narrative and watched as a disen-gaged Quint scratched his neck while Braken exam-ined the digits on his left hand and buffed them with his right forearm.

Braken spoke to his short talons. "Didn't it seem odd that there were no people in a planet loaded with sentient life forms?"

"Yes, sir, it did. I discussed this matter with

Forkus, my second in command, as well as with my immediate crew and concluded that in the years since the scout ship's report and our arrival over 20 Earth-years later, there was ample time for the human's to kill themselves off either through global warfare, pestilence, or by some other means. We've seen those circumstances occur on other worlds in a lot shorter time period and it appears to be a norm. Why should the humans be any different?

"In this instance, their cities were intact and we could detect no excessive radiation from nuclear warfare. From everything we could ascertain, there weren't enough humans left to matter."

Patel soon found that the search for extra-terrestrial life can be time consuming. It was okay if you wanted to make new discoveries and write papers for astrophysical journals, but discovering a true alien species couldn't hurt one's reputation.

Based upon the relative locations of Earth and its moon when the signals had been sent, received, and triangulated, a small sector of space became a priority for examination. The Very Large Array in Socorro, New Mexico, located a double star in an area of space relatively free from other stars some 8,000 light years away. Its location matched the diagrams found in the charts and it possessed at least one planet within a habitable life zone.

To Patel and others, they were looking at a civilization that had possessed electronic communication for at least 8,000 years and more importantly, they suspected the direction from which they might come.

By this time, progress had been made in deciphering the numbering system in the Kurlian language. The figure written on the line from the double star to Sol was taken to mean 25 Kurlian years or some 20 Earth years.

Trying to create a plan that required billions of disparate people on Earth to act as one sounded ridiculous. How could it be done? Many wanted to attempt to reverse-engineer one of the ships without destroying its function. A compromise resulted in the decision to sacrifice a single shuttle with the goals of trying to determine more about their drive, their hibernation, and their cloaking mechanisms.

Yet, these new discoveries could be meaningless for self-defense purposes. In today's world, humans could never fight off an invasion by aliens hell bent for whatever they wanted to do. Some military experts proposed that, through international cooperation between superpowers, new weapons might be developed to fight the aliens, but with man's propensity to use new tools of war against himself, there wasn't much merit in that idea.

One thing did become apparent in reviewing the manuals. These aliens had a lot of experience and were absolute detail freaks. They knew about humans, their ways, and their weapons. This was not a single rogue nation that could be negotiated with or bombed or starved out. Every human life could be at stake, but probably not destruction of Earth as a planet, or it would have been gone already. There would either be servitude or death. The aliens were not here to negotiate. When they did arrive, it would likely be a bad day for everyone.

With this realization, perhaps one grand trap could be set with all of humankind as bait. Time served as the great transporter carrying the human race along for the ride to meet its end in a little more than a single generation. A planet-full of people would be called upon to stop their bickering and to take this seriously—the hardest task of all, because worldwide panic had already begun.

Trak took a deep breath. At least they were letting him speak. He dropped the tone of his voice to a respectful default. "After we landed I ordered our ramps to be lowered for our citizens and soldiers to depart. This takes perhaps two hours. I don't give the command to drop the ramps until our command ship is off-loaded, as a cautionary measure. I believe that was also your recommendation." Here he addressed Braken.

"Immediately after we disembarked, I did give such a command. Once this was completed cargo bay doors would be opened and tractors would bring out all the equipment and supplies both from those doors and through our side doors. Everything was on schedule so, once again, following procedures, I sent my flight crew back to assist the departure of some 1200 Kurl.

"I was preparing to open the cargo bay doors

when I heard Forkus yell and fall onto the console with blood gushing from a wound above his eye. I stared at him for an instant and looked to see a human girl who was loading a second missile into a toy. I started toward her and she disappeared through the doorway through which she had come. This doorway leads to the crew's quarters and from there to the main hold where one of our port ramps is located.

"I looked out the view screen and saw nothing at first but the ramp. I was trying to make sense of it all and continued to watch. I saw the girl run down the ramp. A human stood at the bottom yelling and gesturing at her angrily.

I thought them to be two lone stragglers. It wasn't until I broadened the view that I saw humans swarming out from the aircraft hangars and shooting most of our citizens and troops and capturing others. They were all military and wore gas masks. Our troops fought back, but speed and surprise were on the human's side and we were soon decimated. We got massacred, although I have no doubt many were captured.

"I saw another mass of soldiers running toward my ship. Each group was fronted by a number of soldiers.

"I raised the ramps immediately. I needed to warn the other ships, because their ramps would soon be down if they weren't already. All this occurred in seconds.

"I hauled Forkus' body off the console and found

that the communication switch was shorted because his blood had run into interior electrical mechanisms. I could neither send nor receive.

"The captains of the other ships knew enough to pull out once they lost contact with me, or if danger to their ship was imminent. Likely, they had not yet encountered any danger, but I wasn't able to warn them.

"They would have closed the ramps regardless of what or who was on them in order to save the ship. Unfortunately, they were still lowered when the humans attacked. Seven ships did manage to escape on their own.

"For us, it would have been pointless to open the cargo bay, so I lifted off and took the moving walkway back to the cargo hold where the crew awaited my order to open the rear doors. I quickly told them what had happened.

"Returning to the control room, I had a sudden impulse to flame jelly the entire area beneath us for miles around, which is what I did after lifting off. Then I dropped a small nuke on the location andI flew off to check conditions elsewhere."

Beyond anger, Braken replied simply, "You didn't hear any talk over their airways?"

"We received isolated chatter, but we couldn't understand any of their languages and even if we could, who cared? I started to fly over the other landing sites and saw the humans overrunning our ships. The skies became filled with their war planes wherever we went and in truth it became dangerous for us to remain. We destroyed a number of them, but they did have nuclear tipped missiles and we couldn't have gotten them all.

"I pulled my own ship into orbit when their satellites also began firing at us so we pulled back to their moon, our initial rallying point, where we met the other seven survivors."

"You're blaming this mission's failure on this little girl?" queried Quint, jutting his head forward to stare hard at Trak.

"Oh, no, only the part where we could have gotten all our warships into the sky and poisoned to death every human and owned the planet. Sir. There were plenty of other factors that contributed to mission failure. Sir.

"To continue, my engineers began working on the com and made necessary repairs so that we could discuss the situation with the other ships' commanders who had landed."

"Near the scout ship?" asked Braken.

"Yes, at least where it was supposed to be." Trak let his words sink in.

"Did you try to contact any ships on the ground?" asked Quint.

"Of course. I got no response from anyone."

Braken interjected. "With your eight warships, why didn't you reconnoiter and go back and pound their civilization into oblivion?"

Good ole Braken, thought Trak—all business all the time. He never had an instant of compassion for the countless billions of lives he'd taken on other worlds.

"To what end?" responded Trak, in answer to them both, peacefully, calmly, lovingly. "First, we didn't have enough ships to gas the planet. As I started telling you before, we require a minimum of twenty ships flying in tandem at mid-altitude. And do what, kill 50,000 of our own colonists and troops who were already on the ground?

"Second, that would defeat the purpose of destroying what we came for. We want as much as we can get and we want it intact. I mean, why ruin cities when our people can move right in?

"Third, we didn't have enough room left in our eight cargo holds to collect anything worthwhile even if they gave it to us. Our eight ships hadn't offloaded much except for colonists. It's the cargo hold that takes a lot of space and they were all filled with food stores and equipment. Which, I might add, we did return with us."

"Damn it, Trak, why didn't you call and report to us once your com got fixed?" asked Braken who was feeling for a way out to find that every crack had been sealed. He had no wiggle room.

Trak faced the council members as though they were delinquent children. "Let me be clear so everyone here understands. The Earthmen had taken the scout ship and the team. They probably got minutely dissected. That's what I'd do to find out what I could.

"It's obvious they knew about us and probably deciphered our signals—possibly even the ones we were using to speak with each other after we had landed on the moon. Maybe they even had an early warning system. If I had called home, they would capture and translate what I said and learn even more. Frankly, this mission was doomed from the start.

"So, to continue, I met with the other commanders and we waited for a few days, but the enemy's position continued to strengthen. Their nuclear silos were going on-line by the scores and thousands of warplanes were in the air all day and all night. They, too, were heavily armed.

"Look, our ships are attack vessels. We've never had to actually create defensive weapons until this point. We never could defend against a nuclear warhead that might explode in our faces. There was nothing left to do but return."

"No, you could have finished the job," declared Braken.

Trak had found himself so disgusted with conquests that a part of himself felt relieved. The aliens on Earth had conducted a shrewd fight.

Braken opened his mouth to speak. He could only return to what he knew best: accuse, insult, intimidate.

Trak wouldn't let him speak. He found himself shouting now. He was red-lining. "What were our previous jumps; three, maybe five years at most with lots of rest before returning home? Well, twenty each way with no rest is too damn long for Kurlmen. We never recovered. Nobody thought to experiment with hibernation for that length of time. You assumed it would work so you could rush over to Earth instead of doing it the right way. Are you all insane?"

The council sast stunned at Trak's behavior. Even Braken seemed dazed. He wondered what kind of mood Trak had been in when he decided not to gas the planet or not to return to Earth from the moon and wreak havoc. He wondered what he himself would have done if he were commanding in place of Trak.

More than twenty-five years passed on Earth since Patel made his initial discovery. Harwick had died. The time had come. The militaries were onboard, the people were not.

Years ago, the captured shuttles had toured the solar system and spacemen brought back great knowledge. But riots had begun at the start of the discovery of aliens on the moon, riots which were now unquenchable. Doomsayers had their say and their way, while humans continued to riot for whatever reason they found convenient.

There remained unfinished business. A portion of the alien's last message had always rankled him, as it had other translators. He had stayed on top of the entire matter and could name all the stars in the Kurlian Empire. He knew the Kurl language as well as anyone, having spent years as an understudy of Altman.

Time had expired. Scientists had unlocked the

secrets of the cloaking mechanisms, the printing process that permitted two dimensional figures to appear three dimensionally, as were presented in their star maps. Patel mused there were few volunteers to be the first to see if they could travel faster than light. Good luck finding your way back. But all of that served as busywork, while waiting to be destroyed by a war fleet from outer space.

Patel did find it interesting that the physiology of the Kurl was remarkably similar to that of humans. Their hibernation gas also interested him. The components of the gas were long since identified and thousands of experiments on animals and then human volunteers found that it possessed the properties of short to long-term sleep. Disorientation by the subject always occurred after awakening, yet this had tremendous medical implications. Care had to be taken in administering the gas because at too high a dosage it would lead to immediate death.

With his great mathematical skills that had been focused on interstellar gases, Patel turned those skills toward Earth's atmospheric conditions. Patel drew on his dragon's fire approach toward learning. He taught himself meteorology and developed a grand plan, something that might be presentable.

There existed great uncertainty about the time of the imminent attack and the final conclusion. the world had no means to defend itself. To Patel, his idea had merit.

The logistics of the plan would be relegated to minds more suitable to think in those terms; say, the military.

Braken began daydreaming about where he'd like to go immediately after this hearing concluded and it wasn't local. He already contacted his families to get ready to abandon their homes and to expect a long vacation. How does one relocate a litter of five babies, plus how many grandchildren and their extended families? Worse, his latest mate insisted he buy her the best space yacht on Kurl. He declared himself to be penniless, graft notwithstanding. What to do?

Trak thought through his own quandary and reinforced his feelings. Braken wanted to plunder Earth for something more than feeding people for a short time. That served only as an excuse. He wanted the raw materials for himself and not for infrastructure repair, which was a money black hole. You couldn't eat metals and concrete. You could, however, enlarge the number of ships ten-fold and move forward toward regional space conquest; even to turn Earth into a regional center to specialize in the manufacture of warships and superweapons.

Braken once told him more than once that, if he could find the right planet, he'd create a terrible armada of warships. After his scientists discovered Earth, he sent a scout ship which soon sent in their first report. He hadn't felt this exhilarated in years. With Earth in his possession, he would begin the ship building process by melting down a mind-boggling amount of metals and plastics already present in countless airplanes, 500 million steel shipping containers, road vehicles, ships, railroad tracks, trains, and bridges, along with unmined ores; perhaps more than a trillion tons in all.

Braken slammed a hand onto the table and stood. "Do you know what we're going to do Trak? We're going back."

"Going back? To where?" Trak asked.

"To Earth. You and me and eight warships filled with neutron bombs. We'll fire them from well outside their atmosphere. Lots of death and enough radiation to kill humans, but leave radiation at a minimal level. This time we're going to do what it takes to own that planet. Forget colonists for now. Their space will be used to load food in cold storage and establish operations over there and . . . "

The sounds of heavy artillery shook the palace. Quint yelled, "Revolutionaries are on the palace grounds."

Everyone looked around quizzically. The council members hurriedly rose to look out numerous windows that opened onto gardens. The council members all expected to see onrushing citizens either clashing or siding with military firepower which is exactly what they saw. Surging, hungry mobs trying to enter the palace grounds were met by pro-government forces, both sides using artillery.

Suddenly, booming-cracking sounds came from above. Both battle groups looked upward. Artillery ceased firing. Still, the sounds continued. The building shook continuously. Braken led them outdoors for a closer look.

The skies were filled with warships. Sonic booms continued as more ships entered the atmosphere and began to align in some sort of formation.

"My fleet. We're saved," exclaimed Braken.

Trak began to laugh uncontrollably with a showing of teeth and fangs. "It would appear so. I suspect the remainder may arrive momentarily."

Braken looked from the sky to Trak, totally confused by his laughter and his statement. Everything had turned into a dream comprised of disconnected events. His new reality consisted of water running between his fingers.

Trak continued, "As a rough guess, I'd say Earth's savages are more warlike and enterprising than we gave them credit for. They are probably piloting those ships. In fact, they may even have a few of their own colonists aboard those vessels—say, 1000 each along with their soldiers."

"But how did they find us?" stammered Quint, jaw agape.

"Probably because the star charts and homing devices built into each warship and freighter they captured, not to mention what they may have figured it out on their own," replied Trak, with a mix of great fear combined with a sense of satisfaction—an unusual blend of emotions.

Trak felt it necessary to add, "Oh, and let's not forget the captured soldiers and pilots, who doubtless, turned traitor and who might have aided in translating the manuals and voice recordings to provide assistance in piloting."

Trak added, driving in the nail further, "I'm quite certain our captured soldiers provided them with a few details about our operation."

Braken tried his best to process Trak's words. He couldn't even formulate a question to ask. He wondered, *Is this what they all felt like?*

Worse, the eight remaining warships that had returned were on the ground, their captains in lockdown for purposes of interrogation.

Quint began to cough and rub his eyes.

Braken slowly bowed his head downward and slowly shook it, as every piece came together.

"I do believe it's our own gas from our own ships and I don't think they want us to take a short nap," said Trak, who also began coughing and rubbing his eyes."

The booming continued as more ships plowed into the atmosphere.

"What will happen to all our worlds, our technologies, our empire, our families?" Braken began to ramble as he stared hypnotically into a darkening sky.

Trak pointed his hand and said, hoarsely, "It looks like we have new landlords who will soon be moving in. I'd say our leases are expired. In fact, I'd say we're about to get evicted."

Braken looked at Trak without seeing him and asked, "Why did the scout ship tell us the humans were engaged in so many wars they didn't think any of the idiots would be alive when we got there?"

"Wrong thing to say," answered Trak, facetiously. "I'm thinking our messenger might have provided them with an idea, along with getting them mad, if they deciphered our language, as primitive and idiotic as they are."

The effects of the concentrated high density gas became stronger as the fleet above them began a mid-level circuit around planet Kurl.

Epilogue:

History will record that, in both the beginning and the end, a little boy from a fishing village dreamed of the stars. In so doing, his discovery of the signal, along with his idea to gas his own world and put it to sleep immediately prior to the invasion, were the two most important events leading to the new Empire of Man.

The planet of Kurl was renamed Patel, who lived to see it all happen.

THE MAGICAL POWERS OF LASZLO PEARCE

ONE

Prison sucks. I've been here two hours and I'm already stretched to the limit. At one time, I thought knowing trivia about the average citizen would make me crazy. This place has supplanted that idea and has provided a hell-hole filled with black thoughts.

Guillermo Sanchez, client extraordinaire, is in for three more years for cocaine smuggling. As a real estate agent, I met with him and his attorney at the prison to conclude the final signing of papers they had both reviewed. That was when I found out about both of them and walked out.

I know a lot about a lot of people, maybe least of all about myself. Certainly, taking a little money from those who can afford to part with it isn't what I would describe as real crime, but it doesn't offer a lot of meaning to life.

It hurt to turn down a commission on a multi-

-million dollar mansion Sanchez wanted to buy in Carmel, California. No doubt, life would be less complicated if I personally went on the straight and narrow. Easy to say, hard to do.

Later, I had a stern talk with myself and made an anonymous phone call to the detective in charge of the Sanchez case. I told him Sanchez had committed a murder, where he could find the body and the evidence to link him with the murder. The call took all of twenty seconds.

You'd be surprised what one can learn about others: schemes gone wrong, personal problems, terrible crimes committed, dashed hopes and despair—when receiving messages from your immediate environment.

If you are surrounded by very bad people with very dark secrets versus good people with good intentions, it's like having fetid dragon-breath monsters slathering over your body in darkness with not even starlight to brighten the gloom compared with dancing in the warm sunlight. More than anyone, I can understand that it is not just the dark thoughts of distrust and rage that run through the average mind, it is usually the strange dimensions of the average that is the most disconcerting.

The images I received from previous meetings over the years in that prison room, the tales that had been told in secret by those who had spent any time there at all, overloaded my capacity to process the information. The channel was open all the way, the reception was good, but the mind lacked a spillway, a scupper. Nausea overcame me, and for the first time, I lost the ability to close the channel.

A terrible foreboding enveloped me. I fought the nausea and knew only one thing for sure. I had never been a religious man, but I swore an oath that there must be a God who gave each person on this earth a potential to achieve greatness. For me, I might become something better because I could see ahead. There could be something far worse, and I felt tremendous fear. This was not a fear associated so much with those of us in the room. We were in it for a business deal. Instead, I saw myself for what I might become and didn't know what the future would hold, should I continue along my present path. Something had to change. Insanity must not be an option.

That said, I still possessed a boatload of human foibles. Despite those, I believed I could dedicate myself to a greater good. Somehow, it always came around to income.

TWO

My grandparents came to Minnesota prior to the Russian revolution. Dad was seventeen when he married Mom, nine years his senior. Three months later they separated.

My two maternal uncles and my mother were a part of the Big Band Era. The three of them quit high school and toured the country. Mom sang, tap-danced, and played the piano, while her brothers played clarinet, sax, trombone, drums, and violin—you name it, they played it.

Long gone on a tramp steamer, my dad did not know of my birth. Mom gave me to her parents in order to keep him from learning of my existence, in case he should contact her again.

Eventually everyone moved from Minnesota to Southern California where I grew up. My own grandmother, Tania, worked tirelessly while my grandfather worked a five-and dime. I loved and respected both of them dearly, more than today's tears can tell, but I never told them. I was too spoiled and never learned how to say "I love you," something that nobody had ever said to me.

I spent kindergarten on the sandy beach of Southern California inside a small area contained by a picket fence, separate from the girls' area next to us.

My salesmanship abilities might have been born when one of my playmates offered up a bug and said it would be fun if it could crawl along the grooves in my ear. Takng a close look at his ear, I offered that he had more grooves than I did. Subsequently, after the bug had entered Joey's ear canal and he began to scream, the headmistress arrived, grabbed both of us and hauled us into her quarters. She removed the bug from Joey's ear, spanked him with a coat hanger and told me to leave. I recall her words today: "Anybody stupid enough to put a bug in their ear deserves to get a beating."

In the second or third grade, I got into trouble and earned a reputation that lasted a number of years. It had to do with undeveloped powers, but I didn't understand them at the time.

The tops of our desks lifted up so we could keep our books and supplies inside. During tests, books were not permitted on the desktop. I received top grades. However, one day my answers were too pat, too exact, and a few sentences I used in my elementary essay matched the book word for word. The teacher caught this and became suspicious. When she compared other written answers from other tests I had taken, she found virtually the same identical phrases and passages written in our reading text.

Accused of cheating, the teacher forced me to take further examinations away from all books. My grades fell from exceptional to above average, and no more direct quotations from the books took place, thus proving my guilt as a cheater in the eyes of the teacher and the other students.

Protestations proved useless. What explanation could I give that would carry any credibility?

I remember impressions. Somehow, and from somewhere, had come impressions. The lesson there? Turn off impressions. Unfortunately, this turns off a person's sensitivity to others, but that's what happened.

A lot of people think that in order to be psychic you have to be a sensitive person in harmony with the mysterious forces of nature; however, your average scam artist, who just happens to be psychic, is not someone you would expect to become incredibly wealthy and eventually move to the top of the food chain. One might expect this person to have some fun at magic shows or open up a phone-in hot line. There is no real money in becoming a detective and solving crimes.

When I was eighteen, I had moved out of my grandparents' home, with their blessing, and, spoiled rotten, started college. I had a bent for the mathematical sciences and a leaning toward accounting. People used to say that I was well balanced with a chip on both shoulders and both feet firmly planted off the ground.

There existed inside me a hostility, the origin of which I never fully understood. At some point in my college years, I wisely realized that a person's aspirations toward better things in life stood a good chance of making a solid living when certain positive social behavioral patterns were cultivated. These included the development of strong self-confidence and elimination of self-indulgence. Politeness in general would be required. Honesty, however, did not factor into the equation as I saw things unfolding. Nor did sensitivity to others, I might add.

I possessed gift of gab, a sense of neatness about self and home, faith in myself, and the awareness that it is the nature of people to trust in others, unless, of course, business or politics is involved. These attributes will always serve to reinforce the talents of the successful con artist, a true sociopath, who desires nothing in life but to reach a good level of excellence. What I needed was a product to sell, a bug to put into someone's ear.

While in college, I answered an ad in a newspaper looking for trainees to sell health and life insurance policies.

I applied for and got hired for the job. That turned out to be a good gig so I dropped out of college.

As a lover of garage sales, I'd purchased an autograph book at a local home one Sunday. The book measured about fourteen inches by twenty-four inches and was two inches thick. According to the woman selling the book, it had belonged to her dead husband, a career military man. This man had collected signatures of comrades and commanders during World War II.

I need to describe this autograph book in detail, because it turned out to serve a central role in my life. The book's clothbound cover gave it a striking appearance. The cover and backing appeared to be hand-woven, with brightly colored black and red floral designs on a tan background. Within it were over 100 fully-lined pages. These had been stitched by hand to the backing between the covers. Tan tassels hung from the stitching. Signatures covered half the yellowed pages. I lugged the massive tome back to the car. Later, at home, after poring over the behemoth, I put the ten-pound creature into storage.

The next important event occurred five years later when I joined the Society of American Magicians and began studying for my real estate license at the same time. I understood that the art of magic could teach a person about manipulation, distraction, eye contact, and numerous other positive qualities necessary for a budding businessman. These qualities would be required for a man destined to succeed in a world already rife with people who desired to lean toward certain challenges, which are not, shall we say, totally acceptable by a wide variety of authorities.

While I practiced skills with cards, cups and balls, and the basic presentations, my learning progressed rapidly. No doubt this had to do with my analytical mind, dedication, and fairly good looks. I had grown into a physically fit gentleman with lots of slick black hair which I liked to part down the middle, although, there was enough of it to style it in various manners. My black eyes were not sunken and I possessed a genuine smile. I suppose if I had grown mustache and wore a black hat, I might pass for a riverboat gambler, or possibly a pirate out of the movies.

My true interest in magic, however, leaned more toward the psychic rather than the traditional in-your-face trickery. In the eyes of the masters who were ever diligent, I maintained the status of a rank amateur. In this writer's eyes, total belief backed every manipulation and every drama I performed. This unflagging faith to accomplish anything in life served as a catalytic converter. This faith can separate the rank and file idealist who is looking at the world through rose-colored glasses, from those who knew how to become the rose.

And so, one day, I performed a feat that left everyone in awe. As it turned out, this included me, suddenly shocked to the core. The sleeping giant from my boyhood had yawned and stretched.

I arrived early and set a music stand at the front of the stage in the auditorium where we had our monthly meetings A small table stood to the right of the stand, as viewed from the audience. I had covered the table with a large black spread that fell to the floor, hiding two boxes underneath the table that contained a total of twenty-four books. I could have loaded them with a hundred books, but twenty-four would prove the point.

When the curtain opened, soft Slavic music played and the ghostly swirl of dry ice flowed about a *Cossack* who carried a large object covered in a colorful blanket woven in Persia—the autograph book. I had made the decision to work the script around the book only the day before in a flash of intuition.

The audience saw the Cossack stroll to the front of the stage. Dry ice flowed about his feet and an off-stage fan blew his loose raiment into pulsating waterfalls of color. He wore a loose fitting yellow-orange blouse made of silk, loose black silken trousers and black slippers. His hair was slicked straight back and caught the light.

He set the book upon the table, unwrapped it slowly, and placed it on the music stand to the right. "My name is Nostros," said the Cossack in his best Russian accent. "My Great Grandmother named me Little Gazietta, which means 'little newspaper' in our language. She gave me that name many years ago because as a youth I was good at reading books.

Without opening them."

I spoke the words slowly, paused for effect and smiled slightly. Looking straight into the audience, I stroked the top edge of the book, right to left in an exquisitely delicate and sensual manner. "This book is over a thousand years old, and now with the passing of my grandmother, the Great Bookkeeper, I am the Keeper of the Great Book and you are the first public audience to view it. Inside are the names of our ancestors and relatives, all of whom came from Lithuania and all of whom had psychic skills."

I propped open the book and turned it toward the audience, turning the pages one by one. Hundreds of names were already listed. I had gone through it the night before and placed bright asterisks next to random names.

"Each of these names has a code next to it describing that person's particular ability. Only three names have the sign of the yellow star, which means Object Projection. Little Gazietta's name is in here as the only living person with this ability."

Now the Cossack closed the book and stepped to the left behind the table, knowing that fifty pair of eyes were locked onto his movements. Spectator awareness had been titillated, ratcheted up a notch. What the audience didn't know is that little Gazietta had practiced his routine to perfection, but never before an audience. Distraction was always an element any amateur performer must consider.

"There are a number of different psychic powers," I continued. "Telepathy is probably the most written about, but the least well understood. There are perhaps a hundred true telepaths in the world; two of them are generals in your own army. Contrary to popular opinion, telepaths can read only the minds of other telepaths.

"Clairvoyance is another psychic skill, the ability to know where someone or something is located. Police have used clairvoyant persons for hundreds, perhaps thousands of years, to find lost persons.

"Teleportation is the ability to move an object around with your mind.

"Precognition is a favorite and very dominant skill of mine. I will dream about whatever appears on the front page of the newspaper the next day. Sometimes, even specific words appear in both the dream and the newspaper.

"But what is object projection? This is the rarest of the psychic powers, but now, for the first time in a thousand years this phenomenon will be demonstrated before a live audience."

The audience sat spellbound, their senses heightened. I had practiced the routine numerous times and spoke in perfect cadence to the beat of the soft, but demanding Russian music. This music served to accent the moment, as nightfall and light breezes serve to accent the lapping of waves against a shore, the moaning of wind through trees, my clothing fluttering as colorful flags. Golden bracelets caught the stage lights and chimed ever so slightly.

Some being within my soul pushed itself outward of its own volition, some inner live thing struggling for birth into the world.

"Inanimate projection is the ability of inanimate objects to speak to us, to tell us of their absorbed secrets. How much we could learn, if only we knew how to listen. Imagine going into the halls of an ancient library or university building and feel the smells, sweat and blood of the ages, of the lives that had toiled therein. Imagine what the chairs you are sitting on would say if they could look up and speak of those who sat before you."

Here the audience chuckled at the thought of chairs looking up at them. The timing for laughter allowed for release of the pent-up tension I had created. The watchers would come back stronger. "Only Little Gazietta has the ability to listen to these objects and to tell you what they say."

Now I called upon a female member of the audience for assistance, introduced her (Judy) and assured her she would not be embarrassed or hurt. For this act to work, I needed somebody who would be totally compliant, not on her own agenda, and would not try to screw me up—definitely not a schill. Out of all those who raised their hands, I chose this teenager who appeared to be fairly conservative looking and with her parents present. Granted I had met virtually everyone during my membership, including Judy. I did not need some smart kid trying to fake me out.

Once our typical jean-wearing Judy walked to the front, I thanked her for participating, then reached underneath the table and took out the two boxes of books. The boxes were placed on the table where I overturned them and allowed twenty-four books to tumble into one great mass.

"These books were chosen at random," I declared. "I don't know how many are here, but it doesn't matter." Both of those statements were untrue.

In a true performance, I would have looked out into the blackness because the house lights would have been off with only the spotlights on me. "All of these books are talking to me and relating what is inside of them, but, it is difficult to tell one from another because there are so many. So Judy will choose a random number of these books—let's say twelve."

Judy chose the books and, following instructions, threw them back into the box. "She chose a dozen books and we will reject them."

I asked her to choose another half dozen which I rejected as well. Six books remained I asked her to choose three and I rejected the other three. In the end three books remained out of the original twenty-four.

Then I asked Judy to pick one of the remaining books for herself. I chose another, and announced that the third book would be the "Psychic Book." This I placed to the side.

"Now I know with more clarity what's in these books, because there are only three of them and my mind is not overloaded with much information. Judy, would you please open the book in your hand to any page and read out loud the number of that page?"

Judy did so.

"Now, Judy, I will flip through the book I hold and you just say 'stop' whenever you want." After she did so, I proclaimed the page number. I added the page number in her book to that of my own and announced that if Judy would pick up the Psychic Book and turn to that particular page, I would tell her what was written on that page.

"Now Judy," I needed to reinforce the moment, "you chose all the books down to the last one. You chose a page number on your own in your own book. Isn't that right?"

"Yes," she said.

"And isn't it true that you also told me where to stop in this book I am holding, and therefore, you chose that page number, as well?"

"Yes," she replied.

"Have you been coached in any way? Have I ever talked to you about this demonstration?"

Judy shook her head and said, "No."

I called for another member of the audience to join the two of us on stage to corroborate the final step in the presentation.

With great drama I revealed the writing on the page of the *Psychic Book* that Judy now held in her hand. I asked her to read a few lines on that page and then stopped her and continued to conclude the paragraph she had been reading from, with true and unblemished accuracy. Dumbfounded, Judy and the new volunteer could only nod their assent. "He's right," they both said, a little weakly.

"And that is Object Projection. Little Gazietta thanks you." I bowed and backed to the rear of the stage with Russian music dominating the audio scene.

No one was more surprised than me. I had committed two major mistakes in terms of book and page selections, yet everything worked. Compensating errors just don't occur in this kind of trick and once the magician realizes he blew it, there is no way to recover. It's all or nothing.

Later that night and for the next several days I pondered over what had gone wrong; or, more mysteriously, what had gone right. The numbers were wrong and so was the book; yet, I saw the page as clearly as if a giant screen had presented numbers and words.

Did a spin-off or magnification of my childhood abilities, long suppressed, suddenly evolve into a new ability which burst forth? If so, it would seem to be some fairly useless ability at first glance, unless I wanted to earn a living by traveling around as a Cossack who performed dog-and-pony tricks for a living.

After that, with my faith temporarily shaken, information inside closed books and other periodicals remained less accessible to me than they had during grade school and middle school, years earlier, when I had been accused and punished for cheating.

The following week resulted in numerous phone calls from magicians who had attended the monthly meeting, all congratulating me on a spectacular performance. One or two members suggested that I enter the upcoming statewide competition.

It came to me in a jolt. I strongly suspected I possessed magical powers and had been in touch with the Other Side. Faith and confidence had unlocked and opened a portal heretofore closed, thus permitting true Object Projection to assert itself.

Call it serendipity—the ability to recognize left-field opportunity when it comes along. Object Projection was real. I proved this to myself by mentally selecting pages within books at random, reciting words on the page, and opening the book for confirmation. More importantly, my ability now transcended that of the world of magic alone and pertained to that which belonged to the spirit realm.

Nothing had clarity. Underneath it all, clutter and confusion reigned. What use could be made out of reading books without opening them? It wouldn't work in a racetrack or gambling casino where reading the future would be much more beneficial. There had to be a way to make some easy money with this rare skill. At last, late at night, as my mind relaxed and sorted through it all, enlightenment dawned.

If books can reveal the printed page, then walls can emit the spoken word. Practice and train, yourself, Laszlo. Practice and train. Get away from your apartment. You are too familiar with this place. Go to the oldest university building on campus. Spend the day there and listen to the voices from the past. Try to relax and concentrate. Above all, have one hundred percent confidence and commit yourself to this project. If it doesn't work, then fine. You can move on to something else.

Curiously, I felt no fear. Instead, I felt a calmness, as if a path were being opened to me with soft hands touching my shoulders, pushing me gently forward.

Within days, one cloudy August morning, I went into the old biology building well over a century in age at the University. Darkness had steadily grown outside; roiling gray clouds promised monsoon rains and high winds.

The surrounds cast a surrealistic nature to the affair. This perception acted synergistically with the ghosts in the old building. Faint indefinable odors exuded from the walls. All this served to heighten my awareness of unknown powers. The old brownstone became a truly living entity, its guts always vibrating in some frequency, whispering to those who could hear. Even the least sensitive person might be able to feel a palpable presence within the two great halls of the structure.

Once inside and within only moments, I heard new voices. It seemed that some of them repeated themselves. Perhaps those voices belonged to those who had spent the most years in the old biology building. Or, perhaps, they belonged to those with the strongest personalities. All in all, I heard complete sentences and even short conversations.

These voices spoke in a language to which I could barely relate. They spoke arguments once originated by Socrates, of wonderful chemistry no longer practiced, of the germ theory of disease when germs were still controversial. They spoke of the future of travel to the planets and the possibility to communicate through radio waves. My grandfather had once told me that he remembered the advent of radio, television, and all electronics along with penicillin and so much more—all here for me, including the social undertones of sexuality and who did what with whom.

Feeling both afraid, yet newly empowered, I now discerned the difference between weakness and strength—discerned the difference between giving up, or boarding a steamer to leave the Old Country for America; between getting sucked up into the Great Depression or wheeling and dealing in the back room of a tailor shop to help form labor unions.

While the line of demarcation between failure and success may be sharp at times, resolve to overcome anything will almost always push one over the edge. Knowing that going in didn't help prepare me. Nothing did. Instead, panic suddenly hit me hard,

The voices arrived in a torrent. There was no background of noise, as if muted words came from a crowded room. No, these were ghosts from a darker world that interlaced with our own, ghosts of the past who lived on, to speak to he who would listen and could listen, ghosts who expected no reply. Finally, intellect prevailed and helped to force down the fear.

After a single hour in the building, I had seen not a living soul. I looked at the displays and walked the hallways gently touching the bricks and leaned up against them to contemplate and to feel, to listen.

At last I left for home, physically and emotionally drained, to reflect on what had happened. I thought, there could be no future in this.

I didn't want to become a famous man with a good theater act. Learning about a person's past and confronting him or her with extortion in mind had too many complications. How did a person have this power, stay out of the public eye, and still use it to his advantage? At this point, my abilities were primitive. If there might be potential at all, the skills needed to be honed to a fine point before I could make an informed decision, which required more data.

Nothing good comes without effort. I became a driven man, forcing myself to release years of skills that had been submerged beneath the cover of fear. Now I dedicated several months to sharpening my book-reading-skills and building-reading-skills, in the hopes that more profitable discoveries would be made.

You can imagine all the images I received from the walls of old and new buildings. Arguments, love sonnets, cries, laughter, one-person conversations, raw gossip, and drunken orgies—all the elements of human life bared themselves. I opened my mind at work, as well. Any environment can be fascinating when you know who said what to whom in your absence.

Before long, I could go into newer buildings and hear the conversations of those who had occupied the room during its construction. Eventually, I could take any piece of structural material and hear the conversations of those who had spoken nearby. Tile flooring and brick were better at sound retention and reflection than more porous materials, such as sheet-rock and soft furnishings.

The passage of time did not seem to affect the memory of the inanimate object itself and I became skilled at detecting variations in time, back hundreds of years in some cases. Visiting antique stores offered a rich medley of experiences and a fresh perspective on Man's sordid history. My mind unfolded like a flower.

Many times the language changed the farther back in time I searched. I learned to discern male from female voices, young from old, and the difference between ethnicities.

Overall, the pettiness of the human prevailed over his intellect. As I listened to this pettiness day after day and month after month, it became a distracting and disturbing hindrance to the learning process. I saw too clearly an unholy trinity embodied in the human race—a sprint to the finish line between three components of Man: gaudy and cheap flamboyance coupled with wholesale rapine and plunder of the earth; the second, intellectual and humanitarian efforts of magnificent proportions that paled in proportion to the flamboyant rapine; and the third component, a desperate need to self-destruct versus the need to survive.

All this might be interesting to the historian and to the sociologist, but big deal and where's the buck?

Let's get real. I felt in no mood to over-philosophize about my role in the universe. This magician needed to make serious money. One potential scheme did gain in appeal to me: move into the sale of high-end real estate with access to wealthy homes.

Because most people have spoken their names, credit card numbers and other vital pieces of information over the phone, the home retained the memory of those pronouncements. With higher credit limits awarded to wealthier persons, a great deal of money could be made from this plan, if indulged in cautiously. The money could be funneled to an off-shore account in a circuitous manner. With the emergence of my new abilities, in no time at all, I could be a very wealthy man while dealing in my profession of selling homes.

Aspects of this gift of mine scared the hell out of me. Fear is a great motivator. If I were going to play with fire, I damn well better have a good fire extinguisher at hand. This talent required a solid shut-off switch, or Mr. Laszlo Pearce would become seriously insane, hearing voices constantly in his head forevermore.

Out of necessity, I cross-trained. Power on, power off. Power on, power off, all with the purpose of developing my psychic skills to razor sharpness.

This area of high-end home and business sales was jealously guarded by my broker and a couple of associates, so I quit them and joined a larger firm. Soon, my life changed when I met Rachael at World Travel, where: *We Bring the World to You.*

She had just joined the company, having trans-ferred to the area from Portland. We hit it off from the start: Laszlo Pearce, real estate merchant, tall, debonair, destined for great things, and Rachael "Red" Sawyer with long red hair, adventuress and travel agent first class. Neither of us wanted chil-dren for a variety of reasons. This served to bond us, including minor surgical procedures to ensure the absence of accidents.

We dated for two years, and the more time we spent together, the more time we wanted to spend together. During that period, I wrestled with the de-sire, the need, to tell her about Object Projection, until one day, while browsing in a bookstore, the truth came forth.

"Yeah, sure, Laz. And I would rather have a full bottle in front of me than a full frontal lobotomy."

Laughingly, I shook my head at the non sequitur, realizing Rachel skirted what she really wanted to say: "You want bullshit, try this one on for size."

I smiled and asked her to pick up any book in the store hand it to me. So, with her own smile that smacked of facetiousness, she said, "This ought to be good," She picked up a collection of stories by William Faulkner, and turned to page two hundred forty-two. I told her that it referred to a country boy who ran away from his father. I told her that if she needed verbatim the words on the page, I would be happy to comply. I did so, to her delight. She gig-gled.

She picked up a book on the history of the world,

handed it to me and queried me as to page seven hundred seventy-six. I responded that this entire section related to the modern Post Christian era beginning with the Protestant Reformation spearheaded by Martin Luther. I gave it back to her, whereupon the opened the book and turned to the appropriate page, confirming what I had just told her.

Thus it went for an hour. We went from Bradbury to King to origami to the telephone book. We went from Astronomy Magazine to Custom Cars to the Science of Love.

"Isn't all of this psychic stuff supposed to get you mentally worn out?" Rachael asked, excited after what she had witnessed, finally putting down Robert's Rules of Order. "I mean, after so long, I would think you would begin to fade."

I led her by the arm, walked her to the exit and opened the door. "It's not like that, dear, at least not with OP. It's just a matter of opening a channel and letting the information flow in. There really is no significant effort on my part. Of course concentration plays a role, but only to keep the channel open."

She looked at me quizzically and decided to digest what she had been fed.

A half-hour later, we sat dining at at the Spaghetti Factory. Rachael couldn't stop blabbering about what she had just witnessed. She had one of those almost pixie voices, cute, but not annoying.

"What can you do with this ability, sweetheart?" she asked. "This is astounding, but what use can it be to you? Can you use it in your work?" She sipped from a glass of white wine, leaning back in the booth, contemplative. I drank tea and declined stronger beverages, fearing some uncontrollable increase in my powers, notr becoming a blathering idiot.

"Tell you what, Babe. Let's talk about our future now. As far as OP, we'll talk later, okay?" I said, not in the mood to incur excess baggage at this point. I'd kept so much inside for so long that spontaneous sharing was a non-option. For some reason, after an hour of showing off in the bookstore, I had become an introvert. Despite my protestations, I felt a great sense of fatigue and wondered if I simply required a good night's sleep.

With wonderful awareness, Rachael didn't push the point and kept the conversation to small talk, although it didn't take a genius to see she wanted to discuss more about our future.

That evening, after dinner, we took a moonlight stroll around a local man-made lake, and Rachael Sawyer learned about Object Projection. She learned the entire story of how it had come into my life. At that point, she broached the subject, and within moment's, I agreed that marriage was in our best interest.

After my tale, she seemed somewhat distant for the rest of the evening, apparently deep in thought. At last she said, "You know, Laz, the thought did not escape me that if one were so inclined, one could make a great deal of money with OP by taking it from those who no longer needed it—if one were inclined in that direction, of course."

"By 'one' I presume you are referring to me," I replied, in all innocence. "And how would that work, exactly?"

Hoping she would come up with a good idea, I said, "Doing what? How much money can we make? You earn an okay living in your business and get us almost free travel anywhere in the world, and I've got over a half-million in cash and rental properties. So, why steal, even if we never get caught, or take money from somebody who doesn't deserve to have it? It's just more money."

Not long after this, a perfect opportunity presented itself to loft me to the heights of a real player in the game of thievery. As a real estate agent, my general practice had been to visit the homes of buyers and sellers in order to obtain all the personal information needed, and then transfer money from their account to other accounts I had set up under different names. I did this methodically and with great planning in each case, accomplished weeks after visiting the home to minimize the chance of coincidental occurrences, that is, my visit and their missing money.

On one of my typical jobs, I took a lot of money from a nice elderly couple, who had a home for sale and who could afford to lose a few dollars. With the use of OP, their bank account numbers were available from a number of furnishings.

A twinge of guilt assailed me. I never believed in the scales of justice. When a person gets into a terrible car wreck, he or she doesn't win the lottery.

A lack of bad luck on a given day is about the best a person can hope for. Now, I'd have to revise my thinking. After what I'd one, a run of bad luck might be in my future.

At this point in my life, I encountered Guillermo Sanchez, whom I described earlier. Even before I left that prison, a suffocating and forlorn feeling had swept over me. I didn't want to become one of the prisoners. Somehow, life had to mean more than just taking money. Where did this path lead and where did this dissatisfaction come from?

It had been my philosophy that people like to be losers. That's why they go to places like Las Vegas or Morocco, not to win, but to lose. They need to relieve the pressure that is visited on their house by money. People scrimp and save almost every minute of every day, turn out the lights to save on electricity, shop for a cheaper hamburger, or seek lower prices for automobile gas. You laugh, but it is a terrible scourge, this money, and some people, like me, serve as an alternative to the casino.

In terms of pressure release, let's take another example. Suppose we decide to go on a serious diet or to quit drinking or smoking. After a period of time, things get pretty rough. Backsliding can be a good thing, which means that when things get tough, eating a bacon-cheeseburger, having a couple of shots of booze, or smoking a cigarette is good. The pressure is gone, no real harm is done, and one can re-engender the diet. Obviously, it takes discipline to learn when to slip and slide, but not nearly as much as total abstinence.

After the dark experience with Guillermo Sanchez, I spent several days alone trying to work out some direction to my life. I finally decided to take positive action.

Rachael became my confidant. I explained to her something I had not quite understood myself. Since I could easily discern the cards held by other players—not from their minds, but from the cards themselves—earning money from a card game had a certain appeal. It was just something I'd not gotten around to and told myself that cheating at cards lacked ethics. Besides, I was a thief, not a cheat. Furthermore, sitting at a table for hours on end made me feel cloistered and whenever I felt that way, the uncomfortable feelings and fears that had assailed me in the old biology building reemerged.

Some people have tunes that bond them together. We had our regular bookstore and its cappuccino. Like horses facing each other and touching heads, we sat huddled together, sipping and talking quietly. We decided that the money taken from the elderly couple's account should reappear just as mysteriously as it had disappeared. We also decided that all potential rip-offs be discussed with Rachael for her consideration. There existed an untapped potential to do good, she admonished, now that we had broken the ice and could share the adventures, something she became more excited about as we fomented some grand scheme.

Our first test came when I represented a seller,

who, I soon found out, had murdered his wealthy wife the previous year. Aspects of the house told me that she had been highly allergic to the quinine, such as is found in tonic water. As she had related to her husband, the wife would go into anaphylactic shock if she ever consumed any liquor that contained quinine. But somehow, while drunk, she had consumed a new brand of tonic water that had been brought to the house by a friend of the family. A terrible tragedy occurred.

The husband inherited a considerable sum of money. We can safely round it out to tens of millions. It turns out that the murderer had explained the plot to the friend who agreed to bring over the quinine. This kept the husband out of the line of fire so that he wouldn't be directly implicated. The friend earned a large sum of money for his efforts. Of course the friend appeared to be devastated to learn that it was he who had caused the terrible tragedy.

After I found out these basics and related them to Rachael, the two of us met at Pat's Famous Chili Dogs, under a clear sky and in ninety-eight degree weather. Spooning up a glop of chili that had fallen onto her plate from the hot dog, she said, "Sweetie, you can't take that money."

Taking a bite out of my own chili dog I replied, sighing, "Yeah, I know, it belongs to the dead wife's children or to charity."

"If it makes you feel any better, you can turn in the husband. Of course, that's just one opinion."

Following Rachael's advice, I tipped off the cops in an anonymous phone call from a public phone in the library. The cops put pressure on the friend, who eventually confessed to his complicity in the crime.

The broker assigned me to sell the home, which I did and made a very nice commission. It wasn't thirty-three million in clean profit, the amount I would have made in the old days had I outright emptied the account of the bad guy, but I earned honest money. Somehow, I felt truly clean inside and hadn't realized how much weight my previous life had placed upon me. With the weight gone, my powers increased. Zen must have been in operation because some actions lessened my power and some enhanced it. Perhaps someday it would all gush forth in a torrent.

The husband got sent to jail with the possibility of a date with death-row for premeditated murder and the money went into probate, the disposition of which would be settled on at a later date.

To lose out on that much money would have hurt the old Laszlo Pearce. What did hurt was Rachael's insistence that the money in my offshore account (yes, I told her about that too) had to be donated to charity. I countered that the money was secret and to donate it might arouse suspicions regarding where I had obtained so much wealth. Her counter was that the money could be donated anonymously. She lost the argument. "Tell you what, dear," I said. "For now the money stays where it is, but I will think about what to do with it. Okay?"

I kept OP active for a simple reason. Use it or

lose it. Object Projection is like a sharp knife. You have to strop it in order to maintain its sharpness. The OP ability needs attention to retain a high skill level, just like anything else in life that is worthwhile.

In truth, I had little use for the gift, or so I thought at the time. To cheat and steal just for the sake of cheating and stealing had a value at one time in my life. Now it had none. I had arrived at a better place. How much money can two people have? It came down to staying healthy so we could make our charitable contributions in a timely manner.

More than a year after the quinine episode, the broker assigned me to represent a buyer for a palatial mansion in Paradise Hills, another of the many ritzy small communities near Phoenix. The seller wanted six-point-five million for this twelve-thousand-square-foot home. I stood to make close to three hundred thousand in commissions, a good honest sum for me at the ripe old age of thirty-eight.

The messages were too juicy to enjoy alone, so I shared the information with Rachael. We were now playing in the big leagues, or so we thought. We had a lot to learn in that regard.

"You're a genius," I proclaimed, appearing astounded, after she suggested a game plan.

"I'm proud of you, sweetheart," she smiled with that lovely befreckled angelic face of hers. "It takes a true man to his take his wife's suggestion and admit to it."

What happened was this: Two Iranian brothers

had owned the home outright and had lived in it for a number of years. They served as point men in oil contracts between Iran and the United States and received nice bonuses for each oil contract signed, say around a couple hundred million for each contact signed. They were on a par with another Iranian who had received $400 million for signing a contract with Boeing for jetliners.

Thanks to OP, I learned that the brothers had held regular meetings at the home with other Iranian nationals, as well as with American counterparts. Because of the presence of Americans, all the important conversations were in English.

See, with OP, things just don't come out in sequence. It all comes out of the structure and contents at one time and has to be sifted through to figure out what is recent and what is old. That's the hard part.

What goes in comes out. Speak Swahili in the house and Swahili comes out. It's not one of those science fiction telepathy concepts where people automatically understand your brain waves no matter which language you speak.

The home itself defined sterility in all it's glory, despite its value. Constructed of marble and stone, the residence had ornately carved pillars that decorated the main living area, lacking an ounce of warmth in the dwelling, despite the appearance of expensive furnishings.

The thugs (read terrorists) planned a Big Bang, as they called it, on the Bank One Ball Park in Phoenix to occur shortly after the stadium let out for a game. They were to haul the "goods" to the ballpark in a few days as part of the crowd. Among numerous vehicles, they owned a long-bed Chevy six-wheel pickup truck that would make the trip from Scottsdale, just a few miles away.

With her kind words, Rachael and I had earned a guided tour of the home. The owners gladly showed us about while we openly admired their taste in elegance.

These boys did have a sizable bank account that must be weighing heavily on them. Before they transfer the money back to their homeland, we wanted lighten their load, relieve their pressure.

With Rachel's permission, I went to work, obtaining other relevant details (the walls have ears) such as the bank account numbers, credit card numbers, and as much vital information relating to their respective accounts anyone would ever need in order to do a little creative accounting. I commit these things to memory. This takes practice, but keeps recorded messages out of the picture, just in case the situation heats up.

Fortunately, the funds were held in American banks so the account numbers were spoken in English. I had no desire to purchase a Berlitz book on *Teach Yourself Arabic,* or *Farsi,* or whatever.

By the time the day was out, I transferred some forty-nine million dollars and change through six routing positions that would ultimately fatten our personal account in the Grand Cayman Islands. They had been selling out their investments for some time and had consolidated their funds in anticipation of the great day, after which they would return home to the real bonus money.

The easy part completed, the real challenge came in stopping their forays into human deaths. Rachael was very scared and rightly so. Her previous involvements with OP had to do with words in a bookstore, and thieves. I reassured her that, at the very least, we would give it a try, and at the very best, we would stop the plot. Okay, and make a few tens of millions. She said she felt better once I explained it to her.

I should have given Rachael more credit. She was well ahead of me and had a Persian customer in mind, a man who would do anything for her and who had been in love with her, yet respected her marriage to me. He had no idea what his own countrymen were up to and she didn't, couldn't, say a word. She called him from a pay phone after we left the house to set up a private meeting.

At the rendezvous, she gave him ten thousand dollars cash in small bills for two minutes of work with another ten thousand, if the plan succeeded. The plan called for him to phone the Phoenix branch of the FBI. In heavily accented English, he identified himself as Iranian and asked if they were interested in the presence of explosives destined for the baseball stadium. He gave them the license number of the truck and when they could expect it to pull into the parking lot of the ballpark. If they tracked the truck to the owner and moved in too early, they could miss the explosives.

Authorities found a man sitting in the driver's seat of the truck listening to the radio and found a large crate in the bed of the truck containing enough C4 explosive to kill hundreds and maim countless others. When confronted with a guns, rifles, and shotguns in his face, the driver of the truck confessed that he was also a spotter, in case the ball game went overtime, while he listened to it on the radio. In any event, his instructions were to activate a 30 minute timer once the game ended and walk away.

The brothers were picked up at the airport preparing to leave from Phoenix to Paris. The feds wanted to know what the now-destitute citizens of Iran had done with the large sum of money that had been deposited into their their bank account, surmising it had been shipped back home earlier. Naturally, the brothers denied any knowledge of the whereabouts of their money and are still trying to figure out what had happened to it. No doubt, their own government is still trying to find out the same thing.

I gave up on the sale of the mansion. The feds would appropriate the home, as they always did in these cases. I hate to lose a good commission.

For my part, the reader needs to understand that a few paltry millions of dollars stashed hither and thither did not placate my desire for more money. Don't forget, I had a wife to take care of and contributions to make. I will confess, though, that a deeper well-hidden itch rquired scratching.

Back at our regular bookstore haunt, oper two

large espressos, I explained my inner feelings to Rachael. She suggested it might be worthwhile for me to change careers, at least temporarily. Working Wall Street might be more to my liking. I explained that the gig required too much complicated work with too many deals and too many voices coming off walls and too many checkbooks and ledgers to read and numbers to memorize.

We couldn't come up with a solid game plan until she chewed on some hair, thought a moment, and suggested I turned Object Projection toward politics, where the real money of the planet could be found—where the driving force behind Wall Street lay. That one hit home. It felt comfortable to me. She presented a simple scheme. I had to work myself into the White House and a tourist trip wouldn't do. I needed *time* inside.

A good memory can sort through a thousand conversations that occurred over the years and pick the few that are currently relevant. The same is true with OP. However, after years of hard effort, I had learned to date conversations though rational thought, which amounted to the equivalent of carbon 14 dating with a human memory, not due to OP alone, but through common sense. Presidents and their myriad of advisors and esteemed guests who had entered the Oval Office could be identified, not just through names, but also through discussion of private deals.

A lot of thought about the problem led to the following conclusions: My donation had to be worthy of the effort and avoid the eyes of the tax people who compare donations with income stream and posted money. Additionally, almost every president has the walls freshly painted and some, if not most, install new carpeting and furnishings. The standards are the desk and the walls which will seep information, albeit limited in strength through the paint. It isn't like the old brick biology building where I had first trained. This required more than a single visit before I had enough quiet seconds between conversations to become attuned to the messages. If the president wanted to have Secret Service agents present during our conversations, he would hear no objection from me.

The mind is a computer and will accept a flood of information. If you leave it to itself after that, it will automatically sort the data and provide answers relevant to the data you entered.

Did I work my way up to gain entrance into the White House after years of effort? Nothing so romantic. Instead, because it takes money to make money, I donated a million dollars to the president's reelection campaign fund. That got us noticed.

This did not happen out of the clear blue. Rachael and I had long been nationally recognized as donors to children's cancer funds, to homeless shelters, programs to build businesses in low-income areas of America and of course, to the president's re-election campaign fund—serious donations. In short, we received an invitation to the White House.

You want to talk about insider information? Try eavesdropping on a conversation between the President of the United States and the Army Chief of Staff regarding the future of American Military involvement in oil-rich Middle Eastern nations as a primer.

This course is called Investment Made Simple. First, you learn whose relatives and party contributors will get the defense contracts and what kickbacks everyone will make on the deal. Then you invest. The process goes on every day, everywhere around the planet—always has always will. That's not illegal, is it? Okay, maybe immoral, but what is the definition of moral? Or legal, for that matter. Come on guys, you know what I'm talking about. Rule Number One: No politician ever goes to prison in our county. Their scapegoats might, but not the guilty. Once we belonged to the president's inner circle, we could do as we saw fit, although, crude as it might sound, Rachael and I had a method to our madness.

We worked as team, investing in pharmaceutical and construction companies under government contract, which helped our financial coffers immensely. Within a three-year period, we had increased our portfolio more than one hundred-fold. The president got re-elected. A war served as a great assist to our bank account, as did the entry of various medically related products for public consumption. We were now multi-billionaires.

Learning the nuances of my ability was like star hopping to the amateur astronomer with the use of binoculars. If you wanted to find the Andromeda galaxy, you first had to find Cassiopeia, and then look for the appropriate star in the "W" and drop down a couple of degrees. Sometimes, a half a dozen hops would have to be taken in order to find the star or galaxy you sought.

In my case, I didn't know what lay at the end of the trail. It took me many years to learn the skills necessary to excel in Object Projection. These skills enabled me to do my own star hopping into reading the human body and diagnosing problems inherent in every human being.

Somewhere along the line, it became glaringly obvious that the ability to receive words from walls should not differ greatly from receiving images of poor tissue from healthy tissue. This might not have been true in my earlier years, but decades of hard training to achieve a much higher skill level brought forth abilities that had heretofore remained latent.

As an experienced evaluator of business opportunities, I didn't see a big profit in telling people what might be wrong with them, so I *hopped* to tapping into reading the future health of any person, as well as the manner of their demise. This is a black skill that is not meant to be, especially when, in a moment of loneliness and weakness, I subjected myself to self-analysis and found out the truth about my own future.

Burdened heavily with this knowledge, I quickly gave up trying to know more about the health of people, and never told a single soul his fate, leaving each person to his own unknowable destiny, sharing this information only with my tormented soul.

Had it not been for Rachael, I might have been forced into a dark corner where I might have resided for many years accompanied by the unwanted partners of loneliness, lost loves that might have been, and social relationships with bad people.

During the occasions when my wife and I were White House guests, we chanced upon a great discovery. As one of the president's national economic advisors, I had occasion to tour various research laboratories around the country which were receiving federal money. In so doing, I visited the now famous University of Oklahoma Klein Memorial Laboratory where Aaron and Wilma Klein had been killed in a fire two years earlier. The couple had spent two decades treating thousands of human subjects. They tested a combination of ingredients that previously had worked incredibly well on experimental animals in both preventing and curing skin cancer.

Today, of course, everybody knows about the specific formulation that included extract of tomato seed and grapefruit seed, wild mustard, thyme, and rosemary. Back then, the Kleins had the evidence, but died before they could publish. Everyone knew they were notoriously tight-lipped and were working on something terribly important. The scientific world and the public at large bemoaned the fact that their notes and records were destroyed in the fire.

When I went to visit their lab one morning, I discovered otherwise. The laboratory had never been reconstructed, but was left as a memorial to the couple who had spent so many years of hard work there. Granted, the shattered glassware and equipment had been removed and the water damage had been cleaned up, but charred walls and counters were a testimony to history.

At first, I truly believed that fire would have destroyed any psychic evidence, although in truth, I had never investigated a fire-related incident before. In my mind's eye, if nothing else, the smoke would have obscured any readings from the walls. Instead, just the opposite effect occurred. Through some mechanism I couldn't fathom, the fire enhanced the effect of my readings. Object Projection never spoke so loudly and clearly to me as during the few minutes I spent in that room. If I ever needed another job, a future in arson investigations awaited me.

Shocked to the core regarding what input overrode my senses during that visit, I shared this information with Rachael who counseled me on how to proceed.

Then the two of us met with the university president for a supposedly private conference in his austere office. From what we'd heard, gray-haired, Jimmy Cantrell—a country-born man of integrity. who ran a tight ship, and a likely candidate to make history. We shook hands and took our seats again. Rachael opened the conversation by explaining that her husband is a psychic.

Cantrell looked at me askance, with a suspicious grin on his face. He knew of us, but must have wondered why the president had let loose these people in his house. He glanced at Rachael. She nodded slowly and simply smiled.

My time had come. Perhaps this might be the fruition of it all. "Jimmy, I'm bowing out. You don't need to advertise our visit to the world and you can have absolutely all the credit. You have our word on that. With what I'm going to tell you now, you can up your request for more research funding in any department you choose. You name the price, my friend, and we'll make it happen."

To his credit, Cantrell obtained a bemused look, sliding his suspicioius eyes over to Rachael, who smiled ever so delicately. He turned his gaze to me, waiting for the punch line.

This wasn't my first rodeo, nor his. I said, "Don't ask me how I know, because I won't tell you, but, my friend," here I paused for maximum effect, "like all good researchers, the Kleins had a duplicate set of notes."

UNIVERSITY PRESIDENT FINDS MISSING KLEIN NOTES

Associated Press

In what can only be described as an astounding find, Dr. Jimmy Cantrell, President of the University of Oklahoma, said that angels came to him and told him where he could find a duplicate set of notes written by the Kleins.

Aaron and Wilma Klein were on the fast track

to preventing and curing skin cancer with a simple cure when they were killed in a freak fire in their laboratory. They had published a number of papers in peer-reviewed journals describing the remarkably successful results they were having with thousands of test subjects.

In a fairy tale of romance, the Kleins met as graduate students at the University of Oklahoma and fell in love immediately. Brilliant as students, they married and over the next several years became front-runners in the field of geriatrics. Finding themselves unable to obtain enough grant money to fund their progressive ideas, they decided to turn their talents to cancer research, where money was more readily available.

Reportedly, they were in the final stages of data correlation and were preparing a large concentrated batch of their extract, based on natural herbs and spices, when a mysterious explosion and fire occurred in their laboratory. Foul play was suspected, but no one was ever apprehended.

President Cantrell said that, on a hunch, he personally discovered the Klein's research notes, complete with data from the numerous test subjects and the exact proportions of the ingredients for the cure for the particular type of cancer in a completed final form. The notes were located in a storage room adjacent to the laboratory in an old chest freezer. The freezer had been padlocked and unplugged. President Cantrell stated that this touch bespoke of the brilliance of the Kleins in that the freezer is airtight, waterproof, and fireproof.

Cantrell is being lauded worldwide for his find, which will rank along with the greatest of archaeological discoveries, including the Rosetta Stone by Heinreich Schleimann in 1799 and Carter's discovery of the tomb of Tutankhamen, should the data and records be as applicable as other scientists believe them to be.

Almost, in anticlimax, Cantrell announced there was a new suspect in the laboratory accident that killed the Kleins. He expects to make a statement to the press within a day or two and an arrest is imminent.

On camera, Cantrell stated, "I can't speak for the rest of the country, but our new research emphasis will be to isolate the virus associated with human DNA that many scientists believe contributes significantly to the aging process. According to the newly discovered notes of the Kleins, they were secretly involved in their original love, the aging process, and now, for the first time, we have solid data linking removal of this virus from the human genome and longevity. And thanks to the Kleins, we also have the methods to remove the virus and thus, provide the method for all of us to live longer."

After the Klein incident neither of us had the inclination to pursue OP further. We had made our fortune and had done our good. There will no heirs.

Now comes the fairy tale, the story of the poor boy who, at the age of seven dreamed of finding a city, and who thirty-nine years later, went forth, sought and found not only the city, but also treasure such as the world had not seen since the loot of the

Conquistadors. This fairy tale is the life of Heinrich Schliemann, one of the most astounding personalities, not only among archaeologists, but among all men to whom any science has ever been indebted. *

In our penthouse suite overlooking the Caribbean Sea in Cancun, Mexico, the yellow sun is beginning to peek up over the lightness of the blue horizon that is based by the darker turquoise-blue sea. No significant amount of airborne dust is present to turn the appearance of the sun to less than golden. The water lies as still as glassine in the windless air. Not a wave can be seen, not a single ripple in the entire observable ocean, an immense blue-green animal that has stretched out for a short nap along the shore. It almost feels as though the Earth had been traded for another world that orbited a distant sun, which coincided with our decision to retire OP and try to live a normal life without any magic whatsoever, save that belonging to the glory of each and every day.

Gods, Graves, and Scholars, C.W. Ceram, Bantam Books, 1967, P. 30

ENTITY

ONE

The *thing* got into my mind—into all of our minds. In truth, it scared the crap out of me. What happened from when it first started, I don't think even the *thing* knows or cares.

You can call me the head man, the head honcho, the head camper, or just Jackson Walcott. After several summers at this lodge, I knew it inside and out. I knew where to find the king snakes, the tarantulas, and the alligator lizards. I could follow the cycles of the moon and perhaps, one day, I can become a spaceman.

This particular summer, our troop consisted of twelve members, all boys between the ages of eight to thirteen. We were the elite, the sons of starmen or the sons of the bosses of starmen or sons of the administrators who ran the few remaining corporations that controlled the declining space industry.

I began attending the camp at the age of eight and

had come here for eight weeks each summer going on six years, straight to my present age. This was thanks to the directive of my father, who owned the largest space shipping fleet on the planet.

In the evenings, we sang the usual dumb campfire songs and ate our roasted wieners and marshmallows. Our counselor even made up a special batch of his hot cocoa for us and insisted on toasting to the future welfare of the human race, whatever that meant.

At the end of the first week, I led the other men-to-be in a pissing-on-the-campfire ritual. As an experienced camper of this facility, I knew enough to stand upwind and let the younger campers, who didn't have my experience in life, stand downwind. If you want to talk about my sense of strategy, there was a perfect example. No doubt, I am destined for greatness.

Without question, pissing on a campfire is strictly the domain of man. This is something no legislation can negate. They cannot demand equalization of sexes and insist that women should have equal rights to do it and penalize men for not letting them do it. I say, go for it.

Marty Bordeaux, our counselor, then gave the order to pour plenty of water on the glowing wood. He stirred the residue with a stout branch to ensure that the campfire had been completely extinguished and poured more water on it after he had declared the coals to be dead. The smell of pee brought the sounds of disgust and feigned retching from the other eleven boys, each trying to outdo the other.

One of our more dramatic members grabbed his throat and fell to the ground, kicking his heels and feigning severe contortions, as though a snake had coiled itself around his scrawny neck and had begun to squeeze. Some rushed to his aid, offering a variety of enticing treats to provide him solace.

Finally, we were ready to settle down in the cool air of the Ponderosa Pine forest near Flagstaff Arizona, some seven thousand feet in elevation. The stars were a long way from being out in full, yet the primary ones visible through the trees could be identified by virtually every camper there, whether it be by name, magnitude, color, whether single or binary and distance from Sol.

Upon Marty's command, the troop hiked down about fifty meters to where we had previously laid tarps a few hours earlier over the pine needles in a level area. We opened our bags and formed two rows of six, exactly three feet between the rows and two feet between each bag. My spot, as the head honcho, the man of seniority, lay at the top end of one of the rows and closest to where the counselor would station himself. Joey, my best friend, lay directly across from me. Everyone laid down with head outward. The other kids, all younger than Joey, my best friend, and I, were looking forward to the first sleepout and first ghost story of the summer.

We took off our shoes and placed them under our heads to serve as pillows and bug-buffers. Then we climbed into our respective bags and zipped up, not so much to keep in the warmth, but to keep out the insects; partly real, but mostly imaginary.

The quarter moon rode at a nice angle where we could all see it if we turned our heads eastward, just above the pines. To me it was as though the wind were whispering a soft string melody as it flowed through the countless little pine needles in a soft, almost continuous, swoosh.

Even in early summer the air was still quite cool at this elevation. A rogue storm had passed through a couple of days back and had dumped several inches of snow. Things warmed up a little after that. The sun came out and the snow began to melt. The air felt crisp and clean in my lungs.

Marty eased himself down and hitched backward, settling his back against the deeply gouged bark of an old Pinion pine a few feet from where I lay only feet from him.

Me, I'd heard all the stories. I'd heard about the bats in the cave, the ghost ship, vampires, rats in the crypt, dead humans who walk in the night looking for campers to feed on, and rats in the lighthouse.

Feigning boredom, I still felt an energy, an enthusiasm of expectation. I think we all felt it. My fun would come watching the reactions of the others as the story unfolded, and then I could drift off into an easy sleep and the next morning hear about how scared everyone had been and how I'd missed the best part.

Marty was a first-year counselor and no-year college student. Joey and I couldn't figure out how he even got here, especially when he claimed to be a specialist in soil microbiology. To me, the man was a big, strong, not bad-looking guy with lots of short black hair, green contacts, and a little space between his front teeth. A friendly man, he liked to shake hands, hug, and put his arm around you. It didn't take us long to find out why he did that, and it's not what you might think.

Marty couldn't have been more than nineteen years old. This night he wore what we all wore: sneakers, blue jeans, and a green Tee-shirt and base-ball cap with the words "Camp Oninococ" printed in red letters. Over the shirt he wore the green wind-breaker of the camp.

Oninococ is Coconino spelled backwards, the name of this national forest in which our camp had earned its great, and expensive, reputation.

Marty was the kind of guy you liked the moment you met him when my mother dropped me off the same time the other kids came in. Even without knowing his background, I respected him. He just gave off good body signals. Rumor had it that he might be connected to the system in some way.

At last, drawing out the moment, the camp coun-selor began his strange tale. "I guess this story really begins when I had a chance to take off a couple of years ago to earn some extra money. I lucked out and got assigned a short stint on a good Earth-like planet that orbited Canopus. The ship had to make the circuit on a number of jumps before Canopus with the purpose of dropping off the dozen of us explorer types at their various assigned station planets."

Already I'm seeing giant holes in his story, but I let him dig himself in deeper before I pounced.

"On the ship I met the two middle-aged scientists with whom I would wind up spending a lot of time. One, Ken Hunter, was a walking encyclopedia. The other, Jocelyn Jones, was a truly gifted machinist and inventor."

Marty fell silent a moment, as if recalling details of the story, ot more likely, making it up as he went along. "Hunter was as average looking as they come with the personality of a rock. He said that he knew it to be a problem, but he didn't know what to do about it, except to say that he had improved over what he used to be. He was small and slight in stature, standing maybe five-six and didn't weigh more than a buck and a half. He kept his brown hair as long as regulations would allow and if he had a sense of humor at all, only he knew about it.

"The way Hunter told it, the Federation had been trying to recruit him out of the University of the States for the past few years. His specialties were Planetary Formation and Paleontology. They figured to ship him to Canopus to get more info on the planet before opening it up for colonization.

"Jocelyn, a little gal who didn't talk much, could fix or create just about anything, anytime, anywhere with nothing to work with as far as tools. She also had a Doctorate in Mechanical Engineering and owned a machine shop with her sister, Rebecca.

They owned a number of patents for their original devices."

Marty paused to take a couple of tokes on his pipe. "It took us nearly a month to get to the Canopus system, with all the stops that we had to make to drop off other teams at other planets."

I'm listening to this and thinking, *Yeah, right, and you're traveling along with minds like Hunter's and Jocelyn's. I don't think so. Maybe you're getting boring. How about that? The man is so full of it. I knew Joey was thinking the same thing.*

If he's trying to tell us how great he is, I'd come back with stories about my old man. He's a pioneer in his own way and owner of the biggest space fleet in the known galaxy, or did I already mention that? He personally loves to pull freight and ought to know what he's talking about. He once told me that being chosen to explore another star system was a complicated process that combined incredibly rigorous mental and physical testing, background checks, and great luck. Political pull and lots of money didn't hurt. Millions wanted to go, but only handfuls were selected. The vast majority of those were rejected; or, they deselected themselves before ever climbing onboard a ship.

The rumor that space sickness would kill you before you ever got to another planet had spread far and wide, and for a good reason. Like most rumors, this one possessed an element of truth. I was to find out why.

Almost disturbingly honest and as dedicated

as military commanders, these star travelers were worth their weight in platinum upon their return to earth. In a word, you don't serve as point man for the human race going to the stars because you filled out a form. And to get selected with only a year or two of college under your belt was darn near impossible; no, it was impossible.

Yet, here was a man who claimed to have been selected to serve on another planet without a college degree. For all I knew, Marty had never shined shoes. Maybe he figured we were too naïve to understand the nuances of the selection process and wouldn't know the difference between total honesty and bullshit.

What really disturbed me was the thought that he knew whose children he would be counseling. I dismissed the thought and began to facetiously congratulate myself for my analytical thinking while our counselor told a stupid story that was heading nowhere fast.

In the darkness underneath the stars, a cloud passed in front of the stars directly over us, which served to add an air of mystery to the night. In their turn, the stars somehow seemed to become brighter and much more numerous after the cloud had passed, as though my eyesight were improving.

Marty went on with his tale. "Canopus Four consisted of lots of grassland along the coastlines at the periphery of two continents. The grasslands were fed by soil runoff from mountains and foothills. It had two huge, but fairly shallow oceans, with dark blue-green water, which suggested the presence of smaller sea life such as plankton and shellfish along with plenty of carbon dioxide to make the shells."

Suddenly, Marty lapsed into a softer voice, as though he were speaking to himself, and said, "That's where it came in from . . . the sea."

As though he hadn't made that statement, he continued, "The inland areas of two continents consisted of lush tropical forests. For most of the beach front, up and down the continent where we were stationed, the continental shelf must have been very shallow because the water lacked any breakers. It lay as calm as a small, lapping lake driven only by the wind, and there was plenty of that.

"Because 80% of the planet consisted of water, the humidity remained elevated. It rained a lot and storms from black and billowing cumulonimbus frequented the sky. The gravity and air were fine. Absent the overcast or clouds, the sky turned out to be blue to turquoise and the nights spectacular with lots of great new constellations begging to be named. The planet screamed for the presence of resort hotels and human decadence.

"Our ship landed near a gray plasti-steel tower called the lighthouse that the first team had constructed some years before. A big ugly thing that didn't belong, it sat at the edge of a granite spit, which extended out into the water. Its base, measuring some twenty feet in diameter, tapered toward the peak.

"I wondered why somebody would build this

structure at the edge of an ocean when no ships sailed the seas. I doubted the Federation had anything to do with the construction of this monstrosity, which pointed to the station crew as its authors.

Willy, one of the youngest of the group laying at the bottom of one of the rows, asked, "Marty, why would they build it without approval?"

"Shut up, Willy," yelled Joey, but not loudly enough to disturb the mood of the story.

Marty chuckled. "Hang on, Willy. We'll get there. Where was I? Oh, the ship set down about two hundred meters northeast of the tower. The grass glistened with wetness from an earlier rain. Nearby, there stood a fairly large electric two-seater flatbed ground car and a single long-range two-man flier. On the land, about three hundred meters up the beach before the spit began, I saw a compound consisting of three buildings; two of them appeared to be small basic houses and one clearly served as a storage shed with a durable, moderate sized greenhouse located next to it.

"I recognized the nuclear power generator, a two meter-high dome, situated on a large pedestal constructed of reinforced concrete. Next to the generator stood a fresh water conversion tank. I couldn't see it, but I figured a water well would be found nearby.

"Although the tides were low at the moment, in orientation we were told to expect severe storms several times during the year. These monsters could crop up from nowhere and, similar to the sand storms of Mars, might occur planet-wide. They could last for days and even weeks. One of our assignments was to learn more about climatic patterns on Canopus.

"Which was why the compound had been set back from the shoreline several hundred yards. It also told me that the lighthouse wasn't just sitting on a slab poured onto the ground, but had probably been anchored by thirty foot caissons set deep into the granite rock drilled out by atomic lasers. More importantly, it told me that the people who lived here took some kind of project seriously enough to cut back on their regular work-load to build it.

"No sooner had the three of us stepped out than the four inhabitants came from the tower to greet us. The ship's captain and co-pilot exited the vessel, as well, always happy to plant their feet on solid ground and see real sky and inhale fresh air.

"Introductions were made all around and everyone helped offload the equipment and supplies we would need for our stay. The captain hit a lever to drop down numerous large and medium-size boxes from the ship onto the flatbed ground car where we carefully stacked them. The car pulled a large sled onto which we loaded bags of cement, sheets of plasti-steel, plant seeds, scientific equipment, food supplies and other materials we would need for our stay. Somebody drove the car to the lighthouse and rest of us followed on foot.

"Alex ordered, 'Let's get these loaded into the ground floor for now and leave everything on the pallets'. The exterior door needs to be rehung. It leaks around the edges and at the bottom so the floor floods when it storms and we need to keep everything well above the ground. We'll readjust things tomorrow or the next day. And yes, we do have a nice little pump with exterior hose to remove the accumulated water'."

Marty took a toke from his pipe. "No one suspected that most of our lives, including yours, would change forever only a few days later at the arrival of the next storm arrive."

Right now, I'm yawning. Let's get to the part about the rats, Marty.

"A no-nonsense bearded brute, Alex, our geologist.Alex, when not prospecting, occupied one of the cottages. The man seemed to get smarter every day. In truth he did, for reasons that will become clear in a few minutes. He had just started his third two-year tour on Canopus; in fact, he belonged to the first crew four years prior to our arrival and had been appointed station chief even at that early date.

"Once off-loading had been completed, we all crowded into one of the small cottages, ate steaks and drank clean water and alcohol and gossiped about earth and other developing colonies.

"Federation regulations demanded a virtual zero-time transition period between outgoing-incoming groups. The next day the five would be gone.

"At this, our one and only get-together, nobody asked about the lighthouse and nobody volunteered any information. Even prior to coming to Canopus, I heard the Federation was still furious at Alex for breaking regulations and diverting resources to build it. He still hadn't come up with a plausible reason for the construct. One bureaucrat had proposed cutting his retirement pay to make up for what the structure had cost, an idea without merit, because the cost of shipping the materials added up to 100 times what Alex would be paid.

"What was inside the lighthouse?" Another question from Willy.

"Simple enough answer, Willy. The tower had a small lift in the basement that could take us up one at a time, along with some materials. Also, a narrow metal stairway set against a wall curled to the top. Up one story is the next largest space with the laboratories, work benches, and three computers inlaid into the circular wall. Remember that these computers were connected to the central library on Earth, as are all the libraries on colony planets.

"Go up one level and you find the kitchen and small eating area. The third level held a bathroom and tight sleeping quarters. At the time, I didn't understand why a couple of small cots might be present when the cottages were nexrt door.

"Finally, and most importantly, the gallery occupied the highest area where which had a 360 degree view and from where the searchlight could be controlled.

"When I looked at it, my own thoughts strayed to calculations based on what little nautical knowledge I possessed. My calculations told me that a one hundred foot tower would provide a line-of-sight to the horizon of nearly twelve miles. You take the square root of the height and multiply it by one point one seven to get your distance to the horizon in nautical miles. This one wasn't that tall, but apparently Alex was damned serious about seeing something more than 10 miles away.

"After only a few hours of eating, recreational drinking and trading war stories, the captain and co-pilot said goodnight and retired in the home where we were partying. They might have been traveling between the stars, but they still had a schedule to keep if they wanted to get paid. The three retiring scientists adjourned to the second home, which left the four of us to fend for ourselves. The others would arise at sunup and be away into the void within an hour after waking.

"Hunter, Jocelyn and I were eager to unpack our equipment and play in the lab in the lighthouse the remainder of the evening. Alex spent the night in an armchair in the gallery with a pair of binoculars glued to his face as the powerful search light slowly played back and forth across the waters. This light could also rotate around to survey the land. It would soon become evident why he made it that way."

Not much happening with this story, I thought. Still too early to sleep, I saw nothing but boredom ahead. I stretched and waited for Marty to introduce the part about ghosts in the tower or where Alex turned out to be an alien vampire who successfully sucked their blood while they slept.

I reached out and touched the camper next to

me—a young first-timer about ten years old. He nearly jumped out of his sleeping bag. "Hey, Buddy. You awake?"

"Yeah," he said.

"Scared?"

"Nah."

"Just wait. It'll get really scary pretty soon," I teased.

The wind had been as light as a feather before, bringing the fragrances of the forest, unbelievably rich with scents. With a rustle in the trees, the breeze shifted direction and I could smell what I thought might be some of the campfire pee. Somehow, I knew what comprised the scents, as a dog might key in on any one of hundreds: one-seed juniper, a little sharp and slightly pungent; pine, somewhat heavy, but not unpleasant; soil fungi lending a musty fragrance. Also, I sensed the odor of animal musk and maybe a little fishy smell of algae on pooled water. Funny, I hadn't noticed the differences before. And the myriad of sounds, too. The hoot of the owl, and what other kind of night birds were there and the sky appeared brighter almost by the minute. I saw the dark matter, the blackness between the stars comprising the bulk of the universe, the matrix into which all the stars and two trillion galaxies had been implanted., if one counted all the proto-galaxies formed at very beginning.

Pulling myself back to the story took an effort. I figured this to be a perfect night to fall asleep right here right now. I tried to pull away, but somehow

Marty's voice kept me in tow like the hook at the end of a bungee cord.

"At breakfast Alex gave us our assignments which revolved around biological experiments regarding the dominant species of plant life on the planet and the most curious—the grass."

"Uh, what did Alex do?" asked Dick.

I knew about Dick's father, Doctor William Tremain, a wheeler-dealer with the Fed trading the riches of one world for the riches of another. My father had spoken of him on a number of occasions as one of his most esteemed employees. Notice who employed whom.

Marty answered, "Alex spent his time collecting geological samples from the countryside and plotting geological formations. Within his first year he had found titanium and copper deposits. He knew so much about the planetary geology of so many worlds that he made me sick. I saw him as a man-of-all trades and a master of all of them.

"One thing I'll say against the Space Federation," he continued, on a sour note, "they skimp on equipment for exploratory worlds. As scientists in our own right, we three could recognize a good lab from a bad one and we were in a bad one on Canopus. Fortunately, Jocelyn could either repair the equipment or could build just about anything from scratch.

"The teams before us had planted a large vegetable garden on the land around the tower, separate from the greenhouse. Water came from a well-pump that had been sunk by Alex's first group several years before.

"That first week, we kept busy setting up equipment and getting into routines. Alex taught us about the geology of the planet and reiterated how colonization was right around the corner, given that we find and fix what was wrong with the place."

Which was? I wondered. Now I smiled to myself. Here it comes. I could hardly wait to get scared. I'll give him credit.

Marty forged onward. "Near the end of the first week, Marty assigned me to man the observation tower. This basically meant that one could read, sleep, and do whatever came to mind, as long as I kept an eye on the ocean. For what, he didn't say.

"Let me get to the point. The big mystery of Canopus was its vegetation in that it varied greatly, but only locally near the waterline. We could find no animal or insect life and the oceans had yet to be explored. While there were countless species of plants, my job and immediate concern was the grassland that dominated the low flatlands. It swept as far as the eye could see up and down the shoreline, and for miles back to the foothills where shrubs and trees appeared; at least in the areas north and south of where we were stationed.

"The beach sand had foothill soil mixed in with it. The grass grew at the shoreline of the continents of the planet except where rocky shores prevailed. Here comes the strange part. Most all the green grass grew only a couple of inches in height with the exception of strangely shaped patches near the seashore where the grass grew inland to a height of several feet. This is also where the shrubs grew to a height of trees for several hundred yards up and down the beach, like tall and ripened fields of wheat or orchard trees planted by a drunken farmer.

"These patches of rich green sun-ripened fields were irregular in shape, with rounded margins at the top portions. This pattern would be hundreds of yards long and then disappear; then they would turn into the short stumpy grass again—same for the trees. Short then tall; tall then short. That's why the Fed needed a soil microbiologist, to figure out what caused the differences in height and, if possible, bring home this unknown growth factor."

"Did you find it?" asked Joey.

"Yes," Marty responded, simply.

My mind wandered. *Bordeaux, Bordeaux.* Something rankled me about Marty's last name. Hadn't I read it somewhere? Hadn't my father mentioned it?

The counselor drew on his pipe in the crisp night air. "After several years of research we were no closer to the truth than when the work had started. Nobody, including myself, could find any difference in the microbiology or chemistry of the soil from one area to the next. We could take soil from the short grass and transplant the tall grass into it and the grass still grew tall. And, if we took soil from the tall grass and transplanted short grass into it, the grass would remain short. Therefore, the growth factor appeared to be in the grass itself and not in the soil.

"How could that be, we asked ourselves. Mankind had prospered on planets a heck of a lot harsher than Canopus. On the other hand, we had no clue about what caused this grass and shrub problem. We don't colonize planets on guesswork. We want to know what we have to overcome, who we have to fight, or with whom we have to negotiate.

"Toward the end of the first week, there I am in the tower gallery late one night reading my notes and wondering what I'm missing, I glance outside to rest my eyes to see a storm brewing. If you've ever been to the Midwest during tornado season, you'll understand about very dark low hanging clouds with ripples on their underside. That's what this looked like. One minute a zillion stars dotted the clear sky, the next moment the sky is black and the waves are chopping. The lengthy, shallow continental shelf kept down the height of the waves, but wouldn't prevent the storm from pushing the water a long distance up the beach and flooding the vegetation."

Marty's got up now and began to walk among us. His voice changed in pitch and cadence. He interjected a very noticeable air of mystery into it, as though he had been the sole survivor of a killer rat attack story. "That's when I chanced to notice a strange sight on the water, where the spotlight had just flashed over.Pulling out the binoculars, I stood up and moved closer to the window.

"Alex wouldn't tell us what to look for, just to let him know if anything strange happened. I halted the motion of the light from the control panel and focused the beam. Part of the water actually appeared lighter in color than the rest of the ocean and it also moved in a manner that didn't conform to the motion of the waves.

"The ocean swell just didn't seem right in that area. I set the binoculars on the tripod and quickly adjusted the automatic photo-timer for every five seconds. To this day I can't describe what I saw, but I'll tell you one thing, it scared me more than space sickness ever made me sick.

TWO

"It began to rain very hard and lightning flashed almost rhythmically. At that moment, Alex yelled for people to get to the basement and move things around before it flooded, angry that we hadn't done it before. Hunter was in the computer lab and I heard him say that he'd be right down to help."

Now I'm into the story that is starting to build. Rats on the water wouldn't fit in, nor would poisonous ocean algae like the glow type we have here on Earth. That would make grass die, not grow taller. I figured Marty was hyping up the story to make it more attractive. Or was it just my youthful hormones enhancing the effect? Did it matter which? I knew the other campers must be scared, but none of us could escape the tale any more than a shackled prisoner could run away from his captor.

I resigned myself to be captured by Marty's verbal embrace. As it turned out, the word capture can have a lot of meanings.

"Jos appeared at the top of the stairwell to my left for a stretch break when Alex started his tirade." Almost whispering, Marty said, "Without a word, I pointed outward. The thought came to mind of a story my own camp counselor had told me years before when I was your age. The story was about men in a lighthouse on the coast of Norway who espied an old sailing ship coming toward them out of the fog. The ship had lost its rigging, but still had its masts intact. The entire ship seemed to shimmer as it moved. One of the men picked up a pair of field glasses and saw the entire ship overrun with rats by the tens of thousands, whereupon the ship crashed upon the rocks and the rats left the vessel to attack the lighthouse and the men inside."

I knew the story by heart. I might not have been able to tell it as good as Marty could, but suddenly I stopped being a fan of the story once he made that little analogy. I had to laugh to myself. He's telling the same old tale with a different twist.

In no particular hurry, Marty took a toke or two off his pipe before looking up into the blackness for a long moment. I could almost see his mind fly outward to some distant place. "Well, here was this unknown area or mass approaching the shore. Our eyes were riveted on the sight. Rain and hail pounded against the lighthouse glass and the roof which made it became difficult to see.

"The minutes flew by, the rain fell in buckets. The thing had almost reached the shore. "'Men, get up here. You have to see this'," I yelled into the house speaker.

"'No can do'," replied Alex. "'We've got real problems here'."

"'You can and you must'," Jocelyn replied back. "'It's sparkling'."

There was a slight pause, "'Then it's back'," Alex stated, flatly.

"Jocelyn and I looked at each other and shrugged, turning back to the window. A few moments later the lift door opened and the bearded man stepped out. It would appear that he'd left Hunter alone to deal with the flooding of the first floor.

"Alex removed the binoculars from the tripod and looked at where I had stopped the searchlight for a few moments. Then he turned the light one hundred eighty degrees, dropped the angle and broadened the beam. He quickly walked to the land-facing window, bringing the tripod along and reset the binoculars. We could see sparkles washing onto the shore, following behind the sea foam that lapped even higher as the storm worsened."

"'Oh yes, my dear, I see you'," Alex said, with a gentle smile, as if a long lost lover beckoned to a man on the edge of madness.

"At that moment, Hunter's voice came over the speaker. "'I'm going to need some help down here. We've got some funny water coming into this place'. You could hear the engine of the mini fork lift whining in the background.

"Alex ordered, 'Marty, you come with me. Jos,

you stay here and give us a moment by moment description of where that thing is going and what it's doing'. Then he said softly, 'Although it really doesn't matter anymore'.

"Alex and I crammed tightly into the lift and went down to the ground floor to finish stacking pallets and moving equipment. On the way down I said stupidly, 'Looks like you've got a fluorescent algal bloom. It's somewhat greenish which suggests it's photosynthetic'.

"Alex remained silent, apparently deep in thought, because with all that beard, he scratched his forehead.

"By the time we reached the ground floor the water was three inches deep. We all wore casual work sandals and we sloshed around in them performing our tasks. I quickly explained to Hunter what the three of us had seen, as we set to work.

"Jocelyn's voice echoed off the walls. 'It looks jelly-like and it's definitely oozing way onto the shore and washing all around the base of the tower and up to the compound. I can't tell whether this thing is independent of the water or is part of it'.

"'It's both'," Alex muttered.

"Weren't you scared?" asked Dick.

"Shut up, Dicky," I said.

Several suspenseful moments passed.

"More than at any time in my life," answered Marty. "We never heard of this kind of thing before on any world."

He took several moments to tamp and relight his

pipe. What was that all about? Was it to calm him or to calm us or to add chill to the story? Even in the darkness I could visualize the billows of ghostly smoke coming from the pipe and his mouth.

At last Marty went on. "Then Alex ordered, 'Jocelyn, get down here'.

"We were almost finished with our work, standing in about four inches of water, when she arrived. The pump was working full speed. We wallowed in the water like kids in a wading pool trying to finish our work fearful of the sparkling water washing around us."

"You mean the jelly sparkles got on you," asked Joey, a slight quaver in his voice.

"Not only on us, but *in* us," declared the camp counselor, slowly, meaningfully. "Sort of like drinking something and it gets absorbed into your body. No, more like it was absorbing you."

I said, cutely, "Or like hot chocolate from the inside," remembering the batch Marty had prepared for our dinner.

"Exactly, which is my point," Marty stated, emphatically.

He had just frightened the piss out of a dozen boys under his charge, negating his promise to ensure their physical and mental health. In fact, two campers unzipped their bags and took off for the nearest porta-potties.

Marty rolled on, "I guess you couldn't really call this thing a jelly creature, because it didn't appear to have any mass. I'll call it sparkles of energy, some kind of force, spreading over the water and the land like a giant amoeba, sending out pseudopodia tens of meters across. On the surface, none of us seemed to be affected in any way by the creature, nor had even thought that such affectation could be possible. Perhaps the word 'creature' gives it too much credence; apparition might be have been a more appropriate word at the time.

"We piled the equipment high enough to escape the flooding on the first floor. Some of the more valuable items we took back up to the lab.

"For whatever reason, it seemed to us that this creeping, sparkling thing had been on the planet for a very long time. We found out later that Alex had walked in it along the shoreline just up from the station during a sudden storm after he'd been there only a couple of months. Right after that, he directed the construction of the tower to watch for it in the future.

"We went back upstairs and searched for this strangeness. We only saw sheets of water on both sides. Alex went outside on the parapet to look for it. Finally, we gave up. Because we could no longer see it on the land or in the water we surmised that it had left with the current.

"Alex heard the same tale from the three of us as we sat around the small table in the kitchen eating pizza, each embellishing upon the story.

"He got into a serious scratching of his forehead and said, 'I've seen a lot of strange creatures on a lot stranger worlds than this one'.

"'Just look at Earth. Try growing up on a nothing planet like this and then going back home with its ten million species, only to return here trying to describe what you saw'."

"After a few moments, he told us about why he had directed the lighthouse to be constructed.

"'Thanks to this evening, we now know its period and where to find it," he said, 'which was my original intent in the first place. It's been nearly four years since I saw it, since it's last circuit'."

"Alex insisted he and I take the little scout ship and go find out where the thing went. Why me? You'd think he'd want a soil guy to stay here and do some sampling while the trail was still fresh. He said he wanted Jocelyn to take her oceanographic receptor outside at first light and match the energy trail with the grassland so we could keep an eye on what happens to it if it left any trail at all. He wanted Hunter to do the same thing with surface measurements of the dirt where the thing had or had not touched for comparison. That left me for company.

"Alex pulled out some maps of the planet and followed the ocean currents, at least what we understood of them at that time, and figured that if the thing floated on the tides and these were drifting southward along the shoreline, then it should be maybe one hundred fifty kilometers in that direction come morning given the coastlines, the circumference of the planet and the time it took to make its last circuit."

A voice from farther down my row interjected.

"I don't get it." It sounded like Johnny Barrow, a disgustingly rich kid from a billionaire family. If you were—let's be politically correct here—of the middle class, you could hate him with more than a grain of disgust, except that you couldn't hate him for his brains, his looks, or his personality. Just his money. The handsome ten year old lad exuded analytical skills.

Truthfully, Yours Truly occasionally thought about his own future as a spaceman down the road a number of years, but didn't realize that his future would come much sooner that he had ever thought, thanks to Marty.

"What don't you get?" asked the counselor.

"Did Alex build the lighthouse just to watch for the thing? Why couldn't he just wait until it washed up again?"

"Not really," said the counselor, slowly, meaningfully. "Think about the solution, Johnny. The episode only lasted a short hour or two and then it disappeared. Suppose it had washed up at night but no spotlight had been on to catch its sparkles. It only sparkled when light hit it. The light lit up the sparkles and I spotted them. Alex took the chance."

Barrow then said, "So if the tower hadn't been built and the lab was constructed within the compound, as I presume is normally done, then you would have missed the whole thing."

"You got it. As it turned out, when Alex and I left the next morning in the flier, we were only off finding it by a few kilometers. Like many areas of the planet, the grass grew a short in some places and very tall in others. Figure a ten-to-hundred-fold difference in areas that had had more exposure.

"We were hovering about a quarter-mile above the tide line. Unlike our area here, the continental shelf where we landed was even more shallow and when the tide receded, it did so for a quarter mile and when it came in it did so for another two hundred meters and you could walk all the way out if you wanted to.

"When we landed, the tide had come in and there lay the creature, oozing and sparkling in the sunlight and covering the beach. We filled several quart containers with the stuff. We also drank it. We had no fear, only a great need to do so. Further exposure to it did not concern us. After last night, we understood everything we needed to understand. We returned to home base and put the containers into storage and Alex took off to do some exploration. The man liked to be alone more than he liked company; kind of an introvert."

"Wait a minute," Johnny expostulated. "I still don't get why he chose you to go with him over the others. Anybody could have collected bottles full of the stuff."

"Maybe he believed I could do the most good with it—to expose more people, such as campers, who came from very wealthy and influential families."

Petrified, I told Johnny to shut up so Marty could get on with it. I began to wonder if the thing crawled around inside me now.

"I know what you're all thinking," said Marty. "You're wondering about if you are all contaminated. The answer is that you are. You just got a light dose, a touch, a caress. Things are getting reorganized in your minds with or without your permission, that's all."

"*That's all?*" I wanted to scream. "A dose of what?"

"Of life, Jackson," he replied evenly, matter-of-factly.

THREE

I had to clutch myself inside my sleeping bag. The two campers who had run off came back and silently crept into their bags. Whisperings down the line gave testimony to their being brought up to speed on the story.

"The operative word, my friend, is 'unfettered'. It's like a parasite that traveled along with the development of the brain and this parasite has always limited the mind's potential. Now this thing outside sucked off the parasite, allowing our intellect to expand."

"You mean like handcuffs?" asked Joey.

"Yes, Joey," said Marty. "That's exactly what I mean. Imagine yourself and everyone in the world wearing handcuffs from the moment they are born until they die. Everything you do is with your hands tied behind you and because everyone is the same, you think it's normal. Then one day, someone comes along and takes off your handcuffs. You discover you can now do things a lot faster and more efficiently than you could before."

"Before what?" somebody asked.

"Before you drank the cocoa, before the thing entered your body and unleashed your powers," Marty declared.

Another chill crept into me, as I scratched at a spot on my cheek, fearful a bug had sucked my blood.

"But how did the thing know that you were there, on the land, I mean, or in the tower?" This from Frankie, a ten-year-old computer nerd.

"Good question, Frankie. My best guess is that it didn't," said Marty. "We think it found us there by accident when it came up to . . . visit the grass, or maybe just to touch it, and just like we peed on the campfire before, the thing saw us as logs that it needed to pee on. The grass grew very tall where it got touched by the thing."

Another cloud covered the moon. The night had a long way to go, yet.

"It didn't work, though, did it?" I said, with some humor and great hopefulness. "You were strong enough to resist its mind games."

Marty shook his head and said, with not a hint of mirth in his soft voice, "Surely you jest, Jackson. No, my friend, it won. In its own way, it didn't harm us at all, but made us stronger—maybe by accident and maybe that was what it was supposed to do, you know, touch life.

"After it touched us, it made a passive circuit around the planet, touching land whenever it could. I don't have a clue about how it might have affected any sea life. But our fruit and vegetable garden outside the compound that got washed by the sparkling thing in the water became something spectacular to behold. Did you ever see four pound tomatoes or a tree with one-pound lemons?

"Maybe grass and all life can have handcuffs. The data collected by Hunter and Jocelyn found not a single residual, not in the soil or the air; nowhere except in the growth of living things."

"You're just as tall as you always were, aren't you?" Joey asked.

"Yes and no. There was something else, too," the counselor spoke so softly that we had to strain to understand what he said. We all held our breaths. It would be a perfect time for him to yell at the top of his voice and make us jump a couple of feet straight up like a cat that had suddenly stepped on a hot grate, while he had laughing fits. It would be a great ending to a great story.

But he didn't do that. A stronger breeze had come from somewhere and, to my perception, the creatures of the night became more active in their sounds and rustlings. I could identify every one of them.

Once I had taken my mind off his name, it came to me. Marty Bordeaux, alias Martine Renault Bordeaux; the genius prodigy from high school who had gone to the stars; the only person ever to do so without a college degree, and who had returned as something indefinably greater than a genius, or so the press had stated. He had been in the news recently and now I remember having heard the story not long ago when I was about to fall asleep.

So this was him. Holy stromboli, the man was real which could make the story real. I shivered mightily and wanted to crawl out of my sleeping bag and tell each of the others in turn. Surely they couldn't know what I knew. He couldn't have been more than eighteen or nineteen right now.

Somebody had pushed him through. This realization made me listen with rapt fascination, captured as surely as a spider catches a fly in its web and wraps the fly in its silken gauze. We were his fly. No. The thing took the place of the spider and had wrapped up life itself. What would it suck out of us. I swear at that moment I felt a smile from my inner workings that came from Marty. I wanted him to speak without interruption.

"I won't say that the thing tried to communicate with us, but in our expanded-mind-state, we did pick up a terrible pain, beyond anything we could imagine, as if the alien were projecting a memory. Maybe it carried this emanation within its being; maybe it sent the message for our benefit."

"What do you mean by *any* of what you just said?" Dick asked, his voice cracking slightly.

Marty became wistful and his voice waned so softly that we had to strain to hear every word. I swear he wasn't talking to us. "You know damn well what I mean. A heaviness overcame Hunter and Jocelyn and Alex and me in the tower that night. Call it an unspeakable loneliness—far beyond human comprehension—a loneliness gathered over tens of billions of years, created at the beginning of it all, and of years traveled between galaxies and even universes, a loneliness so ageless that time had no way to measure itself unless one counted the beginnings and deaths of stars and maybe universes themselves as units of time as we count minutes or days.

"For all this period, there was absolute cold and hunger and a wonderment of why Mother Nature could be so cruel as to dictate this meaningless fate far worse than death. Then, with some finality, it landed upon a planet rich with an ocean and plants, sunlight and warmth. With that came the some meaning—a contact with something, anything. More than something solid, it found life. What was—is—life to it?"

Those of us listening to that tale shuddered at the concepts Marty had portrayed in his story. Our minds flew to the outer reaches of space and tried to envision what our counselor revealed to us. Then, suddenly, we did. The heaviness overcame our minds and we felt as Marty felt and so identified with the voyager as voyeurs in our turn. I swear we shivered to a man with cold chills and sweat and terror beyond terror, and felt our own loneliness, and then, finally, peace and insight.

Marty told us of his strange interpretation of a

message that had been sent down to us through the ages. "If these unique compact units of energy, such as our unnamed being, were perhaps freaks created during creation—if they had been human, they might have wondered why the management of time hadn't been handed over to some woman more efficient than Miss Fickle Fate. For surely, to travel thusly, waiting through time unmeasured for a world to land upon and to fulfill its misbegotten destiny, gave the meaningless nature of death a meaning after all. What could be crueler than to have survived a journey across the void, only to cease existence because of some inherent universal randomness and indifference? Would there then be any difference between life and death?"

I thought that Marty had forgotten he was talking to a bunch of kids, because of the words he used and the way he used. He would trail off as if he got to thinking about something else. No, as if he *was* something else.

Marty suddenly presented a lighter attitude, yet seemed wistful at the same time. "Well, all this all happened in my fourth month. For the next twenty months we saw the connections between things more clearly and our senses became heightened and these senses are still growing. We could see a mountain with our eyes and without using sensors, detect thousands of color shifts and bulges that would pinpoint locations of ores. Our reading speed and understanding became truly phenomenal.

"As men who understood the interaction of molecules, Hunter and I knew the subtle implications of how minute amounts of organic and inorganic chemicals would affect life or death or cause a variety of diseases. We understood and remembered everything we had ever learned and heard. We also knew how to shut it off. And that, campers is where you are right now."

FOUR

"Alex's skills exceeded those of the three of us in many ways because he'd touched it years before. Both he and I were different in that our senses were better than those of Hunter and Jocelyn, because we drank of it. We weren't just smarter, our ability to understand body language and to perceive changes in the skin temperature of another person improved greatly. I suppose you could call us the ultimate lie detection devices.

"We wanted to return to civilization and transfer what we knew to others, just as the Entity had given us its gift. For example, try looking at millions of colors over tens of billions of years. Not just colors, but sounds and songs of the stars; not just colors, but the entire electromagnetic spectrum from beneath x-ray and gamma rays to above radio waves and to understand what we could accomlish if we only could ask the right questions.

"Now we can ask them and build things we hadn't dreamed of before. What we can do with that knowledge alone will change mankind into a super race of beings. Mankind and other life forms on this planet don't have a chance to stay the same, not after we expose them to this.

"So far, the only thing our friend has learned about life itself is what it encounters on Canopus, such as what it has found in the oceans and the seashore. Then it came in contact with a sentient being, Man. Man will not be the only thing to change. Entity, as we named it, will also undergo a transformation because of its contact with us. It has assured us of that. How long will that take and in what form remains to be seen. Don't forget something: If it has anything, our new partner has patience."

I was freaking at this too real story, even for my advanced senior camper mind. The saving grace for me was my years of experience in the wilderness and my level of maturity. I began to calm and smile, relax, and let Marty's story flood over me, thinking that when I became a camp counselor someday, I would tell the same story.

". . . we all grew and changed until my tour had finished. Hunter and Jocelyn stayed behind to start another tour because Jos could leave so much fun creating devices to measure a new world. She got named the new station chief. Alex came home with me. Everything is different. We learn more every single day. We learn how people think, how to fix our problems and cure our illnesses. I don't even know if I'll go to college next year. What's the point?"

My head had been swimming for some time. I began to wonder why Marty never got debriefed.

So far he hadn't said a word about it. All explorers are debriefed after a mission. Or maybe he was and everybody in the Fed knew but they were keeping their mouths shut. Yet, they let him go so he could counsel a bunch of kids. It made no sense.

Would Canopus be overrun with tourists or businessmen who would want to see *The Thing*? If it did happen, who cared? You couldn't hurt it. But could it hurt you? Or had it already done so? More specifically, could it hurt me and had it already done so?

For some reason, I remembered something my father had once told me. Life is a series of crossroads. You do the best you can each time you come to one. Some people like to choose the wrong one all the time. It makes them feel secure because that's the way they grew up and they're used to doing things that way, even if it is wrong. Those are the losers. Others do their best to make the smart choices and stand a good chance of making a success out of life.

Space was different. You exchange trips in an airplane for traveling through dark space; you trade an average life of good health for space sickness. My father didn't tell me that in this lifetime we would be trading our humanity for the mind of a creature from beyond the farthest reaches of the undiscovered, the unsuspected, the unimaginable.

The next day we swam, hiked, played baseball and performed other camping activities. Marty held his tongue and promised to continue the tale that evening. As senior camper he gave me the choice to make for the group: hear the story around the campfire or in the safety of the cabin.

In the light of the day my common sense took hold and this gave me courage to forget the fears of the night before and make the decision to return to another evening out.

The breezes were stronger that evening. Distant thunder and flashes of lighting occurred from a passing system some miles to the north, somewhere in southern Utah. Marty sat on a log by himself and I sat nearby somewhat closer than the others and immediately wished I'd opted for the cabin. The campfire burned low; still the flames danced their reflection in his eyes and alternately backlit his face.

Once we were settled, good ole' rich boy Johnny started it off. "Marty, a lot of us want to know what you told your debriefing committee when you got back home. Also, do you think the alien grew after it fell onto Canopus Four?"

Marty chided Johnny, "You're behind the times. We stopped having formal debriefings shortly before I came on board because the development of Interstar networking had reached such a high level of success that it became unnecessary. Why spend the money to send people home just for an interview if they wanted to stay on. and hell, I'd already submitted so many visual monthly reports that they knew me better then I did.

"You can bet nobody was going to tell them about the creature and our lying expressions were flawless. To me, the thing grew from something very tiny to something very large and it might continue to

grow, perhaps, in the end, to create a sparkling planet. What the hell do I know except that colonization
really didn't matter much anymore because of the
larger picture.

"Look, guys, in point of truth, it's time to confirm what you already suspected. We're all joined
with the Entity. The information it gained in its travels, whether on purpose or by accident, got spread
among any life forms with which it came in contact.
The grass on Canopus comprehended the information and so do you."

I guarantee we all felt a quaking fear. Marty told
one hell of a story.

Joey blathered, "Do you mean, like, take over the
world?"

"That's exactly what I mean, and also to make us
better in some ways, so it's not a stupid question,"
the counselor assented. "You're going to help do it.
All of you are. Maybe one purpose is to keep us from
killing ourselves so that we can fulfill some higher
purpose. Maybe it's to be more creative, have more
understanding, to live longer, to save the creatures
of the planet—maybe the planet itself. This Entity
didn't go through eternity just to give us a passing
'hello'. Get the picture?"

My father had told me more than once, if it's too
good to be true, then it's bullshit, until proven otherwise. Therefore, Marty was the ultimate bullshit artist, counselor extraordinaire. However, he did have
everyone's attention.

Dickey spoke out. "Yeah, so what I hear you're

telling us is that we don't need to go out and explore anymore. Well, I don't think this scum alien out there knows diddly squat about us."

The other campers giggled or snickered, either in agreement with the statement or in disapproval and embarrassment at his comment. To me, Dickey had a valid point. At least, that's the way I wanted to see it.

Marty shook his head. "Dick, you're still thinking like a little kid. That's always been your problem. The same goes for all of you. This stuff works fast. For the most part. you will act as your personalities dictate; you will also tap into the underlying layers of your thinking process. Dick, do you know anything about relativity?"

I had something to prove, mainly that Marty told a good story and that would be the end. Trusting my intuition, I said, "Come on, Dick, think."

Dick responded, "Think, huh, okay, sure. The increase in speed and mass don't matter a hoot until one reaches the ninety-nine point ninth percentile of the velocity of light speed in a vacuum. After that; mass, length of the traveling object, and relative time change exponentially to the fourth power. You really can't hit the speed of light; the early equations proved that. You could come right up to it and even go faster than light, but not hit it. The Clark drive jumped the gap."

I already knew that much. What stunned me was who had spoken the words. I searched my mind for some explanation of what had just occurred. This was not the mind of Dickey, or perhaps I didn't know him that well.

"That's a start," said the camp counselor. "Chief Camper, do you know anything about the Clark Drive?"

My turn to roast on the spit. This time I refused to say something stupid. "Sure, what Dick just said only applies to one miniscule part of our universe, that is, the part about trying to travel faster than lightspeed. Like he said, you just can't hit that exact velocity. Take a look at the Lorenz transformation equation, There are are a lot of other ways to get around that are much faster than Clark, such as riding on the space currents that connect the stars and galaxies.

"With a score of dimensions of normal space, sub-space, and hyper-space, you can take your pick. In my opinion, the universe we know is just one bubble in a bubble bath with the others pulling on it, and amongst each other, gravitationally pulling all the stars within each bubble to expand outward at an increasing rate."

My heart pounded. From whence came this knowledge? Saying it sounded as natural as singing Happy Birthday.

We all remained stone silent. The fire sparked hard and made us jump.

The camp counselor stood up and slowly paced around the entire campfire, not looking at anyone, seemingly lost in thought. Twelve pairs of eyes stared, transfixed on the man.

Then he said, "Well, my campers, I think it's time

for all of us to talk and figure out where we go from here."

Before this night, when I dreamed about being like Superman, I could never fly more than a few inches off the ground. Maybe that represented my insecurities. This night I dreamed about flying through star systems and always feeling the tugs of gravitational waves, about being grabbed by stars and galaxies and clusters of galaxies, only to be flung outward again, and of something material like water; touching something called life with the single undefinable thing that was me.

I dreamed about making life grow and I slept as if the dreams were induced by opium. It would be at the height of ludicrousness to intimate that a lone and timeless voyage through the ether was the non-human form of insecurity and that finally land-ing on a home world represented happiness. Yet, those strange thoughts had entered my mind that night, perhaps engendered by human interpretation. Strangely, I felt no threat, no fear, as though this were meant to be.

Just before sun-up, Marty woke me gently and beckoned for me to for me to follow him, motion-ing for me to be silent. We stole into the woods, not making a sound, and walked for a distance until the sleepers in their bags were out of sight.

"What do you think of last night's tale? A real story or a tall tale?"

Oh," I sighed, exhaling the word, then looked at him questioningly, as if it were a silly question to ask. "It's real to be sure."

Marty pulled a hip flask from his front pocket, the kind in which one might carry hard liquor.

"What's that," I asked.

"Want a drink?"

Through the trees I could see that the slightest glow beginning to appear at the eastern horizon. I looked at him suspiciously. "Sorry, never before dinner," I quipped. *What was this man up to? And, Why me?*

"It's pure Entity," he said. "At least as pure as I could collect it. You can't separate it from the water and you can't distill it—at least I haven't been able to, but what do I know. It will taste a little salty because I collected it from the ocean on Canopus. But it's real and honest."

The morning scents of the forest soaked into my skin and respiratory tract. Weren't we all a connected unit? What would these massive pines look like or smell like if they watered them properly with you know what? And he wanted me to take a concentrated dose?

"And yes, there's more," Marty quickly added, anticipating my question. "Alex and I went back and collected a certain quantity, which is now safely stored. I left that part out of the story. Our secret, Chief Camper. Are you in?"

I unscrewed the flask took a sniff to ensure he wasn't trying to slip me . . . what? Something I shouldn't be drinking? Then a taste. I toasted the forest, the counselor, and said for the world to hear,

"Dear Lord, please save us from ouselves." Right then, who's to say he did or didn't?

"Why don't I feel any different with all this knowledge floating around in my brain?" I asked, watching a morning Blue Jay fly from one bough to another.

"Jack, your normal mind, the one you're used to, remains in default mode. Once you begin to think, then, well, things happen."

I became accusatory. "So you sloshed in and drank it—who knows how many times. Then you gave out a few drops in some chocolate and messed up the brains of a bunch of kids. Is that what you're all about?"

"Yes and no. I'm relatively new at this . . ."

"Yeah, and I'm Santa Claus," I spat.

Marty laughed out loud. He had a gentle laugh, comfortable, pleasant to the ears.

"Don't forget my isolation on an island with only three others light years from human civilization. I've only been back a short while. Anyway, in answer to your query, as far as Alex and I know, direct contact with Entity is the best method for our growth, which means letting it soak into your skin or drinking it. After that comes personal contact.

"Frankly, we haven't been back long enough to know much more. We conjecture our contact with another person will result in a transference of power, based on the amount of contact; that is, holding someone versus incidental contact with them.

"We also surmise that there will be a dilution

effect as one person contacts another. Much of this remains to be learned. I'd really hate to think that the few of us are the only ones to pass on the legacy of our traveling friend."

"Does that means this power will passed on to my dog or cat if I pet them?"

"Probably. It's too early to know," he replied.

"Okay. Got it. Number ten down the road will develop more slowly than number nine, yet way ahead of number ten thousand. And Alex is number one and you, Hunter and Jocelyn are number two and I am—I'm guessing at this—number three?"

"Not exactly. You were three, now you're a one after the drink you just took. Our campers are number four based on my slight contact with them and the low dose I administered in their drink," Marty said, completing the equation. "We can call them our understudies."

"Our understudies? Cute," I retorted. "They're pretty sharp for being fours."

"You think?"

At breakfast we explained to the others about the transference of power issue. In fact, there were so many issues brought up that we came to loggerheads. We did come to believe the character of bad people would not be changed and they would probably become more diabolical as their intellect grew; in other words, the basic human condition may remain the same.

When it came down to it, we were the top of the power pyramid that could affect the future of the human race and a lot more than that. At the end of the day we had conjectured everything and decided nothing.

Late that night, after everyone else had gone to bed in the cabin, Marty and I went out into the woods and talked more.

He said, "Alex wants someone to bring back a very large quantity of Entity."

"To do what with it?" I responded.

"He wants to take it to various locations, but he doesn't know where. Jos says to leave it alone. It would take forever to change the race and we'll get there over time, anyway."

I said, "Jocelyn's right and she's wrong and so are you. Maybe Entity's not on a schedule, but I am. You and I can go to Canopus as soon as camp is over."

"And do what?" Marty asked, in turn.

"Bring back more. I'm with Alex," I replied. "That leaves a select few of to program the human race." I tried to interject sarcasm into the statement. At that moment, a little tiny seed had sprouted deep in my brain.

In the morning the discussion continued around the breakfast table in the camp cabin. The cabin was fairly sterile with lots of windows and no wall hangings. A back kitchen displayed a sign above the entrance that read CAMP ONINOCOC—ROWING NOT DRIFTING. An attached bunk room led off through another door that contained a gang latrine separated by partitions between the potties, and eight bunk beds to accommodate the clientele of the season, along with a single bed for the camp counselor.

The hired cook came and went and brought our cereal, milk, fruit, and other nutrients that our growing bodies required. Marty just sat back and let events unfold.

"Don't you think the human race will acquire new methods to create mayhem? That *is* one of our gifts," I said in my facetious manner, in order to establish the tone of the discussion.

Then, little Dickey, nee Richard, whom we used to call little Dick, and whose name had gone through a number of evolutionary changes to become finalized as Dick, came out of nowhere and proclaimed, "Excuse me. Aren't you getting a little presumptuous with that statement, Jackson? From the Entity's point of view, I don't believe it was created to destroy us or life in general as its sole purpose. Life has to mean more to it than destruction of that which it touches. We're in this position and forward is the only direction we can go. We have no other choice."

"From whence comes this digression from your normal speech pattern, Dick?" I queried.

Dick shrugged. "My dad's writes a little. Mayhaps some of his poetic license rubbed off on me."

I smiled to myself. His father wrote all right. He wrote speeches for the President of the United States.

The discussion went nowhere and after breakfast we all went on a short hike in the hills and then hit the swimming pool. Marty and I supervised.

"Back to our topic," I continued, seated in a lounge chair at the side of the diving board, certain the idea had occurred to Marty, but also certain he wanted me to breach the topic. "Do you realize how much money it would take to make that turn-around voyage? Because I don't, although, if I have, say, a private chat with my father, he may consent to making arrangements for us. Especially if it means bringing back a couple thousand plasti-glass bottles with the Entity inside."

"Why is *more* better?" The man asked a legitimate question, testing me one more time. "Isn't it better to do a great job with what little you have than a mediocre job with more?"

"Exactly how much stash do we have?" I inquired, throwing the ball back to Marty.

"A fair amount between Alex and myself," he replied.

"That answer tells me that you still don't trust me," I said. "Why not, I don't know. You lead me down a pretty path, hand me a fresh well-scented bouquet, and then leave me. Okay, you have your reasons and I have my own ideas, even if it means doing things without you."

The other kids were diving into the deep end. I needed to be there with them. In one sense I was in way over my head.

"What does that mean," replied Marty, displaying a hurt look.

I wanted to blurt out that more *is* better, but logic dictated that we didn't even have a game plan yet, so how could we have a direction? As they say, if you don't know what decision to make, make no decision at all.

The seed of an idea I'd had now became watered by a living energy both born and borne in the outer reaches. In a word, to hell with the opinions and counter-opinions. I might be able to do this on my own.

Whatever *this* meant.

FIVE

Martine Renault Bordeaux had it completely wrong. The theories of the genius who went to the stars and which were aided and abetted by an alien thing fell far short of reality. Different people are affected differently. While most may follow the same pattern of development, others shoot forward beyond their own control and may continue to grow until they die. What they may accomplish cannot be predicted.

After eight weeks of summer camp I had grown two inches in height and gained in musculature. While I cannot say that what I drank from the flask aided my growth, I can say that, despite Marty's two year head start, I had caught up with him.

No solutions came from the campsite and all the discussions came to naught, rife with arguments and counter-arguments. In response to one person who wanted to meet politicians, Joey might say something like, "Do you think that politicians will be less political and less crafty with the money they take from you? Do you think the crime rate will go down; or will the use of drugs be lessened? Do you think our lives will be lengthened automatically, and if so, why and how?"

My personal thoughts raced. I considered that on the open market a single plasti-glass bottle of full strength Sparkling Entity, as I secretly thought of it, would be worth a country or an empire in value. I blamed my thought process on the commercialized society that had spawned me.

How would Marty do this? Would he pour it in a metal basin and then have us dip our hands in it, then pour it back into the bottle? How would Alex do it? Wouldn't human germs accumulate in the water? What would happen to the germs? Wouldn't antibiotic resistant bacteria conjure up new ways to become even more resistant and continue the fight against a smarter human race? I imagined it all and became so caught up with my analytical processes that I forgot what we were doing for the moment.

Johnny Barrow had argued, "Well, yes. We will be smarter about finding cures for more diseases, including genetic problems that have not been overcome since gene therapy began so long ago. We will be more clever about building bigger ships to take more people to the stars and smarter about adapting new planets to our needs. Our communication with animals and their communication with us will increase to the extent that we can see and understanding what they see and understand. And there is also the, as yet, undefined. To me, that's the biggest factor of all."

"Good thinking Johnny. The great hidden factor of uncertainty," Marty had replied.

To which I replied, dryly, "That's not good thinking at all. We all get that. The issue at hand is, what do you and I do to take positive action? Personally, I'm not inclined to wait for an eternity to become successful and rich. I'm already rich. We're all destined to rise to that level anyway. And how successful and rich can one be? There's no point to it."

We all went home for the year and promised to keep in touch. My time had ended. I was too old to attend anymore. Fortunately, my own game plan didn't involve the other campers, or even Marty. I needed time to myself. I mostly stayed in my room in our Malibu home where I did a considerable amount of work. Mom left me to my own devices, quite accustomed to aberrant behavior from the men in her life. Dad was absent much of the time on a number of space missions and managing his company headquartered in San Francisco.

The day arrived for me to make the big move.

The skip flight from Malibu to San Francisco took less than an hour. Once I flashed the ID chip imbedded in my hand into the reader, a licensed copter driver arrived shortly and took me directly from our home to the roof of my father's building.

Dad is a fifth generation spaceman and each generation had built upon the one before. That leaves some pretty big shoes for me to fit into. He's a good looking man and fortunately, I take after him. He's tall, but not lanky, dark haired, with dark and penetrating eyes, and great teeth. His office occupies the entire fortieth floor of the Pan World Building that looked out over where the old Golden Gate Bridge used to be.

The last war took it out and it would use too many raws materials to rebuild it, what with public transportation as efficient as it is today. A world-wide uproar defined the beginning of that last war because of the amount of money and materials used to design and construct weaponry, but nothing changed for the better. The smart money stayed with weapons.

Dad had darkened the window behind him so he wouldn't be back-lighted when guests sat in the arm chairs across the desk from him. We hadn't had a chance to say other than "Hi" and "Bye" the last couple of times he came home, so I told him about Marty and all that had transpired.

He looked at me as if his progeny had lost his marbles until I pulled out the hip flask I had wrangled out of my counselor as a going away present. My father needed a drink because I heard Canopus calling my name. I first took a sip to indicate that the contents hadn't been laced with poison and handed it over. Somehow, Marty had topped it off. I placed it on dad's desk, where it remained untouched.

I looked out the side window of the high-rise building in a high-rise city and saw a few planes heading to and from the airport and a number of skip fliers such as the one that had brought me in from Malibu.

These days you didn't see a lot of spaceships, or even personal vehicles, thanks to tight regulations. Earth had run out of resources and we recycled virtually everything we could. Most of the major sources of liquid oil and shale oil had been squandered. What little oil reserves remaining were hoarded by their respective countries or traded with friendly neighbors. There still existed a fair amount of natural gas, but you can't make a lot of hard goods with gas.

In summary, while the family ran a huge business, it also operated an ancient, decrepit space fleet. Space travel would soon be a thing of the past and mankind would be stuck on a third-world planet with a bunch of independent star colonies able to communicate by galactic com and that would be it. To my way of thinking, that's why it was such a big deal when Alex found ore deposits.

"Dad, I want to go to Canopus," and told him why.

His reply: "My boy, I love you dearly and I completely understand the early stages of puberty, but don't push it. I can get you to the moon and to Mars, if you need to get away. Will that work?"

"That's not good enough, Dad," which was the wrong thing to say. The man flushed.

I'd speed read a score of manuals from the history of spaceflight to the construction and operation of a ship. "Dad, this isn't a joke. The construction and operation of a spaceship is all wrong. Here's what I've been working on."

I reached into a pouch I'd brought and handed him a diskette. "These two books have been submitted for publication."

Dad's ire diminished when he slid the diskette into a reader and said out loud the titles that appeared. "*An Analysis of Wrongful Construction of Spaceships and the Misuse of such Vessels.*"

The book contained verbal descriptions, diagrams and statistical analyses replete with everything from regression analysis to chi square comparison of screw types used in construction.

Trying my best to keep it instructive and readable, I also explained the wrong usage of the Clark Drive in terms of the point at which it's employed. Also, its design is all screwed up with way too many parts. The books described the problems with the on-mechanism of the drive. In a word, the poor usage of the drive is the cause of space sickness.

The second book described how to construct a better interstellar vehicle and how to improve the drive mechanism to get us farther and faster.

For the next hour he flipped through the pages, stopping occasionally to read. He would go back and forth between them. At one point he sat bolt upright and bent over one of the diagrams. He asked and I answered, always going a step beyond.

"Jack, my boy, I'm impressed. My question is this: What do you want to do? If you're thinking about constructing a space barge to haul stuff, forget it. There's no money or resources for that. There haven't been since well before my grandfather's time.

There are other worlds out there with resources we covet and no way to get them here to make a difference."

"Truthfully, Dad, the answer to that evades me at the moment. Okay, Alex found lots of ore on Canopus and I get that there's no way to get it here . . . at the moment. Right now, I only know that there is a magnet pulling on me like a found lover and it won't let go. "

"Okay," he replied, resignedly, stretching out the word as though it were three syllables long, similar to a preacher who takes three seconds to say the word God in three different tonal modes. He put his hands behind his head and stretched way back in his seat, looking at the ceiling. After a long break, he leaned forward and punched a button on his wrist phone to make a call.

As a parting gift from a good father, he admonished me. Looking me straight in the eye, he stated, "Young man, I don't give a damn how smart you are or think you are, because smart guys come and smart guys go. Call it the tortoise and the hare effect. Fast burnout types. High risk high gain. Get the drift? You'd better come up with something very solid very soon because if you screw this up, you'll be the sorriest janitor who ever cleaned this building."

Four weeks later I boarded a colony ship with another hundred or so poor souls who had each given up a fortune to pay for the one-way trip to a single stop-off world, with me on my way to Canopus.

I never really got to talk to anyone because, for the first leg of the journey, I got sicker than an alcoholic taking anti-drinking medication while hitting the bottle at the same time, then suffering from a bad case of gout afterward.

You don't provide artificial gravity in these short haul trips and even if you did, the Clark Drive would get to your gut unless you were a seasoned veteran. I spent much of my time in dark hatred of myself, the Entity, and my father. Gagging and vomiting played a big role during this period of self-analysis. Doubtless, a maggot-ridden devil crawled from the putrid blackness beneath a rock to attack my soul. And this represented the constructive portion of my journey.

At last, I understood why my father pretended to give in so easily. He probably figured, "All right, Mister Big Shot, you want space? I'll give you space."

For ten days, the thought of him haunted my visions and stirred feelings of passionate hatred that I'd never known before. The man was truly a retched human being, which made two of us, each in his own manner. Although I had written about the drive and had researched it in order to create my thesis, experience is a great motivator.

At last, the ship dropped out of Clark and entered normal space. After another couple of days of deceleration, we made planet-fall to our first stop. During the deceleration period the body begins to readjust to normalcy. I followed the pioneers onto a dreary, foggy and cold world where one could see only several meters in front of them. "The sun will be out soon," said one of the greeting party, as they led the new colonists to their temporary residence, while their possessions were off-loaded. A regular cleanup crew went onboard.

I soon found out that this world tilted so much it blazed hot one-half the year and nearly froze the other half, more so than most areas of Earth. However, a nice transition zone existed between the hot and cold portions, if you don't mind getting blown by hot or cold gale-force winds, whichever decided to blow that day. But at least the oxygen and water were clean. What else can you ask for?

We stayed until the next morning and with me as the lone passenger, we headed off to Canopus, still off-limits to everyone else except for a handful, until colonization got approved.

We began to accelerate for about two days while I visited with the two-man crew before we went into Clark. In the old days, I would have been inquisitive about the operation of the ship. Now I knew more than they did and this naïve fourteen-year-old played the role and listened at length to their war stories and those told by other spacemen. I wasn't about to instruct them on how to use the Clark. That time would come.

A few gut-wrenching days later, Canopus loomed in sight. Two more days of deceleration and we were there. I tried to push the trip back home from conscious thought.

Looking out the window, the beauty of Canopus enraptured me as we began the descent, having avoided several small moons. Three hundred light years away and four-fifths the size of Earth, the planet possessed the gravity similar to that of Earth's and suggested a large core of iron or other heavy metals.

Instead of perhaps 20 people working a new planet, only two worked Canopus, thanks to budgetary constraints. Those two were Ken Hunter and Jocelyn Jones, both of whom re-upping for a second term. My father paid my own fare, hence his demeanor upon our parting. This all indicated how much space exploration had declined. Colony development inched along, despite media press to the contrary.

Recent incidents in space had left hundreds of colonists stranded to die in old spacecraft on their way begin a new life. Lawsuits had been filed against the Federation and the Walcott name. My father had been the unlucky recipient of a billion dollar lawsuit and, although his company could absorb the loss, rebuilding a worn out space fleet would be difficult when contracts for both freight, metal, and colonists had sharply declined with no end in sight.

Both station members had been advised of my arrival with me as the lone passenger. During the time in normal space, I had gotten to know Evans, the pilot, and Bourland, the co-pilot, both of whom had been in my father's employ for many years. They were the ones who had brought Alex, Marty Bordeaux, Hunter, and Jones to this planet.

We stepped out into the humid air of Canopus

and I saw what I had visualized which matched Marty's description. Still, the site of the ocean gave me a feeling of home. Growing up in Malibu, California, and surfing the waves whenever time allowed made me yearn the ocean whenever I traveled. There were no tides here, though, unless you want to rename four-inch rollers. As far as the short and tall vegetation, I could definitely see what he meant.

Jos and Ken Hunter approached and we greeted as long lost friends with Evans and Bourland unloading camp supplies. I must have looked unkempt and starving. Both would be true. I did not tell them about the selfishness of my motives. At first I thought to explain that my father had sent me here to gain space experience and because of my incessant nagging to see the place my counselor had described. Instead, I kept my mouth shut. Doubtless, the pair would know that my silly explanations were a sham.

The three of us were led into one of the cottages with the design of keeping us there for the evening. I figured Hunter and Joc didn't want to let dad's men see the huge fruits and vegetables watered by you-know-who. But why not?

I broached the subject after the men had gone to sleep and the three of us had walked across to the lighthouse. We sat in the small living room which entailed four chairs and a tiny coffee table. A screen on one wall focused on a particularly colorful segment of sky so full of stars that the voids between them looked like lines similar to the white spaces between words on a page.

Jos said, "The fruits? We've got good fertilizer."

"I'll bet," I replied.

Jocelyn turned me on. I just loved pert women and she had the brains and the looks that lent itself to fantasies, at least to mine. Now she sat in front of me. My mind flirted with disturbing thoughts about her relationship to Hunter, the only man on the planet. What had Marty said once about the mind remaining at default setting?

"We're alone now, so let's talk," I began. "Why don't you share the formula for the fertilizer with Earth?"

Jos and Hunter looked at each other, not knowing whether a little kid asked a simple question, or if he knew something he shouldn't know.

I chuckled. "You think you're the only ones who know about Entity along with Alex and Marty? Add a dozen summer campers who drank it and add my father to the mix. Do you think he sent me here because he wanted to get me to get space sick or because he likes to piss away a zillion credits, or do you think he might have other reasons? Maybe you're not ready to talk, but I am," I stated, flatly. "And I've got some ideas."

In anticipation of my arrival, the team of two had completed the miniaturization of two devices for deep-penetrating ore detection and identification (Jocelyn) and a hand held unit that would read micro and macro weather patterns, detect ocean current flow, and make predictions pertaining thereto(Hunter).

The pair of inventions were adapted to the two seat flier, the instruments with sensors located below the landing skids of the machine.

The gray delta wing air vehicle stood nine feet in length and eight inches off the ground with a separate canopy covering each passenger. It possessed a team of tail rudders that would automatically shift and deviate in order to maintain maximum stability of the unit regardless of wind conditions. Passengers spoke by radio. The small craft held a small cargo hold behind the two canopies that could be accessed by a simple lid and double latch. A shielded area located behind the second passenger housed the nuclear power plant.

From the age of eight, I had been flying anything I could get my hands on and a few extra IQ points provided by our friend didn't hurt either. So off I went for a test run.

I had decided to define the parameters of Alex's initial iron ore find as my first task at hand with his copper discovery less than a score of kilometers from the site. A vein of it ran from the surface downward, then concentrated and bulls-eyed maybe a fifty meters downward. Perfect for good old fashion copper pit mining.

Once within range, I radioed the lighthouse with my findings along with a message to send back to Jackson Walcott, Senior. I felt for dad. I know felt hamstrung. "Big deal," he might think. "You could have a planet of pure gold and it wouldn't matter to

Earth. This is a dying world."

He would be so correct, but the findings might buy time for me. The man wouldn't leave his only son stranded on another star system to save, maybe, one hundred million credits for his return trip; would he?

Hunter and Jos weren't working on the grass problem, which is what the Federation wanted because they knew the truth, something the Federation didn't know. Until the Fed received a convincing answer, there would be no colonization. In fact, if they had told the truth, the result would probably be the same. No colonization. The ship I traveled on was probably one of the last to go to the stars, according to dad.

The entire planet of Canopus might maintain a population of a less than a handful of humans forevermore, possibly with me as one of them.

Hunter constructed a larger cargo hold at the back of the flier. We packed it with food, water, raingear, and other items necessary for survival, should it come to that.

I took us up to fifteen thousand feet to avoid wind currents and settled in for a long ride to the second continent. I don't know how to express this, but as we passed over islands, I perceived familiar sense of motion—of things passing me by.

After some time, Hunter said, "See that ring of mountains north of the main chain? Let's head over there and check it out."

Ten minutes later, Hunter walked to the boot of the flier and pulled out a rock hammer still used by rock hounds and began chipping away at the mountain. He did so for several minutes and stones of various sizes fell to the ground, many of them in dark layered strata and others beneath them were tar-like. At last he picked up a smaller flat one and examined it and passed it to me. He said, "This is an old world, Jack."

"How so?"

"I'll tell you when we get back to the lab."

I had never seen a waterfall in person and a fine one presented itself a hundred miles northward as we hit the upper portion of the big continent where a deep canyon lay downstream from waterfalls. The vegetation on either side of the river was definitely lusher and significantly taller than that which we had noted at the top of the canyon. That could be attributed to a higher humidity, soil type, or other factors.

With new eyes, we saw gold was more common the closer we got to the falls. The cascade of water was reminiscent of the great Victoria Falls in Africa, from pictures I'd seen of them where the water cascaded into a canyon for perhaps a hundred fifty meters and where the river was over a mile in width. This was truly one of the wonder spots on this planet.

"Look at the walls of the canyon," I told him, while he hovered the craft delicately amid the spray wash of the great falls.

"It's basalt," he answered.

We turned the ship around and set down in a sandy area several miles south of the falls. Hunter grabbed some of the sand and let the wet particles trickle through his fingers, watching sunlight glitter off the sand. "We've got titanium, manganese and magnesium, typical of basaltic rock," he said. Under the right circumstances, you can build a lot from that. We'll take some back to the lab for analysis."

"Let's get a couple of samples from different locations and move on. My guess is the mother lode will be several miles upstream on one of the main tributaries.

SIX

At last we lifted off with Hunter still flying the ship. Thusly, we explored the continent, criss-crossing and recording in our memories, to be copied later onto a physical map for transmission back to my father and to the Federation, in that order. We had yet to explore the oceans. That would have to wait.

One problem was that we couldn't ship ores to Earth from outlying worlds because liftoff and transportation and downloading would eat up any dollars invested in the enterprise.

After an absence of nearly two weeks, we landed back at the lighthouse. Jocelyn told me my father had called. That would have to wait after I took a long hot soak and ate a solid meal.

Later, in the lab, "Hunter said, "Look carefully at that rock, Jack. Notice the leafy imprint. You don't see that on every planet. You'll see it on planets where certain geological events occurred. "On earth fossils can be located almost anywhere that are up to three hundred million years old, or more. Now look at the tar above it and the shale above that. There are life forms in the tar and in the shale where the shale fragmented and the tar seeped up into it. Shale is like sandstone without the sand, but with clay, which is comprised of much smaller particles. Therefore, it's still absorbent.

"This whole region was under water and over a billion years of silt and mud and tons of plankton piled up on top of the plant life before it got thrust upward. Land masses and rifts formed and deformed. So there was very heavy plant and micro-animal life here at one time—in fact there still is, especially in the oceans. Larger animals never evolved. It happens."

"You're describing to me some of the factors that are necessary for the formation of oil," was my contribution to the discussion, hoping there might be.

"Yes, I am."

"You're saying that there could be some oil on this planet?" I asked.

Hunter shook his head, emphatically. "No. I'm not saying that. What I am saying is that this entire world is filthy rotten with oil."

"You're making that assumption just based on your one find when we were on the ledge?"

"Negative. Based on the myriad of anticline slopes and geosyncline depressions we saw on every land mass we passed over as well as the composition of those slopes. This tells us there is geological uplifting of the strata and substrata, which on Earth, can be caused by a number of factors. These include as ice, fractures, upward pressure, and quakes. Here, it primarily means oil."

"Okay, I'll play. But when it comes down to it, can you prove it?"

Hunter laughed. A good hearty laugh that came from reserves ready to gush forth, like an oil well drill that finally hit the pressure chamber. "Any day any time to any person."

"Ken, how did you see those slopes through all the jungle growth and forests?"

Hunter shrugged, "Like you, Jack, I happen to be part Entity and a trained geologist, so I look for different things in the ground than you do."

You don't argue with Hunter. You don't play the fool and pretend to act the expert in front of a man who teaches Planetary Formation and Paleontology for the Federation; a multi-trillion credit agency that has the pick of the humans to choose from. Okay, they have a few economic problems. Who doesn't? And here was this kid, me, talking to and questioning this guy like we were equals. Somebody needed to slap me hard.

Suddenly, things came together and a shiver ran through me. Was I looking at a ship or a rat? Had we been absorbed into the Entity or vice versa?

My flighty ruminations brought me to the human race and the need for ores. A people that one day might become a genius race might still be stuck on a planet with no resources. At least humans had power from solar, nuclear, wind, steam, natural gas, and wave action. Too bad you can't build spaceships or houses from those.

I called dad who wanted to know how the exploration had gone. I gave him the condensed version promising to send him the details. He told me the publisher who had read my books was excited, and had sent copies to numerous experts for review.

"Dad, it may be outdated," I opined.

Hunter processed the soil samples. We started with the samples below the falls and found an elevated concentration of titanium, platinum and manganese in the basaltic rock.

We all needed a break and Jocelyn informed us that many of the vegetables in the greenhouse were ripe for picking. The three of us walked through the drizzle to the compound and into the greenhouse. Carrots, radishes, cucumbers, and melons had matured enough to pull. Because they were within the compound walls, all were of normal size. We worked at opposite end of a long table, Jocelyn next to me to my right. She looked very attractive with her short brunette hair, pink shorts and matching halter top. Doubtless, the word 'sexy' was not part of her thought process; not so for myself.

I had fallen in love with her. How does the saying go? "Your brain is the strongest most lasting portion of your body, until you fall in love. Then it becomes the polar opposite of itself." How could I not? My youthful hormones pumped at full speed and my intellect told me I would never be satisfied with a female who didn't have Entity running through her veins.

Hunter interrupted my fantasies and offered, "Junior, you look deep in thought."

He knew the term Junior rankled me. I let it pass and decided to have a little fun. I shifted gears while pretending to clean dirt off a cucumber.

"Somebody give me the high school description of the Clark Drive," I stated.

Hunter replied, "It operates line-of-site. Because you can't turn in space for all practical purposes, you run your calculations, line up the star of your choice, accelerate up to speed and engage. The drive goes to maximum almost instantaneously and when it stops you re-enter normal space at same velocity at which you were initially traveling."

Jocelyn added. "History is replete with adventurers who lost their lives and their ships experimenting with Clark. Why the primer, Jack?"

"Our biggest problem is getting ores to Earth, right? I mean from here or from anywhere. Even if they're smelted to a purified state on-site, they would be too heavy to lift into orbit to be transported by ore-haulers that gulp fuel, right?"

Hunter stopped what he was doing and looked a little ridiculous holding a large bunch of radishes in each hand. "Which makes the Clark irrelevant for the same reason. It doesn't matter how fast you go if you can't get the ore to the ship or get the ship into orbit."

"The Clark as we know it," I responded, holding up a fresh tomato to the sunlight for inspection. "Do either of you know anybody who has employed the Clark from a dead stop?"

They both shrugged. "Not and live to tell about it," Jocelyn said, truthfully.

She paused a moment, then added, "So, theoretically, we refine the ores here on Canopus, load them onto a carrier, Clark the whole thing just short of Sol, and transport them down to earth. Turn it into a teleportation machine."

"Almost. We go to Mars first. Its a lot easier to get it there and then to Earth, rather than landing something on the near side of the moon that is revolving around a spinning planet," I added, almost shrugging, as though it were no big deal. "We do it in two steps, It's basic math. First off, we'd need at least one of the Clark Drives to play with."

"Do you know anybody who could get their hands on one?" Jocelyn grinned, no doubt oozing delight at the prospect of dipping her hands into the guts of a Clark.

"The answer is yes. Here's my thinking." I stopped pulling and cleaning vegetables and looked at the others. The temperature inside the greenhouse was warm and humid. We were all sweating. At that moment nobody cared.

"I know where we can get at least one. I did my research. There are only five ore haulers out there.

Physically, they're breaking down, in part from disuse. Only one is in occasional use. The others are being parted out to keep that one operational. "

"How many Clarks are out there? Do you know?" Hunter asked.

"A good dozen, I think. Three are locked up tight in colony ships. You don't move them an inch without Fed approval. My dad has one on his space yacht along with a bunch of rich other guys on their yachts at various convenient locations. There's another one I know about that is one of the first built, a true dinosaur. It's parked on Earth's moon where it was used for mining years ago. Onboard mining equipment is still in place, either on the ship or anchored to the ground. That's the one I hope to get for us.

"If I called right now, everything considered, it would take weeks to get here, given that the Clark is still operational and men are available. If the Clark on the ship is down, figure on eight thousand years to get here. It will take a crew to drive her and the crew will have to live and sleep onboard and give them a percentage of the action. We'd need to offer that up front and if the deal fails, well, as a rough guess, I'd say there's not enough money in my future janitor's fund to cover the costs."

"One slight problem," said Hunter. "This is a Federation planet. You can't do anything here without their approval, the lighthouse notwithstanding."

"True enough, but they can't move an inch without my father's ships, either. And," I threw in for Hunter's amusement, "according to the information out there, the hauler has limited, yet functional smelting capabilities. That'll give us a start. Our new instruments will find us the nearby elements necessary for the oxidation process that will remove impurities. Then we'll toss out the slag.

"So, the hauler sets down where we think is the best location, which is right over there." I pointed. "We pull the Clark and turn you two loose on it. I'll provide the specs for what I'd like you to do with it.

"Before you say it, the Feds don't want an independent for this job. It's too big. You want the best. That leaves Walcott Galactic."

Before speaking, Hunter wiped the remaining dust off a radish, polished it against his shirt, took a nibble, deep in thought, then popped the rest into his mouth. He took his time chewing while Jos and I waited. "How do you plan to convince the old man?"

I replied, philosophically, "It's easier to ask for forgiveness than for permission. However, in this case, there's only one option. Begging."

It didn't hurt the cause when I received a call that my books had been accepted for publication and had received critical acclaims. Many experts called it an intellectual challenge to understand the nuances which were presented; however, no flaws could be found outright. The fact that they were authored by the then thirteen year old son of Jackson Walcott, Senior, owner of Walcott Galactic, brought my father endless pride and the possibility of some new contracts.

Or so it seemed on the surface. Business being

what it is, the prideful father took some hard convincing. I explained the situation to him over the Com. "Just one ore hauler. You know which one, dad. Please. I *can* make this work."

As soon as I said those words I regretted them. I didn't know anything of the sort. I could almost feel my father's mind compute. Finally, he said, "You're killing me, Jack. I'm not saying yes or no. Let me check on a few things. The janitor's spot is still open for application."

We signed off. There was no other way but to tell him the whole story. Otherwise, sending an ore hauler to Canopus for mining an extremely rich world would be no different than sending it anywhere else without a very serious plan in place to make a very serious profit.

SEVEN

Everybody has had that little niggling thought that won't come to the surface. The harder you think about it, the faster it retreats, only to reemerge in the middle of the night. Thanks to Entity, once an idea pops into my head, the solution comes along with it.

Here's my thinking: Scientists believe the Clark Drive operates in either sub-space or hyperspace (it's subspace). The communication system operates in another plane (hyperspace) and is instantaneous. If we could couple the two, we'd be able to move solid objects instantaneously through hyperspace from point A to point B, which we already did via communications between colonies and Earth.

Although my improved Clark Drive should be able to move people faster without the need to accelerate, it probably won't make interstellar travel any cheaper. So economics reared its ugly head again. Whether we would move material objects with my newest idea remained to be seen. Moving people might be a completely different story.

The task of combining the essences of two very heady technologies turned out to be less daunting than it seemed initially. The interstellar Com system we use today had been developed way back in the twenty-fourth century by a team of researchers from the Swiss Institute of Technology. Clark, a visiting American, tried to make the system work for a spaceship and came up with a drive mechanism instead.

It's easy to pull up the specs on the Com. Once we did, it became just as easy for us to see where Clark had gone wrong and had made his two mistakes.

In order to fix the problem we needed to do a couple of things: dismantle the Com and do the same for the Clark. There is no sense doing one without the other. In his vernacular, dad would call my proposal if-come and wish-come rather than income. In truth, I had the same thoughts. We still had to work out the master plan for elements of discovery and recovery. We had to plan for housing, mining, smelting, and identification of the minerals. For slag production, we would need sodium nitrate, oxides, and silica. The sources for these had already been identified.

We could use the ore crusher onboard ship; should it ever arrive. If dad ran the same numbers I did, the worst he could do would be to break even. The best would be a game changer.

We had a lot of mapping and planning to do in preparation for company.

Feelings of apprehension had assailed me since my arrival on Canopus. My presence on a Federation-owned planet was not a sanctioned visit and should arguments ensue, things could get quite nasty with dad at the receiving end. It could cost him their contract and legal action might be brought against him. If that were to happen, chances are he would lose everything.

Two months, in the very early morning hours of heavy rainfall, a rumbling shook the earth. The three of us came outdoors from our respective habitats where Hunter and I were in one. Jocelyn had been in the other; not necessarily out of my newly found hormone-driven desires. We turned our eyes to the murky sky.

Countless tons of flatbed spaceship blocked out the sun, already dimmed by the mist.

The massive bulk was as big as two football fields both lengthwise and width-wise. It was descending to land on a large granite slab almost made for the purpose half-way between the compound and the rolling foothills where Alex Rosovsky had made many of his initial discoveries not so long ago. This behemoth had Triton painted on its side alongside a smaller "WG" for Walcott Galactic.

Somebody had been reading the data we'd sent them and the landing couldn't have been more perfect. Rocket flames came from numerous jets from the bottom of the 200,000 ton ship assisted by six massive turbofans.

At the very front of the ship stood the pilot's cabin, crews' quarters, rec room, kitchen, machine shops and a few other necessary rooms. The ship looked like a small wasp's head on a very long very wide flat body. Doubtless, entire small towns had occupied a space smaller than that found on the upper surface of that vessel.

As we watched from a far distance, we could see that its sides were perhaps five stories tall all around with drop gates on each of three sides where front-end loaders could deposit their wares on the floor of the ship and over the top, if necessary.

From my reading of Tri-D videos available virtually anywhere, I knew the ship had a flexi-steel role-over that came out one of the sides like a swimming pool cover to settle onto the cargo and hold it in place as the vessel went through its various maneuvers.

An ore hauler is the largest spaceship ever built and can carry 50,000 tons of payload. It comes with its own shovel, front-end loader, forklifts, and a couple of shuttle craft that can carry five persons each. Initially, the ships were constructed to land on low gravity worlds for discovery, harvesting, and returning ores to earth. Nowadays, the economics had completely turned around and fuel for these monsters was in very short supply. A year's supply of petroleum for a moderately sized community had just been squandered during that landing.

In addition, even with nuclear power available to operate the turbines, no more materials were available to build more of the ships. My dad was risking his company on my mission, a thought that scared me in terms of insecurity, rather than possible insanity. It didn't make me feel too good to know an alien was rattling around in my brain and coursing through my veins. The new thought that, if I failed, Walcott Galactic could crash and burn overnight, helped me grow up real fast.

It takes about a couple of hours to shut down one of these beasts and let things cool off. If the ship begin to settle too quickly, you'd better blast off find another landing spot before you sank so far into the earth you might not get out. We knew the crew would be checking instruments moment by moment from a number of locations throughout the vessel to ensure that they could blast off quickly, if necessary.

Close to two hours later Jocelyn and I took the flatbed in the rain to greet whomever, while Hunter prepared our compound for a large number of guests. The captain, my father, stepped out first. Behind him came as rugged a crew as one ever saw and seemed to fit right in. They must have been recruited from a pirate ship through some sort of time warp. Nasty looking blokes. Even dad had a scruffy, unkempt beard.

"Well, my boy, is that what you had in mind?"

Dad said, objectively and dispassionately, swinging his arm outward to encompass the huge vessel.

I nodded, grinning from ear to ear. "It's a start."

I'd grown another inch or so and gained another fifteen pounds since he last saw me and looked a little like his younger brother. We hugged and he introduced the crew one by one. Not really looking at them, each nodded in his turn and stepped forward to shake his callused hand with my unworked pretty boy hand, to my embarrassment.

Remembering Jocelyn, I introduced her to the savages. She just nodded while they tried not to leer too obviously.

Dad said, "This is my first mate, Alex Rosofsky. Marty Bordeaux, my project director of operations, has other duties back at the office."

My jaw had a bad habit of dropping as of late. How did my dad know Marty other than what I had told him in his office. I wanted to pursue the issue, but that could wait. I did not need these ruffians to know that Marty had been my kiddie camp counselor only months before. My dad must have sensed my concern regarding disclosure of this fact and said nothing further about the matter.

There stood Alex the legend, now sixtiesh, who had mined colony worlds for various corporations before he went to the Fed and got assigned to Canopus. The man possessed a strong black beard well-trimmed with a trace of gray running through it. He stood of medium height and I surmised he could hold his own in this bunch of space sailors and may have done so in the past. His face held a number of scars, which Marty had failed to describe during our sleeping bag sessions. He and Jos simply nodded at each other.

"All right, Jackson, let's see what you've got," said Alex.

Alex led the way to the meal room. Jocelyn brought along a large maps we'd prepared and un-rolled it onto a table where she displayed the first map depicting sites Hunter and I had identified on the land masses. She explained all thirty seven of them one by one.

The second map presented the immediate area, along with a basic Tri-D image pictorial of the titanium, platinum, and copper finds. Alex made a few suggestions in terms of who did what. My father had already seen crude versions of them weeks before when Hunter had commed him.

The fields were huge finds because they held the metals most needed on Earth. Gold had long ago faded into insignificance and served primarily as ornamentation. The race did need more gold and rare earths for electronic technology. For that reason, a large supply of refined ores of this type would pay for an entire round trip and a lot more. Unfortunately, up to this point, it had been many years since unprocessed ore had been hauled back to home base. We planned to process it and bring back the pure refined metals. We'd start with gold that, in today's world, sells for about $10,000 an ounce. If we ship back, say, 35 pounds of the stuff, the weight of a gold bar, that would be worth over half-a-billion dollars. That could make somebody happy enough to give us the time of day. But that would be down the line. Right now, we had copper and titanium in front of us we could use as a teaser.

In few words, the job of the crew was to grab a scooper full of ore, enter it into the furnace, slag off the oxides, pour the metal into crucibles without causing them to explode from heat and gas expansion, cool the crucibles, dump the residue, and move on to the next batch.

One seemingly insurmountable problem bothered me. Earth had depleted its resources because Mankind had done a Class A-1 job of stripping it of available resources. It would seem that Canopus might be next in line.

Is that what worlds were for? Is that what Man was all about. Is that a necessary basic component for survival? Maybe it isn't a problem for mankind, but it had become a problem of mine. Or is that Entity speaking through me?

More than that. Did Entity even give a damn? Maybe Walcott, Canopus, Marty, me, and the rest of us were just incidental bookmarks that might represent absolutely nothing when compared with its past and its future, although the species would be long dead before a single second passed in its life.

Dad didn't get to stay on top of Walcott Galactic out of thoughtlessness. These were tough men and, if they wanted to get paid, they would work tirelessly come rain, shine, night, and day.

Jocelyn itched to get at the Clark Drive. She wouldn't admit it, but I'd come to know her a little and she feared disabling it during her investigations. None of us would be too worried about that because my father could order up another ship to get us off-planet. The bad news? If that happened, the entire mission would fail and so would he with a monster ship stuck here.

I called Hunter and asked him to bring over the flier and to assist Jocelyn, who had already bolted for the engine room. Dad left the ship in charge of Alex who'd mined worlds under my father's direction for several years.

Alex directed the men to get the ship ready to begin loading and smelting operations. They'd been instructed to bring along a deep-hole digger for ore extraction.

Hunter remained onboard with Jos and I drove dad through the short grass and the long grass and the incredible super-sized peaches and other fruits just outside our compound where the sea water and Entity had been free to roam and foam. We entered one of the bungalows and each found a recliner we could claim as ours for the night. He chose to spend the night off-ship.

Before we began our visit, I went to the cupboard and pulled out a bottle of Essence of Entity and tossed it to dad. "For your crew."

After we talked about my mom, the various space colonies, wars and politics on earth, we spent the night going over the grand plan as we saw it, from the new and faster Clark Drive that, hopefully, would be outdated before the publication even hit, to its tie-in with the Com, to colonization of Canopus. Neither of us mentioned the word *Entity* once.

We finally got a little sleep and, after my morning exercise and run, Jocelyn had returned, showered, changed into cooler clothes, and grabbed a pair of gloves for herself and for Hunter, then returned to the hauler.

Soon after we had toured the greenhouse and compared the edibles with what grew outside the structure, Jos and Hunter returned with the Clark Drive. Only the size of a shoe-box of old, the drive consisted perhaps a thousand components, mostly chips tied to one another. It had performed its function so well over the past three centuries since its invention, nobody had made any significant changes to it.

The four of us crowded into the lab in the lighthouse. The moons were up and the rain fell heavier than ever, while Jocelyn opened the case and we crowded around staring at the innards. While anybody could easily obtain the schematics for the device, it was a different matter to actually the components.

Full of micro and nanochips, I had condensed the thousand to a third of that number in my book without ever having seen the unit.

We planned to leave a couple of leads open which would be connected to a rebuilt subspace com system with goal of setting up a receiving station at one or more locations. Which meant . . . ?

I said, "Jos, once you hook it to the com, get me leads long enough to hold in my hand along with an ON/OFF switch.

She got to work.

"Dad, is there another Clark somewhere we can get our hands on??"

"Nothing that's not being used," he offered. "Except for my own personal ship, of course," he added jokingly.

"That'll work."

"Work for what?" he asked darkly.

"For what I have in mind. Is anybody on your ship?"

Suddenly, they all understood the plan.

My dad looked at me sideways with narrowed eyes. "Not at the moment. It's parked at the spaceport where we've always kept it."

"Can you get somebody on board to fly it to Mars, then start the engines and turn on the Clark drive?"

"They'd have to start the reactor for electricity in order to get it up to the voltage necessary to generate a field large enough to encompass the ship," he said, as if I didn't know that.

On the other hand, the Clark we were playing with required a minimum of one hundred thousand volts because it had come off the hauler. Right here we'd only need about a thousand.

"Can you build a second one from this if something goes wrong?" Dad asked looking over Jocelyn's shoulder in the lab.

"No," she replied simply and paused in her work. Nobody said what we all thought. A lot of people could be stranded on Canopus for a very long time.

In the end, it worked. We transshipped about five pounds of platinum worth about $25,000 an ounce and another block of titanium. A tremendous amount of work lay in front of us, not the least of which included setting up permanent receiving stations on Mars, Earth and its moon, and on the colony worlds. Whether it would work for human transportation remained to be seen.

My father and I sat in a pair of armchairs munching on the sweetest and most tender garden fruit in the known galaxy. The rain had let up and clear skies were expected. I had to ask, "Okay, Dad, how do you know Martine and how did you get him through the Federation screening committee?"

"Who, Marty? As you know from experience, I sponsor promising children who show a propensity for genius and try to guide them toward space. When Martine left grammar school and went private he had wondrous potentials—a true prodigy—one in a hundred million. By your age, he knew each committee members' professional specialty better than they did, long before coming to Canopus."

Dad's thinking was clear. Things couldn't go on as they were. He had to toss a couple of rocks in the pond to create ripples.

"By the time he'd hit seventeen, I had wrangled

my way onto the Federation selection committee. A couple of the members owed me big favors. I can tell you a lot of stories about who went where on my yacht and what they did. That sort of thing. When Marty returned from his tour of Canopus and before he began to teach summer camp, he brought along a bottle of water for me."

"You mean all this time you knew..."

"A lot," concluded Jackson Walcott Senior.

"Dad, what do we do with this planet? It had lush vegetation perhaps tens to hundreds of millions ago. We've got shallow seas, mud, anaerobic bacteria which we've identified in the lab, and other factors that go into the creation of biotic masses that convert plant waxes and oils into linear hydrocarbons. You got uplifting of earth and further burial to provide pressure over time and possible up-migration into pockets. Everything is there for biotic conversions into oil and maybe even natural gas."

"And then what?" he asked. "Oil rigs all over the planet, on land and sea? What about open pit copper mining? That'll be a wonderful eyesore. Look at the hole we already have after just a couple of weeks," he bitterly complained.

"Jack, back in the old days on earth those open pits could measure a mile across and a mile deep. They got the copper all right and got it best in dry climates such as in the Desert Southwest and other dry areas of other countries. Why self-limiting? Because there will be landslides as the sides caved in; the aquifer will flood the pit after the water table is hit; rains will create a blue-green lake at the bottom. That's what would happen anywhere on Canopus. So, copper mining is pretty much out of the picture here."

I said, "All of us here need to ensure that Earth will get materials, albeit slowly, and Canopus will get engineers and settlers. The Entity can't create a good person out of a bad one; it can help people make intelligent choices about the future of these and other planets they've settled on."

"What about you, Jack, what do plan to do when you grow up?" my father asked.

What with everything in flux, I hadn't thought about that. I scratched my head. "Well, school is out of the question for obvious reasons. Like Marty once told me, what's the point? So, if you've filled the janitorial position, I hope to start working for you in some other capacity. Inventing and geology are two areas that attract me." I didn't mention my fantasies about Jocelyn.

EPILOGUE

Over time the peoples and domestic animals of Earth became blessed with endowment. As I look back, my life might have ended a number of times without the advent of cancer cures, reversal of the aging process, nutritional successes, and elimination of genetic ailments. Truly extended longevity became the norm, until the Earth became overpopulated. Then the Great Incurable Plague came out of nowhere and caused a reorganization of civilization with efforts to turn the page toward a more conservative life style.

We became brilliant when compared to what we were. Despite this setback, the smarter and more driven humans forced explorations of the inner and outer universe that became a thing of beauty. Our lifestyles changed from fractional to what we conceived to be wholesome and practical. The number of heroes and geniuses that flowered in every field of human endeavor astounded even the mind of the new human who struggled to keep up with it all. This flowering did not occur overnight and took many years as Entity spread it tentacles.

The characteristics that made up a human did not change. As even young campers we had guessed that the more things changed, the more they stayed the same. Criminals became more ingenious and more destructive which challenged law enforcement to keep up with their ingenuity. The upper, middle, and lower classes remained. Granted, the people lived much longer lives, but the relative distinction between the classes did not vanish; nor did the relative level of graft, corruption and income.

In a simple summary statement, Earth remained a dirt-poor planet. There were no towering spires of the vast cities, no floating cities on the seas, only rundown buildings refreshed by occasional influxes of materials from outlying worlds.

The Entity had accomplished its purpose; at

least, what we had imagined it to be: to spread its intelligence among the life forms it encountered. On the good side, we developed environmentally safe methods to tap the oil and gas on Canopus without the creation of unsightly derricks and pollutant gases.

I do believe, that the message of Entity is beyond that of the sheer unveiling of growth potential. In my mind and sadly said, the problem lay in the fact that none of what we were all about had any purpose. I'm trying to figure out what that purpose might be.

Of all the worlds people now populated, only one remained free from strife: Canopus. Early on, my father, head of the self-proclaimed New Interplanetary Council based on Canopus, finagled ownership of the world. That's how rich and powerful they had become. All right, I had a hand in it and still do. Because of private ownership, people were screened before being permitted to move to the world—only a small part of what made Canopus a special place. The screening process retained only creative people. Curiously, nobody could ever find out if drinking more Entity water made you smarter. We only knew that it didn't seem to hurt.

Many of the original group of people who had first encountered the Entity so many years ago now live on Canopus including Marty and many of the original campers.

Jos opted to stay on Canopus and her sister, Rebecca, joined her. Rebecca and Marty became an item, got married, and are inseparable.

After a period of time, Jos and I also got married. To those of us who lived on Canopus, the life is satisfying and our first generation Entity-Human children blossomed into intellectuals who found the time to dedicate their lives to creativity without the headlong rush for instant success. She talks a little more than she used to and we decided that a few year's difference in age doesn't matter much anymore. We both discover and invent and have become happy together along with our children. I still exercise in the mornings and for what it's worth, carry a bottle of sparkling water with me whenever I travel the stars.

In the grand scheme of things, what had been accomplished? Master Jackson Walcott was not the simple camper he was not too long before. He had become part of a *Being*, traversing the universe for countless ages, seeing things no person had ever or will ever see. *Alone virtually forever.* The human part of me began to cry. I didn't understand. None of us who had tasted of the Entity, or had touched those who had, would ever be human again.

SPLIT TIMES

Arnold Chambers, your boiler-plate accountant, had gone through school with a Hewlitt Packard Do It All calculator strapped to his belt and thick glasses to adorn a pudgy, placid, unexciting face. He couldn't completely hide a middle-aged spread by a dress shirt that never seemed to be completely tucked into his pants.

The split in the space-time continuum, just millimeters wide, ran vertically through the body of Chambers while he sat at his desk.

As these things go, the rift hit instantaneously, from top to bottom, well off center, from his head down, much more to the left than to the right. The accountant suddenly and simultaneously possessed both the temperament and intellect of a human being far in the past and another human only a few years in the future. As time rifts go, this one disappeared forever from that particular point in time and space.

Chambers lived a simple life. His relaxed marriage of thirty years had been unmarred by scandal. The couple owned a small home only minutes away from his place of employment at a large furniture store where he worked as an accountant.

The couple lived in Sierra Vista, a small community in southern Arizona. This community found itself affixed by the umbilical cord to Fort Huachuca, a military base that oversaw operations in Central and South America.

Now in jail for the gruesome murder of two employees, he refused to talk to police interrogators who had been assigned to his case. The community had been rocked by the murders.

A single light bulb hung in the interrogation room. Chambers was seated at a small table in the chair reserved for the guest of honor with hands cuffed in front of him. Across from him sat Jeffers, a clean-cut police Lieutenant, and a man named Brodsky, a grizzled homicide detective with nearly twenty years on the force, soon to retire.

Brodsky refused to become excited, although after two decades as a detective, he thought he'd seen it all until this new one popped up.

Brodsky calmly asked, "Once again, the question is, Mister Chambers, do we hang you for Murder One or send you away for the rest of your life for Murder Two, or do you cop the insanity plea? Why did you kill them? A simple statement will do."

After twenty minutes of questioning, Chambers spoke for the first time in perfect English. "Sorry for the late response. It took me a while to figure out your verbal patterns. Your body language contributed significantly to my knowledge base. Then there's your aura, your subdermal skin temperature, eye usage, facial expressions, social distancing, manner of dress, personal hygiene, and other parameters of human expression."

The detectives looked at each other and pulled their chairs closer. *Insanity?*

Chambers centered his glasses using both hands and spoke to the men. "To answer your last question, Sharon pissed me off because I asked her to bring me a particular file and she told me to wait a minute until she had finished with her customer. Personally, I don't like to be kept waiting.

"As for Lefkowitz, I just didn't like the way he combed his hair, so I did him while I was at it."

"At it?" asked Brodsky.

"Right after I bashed Sharon. Do I have to explain everything?"

Jeffers looked in astonishment at Brodsky, who made a circling motion with his right forefinger near his head.

"So you grabbed a paperweight and clubbed both of them to death just like that," said Jeffers.

"That's about it," replied the accountant, as open and honest as if he were in a confessional. "Nothing complicated. Fortunately for me, Lefkowitz was close by when I was finishing with her."

Brodsky looked through a file folder. "Arnold, from every indication, you've been a model citizen up until now. Maybe we're not too bright, but we don't understand. Help us with this."

"Look," said Chambers, "it's really very simple. If somebody pisses you off enough, you solve the problem. If you're asking me about the paperweight, it's all I had. Believe me, if a large sharp rock were present, I would have preferred that. One swing and splat. You're home free. I think I pulled a shoulder muscle."

"You're home free?" said an astonished Brodsky.

"You know, 'more muss, less fuss', as the saying goes."

Chambers needed to explain further to his inquisitors, who appeared to be slow on the uptake. "It solves the problem, it ends your frustration, it helps reveal your testosterone level to your peers, it makes you king of the hill, it expresses irrefutably the need for society to maintain stability in a world gone mad with unexpressed hostility."

Brodsky pulled a cigarette from a pack. "You know, I've killed for less than that," said Chambers, pointing at the cigarette with his chin. "But you already know that."

Brodsky put the cigarette back and said, "You don't sound as if you have a bit of remorse about what you did to two innocent people."

Chambers didn't reply for some time.

"Are you thinking about remorse?" asked Jeffers.

"Just extracting cube roots in my head for something to do. You're boring me," continued accountant. "It's like having to explain why gravitation, electromagnetic radiation and magnetism all exhibit the inverse square law if they are associated with a spherical body. Hell, that's just basic three dimensional Euclidean geometry."

Noting the expression of puzzlement on the detectives' faces he added, "It's like having to explain why we have to scratch an itch, okay?"

Jeffers leaned back in his chair. "Arnold, "What I don't get is that you appear to be a bright guy. My question is, how can anybody as smart as you be so stupid at the same time?"

Chambers shook his head. "You're not looking at the big picture. Humans have changed a lot over the ages."

"I'm sure they have," agreed Brodsky, looking at Jeffers, who merely shrugged in agreement.

Chambers explained, "A very long time ago—I couldn't pinpoint a date for you—Man had a highly advanced peaceful civilization throughout virtually the entire world—a civilization of great intellect. Mathematics, arts, and sciences flourished. We possessed a great understanding of our role in the universe. Ice ages and warming periods can come upon us within decades or even years for reasons of shifting contintents, orbital fluctuation, 12,000 year sun spot cycles, planetary wobbling, shifting ocean currents, and so forth. So, a great ice age befell us and drove us back to primitive conditions. Over time, civilization rebuilt itself to this present world. I demark this as the period of the clueless here and now. The present civilization will be destroyed in twenty-five years, three months and two days by a terrible nuclear war. 'Just saying', in your vernacular.

"My intellectual side is from this past, before destruction of the great civilization. My violent side comes from after the next twenty-five years, when we rule by the club, that is, those who survive the nuclear war. If you don't believe me, undo these handcuffs and try me."

As one, the two detectives rose from their chairs and helped Chambers from his, leading him from the room. "No, Arnold, we'll leave that to the jury." said Jeffers.

THE MUSHROOM CAVES OF PALAU

One aspect of Jeff's insight was chemically induced. He knew that as sure as he knew his name.
Now, remembering and seeing the future at the same
time, he still wondered the same thing.

Jeff's claustrophobia had brought about profound
nausea. His impulsive nature had flown in the face
of common sense, yet it was this same impulsive-
ness and the same regrets he was so familiar with
that had brought him great successes. One of these
days it might lead to a long and slow death. The way
things were going, that day could be today.

Trapped in a tunnel constriction well below the
surface, Jeff's broad shoulders prevented him from
moving forward or backward, and just ahead of him,
Talley, also trapped, had begun to panic.

The guide kept kicking Jeff in the head trying
to go back and in his turn, Jeff yelled at the native
guide to relax, a difficult thing to do in the pitch
blackness. Just the thought of the horror of losing

his sanity and dying while he did so kept him sane. If he died here in an underground tunnel on the island off Palau with the obscure name of Babeldaob and was never found, his life would not have been in vain. At least he would die doing what he loved.

Small stalactites and sharp rocks were present at the constriction, which the diminutive Talley had discounted as he hugged the ground during his forward crawl. Now, they tore at Jeff's shoulders, back, and upper arms, gouging through his protective clothing as though he were in the maws of a shark.

The two had been underground much longer than Jeff had anticipated. Dehydration had become a serious consideration. Although the temperature and the soil remained relatively cool, the high humidity caused the men to sweat profusely. The damp passages and the presence of stalactites and stalagmites meant that water would be in the form of seepage from above, but may also be in the form of frank flooding of many of the passages. He understood that immediate escape was crucial because of this reason.

His mind went off into dark tangents driven by the psychotropic drug produced by the growth of the prolific mushrooms and which now commanded his mind. Its gases lived within him as an alien life form that may have waited through eternity to capture a human body. But wouldn't that alien have to escape in order to transfer itself to another body? He saw the entire event as a setup, a devious macabre plot to bring him to this place where he would conveniently vanish without a trace and the perpetrator would escape.

Time had slowed to a crawl, although he had no references anymore by which to gauge its passage. Did that mean his thoughts had sped up or had the movement of time become slower? He always did have trouble figuring that out.

The insects arrived. The fucking insects were everywhere. They crawled over his face and beneath his clothing and into his eyes; everywhere he couldn't reach or scratch. He knew with certainty they were burrowing beneath his skin to infest his body, to turn it into a maggot ridden ... Jeff screamed within the tunnel. The echo actually lessened the effect of the scream's eminent message: Death has arrived.

Above the scientist, Talley kicked and returned him to his fear of enclosure. Jeff forced himself to relax. He tried to twist onto his back with one arm pinned beneath him, the other trapped above his head. Twisting around a centimeter at a time, he finally managed to get onto his back and in the process, dislodged enough dirt to clog his eyes and his mouth. This momentarily distracted him from the scourge of the insects. He sputtered and spit, but could not yet reach his eyes to wipe out the soil that stung eyes like acid rain, or was it volcanic ash?

In his imprisonment, Jeff was also concerned about lingering volcanic gas killers such as carbon monoxide, carbon dioxide, and various sulfurous gases, of which he detected a faint odor. Or was it the odor of the mushrooms?

Jeff tried to keep his head as low as possible, but didn't succeed completely. A sharp projection carved into his forehead above the left eye. With blood streaming down his face, Jeff dug the heels of his boots into the passageway, and after several attempts, managed to pull himself backward enough to free both arms.

With the small powerful flashlight still in one hand, he shined the light around him as a reality check. Instead of white light, Jeff's mind saw a kaleidoscope of swirling colors, as if multiple prisms were rotating about one another. Time stopped. He became infatuated with the patterns of color.

While Talley's light had burned out, the guide saw Jeff's light and began to calm. However, nausea assailed the scientist once again, which, for him, had the opposite effect. The darkness calmed him, while the light only served to remind him of his claustrophobia and brought about a sense of panic so terrible that ,he realized, had to be chemically induced. What to do about became a separate matter.

Jeff had first heard of the elusive mushroom when reading a scientific journal that described its properties. The antibiotic potential of the rare variety of the *Agaricus* mushroom could not be overstated. Unfortunately, it could not be kept alive in the laboratory after recovery from its rare native habitat on the shady surfaces of Palau where it had first been recovered.

The mushrooms could be identified by their

heady, almost fetid odor, once they had been spotted. Much more potent than penicillin discovered by Fleming, the *Agaricus* was reputed to leave a broad sterile zone in which neither bacteria nor viruses nor other fungi would grow.

Jeff contacted the authors of the report and his follow-up phone calls took him to an underground guide. Talley, proud of his Philippino decent and his near perfect English, told Jeff that he knew many of the tunnels of the island chain and reported such odors in some of them he had visited while gem hunting with other tourists. Jeff planned his trip. Thus, he prepared to take an arduous journey to the island of Babeldaob, 600 miles west of the Philippines. He could expect an abundance of rain with an average relative humidity of 82%.

In his experience with tropical rain forests in Asia, Jeff's initial hunch was that they might not be found associated with the forest which covered the island archipelago. In fact, the mushrooms might grow in association with caves back in the forested land of one of the Palau volcanic islands, Babeldaob, where they had originally been recovered in limited quantity.

The more he studied, the more he came to the realization that the presence of past volcanic activity and associated tunnels on the island tunnels might just be the true and likely home of these peculiar life forms.

Three days before departure for the islands, Jeff had been conducting research at his own institute while teaching one course of medical mycology at the University of Oklahoma medical school. The thought of the elusive and rare variety of *Agaricus* mushroom had begun to consume the scientist and when that happened, the rest of the world didn't exist.

His obsessive-compulsive nature demanded action. He contacted a friend in the state department to hastily obtain the necessary permits for removal of mushrooms from the Republic of Palau and for their entry into the United States. He turned the business over to Carmen, secretary at the time, and left the country during spring break.

After a twelve hour flight to Guam, he boarded a smaller plane to Koror, the capital of Palau, where he met Talley.

After a night in a hotel, the pair traveled by a series of small planes and boats to their final destination. Jeff planned to get enough of the soil and the life forms together to help them survive, especially if they were producing spores when they were plucked. He believed that he and his graduate students could propagate them enough to isolate the antibiotic that might work in the treatment of a wide variety of diseases, possibly including cancer.

Shortly after entering the cave mouth Talley led them down a tunnel born eons before through the action of escaping volcanic gases. Occasional offshoots of tunnels presented themselves.

Talley told Jeff he had gone gem hunting before, but had not gone as deep as they were now descending in this particular series of tunnels. Crawling down the main trunk they could smell a slightly fetid odor emanating from somewhere ahead of them.

At Talley's suggestion, Jeff had brought with him a two hundred and fifty foot roll of yellow twine as a trail marker to run behind them as they crawled. The guide had thought that this would be enough to serve as a sure method for their return.

After the string had run out, they crawled another fifty feet on a nearly level plane and came to a crossroads where three other tunnels intersected with theirs. They'd chosen the passage that had the fetid smell and before long found themselves in the midst of a field of *Agaricus* that could be numbered in the thousands. The odor became overpowering and Jeff became concerned that their lungs would soon absorb enough of the volatile compounds to poison their systems and cause unknown effects. These might include hallucinations and seizures, such as had occurred in Salem, Massachusetts, during the late Seventeenth Century. Indeed, disorientation could not be ruled out. He limited his breathing and told Talley to do the same.

Jeff collected as many mushrooms and as much soil as his waterproof nylon bag would hold. He dragged this container behind him. The air was heavy, humid, and oppressive. Except for occasional flashes from Jeff's light, they failed to realize how disoriented the mushroom's chemicals had made them. When they had returned to the crossroads, in a rare error of judgment and under the effects of the poisons coursing through their systems, Talley mistakenly chose the wrong passageway, which led them to their present predicament.

Still, in Jeff's mind, he had accomplished his goal. He had won. He rationalized that this investigation was for the good of mankind, but as a character flaw, knew that it was best for the good of Dr. Jeffrey Shenero.

Jeff tried to calculate how they had gotten where they were. The initial tunnel had a downward slope, sometimes gradual, other times steep until it fairly leveled out as it came to a central crossroad. At that crossroad intersected three other tunnels, one of which clearly headed upward where they had found the mushrooms. A third was level and resembled their entry-escape route, but soon headed downward, and the forth clearly went downward. Very small tunnels descended straight downward from the cavern floor and made walking treacherous.

Jeff could inch backward, but got jammed again when his belt snagged onto a sharp rock and he had no way to get his hand underneath him to free it.

Then the sound of the ebb and flow of water entered into his senses. He paused in his effort to escape and listened. "Is that water I hear, Talley?" he asked, wondering about this new sound in their limited environment, until the realization occurred that the tide was coming in and he and his guide might be drowned even while they lay entrapped.

"Yes, Mister Jeff, it is the water," replied the guide, in a tone sugggesting death might be imminent. A chill ran over Jeff as he realized the tide would be the highest now and that they had lost all sense of time. Water would be entering the cave mouth, running down the entry tunnel into the cavern, and into the two passageways that led downward, one of which held them captive. It would not be entering the upward passageway that held the mushrooms, yet would pour into theirs for the next several hours. They had not found water in the crossroad because it would drain off through smaller holes in the earth, as well as through the downward tunnel they were now trapped in.

Soon the water rushed in to soak Jeff's feet. In a time-altered universe created by hallucinogenic volatile organic compounds, the sound of the water became magnified.

One instant his mind calculated at lightning speed as he saw solutions to problems that had plagued him for years. The next instant he could see a kaleidoscope of swirling colors as beautiful as anything he had ever imagined. Horrid panic gripped him. He laughed out loud when he thought of volunteers that would be needed for the study of these mushrooms. He considered himself to be an involuntary volunteer.

Talley might have some words of advice. After all, this was his country, his territory, his caves. But peace did not to come to the small man. He panicked anew and tried to kick himself downward at the sacrifice of Jeff's head.

Years of tunneling had inured Talley's body to

the harshness of crawling through the lengthy holes in the ground. Not so Jeff, whose knees and elbows were cut and rubbed raw and were bleeding freely. Every muscle ached and shooting pains traveled from one shoulder across his neck to the other. He figured that if he and Talley ever escaped their predicament, he will have crawled the equivalent of three football fields, much of which was over smooth terrain and much more over sharp volcanic rock that had melted and fused into itself to resemble coral and now seemingly fused into his skin and muscles

He managed to muse: *And how was your day, Doctor Jeff? Oh, just dandy. The tunnels carved me alive from the outside-in and the chemicals destroyed me from inside-out. The brain? Well, that's another matter.*

With a last bit of sanity, Jeff shook off the oxygen deprivation and the toxic chemicals that were obviously winning the battle between fantasy and reality.

Jeff finally freed himself and began the upward and backward movement, an insane movement against balance, against the natural order of motion; as the incoming tide kept pushing him back down the way he had come and into Talley feet.

Some indeterminate time later the pair finally reached the crossroad, but fate gave the two men little chance to reconnoiter. They stood in water up to their shins and every few moments more sea water would surge in. Unable to see the tunnel holes that permeated the floor itself, there was a good chance that one of them could step into one of them and break a foot or a leg. Water swirled around them as it drained into the holes and into the downward tunnels, making it as difficult to stand as it would have been had they been on a shore with receding waves sucking them back into the ocean.

The men checked the three remaining passageways with Jeff's waning light. Water gushed from one of them—their way out. With Talley in the lead once again, the two crawled forth into the flow and into the surges of ocean water, gasping and turning their heads for air every few feet until the string was found. This gave them the reassurance they needed and Talley lost his panic and felt confident of their escape.

Every few seconds, however, water would surge into their tunnel in a great torrent and wash over the men. They had to cease their movement and hold their breath until the wave passed and then they would begin to crawl upward.

Every seventh wave or so would be the worst and a huge quantity of water surged into their black hole to wash over the two desperate men. By the time the ocean water had drained from around them, the next wave would be upon them. Jeff's inner thigh muscles, his shoulders, and his butt ached beyond anything he could remember.

The salt water that washed over his torn knees and elbows added stings onto the aches. The bag that Jeff dragged behind him acted like an anchor not only in its weight, but would pull him backward several feet when the water pushed it downward in its own gravity-driven pulsations. Fortunately, he had ensured that it was waterproof before he brought it with him from home; otherwise, the water would have soaked the soil within it and its weight would have been an impossible burden.

The steeper the tunnel became, the farther back down the men would be washed. Struggling against the tide, they learned to wedge themselves against the sides of the hole, when the waves came in, to prevent them from ending up where they had started from. The near-drowning, the pain throughout his body, and the focus of his mind on escaping the dreadful tunnels served to wash the potent drugs from his system and he regained his desire to survive the ordeal.

In the lower reaches of the exit tunnel through which they crawled, the water picked up velocity as it would in a constricting pipe. Crawling a few feet at a time, stopping for several seconds and crawling again, it took perhaps an hour to get to the surface.

The most difficult portion of the climb occurred when the tunnel widened sufficiently for them to crawl freely, but the explorers could not wedge themselves to be pushed backward anew.

Desperately, between waves, they sprinted on their bellies as quickly as possible, were washed backward and sprinted anew, somehow gaining ground until daylight became visible and the men exited the tunnel into fresh air and sunlight. A change of clothing awaited the explorers, each man standing and stretching in the warmth of the day, dripping water, scarred and haggard. The day's work was complete. The hour was not yet noon.

The men relaxed but a few minutes before beginning the trek back to civilization. An emergency clinic in Babeldaob would be their first visit to stitch the Jeff's head and to ease the pain of the scrapes and bruises each man carried over his body.

Then Jeff could plan for a long and painful journey back home with his bag of mushrooms locked in a trunk and stored in the cargo hold of the planes he needed to take. He could only hope too many people would not complain of their smell.

SOAP OPERA

Part I – Cover-Up

FADE IN: INTERIOR OF FLYING SAUCER, CONTROL CABIN

"This is Anor Quinn broadcasting with the Galactic News Agency on site at planet Earth." He swept his three tentacles over his head and, with his middle arm, ensured they strung properly down his neck taking it easy on the long one in the middle, or sensory tentacle, used for mating purposes.

"Be advised: This is our season finale of our comedy series, *For the Love of Earth.* Today: Will the Earthlings survive the arguments with their different linguistic, ethnic and political groups. Our experienced forecasters predict that they will not. We'll listen in during the private conversations for some real hoots, so hang on to your vitals. Many of our paid subscribers ask the question: Who cares?

It would be in their best interests to at least hope that *something* occurred. As it stood, the moderately popular series featuring Earth's inhabitants had been slated for cancellation with sponsorship increasingly difficult to obtain. For general purposes, Anor did not want the planet to become a wasteland. But ratings were ratings. He was in the broadcast business, not the free-lucky-charms business.

FADE OUT FOR ADVERTISEMENTS BY THE SPONSORS: UNIVERSAL HEALTH FOODS, GALACTIC TOURIST LINES, DRESSES AND TRESSES FOR THE RICH AND FAMOUS, AND PERSONAL SECURITY BEFORE FAMILY

Now off the air, Anor declared to Jado, his identical twin brother, "These humans make me crazy. How the factions coexist is mind-boggling."

"That's just it, Anor, they don't, which makes for a successful comedy," Jado declared with mirth, "especially when they try to coexist." Jado had been a mercenary for a couple of centuries. Tired of arms running and barely escaping death on a number of occasions, he finally decided to call it quits and contacted his brother for a legitimate job. Always bonded, but rarely in contact, Anor jumped at the chance for a partnership and got him a job with Galactic News Agency, or GNA, as their first and only weapons specialist. Since then, the two joined to become a news team second to none. The fact that a number of worlds listed Jado on their most wanted list did not concern anyone other than those who wanted him. Others lionized him as a freedom fighter. You couldn't ask for more press. The reborn Jado Quinn had become engaged in a new career; that of making an honest living. His word was his bond, which he gave GNA; up to a point, of course.

They had parked their flying saucer on the dark side of the Earth's moon months before over intervals of several years. In between, they would record more exciting events in the galaxy and always argued that a lesser reporting team could cover Earth. Now, the time had arrived again to close out another season of broadcasts. Their ship carried twenty beings from various worlds, all of them expert in the fields of audio and visual photography, sound amplification, linguistics, intra-galactic navigation, nuclear physics, weaponry, and nuances pertaining thereto. The ship also contained the Quinn brothers, experts in theatrics and broadcasting.

Their saucer belonged to GNA, which operated many such news vessels within the galaxy. Their electronically replete personal cabin contained a multi-species bathroom and a small bedroom with two bunk beds to house whomever might be sheltered there for the voyage. A score of screens were present around most of the saucer, each featuring a different drama recorded from around the galaxy. Two exercise areas and a central galley provided enough food and supplies for every meal taste.

Beings from every world wanted to belong to the

Quinn team. Only the best were approved, and cared not where they might be stationed, as long as they were together as a unit. In the end, on paper, Anor made the final decisions,

Anor, all seven green feet of him, stood and stretched, waving his arms about. He checked the instruments were off to ensure his voice did not go out over the airwaves. "They just won't let it go. They won't destroy each other and they keep teasing and teasing . . ."

"Anor, so don't get wrapped up in minutiae" declared Jado, and snapped a few of his digits. When the drinks arrived, Jado offered his brother a pair of medication tablets. Anor gratefully took them and swallowed. Soon, a door to the broadcast cabin of the spaceship opened and two attendants appeared carrying mind altering substances in liquid form. Both Anor and Jado threw down the drinks in an instant. The attendants disappeared.

"I get that, Anor. I appreciate everything we have built and the money and position . . ." Jado sounded drunk as the alcohol and the medications began to take effect.

Inebriated or not, Anor did not exaggerate. Countless toys and do-dads were sold across the galaxy, each with images of himself and his brother to bring incredible wealth and fame to them both. He should be appreciative, Jado thought; although in all fairness, Anor had been popular well before he had stuck himself into the contract with GNA.

Jado waited patiently, watching the view of Earth

on one screen and commercials appearing on another. His brother carried the Quinn blood and as such, had a tendency toward eccentricity. Once off his medication, he could become unpredictable. Curiously, that contributed to his popularity: because, like his subject matter, he might go off the deep end at any given moment. The audience loved a narrator with personality and flavor. At one time, when he had been younger, Jado could remember that beings preferred warm and stable broadcasters who were bipeds. Anor changed all that in so many ways. Times are different than in the old days.

Anor stood and lectured his brother, head tendrils and body arms waving in all directions, manipulating keys on the console. The spacecraft drifted upwards to clear the edge of Earth's moon to present them with a wondrous view of the planet in full sunlight. "A thousand years ago our people found this planetary dung heap and forecast that it would never amount to anything. So far they've been right. Virtually everything they've done has been predicted and it's been a hundred years since Network picked them up as a late night time slot—a cheap date, as it were. I get that it's not prime time anymore, but, hey, we've done it all. "

Jado held his brother around the shoulders and gently pushed him into the captain's chair. The seat instantly conformed to his shape to hold him securely and comfortably. "No argument from me. They're simpletons bent on self-annihilation and p;rovide good entertainment for a largre portion of our viewers."

FADE IN: OVERVIEW OF PLANET EARTH

Miniature and undetectable video cameras had been shot into orbit from the GNA saucer and surrounded the blue-green world. These saw and recorded anything the occupants of the ship wanted to record and had done so for a long time. Other cameras and recorders had been secreted in locations that might be handy, if called upon. Movement of persons and voices within buildings could be seen, heard and monitored. As a drama unfolded in one or more hot spots around the planet, the technicians would focus on that event around the clock, present Anor with the backdrop, and help him understand the unfolding events, better enabling him to narrate the occurrences that the galaxy-wide audience would see.

Anor contemplated what they needed to do next, now that this season's broadcasting had finished here. As per standard procedure, they'd need maybe a week or two of follow-up to ensure that there were no odds and ends. Their ship would leave the moon and would move faster than could be detected by any technology the earth people possessed. Even if they were detected upon their departure, what was one more saucer sighting?

The dictum of the politicians who owned and ran GNA held to a strict hand's-off policy and zero tolerance. Great broadcasters had been brought to ruin for even slight infractions. Well, too late now, Anor reflected. If things panned out, new events could certainly help next season's ratings and then do what . . . bring in more wealth? More fame? More glory? A dead world? They risked losing everything if the present turn of events could be traced back to them. So far they had not needed to do anything here except for permitting the earthlings to see their spacecraft on occasion. Big deal. A tease always stirred up the pot. That's not like creating an earthquake or assassinating a key figure or flooding an entire continent. They played the game within the rules, with a lone exception.

To swear they had never manipulated events would be a flat-out bald-faced lie. They and the audience had been aware that a Pakistani general, in league with terrorists, had given the terrorists access to one of the nuclear vaults in Kandahar, the capital city of Pakistan, with a population of some 600,000. Fine, unto itself. But in a drug-induced state, and not willing to let tens of millions die, Anor wanted to explode one of the bombs, which would result in the death of a large portion of the city, but would also take out the other bombs. If the explosion happened because of something they had done and it could be proved as a result of an investigation, their images would be hung in effigy, even in a universe full of beings who were tolerant of a lot of misdeeds. A galaxy full of sentient life would not be tolerant, if they knew that Galactic News Agency had the means of bringing about the death of one world, and as a sequitur, had the capability to bring out the death of their own.

As fate would have it, the shoot had concluded. Anor called the technical crew, congratulated them on a great job, told them to wrap up and prepare to go on home after they did their usual after season follow-up. They'd all meet at their usual pub in a couple or three weeks if another assignment didn't present itself. This was a real possibility because a love affair was ongoing the King of Canopus, Kredo Quinn, another of their brothers, and the Queen of Altair, both married to their own races on their home planets and both totally alien to one another. This affair promised to continue with hot and steamy episodes.

"That's our king," exclaimed Anor.

Jado nodded. "And our brother. Word has it he's sexually over-endowed. An issue of heredity," he confessed, pridefully. "In his case, he's in love with threes, but is shifting to ones and twos?"

"Huh?"

"You know, three eyes, three tentacles, three breasts, three arms," responded Jado.

"What's the matter with threes? I'm kind of proud of mine. It beats bipedal or quads."

Once Anor signed off with his crew, a chill of fear overtook him and gave him a bad case of the shakes. "Let's finish what we have to do and get out of here."

Jado stared at his brother. "Look, things will take care of themselves. You know we may make things worse if we meddle."

"We've got a little time here for follow-up. Once we explode a nuke, we could have a problem with GNA when they review the footage," responded Anor, saying the obvious.

"You didn't hear what I said, did you?" replied a frustrated Jado. "Look, I feel badly, too," Jado relented. "If we did this, at least you and I will be the only ones who know the truth. We'll keep the crew out of the loop. "

The two shook six arms and sat down to compute a plan of action. Jado ticked off points on the ten digits of his right and primary arm. "We know they brought in seven large trailers to haul off the bombs. We also know those trailers had been on stand-by since the new president came into office. That was back in episode four of the series before we switched to the typhoon off China. We followed the inspection of the nuclear storage facility by the United Nations and spied on the general when he called the terrorist leader to give him the eight digit code to open the electronic lock on the steel door to the concrete warehouse where the bombs were stored. Okay, so far?"

Anor assented.

"If you recall, we dedicated the next episode to the volcanic eruption in Sumatra where 100,000 people tried to flee the pyroclastic cloud and either got asphyxiated or burned to death before being buried under 10 million tons of ash. Great episode.

"After that, in the next episode, the big trucks, already on standby, load up with terrorists and move into the compound, kill the scant number of guards who are drinking and carousing with the local whores and not paying attention to their duties. The general has flown out of the country to a luxury villa in France, soon to be the world's most wanted man, while the terrorists enter the numbers given them to the vault, pick up five hydrogen and two neutron bombs with heavy forklifts and load them onto the vehicles. Our ratings skyrocket. End of story and end of the season."

"In for a finger, in for three arms. We trigger one of their nukes and blow up all the bad guys," Jado stated flatly. "It'll look like they did it to themselves out of stupidity."

"Exactly." Anor's voice slit finally turned upward. "Now you're starting to use your brain."

"Here's the bad news," Jado expostulated. "The seven nuclear weapons have multiple safeguards. You can't set them off with explosives and you do have to set them off with a coded sequence and you have to know that code and you have to know how to arm them. The general gave them all they needed to know."

Anor thought for a moment. "Okay, we know where those weapons are. Any school child can operate nuke sensors and pinpoint radioactive weapons from outer space. But we don't have the codes to blow them."

Jado clapped his brother on the shoulder. "Anor, here's a bit of good news. That technology is ancient. We can detonate one of the bombs with a pinpoint laser set at a thousand degrees and hit the junction past the timer and the input into the atom bomb that is used to trigger either the hydrogen or neutron bomb. Simple stuff.

"So while you've been working and translating the story dialogue into Galactic Universal for the show, I've been on the job tracking the trucks. Bet you ten-to-one the cult leaders are nearby, certainly within the radius of a nuclear blast." Jado pulled up a screen that depicted seven very slow moving trucks, each covered with a tarp. He penetrated the tarps to reveal the different weapons. The last two were the neutron bombs.

There was a lot Jado had not told him about his years as a merc, but when he signed on with GNA, he'd insisted that if they were going to permit him to fly with his brother, their saucer must be outfitted with the latest in weaponry, second only to a battle cruiser. He rightly argued that a number of the GNA ships had come under attack by pirates in open space and insisted on better protection. He presented his list of equipment and GNA, tired of losing ships, relented.

"If we blow one, won't they all go?" Anor asked.

"No, you can't trigger a nuclear bomb to go off with another nuclear blast, not even with these old relics. In any case, we want to blow up one of the neutron bombs. That will still kill people, but will leave structures intact. We don't need a radioactive cloud blowing into a large foreign population center.

"One more thing. We're going to have to hurry

up because the military should be around pretty soon and the force from the blast will shut down the electronics of their vehicles and their planes. Remember, those are the good guys."

"That could mean the end of our show here," Anor lamented, wishing he could have another dose of medication.

Jado commiserated. "Maybe. Don't forget that there is no lack of terrorists on this planet. And, dear brother, if it is the end of the assignment, so what? The show is as much about us as it is about subject matter."

Jado operated the controls and shut down all the screens on the ship, standard procedure after a shoot, except for one in their private room. At the weapons console he punched a button. A cross-hair appeared hovering over the trucks. He adjusted the crosshair, sharpened and minimized its image, moved it to the last bomb in the chain, enhanced the image, and depressed a red button. A bright light filled the screen.

"That's it?" inquired Anor.

"One and done," answered Jado.

"Now what?" asked Anor. "Stay here a few days and make sure everything is clean?"

Jado scratched himself. "All we have to figure out now, before we send in the footage, is explain what the stupid terrorists could have possibly done to a bomb in transit to make it blow up on its own."

Anor groaned.

Just at that moment the incoming call button flashed from GNA Central. The brothers gasped in unison wondering how their employer had found out about what they had done. Rumor had it they had psychics on their staff.

Shakily, Anor pressed the receive button. "Anor here."

A voice on the other end spoke, "You guys about ready to finish out there?"

"We're just preparing for follow-up, sir."

"Well, send in what you've got and get over to Altair. War may break out if the king of Altair finds out that his queen is making babies with the king of Canopus. Not only that, but you've got the only warship in the fleet. We need you there *now*."

"Yes, sir, we're on our way. Quinn out."

"If any crew member saw that explosion, he'd get suspicious," worried Anor.

Jado responded with a sly smile, "It'll be perfect. We'll put it on GNA."

"How so?"

"GNA will be between a rock and a hard place, as they say here. They ordered us to leave. Fine. The explosion will be a perfect wrap to the season—keep the viewers itching for the next series to begin. We'll title it, *Will Earth Survive?*"

They couldn't get away from Earth fast enough. While Jado got on the intercom and informed the crew of their new orders, Anor programmed the ship for the flight to Altair only about a dozen light years from Earth. Perhaps they would have a chance to get back home to Canopus, about three hundred light years distant. Just a short trip to each. The Quinns had taken longer in terms of hours to travel by ground car to visit their respective girlfriends back in the old days. The trip to get to Earth from GNA Central nearer the heart of the galaxy was 20,000 light years from where they were presently stationed.

During the next several hours, the brothers worked feverishly to complete their past assignment, crossed their tentacles, and sent the script translations, and footage, sans explosion, to GNA who, they fervently hoped, would accept it at face value.

When they returned to Earth to begin the following season, what they were to surmise upon seeing the dead world was that Pakistan had assumed that India had nuked them and returned the favor. Missiles flew back and forth until an errant one hit on the outskirts of Tehran. This brought the Iranians into the act which brought in Israel, then Russia. Ten thousand missiles flew from silos and submarines.

The developing civilization, such as it was, never had a chance to evolve to a space age race and had been set back a thousand centuries or more.

GNA would be thankful. Earth had to be eliminated from the series. Now, they could cut it for the simple reason there was nothing left to film.

The Quinns would be even more thankful, since they were at the least, the immediate cause of the death of a civilized planet. Hopefully, GNA would never find out. The job can be stressful at times.

Part II—Queen's Gambit

Anor and Jado Quinn, along with their crew, managed to grab a few hours of food and rest while the crew landed the vessel out of sight to observe the seventh planet, dubbed Altair, after the star. Similar to Canopus, Altair shines several times greater in magnitude than Sol and its habitable planets have to be located relatively distant from it to support life.

Once they settled in, the crew chief contacted Jado in the control console. "Sir, we've got the palace locked on. They must know we're here because they're sending ships to greet us."

Anor replied, "No problem. We've got distance rights. Zero in on the castle and see what the queen is up to."

Jado inserted, "Under no circumstances do I want them to believe we are anything but a news ship until I give the okay."

Almost instantly, a close-up of the castle appeared on one of the monitors. The queen's chamber appeared in another. Audio came on instantly. The military of the planet might see the GNA ship, but apparently the queen didn't. Not a fan of video dramas, she didn't care about being informed about anything but the latest in wearing apparel. The rest she left up to to her king.

Now in the presence of her handmaiden, the queen succumbed to her ministrations. Her skin gleamed with bug oil, her single breast shone in the light of the fluorescent lamps, her two loosely jointed arms waved about. The single eye in the middle of her forehead gleamed with excitement and expectation.

"Your husband has been gone for a long time my queen. So far there has been no word from him regarding your last baby. I shudder to think about what he would do were he to find out," offered the handmaiden, expectantly awaiting to hear more intimate details.

The queen shrugged and gave a slight laugh. "I will make many more before his return. They will all remain with my sister until I can find a way to get rid of the tyrant."

"You cannot divorce him," replied the handmaiden, soaking in the words.

"There are other means," answered the queen, running her hands over her body sensually, especially between her thighs, in apparent expectation of her meeting with her lover.

The film crew captured the scene, which would soon be transmitted to the tens of billions of sentient galactic beings, after video clean-up by production and GNA Central. Normally, this took a matter of seconds—minutes at the most. "My special king is on his way to feel the silky smoothness of my skin, the ripeness of my sexual organs; how he lusts for them. Soon he will have it all and then some."

"Rumor has it he is may be amassing his forces to capture you, your highness; away from your tyrant king," contributed the maid, teasingly, hoping to go along for the ride, if it should ever happen, perhaps even to be captured herself.

The queen gave a smile as smooth and the rest

of her body, "Oh, yes, it is so exciting that my pulse quickens and my juices flow." She shuttered to such an extent that the watching camera crew breathed harder.

"This beats terrorist scum on earth," said Anor, his sensory tentacle swelling with delight, as he spoke Jado's ear.

"Shut up, I want to listen," whispered Jado, lightly fingering his sexual tentacle.

A tiny dot caught a ship leaving Canopus. Another film crew already in orbit at the planet zoomed in on the tail markings and identified the ship as the private yacht of King Kredo Quinn, the third brother of Anor and Jado, just before it entered the netherrealm of subspace.

The scene switched back to Altair, where the queen's private phone rang. She picked it up, read something and smiled. Her prince in shining armor would soon he here.

In a bold move, six space ships, heavily loaded with armament, appeared from the backside of the planet. They weren't the GNA saucer types, but actual spaceships. "Do they belong to the Altair fleet?" asked Anor. Do you think they're going to attack Kredo when his yacht appears?" asked Anor.

"No, there is no subterfuge here at the present time, according to my sources. I can only think the ships are going to guarantee him safe passage," replied Jado.

"I will admit he's a handsome devil. Voted by women as the best looking three-eyed three-legged three-tentacled being on Canopus, or any other planet of threes, for that matter," Anor stated flatly.

Jada said, "Wait a second, give me a close shot of that lead ship," Jado called in the intercom to the crew as he peered more closely into the tri-dimensional screen.

The film crew focused in on the lead ship only 100,000 thousand miles away in open space. "I know that vessel," said Jado quietly, almost to himself, "and I know the captain. It's Trantor the Traitor. He's done jail time. He's totally demented. He must not know we're here. The creature hates GNA because we got him busted by filming his criminal acts. If he sees us, our mission could be in trouble. No, those aren't part of the Altairian navy; they're pirates and I'll bet you ten-to-one they're going to try to kidnap Kredo when he comes out of subspace. Anything in open space is fair game to this bunch of criminals, but they're not in open space, which makes them criminals."

Jado scanned the surrounding atmosphere near the ships and declared, not only to his brother and the crew, but to the mega number of soap opera followers, "Notice you don't see any military craft after those ships. They must have paid off the military captain because we had no indication of a battle between the two groups. They won't hesitate to nuke a city to get what they want."

FADE OUT: COMMERCIAL MESSAGES FROM ALLSTAR TRAVEL, FLEX CLOTHING

FOR ALL SHAPES AND SIZES, AND PUPU'S PLEASURE PLANET
FADE IN

The handmaiden assisted the queen in putting on her garments. "You'll meet him here, then?" she asked. The camera crew had already discovered the spy hole used by the prurient handmaiden when the queen had previously received her esteemed guest for their salacious encounters.

The queen checked herself in the mirror and unbuttoned the top button of the cloak that covered her single breast, thought for a moment, then unbuttoned the second one. She ran her hands over her stomach. "Yes, and it will be another baby tonight with my love." She spoke the intra-galactic language of the masses.

"Fortunately, your King Goldura will be gone for several more months," contributed the handmaiden, already dripping sweat in anticipation of what she could see and capture from her spyhole camera to review at leisure.

"And that means several more babies," sighed Queen Goldura of the Tresses, turning about in the mirror several times. She placed a long tress of real synthetic hair over her head in the fashion of the rich and famous. The handmaiden began to breathe huskily, anxious to be on her own to watch.

"How are these two races even compatible?" Anor asked in the background, out of sight of the camera, just loud enough for the audience to hear.

"It's one of the mysteries of the universe." Jado explained to the masses, repeating what everyone knew, yet required repeating for a younger generation, similar to the admonishment that everyone keep their hands away from their faces to reduce infection from viruses.

Jado explained, "We do know that Canopeans and Altarians have been compatible ever since they discovered each other back in the old days," assisting the viewing audience in understanding how the ones-and-twos queen was going to make several babies with this off-worlder threes with her gestation period of about a month. "So the children who survive will be mutants. So what? Aren't we all mutants? Don't we all belong a to a single cause?" Aren't we all family?"

"Come on, Jado, that's a little far-fetched," said Anor, speaking more to his audience than to his brother.

"No, Anor, "what isn't far-fetched is this: If the queen's husband is watching our program, she could be in big trouble."

Anor said, "I seriously doubt the king is watching. He's at the galactic star conference 40,000 light years away on the other side of the galaxy and he has better things to do than to watch our program, doesn't he?"

FADE OUT

FADE IN: INTERPLANETARY GALACTIC

CONFERENCE 40,000 LIGHT YEARS DISTANCE

"GNA saucer at IGC responding to inquiry from GNA saucer tracking the Goldura flag ship confirming that King Goldura has not arrived at the conference, which has been ongoing. He called ahead to report ship trouble but he should arrive shortly, pending repairs.

FADE OUT

FADE IN TO THE KING'S ROYAL SPACESHIP

Unseen, a GNA news ship had been tracking the royal vessel once it came out of subspace into normal space awaiting the king's arrival. The breakdown afforded the news ship to hide behind large local asteroid. Amplification of the image shows a dozen or so space yachts parked around the royal ship, still several thousand light years from the conference center.

FADE OUT

FADE IN: ENHANCED IMAGES OF INTERIOR OF THE ROYAL VESSEL WHERE KING GOLDURA IS DRINKING, SMOKING, GETTING MASSAGED, AND ENGAGING IN SEXUAL ACTIVITY

Close up depicts various sentient beings entering and leaving the spacecraft from their yachts. "Can you identify any of those yachts?" asked Anor.

"Yes," responded the crew chief of the vessel tracking the king. "Their signature names and numbers indicate"—here he paused, as if he were referring to a listing—and then gave the names of various well known female species of various races, a few of whom are married, are media stars, princesses, queens, and renown bohemians.

Those names were repeated by Jado, who then said, "Looks like the king has things well in hand," mused Jado on air.

"'Well in gland' is more like it," threw in Anor, or the galactic equivalent word, a statement totally permissible to simulcast throughout the galaxy, where broadcasting and communications were virtually instantaneous, once it got past the eight second delay at GNA Central. He knew he'd get a chuckle from the viewers and kudos from network for making that cute quip.

FADE OUT

FADE IN: GNA 1 SAUCER PILOT'S CABIN
Seven ships suddenly appeared from behind Altair. Jado recognized the lead ship. It belonged to Trantor the Taunter, his old business partner. Jado had to act fast. He instantly ordered a full alert to arm all weapons, including the fusion laser and the atomics, then pulled the saucer into plain sight.

Jado knew that Trantor hated both him and the GNA. Trantor didn't know that Jado presently commanded the heavily armed GNA ship and that GNA had granted Jado absolute authority to protect the vessel from foreign intervention. Furthermore, the watching masses had no idea that the GNA saucer possessed serious armament. They would soon find out.

The pirates drew closer and the image of Trantor appeared, in all his pale glory. A ghostly pale white-skinned bipedal humanoid from the far reaches of the galaxy, he had ruled the skyways for a generation, plundering ships and worlds alike—the most feared pirate in the galaxy, one with whom Jado had partnered for many years. "Ahoy, there GNA captain, do you have the guts to show your face?"

Jado laughed and lit up Trantor's screen with his own image, cognizant that none of the ships in front of him had even activated their weapon's systems, in their overinflated sense of security. Seeing the surprise on Trantor's face, he said, "Hello, Trantor, I see you brought along your mother and grandmother and their little piglets to do your fighting for you."

"Jado. You're still alive, are you?" Trantor bristled with rage. Nobody spoke to him that way.

"Alive and well," Jado smirked. "While we are discussing your mother, the word around the galaxy is that she never did recognize you as a living entity, just another bit of afterbirth."

Trantor's pale skin became inflamed and his entire pale, almost see-through body turned bright ruby red. The viewing audience thoughout the galaxy moved closer to their 3-D screens, perhaps inhaling a more nerve-reactive accelerant in the process.

"Yes, Trantor, you fool. I am alive and I told you once what would happen if I ever saw you again. By the way, say hello and goodbye to a few billion viewers."

"Viewers? Goodbye?"

"Yes, Trantor. You are on the news. The entire galaxy is now watching you say goodbye to all of those who wish you the worst in the next life." Jado pressed the firing stud on the laser fusion weapon pointing down the throat of Trantor's ship. A moment of brief shock passed over the pirate's face while his ill-begotten ship and those accompanying him melted into lumps of metal. Two other blasts from the atomics soundlessly turned the metal into free atoms with only a single ship escaping, the one belonging to Warfoot, Trantor's second in command.

"I always wanted to do that," mumbled Jado Quinn, now a bigger hero than ever in the eyes of the populated galaxy.

At that moment, completely unaware of the happenings at Altair, or the presence of the watching GNA vessel, King Kredo Quinn's ship appeared out of subspace and casually cruised downward for a landing at the castle of the queen while her own husband, Goldura the Fourth, partied endlessly near the other end of the galaxy.

FADE OUT: EXTENDED COMMERCIAL BREAK FROM DRUGS FOR ALL OCCASIONS, SIN WITHOUT GUILT, PLANETARY SELF DE-

FENSE, LIFE AFTER DEATH, AND LUCIOUS LACIVIOUSNESS

FADE IN: QUEEN'S CHAMBER

The one-eyed, two-armed, two-legged, triple-tentacled Altarian queen permitted the green three-eyed, three-tentacled, three legged Canopean to disrobe her; all details captured by the hidden camera.

GNA never revealed how they had obtained interior shots of their subjects, nor the methods which were used to place their cameras, or when they had been put in place. Somehow, the public accepted their presence in light of the greater truth—the drama itself. Like a good novel, sometimes it is necessary to suspend disbelief for the good of the story.

Now Kredo's sensory tentacle touched the special area between the thighs of Goldura of the Tresses while the camera panned in slowly. Beyond a few moans of the aroused camera crew, and perhaps Jado, not a word was spoken. The handmaiden watched in rapture from her spyhole, as Kredo's sensory tentacle exuded the impregnating fluid and Lady Goldura swooned in his arms as she felt the baby being conceived. The child would come out to look like him, or so she hoped, this time a female version with three breasts to complement the first child they had conceived together. (It had long been ascertained that three-breasts held dominance in the gene pool compared over a single breast.)

In six weeks she would be ready to conceive again, but there was no reason why they couldn't practice until then. They spoke of their next meeting quietly, as if fearful of being overheard.

FADE OUT: END OF SEASON'S BROAD-CASTS
NEXT SEASON HIGHLIGHTS

FADE IN
Anor presentd background: "Trantor's second in command, known only as Warfoot, is the only ship to escape the wrath of GNA's beloved Anor and Jado Quinn. To this date, Warfoot's origin and appearance are a complete mystery. Everybody knows that King Goldura is the richest man in the galaxy and that Altair is probably the richest of all our planets. Never mind trade balance, how does this fit into the equation. We ask an important question: Did Warfoot really escape? It turns out one of our GNA saucers followed him to his hideout."

Warfoot turns to his younger brother, Junior, seated at the console next to him. Their mother had given birth to fifteen children in her single litter with Junior the youngest and Warfoot the oldest.

"Trantor caused his own death," Warfoot began.

"Sure," replied the younger brother. "He couldn't stand being taunted, instead of being the taunter. I will allow that he was magnificently bold."

"Yes, but set in his ways," Warfoot asserted. "Trantor relied solely on his spies to keep him informed of events within the galaxy where a being might make a dishonest living. He was all about business, but don't believe everything you hear, news reports can be biased. He did have his immoral code of ethics."

Junior agreed. "I maintain that we still need to tune in to the GNA broadcasts that feature these bothersome episodes. We need to see what that damnable Jado Quinn had to say about the death of Trantor, if anything, and if they have a clue as to where you and I might have gone."

Warfoot pursed his sucker-like mouth. "How had that damnable Quinn arranged to arm the news vessel? Okay, he has a real job. But he was a lot better as a pirate when he worked with us. Too bad he had to develop an honest streak. I wonder if GNA knows about Quinn's background," Warfoot scratched his right ear with his right rear foot. Maybe we can get a message to GNA and give our friend a little embarrassment, such as a firing from his position and public scorn throughout the galaxy."

"I wouldn't make Quinn a project," older brother. "We have other foods on the table. Besides, Jado is fairly easy to read. It's his brother, Anor, who I don't trust. The guy is too quiet, and like Kredo, he loves to party when they give him time off from that flying garbage can—all right, a garbage can a few weapons."

FADE TO SCENE

"Warfoot, I'm glad we didn't capture Kredo, because King Goldura is worth infinitely more than another Quinn brother. The fact that he is stalled for whatever reason is our opportunity. All we have to do is to pinpoint Goldura's flagship and capture it along with a few other wealthy hostages and we'll never have to work another day."

"As far as that goes, we don't have to work, now, Junior."

"That's besides the point. Isn't the dream to own as much as we can, to think boldly?"

"I hear you brother," Warfoot nodded his huge head. "I'll tell you something else. I think Jado let us go on purpose. Why? Because they're in the entertainment business and we lend excitement to their lives and to the lives of their viewers."

"Which begs the question, are we being watched now?" threw in the younger brother.

Warfoot shook his mane as if to say, so what? Gathering more of his forces, he made a few calls and within minutes, received the footage he had been seeking; an approximation of the king's location as broadcast by the Quinn's themselves from an earlier episode.

FADE OUT: COMMERCIALS BY PUPU'S PLEASURE PLANET FOR THE PLUSH AND FLUSH; HOUSE-SIZE SAFES: WE PROTECT YOUR POSSESSIONS; UNIVERSAL HAIR AND TENDRAL PRODUCTS

FADE IN
Split screen shows a sweating and panting hand-

maid peeking through her spyhole as King Kredo in-
seminates the Queen who lathers herself in his now
expressed and voluminous saved-up fluids.

Now laying intertwined, the two lovers offered
an interspecies attraction crossing social and interplanetary barriers. Who could not identify with three
tentacles on the one participant and multi-digited
arms on the other? Who could not identify with the
reproductive act in general? This feature that drew
in most of the viewers to the series and GNA did not
want to dilute, indeed, cheapen their series with a
lack of lasciviousness. Even the sponsors were excited. They'd better be.

"What now?" whispered King Kredo, as though
he might be overheard.

"You ask 'what now'? Why, we keep having babies as long as we are able."

"I'm sorry I was so rushed this time, my queen."

"I was too. We were both hungry for one another.
Next time it will be much slower and much more
sensuous, I give you my promise on that."

"Your king will be gone for some time, then?"
asked Kredo.

"If he returns early, I shall find a way to send
him on some mission. You and I must be together. I
tremble at the thought."

Doubtless, so did countless panting and sweating
viewers, the hidden handmaiden, and the recording crew. The queen's vital signs, as were Kredo's,
were sent to the viewing audience in a scrolling sub-
screen—vital signs spiking to unheard of heights.

These episodes were always scheduled for prime time. Queen Goldura's promise of longer, slower, and better sex when she would next meet her lover would be one of the platinum moments of the soap opera to be replayed uncountable times on individual all-senses 3-D screens to slathering audiences everywhere. The beautiful poetry of the scene would be immortalized simply because of her natural responses and true love, and not simply acts written into any script.

FADE OUT FOR COMMERCIAL BREAKS

FADE IN

Warfoot's pirate ships now amassed only a few light years away from the site of King Goldura's party. Their ships possessed the highest technology available in the galaxy, basically stolen or purchased from militaries, corporations, traitors, and spies. This enabled the pirates to utilize their signals to penetrate even planetoids for information without exposing themselves, similar to, but much more powerful than, the devices used by governments to spy on their own citizens at a great distance. But stationed in open space, the images came in crystal clear. No ships in the yacht party, even Goldura's yacht, were weaponized.

"I should think Goldura would surround himself with a war fleet wherever he went," Warfoot pondered out loud. "Something's not right. This is too good to be true."

Scanning the interior of Goldura's ship and the outer identifications of the visiting vessels enabled Warfoot and his crew to construct a plan of action with the capture of the wealthiest man in the galaxy as the prize.

Newsflash:

It is with regret that GNA will be cancelling any further reporting about Planet Earth. We know many of you enjoyed the low-level comedy that defined the ongoing series; however remote sensors at the site report wholesale destruction of virtually all life forms on the planet. This is due to an extremely high amount of radioactivity. Yes, they finally nuked themselves off the airways.

Instead, we will provide you with another short and fast-moving comedy: the galactic conference now underway.

To be continued

TELEPATHY SCHOOL

"Wow, look at this, Patty," laughed Carlin Ormsted, scanning the ads on-line. The bruise her shoulder had faded to yellow. "And help yourself to another buttered croissant," she offered, pouring herself a second cup of coffee.

Patty Johnson, Carlin's next-door neighbor, looked over her shoulder to see what she was reading and laughed. "Sure beats thigh reduction. What do you think? Want to have some fun? I've heard about the benefits of being a telepath: earning better grades, increasing business potential, learning what other people think of you, meeting new friends, and having great sexual adventures while tuning into another's feelings. Shoot, who hasn't heard of Jerry's? What's he doing advertising? Business must be slow."

"Congress sure has heard of him," Carlin offered. "That's why Jerry's is being investigated, along with all the other telepathy schools."

Patty said, dourly, "Yeah, Feds had to stick their noses into it. Meanwhile, the Asians, Latin Americans, and everybody else is going like gangbusters, running schools all over the place. Who knows how many telepaths they're cranking out. Meanwhile, we're lucky to get a dozen people to show up at one time. Wasn't Jerry the very first one?"

"Yep, he was in the first group of telepaths that appeared, what, twenty years ago after his father developed the serum?" Carlin contributed. "Wait, I remember now. The original formulation was supposed to be a trade secret, not what his father gave to everybody else."

Patty stopped to read more. Her eyes widened. "Carlee, here's a nice twist. Full refund, if you drop out within 24 hours. "Pete wouldn't mind. He'd tell me to go for it, figuring he'd get the whole fifty back after I drop out before the second day."

"Well, Bill wouldn't let me spend that kind of money. Anyway, he left early this morning. He'll be gone a month this time."

"Where is he now, Nashville?"

Lucky me," said, Carlin sarcastically.

Patty pointed to Carlin's bruise. "Bill?"

Carlin nodded.

"What happened this time?"

Carlin snorted. "You know how he guards that phone of his. Well, the other night the thing lit up a couple of times while he was in the shower. Two different names popped up. When I asked him who Sharon and Tiffany were, he said they were clients. I asked him if they bought tractors, too, and he grabbed me hard, shook me a couple of times, and told me to mind my own business."

"You know," Patty continued, in a more serious vein, "This school starts in three days. If we do it, we'll have to pack now to be gone for a month. Tell you what. I'll loan you the money."

"Patty, I'd never be able to pay you back."

"Yes, you will, someday. Let's have some fun. The only thing is, Pete might be mad because he'll have to cook for the kids the whole time, but I'll make it up to him."

Carlin shrugged, compliantly, and said, "Okay. For the sake of entertainment, I'll make the call and we'll see what happens." She picked up the phone and called the number provided in the ad.

Minutes later, two lengthy forms came onto the computer screen, one for each of the women. Carlin printed then out and the women took them to the sofa and sat before a coffee table. A picture window looked out over the sprawling Southern Arizona desert outside of Tucson.

In the yard, eight quail, one parent at the front followed by eight chicks followed by a second parent, walked up to a watering bowl to slake their thirst in the warmth of the desert. Mountain ranges and low hills in the distance offered countless hues and colors. A rising morning sun and passing clouds caused the shading on each of the hills to change from moment to moment.

Patty exclaimed, "Look at these disclaimers, Carly, especially number seventeen: 'Jerry's is not responsible for claims of real or alleged insanity after the student has been accepted to the school, nor is Jerry's responsible for pre-existing conditions of insanity or mental illness'. No wonder they're in trouble."

Carlin nodded soberly. "I've heard that once a person is injected with the unlocking compound— well, if and when they go insane, they can't be cured. Apparently, we lost several Senate and House members that way."

"No big loss there," added Patty, almost cheerfully. "Something like 30% of those injected can lose their mind after injection. But look at the bright side. That puts the odds in our favor, I mean, with two of us. The best news is that the school is only ninety miles north of here in Scottsdale, so, if things get too bad, we can be home in a flash."

The women read the forms completely and filled them out. Sunlight flooded the room constructed of heavily paneled oak and a ceiling with saguaro cactus ribs lining its underside. Patty provided her credit card numbers and Carlin return-faxed the paperwork. Within minutes the adventurous women held two entry passes to Jerry's School of Telepathy.

At thirty-five years of age, Carlin was no beauty-queen and gained weight over the years since her marriage. She stood five-foot-two in her flats and weighed 130 pounds. She had no beauty marks to distinguish her bland face, and her medium length, brown hair always appeared drab, although she had never really taken an interest in doing anything with it. Perhaps a little broad at the hips, she did have an outgoing personality and strong intelligence. She held a Master's Degree in Finance and worked from home. Hopefully, she could prevail upon her assistant to take over her duties for the next month. Her unhappy marriage to a wealthy executive ten years her senior was childless.

Her best friend had both looks, and a figure. A former beauty queen with blond hair in ringlets, she had received an Associates in Arts Degree from a two-year college and married at twenty-two. Now with two teenage sons, she craved excitement outside the gossip of the local country club.

Both women decided to pack lightly for the trip northward. They could always buy new outfits, or make a quick round-trip for a change of clothing, if necessary.

Three days later Carlin drove her Lincoln Town Car into Scottsdale with Patty seated next to her. It was hard to miss the Oberoi Intercontinental Hotel, one of the tallest and most resplendent hotels in the nation. Reputed to have cost nearly a half-billion dollars to construct, the hotel boasted its own national-class golf course with annual tournaments, and a fifty-acre man-made lake stocked with trout.

The women checked in, found their suite, and spent the remainder of the day in the hotel's lavish gift shops followed by dinner at one of the hotel's world-class restaurants.

DAY ONE

Slightly before 8:00 a.m. the next morning, Carlin and Patty entered the small lecture room on the ground floor of the enormous hotel. Five people were already seated at two of them, with another ten tables vacant.

Carlin had dressed in a green pullover covered by a white V-neck cashmere sweater and green three-quarter-length skirt while Patty wore blue jeans, customary attire in the Desert Southwest, pink button-down, and white sneakers. Of the two women, she drew the most stares from both men and women already present.

A man wearing a Brooks Brothers blazer, khaki slacks, and cordovan tassel loafers sat on a stool in front of a head table. He appeared to be fortyish, tall, slender, blue-eyed, clean shaven, and somewhat baby-faced with razor cut blond hair. He possessed creases in his forehead that, to Carlin, suggested a thoughtful countenance. He also had smile lines around his eyes, something she noted with jealousy.

As the women entered, the man stood and handed

a single sheet of paper to each of them, greeted them by name, and invited them to take a seat. The same sheet lay on the table in front of the others. To the man's right, on a small table, stood a pile of large books along with a pile of documents.

"Welcome, ladies and gentlemen. My name is Jeremy Deeds and I am the proprietor of this establishment. Presumably, you are here to learn about telepathy and not how to cook. That is down the hall." Deeds paused a moment to look over his students, then added, "I must say, this is by far the smallest turnout I've ever experienced, but that's all right. It will make things more intimate."

Carlin and Patty took their seats at a table with two others: a young man, apparently in his late teens, and a stalwart older woman, whose tanned, weathered face had the lines of a person who had spent a life outdoors. The woman appeared to be about Carlin's height and, like Carlin, was stout and wore her hair short.

The other three seats were occupied an elderly man and woman, who may have been married by their similar dress and down-turned mouths, accompanied by a suited businessman and a young man, perhaps in his late teens.

Deeds picked up the single sheet of paper and read from it. "The United States Department of Consumer Affairs requires that this statement be read to the class by a Certified Instructor of Telepathy in a clear and concise manner at the beginning of the first day of school.

"A telepathy school is defined as one that teaches the use of telepathic communication derived from exposure to an injectable compound used to unlock the purported potential for telepathy that is stored in cellular DNA. It is called a serum, which has been shown to be effective in a small percentage of persons. Out of every ten persons who are injected, telepathic skills will vary in strength and duration, from none to extremely intense. No effect at all is the norm. A slight effect will occur occasionally. Extremely intense is very rare. Out of those ten people, three will require psychiatric care.

"No improvement has been made in this serum over the past twenty years. In light of these warnings, the desire to learn this mental art should be reconsidered.

"Therefore, all schools of telepathy are required to provide return of money to their clients within thirty days, should they leave the school prior to the second day of classes."

Deeds thumbed through the registration forms. "We have seven students, which include three housewives, one engineer and his wife, one college student, one newspaper reporter, and one owner of a corporate chain of restaurants.

"Thank you for joining our school. Now that you have heard most of the bad news, let me give you more. Telepaths can only communicate with other telepaths and, at that, only when their minds are open for reception, or they are already in sending or receiving mode."

Several members of the class whispered comments to one another. Deeds continued, accustomed to interruptions at this point in the presentation, "Therefore, you will not be reading the minds of the man on the street, or your school professor, or your boss at the office, unless, of course, they are also telepathic. You can't read somebody's mind and know what they know, or what they think about something. A mental door has to be opened, at least a crack, for you to insert your mind and pry it open."

Carlin liked what she saw, but not what she heard. She saw a mature and relaxed man, who told it like it was. She didn't like the odds against significant success. The money didn't bother her. She could cut corners enough to return Patty's money within a few years. She had no children to look out for, but didn't particularly appreciate the potential for indefinite psychiatric care.

Patty looked left and right at the others to see nothing but downcast faces, then raised her hand. "Sir . . ."

"Jerry."

"Jerry, I don't know about the others, but I need some good news."

"All right, Patty," answered Deeds. "Here is some good news. When telepathy works, it works beyond expectations. I am the first to admit there is rare success. Close to a thousand persons have passed through this particular course, but not many have been satisfied with the results. Still, there is a worldwide network of telepaths. Contrary to what you might have heard, there are not that many. This training is dangerous, but it's also fun and different, by anyone's definition. In the end, telepaths make up a close, small fraternity, and one or two of you *might* make the grade up to mediocre, rarely beyond that.

"We don't want money, we have that. We need your potential ability. You have until tomorrow morning to drop the course. At this time, I am going to give out some textbooks and literature. This is a hands-on course. It's touchy-feely whenever possible. Please take a set of stapled documents, as well. Never mind the fact that I wrote the book."

Everyone chuckled at Jerry's mention of the expensive free book.

Carlin looked closely at him. He had good teeth and gave off good vibes. She could detect no dark base to his hair that had been cut to frame his pale face perfectly. No lopsidedness to it. His hair might have been recently dyed, or it was natural. She knew money, and this man had it. He was so smooth and direct with his communication skills that she considered he might be a sociopath.

Jerry said, "Look over this material for the remainder of the day and those of you who wish to return will be injected with the serum tomorrow morning. If you decide to leave the program, you may keep the book. We will provide transportation for your return home.

"We start class promptly at 9:00 a.m. each morning and go until 4:00 p.m., Monday through Friday. You will have an hour lunch period each day, from

12:00 until 1:00. We have housed all of you under the same roof here at the Oberoi, so you can eat lunch together, get acquainted, and also to have time to rest in your individual rooms. You will find the sessions exceptionally taxing. That's why the sessions are only three hours long.

"The course will be divided into different phases. During those phases, you will learn skills of varying difficulty, as explained in the literature." Here Jeremy waved his hand to the right to indicate the stack of stapled papers on the table.

"I have named the various skills: Coping, Finding the Off Switch, Seek and Find, Opening the Crack, Two on One, Gang Attack, Defensive Mechanisms, General Broadcasting, Programming, Target Acquisition, Sabotage, Suggestive Control, and Playing Dead. I strongly encourage you to read about them before you begin each session, so you know what's coming.

"I'm sure you're aware that books on the subject are plentiful. The vast majority are written by pretenders who possess no ability whatsoever. Trust me on that fact. For now, you are excused. Oh, don't forget to wear short sleeves tomorrow for the injection. Our nurse will administer the serum.

"Try to eat lunch together at noon. I've arranged a table for you. I won't be there. It would be a distraction. I want you to get to know each other. Then spend time looking over your reading material.

"One last thing. Diet is crucial. Read about it in the literature, avoid alcohol of any form, and do not eat breakfast tomorrow. Water only."

The others got up to crowd around Deeds. Patty leaned over and whispered, "Carly, this is so much BS. Let's go."

Carlin, deep in thought, began to follow her friend, stopped, then turned and picked up the book and literature from the table next to Deeds. She wanted to find a comfortable place to sit and read, but Patty insisted on visiting the boutiques. Carlin deposited the materials in her room and reluctantly, spent the next couple of hours trying on dresses and playing with jewelry.

Lunch saw the seven persons seated together at a single table. The older woman took charge of the conversation at the table. She introduced herself as Stoney Carstairs a retired reporter who'd traveled the world and was always looking for more adventure. In turn, each person presented a brief overview of their lives. Carlin took the executive, named Roger, to be brash and egotistical, similar to that of his wife. She perceived the youth to be a thoughtful boy, who wanted to be successful in life at whatever he did. Frank, the restaurateur, owned a chain of nationally-renown hot dog restaurants. He was a no-nonsense businessman, who openly expressed disappointment at hearing many aspects of Deeds' presentation.

Tired of hearing complaints from the group, Carlin excused herself early, declaring, "You folks enjoy yourselves. I've got a book to read," and returned to her room, while Patty gave her a quick look, shrugged, and remained to enjoy the ambiance of the hotel and her new friends.

Once upstairs, Carlin picked up the hefty text and leisurely thumbed through it page by page, reading highlights and notations. Deeds was listed as the sole author. Off and on, she'd pick at the pages of other books about telepathy to find them to be flimsy, cheap, purporting to be definite tomes, but could not compare with the quality of the book she held in her hands. This man was either a serious shyster, or a serious telepath.

Just exiting the shower at 5:00 p.m. and wrapping a towel around herself, Carlin exited the bath area to run into Patty who had dropped by for a visit, carrying shopping bags in each hand. She deposited them on the bed.

"What happened to you?" Carlin asked, laughingly.

"Oh, my God, Carly, this place has the most fantastically awesome boutiques. I couldn't resist," Patty slathered.

"All right. Give me a minute. If I like what I see, I might have to let you give me a guided tour," Carlin replied.

At 7:00 o'clock that evening, Carlin and Patty relaxed in the plush chairs of the outdoor area of the hotel dining room, overlooking the well-lit lake.

Patty sipped on a glass of Chablis, accustomed to the ambiance that surrounded good dining. She picked a shrimp from the shrimp cocktail and nibbled at it. "I'm going home tonight," she stated. "I already called Pete."

Carlin looked across the table at her in surprise. "You're kidding."

"No, I don't need to look at the book to know this isn't going to work for me. The odds are stacked against us. It's too risky. Deeds already said they'd give us a free ride home. I'm leaving at 9:00. Come with me. We'll get our money back. Look, Carly, I've got two kids and a husband to take care of. It was fun for a while, but Pete doesn't need to take care of a psycho."

Carlin smiled at her friend in understanding. Patty's argument was solid, but she had other plans. She couldn't have children and had long since come to terms with it. She had an abusive husband and it always rankled her. She had no reason to rush home.

Carlin took a sip of raspberry tea, having been admonished regarding the use of alcohol. For all she knew, the combination of alcohol and serum might be one of the contributing factors that led to insanity. According to the literature she had read, it was possible to be telepathic and insane at the same time, which did sound like an appealing combination.

Carlin said, "I understand, dear, really I do. But as my best friend, you have to understand my wanting to see it through. I'm staying."

Patty nodded, understanding in her turn. "For better or worse, you've always finished what you started. Not me, I'm the starter, but not the finisher. I'm the one who dribbles the basketball down the floor faster than anyone and avoids all obstacles.

The trouble is, I can never put the ball in the hoop."

"Stop it, Patty. This has nothing to do with your opinion of yourself. It has to do with your reality, which is different than mine."

Patty took a long sip from her Margarita. "For me, I've known my share of successes, but I can't take a chance. There's a lot Jerry told us that wasn't in the on-line literature. In short, I'm scared, so I'm done. Just be careful, and call me all the time, will you?"

"Will do. Now let's finish our dinner and talk about something else. Then, I need a good night's rest."

DAY TWO

Deeds wore a short-sleeve, blue button-down, which displayed his muscular arms—no tie. He still wore the khaki slacks and loafers. Many of the tables had been removed and five cots lined the rear of the lecture room for the five students still remaining.

Without the mention of Patty, and Frank, of Frank's hot dogs, both of whom had left the program, Deeds introduced his nurse, Blanda Pickett. Carlin inwardly chuckled at the name. It sounded like someone out of Joseph Heller's *Catch 22*. She surmised the woman to be in her fifties, poised, not bad looking, with sharp dark eyes. She wore a lab coat—her shoulder-length, brown hair was well-styled.

Deeds explained, "Miss Pickett is one of my first successes. She wanted to work with me on the program, which she has faithfully done over the years.

"After the serum is injected, the first thing you may notice is that you will hear voices. These voices are one component of the insanity factor. It is the connection of your mind with the minds of other telepaths who are communicating with each other. When they find out you're there, they'll try to communicate with you. It's like being in a crowded room, except that the voices don't go away because they begin from within. That's where mental discipline comes into play. You need to learn to block out the background noise. Some people are unable to do that.

"Also, you may notice other side effects. Your mind will organize and pigeonhole these occurrences automatically, so trust to the process and don't fight what your mind is going through. If you try to fight it, you may get into trouble. If that happens, Blanda and I will help you with that. Now if you will each find a cot to lie on, we will proceed."

While each person found a cot and tried to get comfortable, Pickett walked over to a cart standing against one wall on which were a number of vials, syringes, and unidentified medications.

Carlin tried to relax. Someone had dimmed the lights in the room. She could hear the nurse moving from cot to cot, until she rolled the cart next to Carlin. She felt the wipe of alcohol at the crook of her arm followed by the soft words, "You'll be fine, Carlin," then the injection.

An incredible rush ran through Carlin's body. The

only thing missing from the roaring of the freight train was the whistle. Her head swam with pressure, as though she were performing a head stand—then darkness. She must have slept because she felt the coolness of a compress on her forehead. When she opened her eyes, she saw both Deeds and Pickett looking down at her with concern.

Deeds said, "Carlin, you're experiencing a slight overreaction to the serum. It happens occasionally, but not often. It is not anything to worry about, because nobody has ever had an allergic reaction to the serum itself. It's something else. You'll feel better in a few minutes. Take some deep breaths and don't panic."

Carlin heard Deeds' assurance, but she was in no condition to question him. He appeared to be in a fog bank and his voice came out muffled.

"Could you please turn down the lights more?" she managed to whisper hoarsely.

Deeds nodded to Pickett, who did so, until the room was in near blackness. Deeds handed Carlin a sip of cool water from a glass, while holding her head up. As she did so, Carlin heard voices began to speak, almost unintelligibly, at first. One of them belonged to Deeds.

Blanda, I think she may be a paranormal. Did you see that reaction?

Yes, responded Pickett, *but I wouldn't make too much of it. Even the Europeans' and Asians' abilities fade in time. The paranormals don't last long.*

Other voices came in. They were somehow different from those of Deeds and Pickett.

Looks like we picked up a madam of the trade.

The other one's a wannabe—she's hungry, but trying to hide it.

My bet is they'll completely lose their sanity. We can have fun with them once they do that.

Voices, too numerous to count, entered her mind. She couldn't distinguish one from another, with one exception.

Allisa Stonebrook Carstairs, the old reporter, who had been seated at Carlin's table, entered her mind. No, Carlin had entered hers.

What Carlin saw was a woman who had begun her career as a high school teacher of English and Creative Writing. Because of her stern militaristic bearing, she had gained the nickname Stoney. Later in life, the woman had become a fearless reporter who had risen through the ranks as a tough roustabout, who loved the bottle and loved men more.

I've heard of you, Stoney. You actually reported war footage front the front lines.

And a lot more than that, sweetie.

Knowing where that last thought had come from, Carlin turned her head to the side and saw Carstairs, in the cot immediately to her right, staring at her, smiling.

So you've gotten into my mind, have you? Well, enjoy what you see. Carlin, are you raw meat or what? Carstairs sent the messages with a mental chuckle. *Can you pick up anybody else in the class?*

Carlin came back, *Yeah, Deeds and Pickett are*

listening in and the kid is starting to come into his own. The others may be duds. That's a pretty high percentage of positives out of one class. It's still early in the game. I'm also picking up a lot of foreign languages; French, German, maybe some Japanese or Chinese, but I can't understand them. I want to say I feel like I'm a goddamn shortwave radio, but I don't talk like that.

No, but I do, Stoney sent.

Deeds entered the mental conversation. *A person thinks in their own language. When they send, it is in that language. When you go into their minds, you read them in their language. If you want to telepath with somebody in China, you'd better know Chinese and I don't care what the science fiction stories say about universality of thought processes.*

There is a least one exception. Deeds continued. *Emotions are dead on. If a person has a black heart, or is a traitor, or a giver, or lover, you will sense that immediately, once your skills are refined enough. That said, there is no end to learning and refining.*

Also, n*otice how it doesn't matter whether twelve thousand miles of planetary diameter is between the sender and receiver. The thought waves act as though nothing is there. It's a physicist's dream. However, there is very little international mental traffic. In addition to language differences, there are also time zone differences.*

Carlin must have dozed again, because when Deeds mustered the class, another hour had passed. Pickett saw her awaken and approached her with an encouraging smile. She helped patient stand and guided her to a seat next to Stoney.

"Glad you could join us, Carlin," said Deeds. The other four were already seated.

As Carlin took her seat, a lurid thought entered her mind. Somebody wanted to do things with her. She poured herself a glass of water and set it on a coaster.

Carlin probed with her mind and found that the impulse had come from Wheatley, the young man seated to her left, on the opposite side of Carstairs, who saw him as mother material, whatever that meant.

Deeds spoke to the class. "Remember when I said that the voices are one component of the insanity factor? Well, another big component is the garbage inside another person's mind—garbage that a telepath will pick up.

"We all modify our concepts before verbalizing them. A lot of these concepts we think, but don't say. With telepathy you dig right into the flotsam and jetsam, the trash dump, the pettiness, and it's not pretty. Many people can't deal with the dirt they encounter in the minds of others, especially when the person, whose mind they enter is outwardly humble, or is very religious. The person might have a warm personality, but lives in a trash dump, both physically and mentally. Then there are the outwardly venomous people, whose thoughts are even worse. Mental garbage is part of being human."

Carlin looked as though she were about to say

something, but hesitated, trying to work it out. Now that she had had a firsthand glimpse into what Deeds was talking about, she finally verbalized her thoughts. "It doesn't sound to me as though telepathy is really a unifying factor among people. I mean, true evil-doers are just as apt to receive this gift as those who are good-meaning people."

"True," responded Deeds. "My company never promoted telepathy to be a unifier, where we all sit around and sing lullabies. Other companies advertise it as such, in order to lure customers. To my way of thinking, it is an end in itself. And yes, a person with ill intents will be likely remain so—in fact, find new ways to become devious."

The wife of the executive raised her hand and said, "All that is interesting, but I want to know when I'm going to start feeling something."

"To be honest, Mrs. Hollings," responded Deeds, somewhat contritely, "if it doesn't happen by the time this course is over, then it's not going to happen. There are cases of very slow buildup. I encourage you to continue to work with us, and we will work with you. We want you to succeed and we will do our best to ensure you get the best we have to offer."

Mr. Hollings entered the conversation. "That makes two of us who don't feel anything. I'll bet nobody else does either."

Deeds smiled and said, "Who here believes they have gained telepathic powers?"

Carlin, Stoney, and Wheatley raised their hands.

Although Deeds sensed the Hollings couple wasn't going to develop, even he had his doubts. There was so very much that was unknown. It didn't matter that one or both of them wanted to fulfill some childhood fantasy. Beliefs and lifestyles didn't matter. All that mattered was some undefinable quality that might or might not be present in someone's genetic code—or, perhaps everyone had the ability but it couldn't be accessed readily. It was a crap shoot. He wanted them to stay with the program.

Carlin and Stoney understood that Deeds feared moving too-fast, too-soon, with any of his clients. The fact that they had already paid for the course was beside the point. He needed as many telepaths as possible to bolster the reputation of the school. But to do what? Why more telepaths, anyway? What was Deeds' end game?

Stoney touched Carlin's foot with her own, as a sign of affirmation that she, too, had questions.

Carlin didn't know how she knew that Blanda Pickett had entered the conversation, she just knew. *We better split up the positives and negatives for the moment,* came the nurse's thought.

Right, Deeds thought, nodding his head barely perceptibly. Out loud he said, "I'd like Wheatley, Carstairs, and Ormsted to come with me. You other folks will remain here with Miss Pickett for some mind stretching exercises."

The three followed Deeds from the room, down the spacious corridor, where only meeting halls were present. Several were in use at the moment, including a lecture on organic cooking, and a magician's conference. Now you see it, now you don't. He led them to a comfortable lounge area where he invited them to relax in heavily padded armchairs. Original oil paintings from various Southwest Indian artists adorned the walls. Deeds wanted his prize students to feel upgraded, to feel they were special, to get what they paid for, to relax in the midst of good art, plush carpeting, and opulence. A large picture window looked out over the Superstition Mountains and the vast sky, something that always came as a shock to persons who visited the hotel from the overcrowded cities of the east coast.

Deeds pulled a chair over to be seated facing his students. "In the early stages, verbal communication, whenever possible, is a good way to reinforce the telepathic message you are trying to get across. That's why we're going to use a mixture of the two. Your abilities are well above average. That's why you're with me and not with Blanda. Activity within the first hour is the signature of a strong telepath. I didn't want to cast a cloud over the others, who may come into their own later in the program and laud only you three in front of the others. Still, it's rare to see success happen when there are minimal results at the start, but it can happen. Converting three in such a small group is almost unheard of.

"Mr. Wheatley, my intuition tells me you will be of medium strength. Don't worry, your flame will always burn and you will be quite satisfied with your performance. If you work hard for many years on your own, you will vastly improve and tend to make up for many deficiencies. We will help you with that and will always be there for you.

"As for Carlin and Stoney, you two are definite prodigies; Carlin more so. Get to know each other well, for you will need each other's support, if you are going to reach your potential. For me, the finding of the three of you at one time makes up for a lot of failures.

"At this point I am going to guide you through a few mind-stretching exercises. Mental strength is like physical strength. You don't see a sprinter training only on sprints. Injury and inefficiency are the result of that type of practice. You see him lift weights, stretch, run some casual middle distances, and so on. The mind is like a rubber band and needs to be challenged in different directions. Rote memorization, logical thinking, mathematical abilities, self-expression, personality improvement, diet, and even physical exercise; these are all part of the bigger picture. That's why I'm in the hotel gym at least four mornings a week. To me, keeping the body healthy goes hand-in-hand with a healthy mind, which provides groundwork for faster learning. If you are going to run both fast sprints, and long distances, you will need endurance. So, I am going to give you all a telepathic drill, which I will monitor closely."

You turn my head with talk of love and ripening of the spirit. I mourn for the life I wish could be, yet I know that this life will not come to pass. Oh, my soul aches for your heart and for your tears. Be my king, sweet love, and I will be your queen.

The three class members looked up at Deeds in surprise, as he began to laugh. "It's Julia. She is somewhat off-center and always transmits communiqués that way. Your minds are still weak and are easy to enter. She's one of the strongest telepaths we've discovered, perhaps the strongest. Usually, I'm able to see her coming, but this time she blindsided me. Don't worry, she's harmless."

Harmless is a relative term, and so is incest. I see, dear heart, you have new playmates for me. Let me help you train them to my satisfaction and I will always be yours.

Leave them alone, answered Deeds. *They are born only a little over an hour ago and have a long road to travel.*

So be it, Julia responded. *Would that I return at a later date to embrace your heart?*

Would that I let you know when it's time to play, sent Carlin suddenly. *I'll let you know when it's time for our hearts to intermingle, or perhaps not at all.*

Apparently taken aback, Deeds smiled broadly at the interplay between Carlin and Julia, while Wheatley, eyes, narrowed, shook his head quickly from side-to-side, apparently receiving only fragments of the exchanges.

"There is a lot in that message Julia sent," explained Deeds. "Some was good fun, some of it raw truth. You see, once you are a telepath, unless you learn how to close the door, others can enter your head and read you to the darkest depths. Your response, Carlin, caught Julia unprepared; not only for your communication with her at so young an age, as we call it, but for the poise you exhibited. This is a rare event, and I feel she is going to need to pull back and reflect on your strength."

Stoney laughed out loud, her mind picturing a double-martini and a cigarette—a picture not lost on the others, even Wheatley. "This is all so crazy."

Ignoring her, Deeds took a moment, appearing to contemplate. "We think she may be a native speaker of American English because the subtlety of her prose and accent would be difficult to translate telepathically from a non-native speaker. She is well-hidden and is likely the product of another American school."

"You've got motives, Jerry. What are they," Stoney inquired, a complete non-sequitur.

"Right on," interjected Wheatley. "I want to go places in this world. I know I'm not as bright and experienced as you guys are, but I still want to know the answer to Stoney's question. If you're not doing this for the money, why are you doing it?"

Carlin glanced sideways at the teenager, curious about his unusual sensitivity, perception, and ability to express himself.

Deeds raised the index finger of his right hand. "Ah, that—the confessional. If I leave my mind bare, which I won't do, you will find that I was probably the first person to reach my level of telepathy, in fact, somewhat younger than you, Thomas.

"Stoney, in print terms, you would call it a flap. I remained at the top of a very small heap and gained my notoriety that way—a big frog in a small pond. Then others came along to challenge me in terms of their strengths.

"A great many people wanted to be what I became, but it didn't work. Doubt began to grow among average citizens about our abilities. The real drawback? There's no point to becoming a telepath if you only have a handful of others with whom you can communicate.

"Understand that whatever or any other telepath knows or experiences is a virtual open book. Get used to it. You now stand naked. In fact, I would rather stand naked physically, than bare my insides to prying eyes. That's where blocking skill come into play."

Carlin felt a mixture of hurt, anger, and confusion at Deeds' words. Deeds never answered the question about his motives. Were they being used as pawns in a bigger game? They had gone from zero to sixty in nothing flat and it was all negative. Everything had limitations or conditions tied to it. Furthermore, nobody wanted themselves exposed and evaluated by other telepaths or getting immersed in somebody else's mental garbage. The rug had been pulled out from beneath them. She felt no sense of purpose anymore, except to finish the school and go home. Maybe Patty was the smartest one of all, getting out while she could.

As if reading her mind, Deeds said, "Honesty is

one positive aspect of mental telepathy. Your reading material talks about at least two basic blocking techniques to keep other people out of your head: the Safe Place and the Image. When I feel other uninvited persons prodding my mind, I think of something I love. So I concentrate hard on slalom and ski lifts to keep others less skilled players from entering.

"Some people use images. For example, most people don't like spiders. But if you concentrate on those, then persons trying to enter your mind will become repulsed. Telepaths, who are good people ,are honest with themselves, if nothing else. This isn't to say a lot of bad people aren't in the mix. Oh, there are a few true nasty elements filled with blackness that have no business on our planet, let alone being telepathic. Such is the condition of Mankind," Deeds inserted philosophically.

Carlin got the sense that Jeremy Deeds did not bare his sentiments and opinions so readily with other groups he had taught. He was also holding back with them, but, hey, it was only the first day after all.

Deeds led them through various light attack and blocking exercises; of one on one, two on one, and in Carlin's case, three on one drills. During the drills, Deeds pointed out that, if they became tuned to it, they would feel a certain mental itching whenever someone tried to probe their mind.

They started light and after lunch, progressed to the more intense. He had included himself in the drills, and then let them go at the end of the day, drained of energy, their mental walls completely collapsed and feeling as though even a non-telepath could enter their minds.

During the first week, Carlin had decided to follow Deeds' advice. She began to workout with him each morning and carefully watched her diet. He showed her the proper way to use the universal weight machine and the other equipment. Soon she gained in strength and stamina well beyond what she had realized during her social country club work-outs. She began to lose weight.

Although Deeds continually encouraged the tele-paths to associate with one another in any manner they could. This night Carlin wanted to be alone. She walked to the windows and opened the curtains to the lighted man-made lake below her and then flopped onto her bed in her spacious apartment, not having the energy to take off her clothes or turn on the TV for mindless diversion. She needed to call Patty. The thought of rehashing another day's activities and responding to her endless questions would be a tough go tonight, so she would cut the call short and claim fatigue.

Too much, too fast, she thought, laying her head back on the pillow, and promptly fell into a dream-less sleep.

Hey, housewife, wake up. It was Stoney.

Carlin slowly awoke and took a deep breath.

About time. I've been trying to call you for the last hour. Meet me and the kid downstairs for dinner in thirty minutes, sent the reporter.

Carlin checked her watch: 7:30. She'd been sleeping for two hours. Groggy and almost zombie-like from the long nap, she took a long shower, starting with hot to ease the tension of her neck and upper shoulders, and finished with cool. She changed into casual wear, still opting for a skirt while trying to summarize the events that had occurred so far.

Unquestionably, she had become telepathic, more so than her instructor had expected. From what she could gather, once a person became so, they were stuck with the ability. Over time, the ability could wax or wane, depending on training or lack of it.

Deeds was still being evasive. Try as she might to enter his mind, she found a wall, so solid and impenetrable, that when she and Stoney had teamed up to break it down or find a way to go around it, they found themselves blocked at every move, even repulsed and mocked.

One amusing curiosity was Julia. Who and where was she and how could she probe Carlin's mind without her feeling it and how long had she been there? Carlin suspected she might be missing the greater picture, possibly something sinister, something Deeds would not reveal.

Carlin checked the time and called Patty. The call lasted less than five minutes. She assured her friend that all was well, and, by the way, she might be developing some powers. Too much intimate information needed to be understood before she could share it over the phone.

On the elevator ride down to the dining room, Carlin tried to focus her attention on the thoughts of the reporter and the young student, both of whom awaited her. She been picking of fragments of their thoughts over the past several days and, not wanting to listen in on their private conversations, left it alone. This time, as she did so, vivid sexual images filled her mind. Over the past two weeks, the couple had already formed an intimate relationship, without performing an intimate physical act. Where was the law against that? Where were the thought police when you needed them? Laughing to herself, she mused, *What an interesting twist to humanity—thought police.*

Carlin smiled at a realized fact: the old gal was a cradle robber. Also, neither one of them gave any indication they recognized Carlin's probe, much as she had not recognized Julia's entrance into her mind. Interesting. She decided to coin a new term: *sliding.* Julia had slid into her mind as slick as oil on ice.

Deeds had it right. Telepathy certainly exposed the inner self. Doubtless, every telepath on the planet, who wanted to pay attention, would also pick up the signals from Carstairs and Wheatley—and mental pictures always transcended verbal language.

That understanding helped her to grow. It hit her like a brick. She must develop her personal blocking skills to the highest order as quickly as possible, if she were to survive in this new world—a world to which she now belonged, like it or not.

I'm thinking that you're thinking like a wannabe, my dear. Watch your snatch around those two. Better take care, love, or she who desires to bite might get bitten.

Damn it, Julia, shot Carlin. "*Don't you ever sleep?*

No, came the response.

A certain amount of entertainment presented itself in the form of telepathy; that is, if one considered entertainment to be laughing at another when they aren't intending to be funny. In this case, Carlin had to admit to a perverse attraction to the mental interplay between Carstairs and Wheatley. At least, their own conversation had presented some originality and had added a tad bit of sensual excitement to her drab life, too long married to a man who, she strongly suspected, had been cheating on her for years.

During a casual and uneventful dinner poolside, Stoney ordered a number of drinks for herself, reasoning that if she already had telepathic abilities, there was no reason to stop drinking. Stoney sent Wheatley a quick message, *Call you later,*" which she broadcast, rather than focused, to ensure that Carlin and every other telepath received it.

Carlin retired to her room to read Deeds' book and Wheatley went to his room to watch TV and await Stoney's call. At his departure, the reporter wandered the hotel to pick up a man, whom she brought back to her room, where they continued to drink followed by sex, until he left in the early morning hours.

A short time after Stoney had finally gone to sleep, the messages came flooding in from virtually every telepath on the planet. Presumably, they were similar to the ones expressed in English.

Hey, Stoney, do you remember what you did last night? We do.

Stoney, was it as good for you as it was for us?

Lady, you sure took care of the poor guy.

We were with you every second of the way.

Let me offer you some suggestions for next time.

What a slut. When can we meet?

After the barrage had ended in the morning, Deeds sent Carlin a thought message before she had completed her toast and cereal in the hotel restaurant.

Carlin, this is a direct communication. Don't worry, I blocked it from my end and yours. Go ahead and finish your breakfast. Just listen. Alcohol causes the leakage of messages from the mind. It keeps the mind open all the time. That's why the two don't mix.

Stoney experienced a hard lesson, but she'll never learn from it. She will never come close to her potential. She always has alcohol in her system and that is why she will always be read by everyone.

Deeds dedicated the remainder of the week to a broad spectrum of drills and the pace increased. Each morning a review of previous drills was entertained. Carlin found herself enjoying the lessons and also found this enjoyment lent a positive aspect to her learning process.

Wheatley had come on relatively strong and improved by the end of the third week while Stoney had hit her limit. She understood that Deeds would ask her to leave, if she came to class too fatigued or hungover, but, to his credit, he stuck by her, encouragingly, trying to show her a life that might offer more rewards over what her current life provided. What those rewards might be had yet to be defined.

Clearly, Carlin stood alone. She gained more and more attention from Deeds as his main focus. The two of them frequently conversed telepathically, without the slightest inkling from Stoney and the boy that they were picking up their private conversations. He assured her that their conversations were blocked and completely private. She wanted to believe him, but a part of her held on to an element of distrust. Despite her reservations, she found herself becoming more attracted to Deeds and he to her, as each learned details of the other's inner self and liked what they saw, distrust notwithstanding on the part of Carlin.

Now only three remained. The married couple, who found fault with their lives in general, had departed. On Friday evening, at the end of the third week, as Carlin lay in bed, Deeds contacted her and sent in-depth graphic images, which left her panting. After it was over—after Deeds had activated the pleasure centers of her brain and he let go—she related to him her concept of sliding.

That is a very advanced and basic concept at the same time, he had told her. *The best way I can ex-*

plain it is to compare it with two fighters facing each other. They square off and one of them makes an attack. The other fighter responds, based on his conditioning, experience, and ability. One great equalizer is the idea of sliding, as you call it. Without any sudden movement, you easily slide into the other's space without tripping off any alarms; in other words, just as plain as day, you just walk up to the man and hit him. If you do it right, it will work every time.

It's the same thing mentally, Deeds continued. *A street fighter who cocks his arm will send a signal; a less than advanced telepath causes another's brain to tickle. You have already learned several advanced techniques. There are more. You will grow a lot stronger.*

The next evening, Carlin received a message. *Carly, Carly, are you hiding in that secret place into which even smooth whispers can't find, even when they slide on oiled glass? Would you like me to guide you to your castle, your paradise yet to be found?*

Carlin awoke as if a bucket of ice water had been flung onto her. Had Julia called? If so, could there be no escape from this woman? She looked at the digital clock and read 4:14 a.m. There was no way to fall back asleep after this without dreaming of voices, not knowing whether they were real or self-manufactured.

She got up, washed her face, dressed in blue jeans, and checked her figure in the mirror. She'd lost more weight, her face less fleshy, her hair was a little longer but still drab, her breasts a little more pronounced with her weight loss. Yet, she was still not pleased with what she saw. She decided a makover is what she needed.

It made sense that, if she felt better about herself, her abilities might improve. She called down to leave a message to schedule a Sunday appointment at the hotel salon, then ordered a tall cup of espresso coffee in a carry-out container from one of the all-night restaurants at the hotel. Her husband had not made contact with her since his absence, an unusual occurrence. With a flush of anger, she surmised that he must have found somebody to keep him occupied during his business trip.

Carlin headed outdoors toward the path that wound around the great lake on the hotel grounds. A thermometer in the outdoor lounge area read seventy degrees. In about two months that will seem like a cold snap down from Alaska, she laughed to herself, since the weatherman had forecast a high of 112° for the day.

In the calm and peaceful early morning air, Carlin felt a sense of melancholy and awe. The brilliant full moon hung in the western sky with the star Sirius just at its top, both reflected in the still water of the lake.

She did some reflection of her own and appreciated the fact that she had learned to attack and defend, both singly and with others; to discern characteristics of other telepaths, wherever they might be. And she had learned that her old home life could offer little in comparison. It now seemed so very shallow.

She considered that if Julia wanted to play, she would find in Carlin a willing playmate—$50,000 worth of playmate.

The hard part was trying to contact Julia when she didn't have an image or a location. Deeds had told her that special skill would be required for that to occur, which she didn't have yet, but obviously Julia did. She could try sending a General Broadcast, but that seemed a little desperate. She made some modest attempts, but either she couldn't reach the other woman, or her efforts were being ignored. All she managed to do was to contact other telepaths and stir up the background chatter.

Carlin had no problem dealing with background noise or the garbage of another person's mind. She had automatically risen above the insanity factors and the only thing that lay ahead was mind-splitting training only a sadist could relish, and relish it she did. She understood that if she wanted to make use of this gift, whatever that meant, she would have to apply herself. For the first time in her life, other than acquiring her college degree, she felt purpose, a true goal worth going after. To what end remained to be seen.

The sight of ducks now stirring the water on the lake made her slow down the pace of her stroll. This was early Sunday morning. An entire day of relaxation lay ahead. When she saw the ducks, she thought about Deeds. What was going on beneath the smooth surface of his facade?

To Patty, she told bits and pieces of her experiences, touching all the highlights. She tried to keep the calls short in order to have time to read and practice her daily lessons.

For her part, Patty couldn't wait for the next episode of Carlin's soap opera and requested she repeat certain events so that she might play word games with her own husband. Things at home were perking up, Patty reported.

Carlin stood in the warm breeze of the morning air; the lights planted around the lake cast shadows of trees on the surface. Some ducks hid their heads tucked under their wings, appearing for all the world as headless decoys.

By the time Carlin had returned to the clubhouse, the sun had risen above the Superstition Mountains and the new telepath had given up thoughts of bolting for home. She had worked out a game plan.

Two hours after the salon had opened, Carlin's hair had been cut several inches shorter, highlighted, styled, and no longer drab. She had enjoyed the intimate relationship with Deeds, albeit strictly mental. She quickly overcame her initial guilt feelings of cheating on her husband—after all, she did have her principles, even if he didn't—by rationalizing what someone had once told her. Thinking is free. Evaluating Deeds' ability and his many years of teaching, training, and experience, she knew with certainty he was more than a good telepath. He could keep himself completely shielded— a skill she was determined to learn, at whatever cost.

The last Friday night, after the month had ended,

the couple sat by the pool, wordless, relaxing, until Carlin got up and announced, "Jerry, It's late. I'm tired and I have to pack. You know, I'm going home tomorrow."

"You can't go now, Carlin. We're just beginning to explore new avenues," Deeds implored.

"I still have a husband to go back to."

"Tell you what. Go home for a week and reorganize. Then come back for another month. Right here. No charge. Carlin, we have got to do this."

"Do what? What's the matter with Blanda? Work with her more," Carlin suggested.

"Come on. She's a registered nurse with mediocre ability. We worked together since forever and she's not going to grow. She reached her peak a long time ago. You're just beginning to learn. Just one more month. Carlin, we need to do this."

"I don't know, Jerry. I got what I came for and then some." She couldn't help but chuckle, realizing the nuances of her own statement, remembering a special night.

"I'm not going to beat you up over it. Do what you must, but keep in contact with me. Will you do that, please?" Deeds implored.

"Yes, I can do that" Carlin consented, in the face of Deeds' absolute sincerity.

THREE

He's been cheating on me, Carlin sent the same day she returned home.

How do you know? You can't read minds of the

non-telepath. Deeds returned.

Carlin sent, *He doesn't know I know. I could sense it the moment I saw him and confronted him with it. I saw the way he tried to lie his way out of it. If nothing else, I've learned to read people very well. I told him I could read his mind, now that I have a certificate as true telepath and showed it to him. He believed me and confessed.*

Deeds returned, *How long has he been doing that?*

Years. Give me a few days to deal with this mess and I'll be back. By the way, Jerry, a few of us were wondering why you weren't married."

I had a rough childhood and swore an oath I would never get married. Nothing complicated, Deeds answered. Then, *In any case, you'll have your own room. I'll pay you a good salary. We'll work together as a team to train people and to challenge each other.*

Two conditions, Carlin added. *I stay as long as necessary to accomplish the goals that we will set forth, and no physicality.*

The first part was easy. They both smiled at the implications of the second condition.

Agreed, responded Deeds.

I'll let you know when I'm ready, Carlin concluded. She wasn't certain why she shied away from a physical relationship with Deeds. It was complicated. She was still married, her blocking skills had a long way to go—the other telepaths would tune in to her activities—and she wanted to maintain a teacher-student relationship.

Once she returned to Scottsdale, Carlin and Deeds spent hours each day working on blocking, probing, and sliding drills, entering the minds of other telepaths, in many cases unbeknownst to them.

Although she had gone home at the conclusion of the course, Stoney was always an open book to read and fun to toy with. The old reporter had retired and, while having no desire to further her skills, served as a source of open derision to telepaths around the world. Strangely, the woman did not put up any resistance and, in some perverse manner, enjoyed their voyeurism at her expense.

Three months had passed. Patty had been paid back and another class would begin within a few days. Never having been challenged to this extent, Deeds was aglow in the growth of his own abilities, while his student had excelled beyond expectations.

Carlin wore a pair of slacks and sneakers. She had lost more weight, down to a respectable one fifteen and shooting for sub-one-ten—self-conscious no longer.

The couple sat lakeside in the warmth of the Arizona evening after a summer rain had passed through earlier, leaving behind the noisy area of the pool. Others sat in lounge chairs some distance from them. Two iced lemonades stood on a table between them.

"I'm ready for Julia, Carlin offered. "I believe I have enough focus to find her."

Oh, are you truly ready, my dear and dearest.

How fortunate that we may by conjoined in a three-some after all this time. I was becoming impatient, Julia sent. *Carlin, as the saying goes, I have taught you everything you know, but not everything I know.*

Clearly puzzled, Carlin turned her head to the left to see Deeds reclining on a lounge chair, hands behind his head, eyes closed.

Still with his eyes closed, Deeds said, "Carlin, I would rate myself at eight out of ten, because there are possibly others beyond me. If there are, I don't know who are where they might be. You could be one of them in the making. For your enlightenment, I am Julia."

Carlin didn't understand.

A voice entered her mind. *Carly, Carly, are you hiding in that secret place into which even smooth whispers gliding on oiled glass can't find? Or, would you like me to guide you to your castle, your paradise yet to be found?*

Had he memorized Julia's words?

He said, "Carlin, I want you to look deep into me." For the first time in their relationship, Jeremy Deeds opened his mind to hers, not completely—that was for no one—but enough.

Carlin penetrated his mind, past the superficial, past the garbage and the forgotten memories and broken dreams, past the hurt and the rage and into the innate self—into the part that had created Julia. The poet. Carlin also saw something that she found interesting. She spoke to the issue at hand. "I'm flattered that you thought so much of me to challenge me. Why Julia at all?" she asked.

"Call it a challenge to my best student, a lesson in entering another's territory without triggering any alarm," he responded. "Call it a little family fun."

Before Carlin could ask whether she should feel violated by his acts, Deeds said, "Carlin, listen to me carefully. Insanity in this crazy art of telepathy will soon disappear because a neutralizing drug is being manufactured, as we speak. It will be administered even before our serum is given, so it's a no-brainer to give telepathy school a try. Cost will start to come down. This will induce more people to start class, like the old days. I need you. You're one of the best telepaths I've ever encountered and you'll continue to grow through the teaching of others. We need to take action before things get out of control."

He seemed sincere in his congratulatory words, but she was puzzled by his last words. Maybe he had respected her privacy and had only teased her with Julia, without plumbing the depths of her mind. And maybe he was a great liar.

Her husband's behavior still rankled at Carlin. Torn by her husband's infidelity and his physical abuse, she found in herself an anger and a bent toward retribution she didn't know she possessed. Perhaps it was this feeling of newfound power that drove her toward greater success. She began to use her husband as an experimental subject, trying to probe into him when time permitted, as a single person with whom she could experiment.

Then, one very early Sunday morning, without him on her mind, she decided to examine her abilities from a different perspective. She arose, dressed, and armed with a cup of coffee made from her room coffee machine, she casually rode the elevator to the hotel roof where a portion was dedicated to a café, still closed at this early hour.

At 2:30 a.m., Carlin walked over to the parapet that overlooked the city of Scottsdale. The moon was crescent with Venus in conjunction. Sirius had migrated to the north.

There existed a handful of great telepaths and many more who were mediocre to fledgling. A small extended family, when she thought about it. She was getting to know many them by their thoughtprint. A pretty average cross-section of humanity in a lot of ways, except for the fact that none of them were dirt poor—telepathy schools cost a lot of money. What if school became affordable to the average person?

She wondered if her abilities might extend into the realms of precognition or clairvoyance. She'd have to experiment with that at some point. Her mental meanderings brought her to this new life, and then to her old life, and then to her soon to be ex. What might Julia say? *Would that I could penetrate thine inner workings to reveal the truest nature of your soul.*

Not for the first time, Carlin sent her focused mental waves toward him. Suddenly she was in. *It had to be the hour of the night,* she realized. He must be dreaming. The dream had opened the door through which the mind of the telepath could enter the mind of the non-telepath—the average person. No, not just the dream, it had to be a particular point in the dream, otherwise it would be common knowledge.

Concentrating, sliding, Carlin easily passed the conscious, which was busy doing other things at the moment, flashed past the ego, past the memories and the garbage pile and found the instinctual drives of the id. Wait, she'd gone too deeply. She had never entered the mind of a person in a dream state before. Telepaths are not dreaming when they send and receive.

She backed out slowly, where she found the junction between the conscious, and subconscious, and there it was. The dream itself; a fanciful nonsensical random jumble of mind-sorting events in the form of him driving in traffic at night in a storm, not quite remembering where he was going.

Carlin sent a blast of anger and hatred at him in the form of a double-semi coming at him head-on with its lights on high-beam, blinding, horn blasting.

She felt his mind scream as he tried to waken, filled with horror. Carlin showed her teeth in a snarl, eyes wide, to replace the semi filling his vision. She froze the picture, kept the horn blaring, then mouthed the words, "I'm watching you. Let's see if you try to beat someone else."

She continued to smile on the view screen of his mind where she held onto him for long seconds, before allowing him to try and claw himself out of the dream. She pulled him back down into it, only to let him claw out, again, and again, to finally awaken in horror, heart pounding, soaked in sweat—a feeling that would stay with him forever, like a branding iron on a cow's hide. Then the image was lost to her as he awoke, hearing his own scream, fearful to ever sleep again.

Carlin took a sip of coffee. "Well, that was certainly a learning experience," she said out loud, taking in a deep breath of night air. "Thank you, Mr. Ormsted, for helping make me what I am."

Then she thought, *What a hornet's nest I had stored inside of me.*

No argument there, Deeds sent.

I had to clean that out. Carlin felt the need to defend her actions.

Deeds sent, *Don't apologize, my dear. Stored energy leads to learning experiences. We both learned a tremendous amount just now. Maybe we should prepare a book of behavioral guidelines for the telepath.*

Right. Like rules work for society. Jerry, don't you ever sleep? She asked.

I need to keep track of you to keep you from getting into trouble.

Liar.

Remember when I agreed to no physicality? I did lie. I'm in lust, Deed's said.

Give me an hour to collect myself and I'll come down to tuck us in, she told him, to Deeds' great surprise, thinking that physical and mental at the same time could be interesting, if not educational, on both of their parts.

They lay nestled in each other's arms. There was no commitment. None was needed. "You let your guard down," he said.

"Do you think any of the others found out?" Carlin replied.

"It doesn't matter," Deeds replied. "We can't keep it a secret forever. Carlin, the world is changing. Man is changing. When telepathy becomes mainstream, we'll have to find new ways to deal with who we are. Above all, we both need to get our blocking skills beyond where they are—to the next level."

"What are you talking about?" she inquired.

"I'm talking about a sociopathic psychopathic serial killer out there who has exceptionally strong telepathic powers. You do not want him in your head."

Carlin shuddered at his words. Afraid to ask at first, she suspected that this person had already introduced himself to Deeds. She had to know. "What happened?"

"You begin to feel something dirty and vile—unspeakable—crawling into your mind, trying to take purchase. You have to shut it down fast before it takes hold," Deeds said, with a look in his eyes that Carlin had never seen before. But it was not a look of fear, but perhaps of challenge. Did her man believe he could take on this monster?

"Was it a male or female, domestic or foreign?"

she asked.

"I don't know, but if it's human, it has to sleep sometime," he replied, grimly, without extending the implication. He had frightened Carlin to her depths.

After that, events moved quickly. Carlin divorced her husband in trade for a new business. He gave her the house and his savings, with the promise she would never enter his mind again. She said she'd think about it.

The school's name was changed to "Jerry and Carlin's Institute for Telepathy."

Thanks to the new anti-psychotic medication, Congress backed off their restrictions and several members signed up to take classes, hoping to further their personal political agendas.

The school and the Oberoi hotel came to an agreement and classes were held there regularly. This brought business to the hotel and continued to provide the classy ambiance the couple desired for their program.

Patty became a frequent visitor to the school. After her sons had left for college and with the new medication available, she joined the school, moving to Scottsdale with her husband. Despite her trepidation, she achieved a fair degree of success in the art to become an assistant instructor.

The school flourished. Carlin and Patty became close friends with Blanda Pickett, Deeds' nurse and aide. The three were frequently seen together at the school and at social events.

Thomas Wheatley, the young student who had

grown up under the nightly tutelage of Stoney, entered Arizona State College and majored in social
work. He and Stoney maintained their relationship,
even after his marriage to a non-telepath.

The ability to read the minds of non-telepaths
during their dream state remained a secret shared by
only Carlin and Jerry. They intended to make good
use of it. How this would be accomplished had yet
to be decided. Neither of them wanted to contemplate a world occupied, if not ruled, by telepaths.
The new breed of humans surely would find a way
to affect the minds and behavior of politicians, busi-
nesspersons, and warriors, in a fictionesque world
gone mad—a world in which they would be living
in a few short years.

TIME VAMPIRE

My wife says that it's a bad mix, me being a sci-fi buff and a conspiracy theorist at the same time. She said I tend to read too much into things. To my mind, I'm a realist and what happened to me was not normal. She actually laughed when I told her the story and, half-jokingly, suggested I seek some counselling. Perhaps I was working too hard. You know the drill. She may be right in both regards.

I'm a crew chief for the city power company. I do poles, boxes, and general troubleshooting. When my super called me regarding Sally Rostovich's complaint, he told me to get out there right now because she wasn't going away.

The woman claimed to be on Section 8—that aspect of welfare which provides limited housing for the needy. The benefit to the management and property owner is that they receive a timely government check each month and don't have to chase after tenants for their rent. The disadvantage is that a strange mix of people qualify for Section 8 housing. The fact that they couldn't be evicted presented a problem unto its own.

I knocked on her apartment door and a woman my height at six feet opened it. She looked about thirtyish, had a pasty white complexion with matching colorless smile and weighed all of ninety pounds, a hundred pounds less than me. Her hair was stringy yellow-brown and she wore a tight drab brown sweater over a surfboard flat chest along with jeans and sneakers. Now, I'd seen the occasional round-woman with a bouffant hairdo, fleshy face, neck and arms, rounded breasts and big belly, but couldn't re-call ever having seen a six-foot tall walking stick before.

After inspecting the electrical work in her sin-gle and uncluttered one bedroom apartment, I pulled out a meter and checked multiple readings through-out the unit. I noted the normal variations and ex-plained, "Ma'am, everything electrical produces electro-magnetic waves including power poles, wir-ing in the walls, toasters, and computers," pointing to the latter two. I did not see a television.

"Well, my waves are intolerable," she com-plained, in a heavy accent I took to be Eastern Euro-pean, "and they make me sick. Just look at me," she commanded.Apartment management called the next day on her behalf and I told them the same thing. No abnormalities with the electrical system. That's what I like—nice clean simple jobs; time efficient.

A day or two later, my super told me that Rostovich called to complain that I walked by the bathroom and hadn't metered it. This is while a storm raged, the city stood at a standstill, and lines were down. I was in no mood to drive across town for a sixty second visit to Rostovich's bathroom.

Somehow Rostovich presented a different picture than what I had been accustomed to. Other Section 8 and welfare clients whom I'd helped over the years owned big screen TVs and new camcorders. Usually, one could find pizza boxes and beer cans strewn about, along with the occasional double-wide refrigerator and a Cadillac or muscle car in the drive. Maybe she should apply to the government for a TV or a car to occupy her time.

The desk phone rang just as I was about to get a maintenance truck out of the lot. It was Rostovich, my fantasy love. She'd gotten my number from somewhere. "I mailed you my results. Do what you want with them," I offered, matter-of-factly.

"What does that mean?" the stick became animated. I could just see her stringy hair flying around. I needed to go.

"It means you can believe them or not. Feel free to hire an independent expert. I'm just a grunt for the city." What else could I say?

Rostovich railed on with a laundry list of items that could make medical history, given they were real. I glanced at my watch. There wasn't time for this and I had to check on downed power to a hospital. I said my goodbyes and hung up.

Only two days later I received a call from the district Section 8 Supervisor who discussed the matter with me. I went through the events and faxed the man a copy of my report.

The next day I returned to my office after sweating out some high voltage lines from a lift. I was getting too old for pole-topping and noticed that Sally Rostovich had called again: four times. I could tell from the caller ID and left it alone.

Three days followed before a lawyer representing our mutual client called me. I advised the man to drop the case because he would lose and spend virtually all his waking moments taking care of Rostovich. In the end he would earn zero money. "This is a high maintenance woman," I advised. And if the lawyer didn't believe me, he could go ahead and take the case and find out the hard way.

In addition to her calls and those from the district and state Section 8 bigwigs, I also received calls from the county and state health departments. I told them in no uncertain terms that I needed to get Sally Rostovich out of my life and did they have any suggestions on how I might do this?

Within the next twenty-four hours, I received a call from the apartment manager, the city manager, the mayor, the state senator, the national Section 8 supervisor, the congressman, and every electrically sensitive person in the known universe. Obviously, Sally Rostovich had found a new project in her life she considered worthy of her time. Perhaps she hoped to make enough money out of her winnings to support her until the next project came through.

The city and I also received a lawsuit filed by a second attorney (the first had dropped the case) named Adrian Lawson, with whom I had had a previous and colorful experience. The man had gained such a reputation for not paying for anything, including his employees, that even the bar association fined him a half million dollars, which he didn't pay. And they still kept him aboard. How does that work? I scratched my balding pate and grinned. This couldn't have happened to a nicer guy like Lawson. I could just picture the corpulent attorney rubbing his sweating hands in glee with the thought of suing the entire city in lieu of following behind an ambulance or fire engine, or people like Rostovich, for that matter.

To the national Section 8 administrator, I said: "There is clearly something wrong with the woman. She has taken the time of the many professional persons who are now so involved with her that they can't do any other work. If you consider your own situation, you will understand what I mean." I could almost hear the man making mental calculations.

A Larry Crabtree called and told me that he owned the apartment complex for thirty years in which Sally Rostovich now resided and had a file three inches thick on the woman, far and away a new record for problem files. He had done nothing for the previous two weeks but log her endless complaints and talk to authorities regarding her issues. He needed to find another place for her to live. Section 8 was resisting.

According to Crabtree, her records revealed the previous complex where she had lived prior into moving to his. He had called the management there and they reported similar occurrences with the woman and had dragged their feet so much (on purpose—this is off the record) that she moved out in disgust. Could I help him?

I suggested that Crabtree file a complaint with his personal corporate attorney and quickly file suit against the woman for anything.

A week later Sally Rostovich left several overnight messages on my answering machine. I saved them. They all dealt with the point that, although she knows that I was only the finder of the problem, I still failed to survey the bathroom and as a result, she is now in grave health.

I contemplated requesting my supervisor to obtain an Order of Restraint against her, but decided to wait until she had received her own lawsuit from Crabtree and the apartment management.

As I closed my office door for the evening and headed for home to my family, I saw her down the hall coming my way. How she got there I have no idea. Our headquarters are on the city outskirts with no bus traffic. It must have cost her a small fortune to take a cab. Maybe she hitchhiked. She saw me and waved, a thin apparition wearing a yellow dress and three inch heels, hair up in a bun, back-lighted by the setting sun—a walking pencil. Frozen in place I could only wait to be erased. I wanted to turn and run into back into my office and lock the door;

to do anything but stand there. Within slow motion seconds, the thing had reached me; had caused me to freeze.

"Sir," she panted, grasping my hand with her bony and damp fingers. "I've been trying to reach you. I think I'm dying from the magnetism you didn't find in my bathroom. I know you are only under the directives of the city, but you can see how much weight I've lost from worrying." Her blue eyes penetrated my soul.

Standing rock solid in place I knew that reasoning wouldn't help. I felt as if one false move might cause her to escalate her barrage to another level. "I'm sorry, Miss Rostovich, I don't think I can help you. Check with your doctor," I stammered. I tried to muster the courage to run back into my office. This had become a dream from which there could be no awakening. I soon turned my back made the move into my office and locked the windowed door, ignoring her repeated knocks, in fear for my life from this creature out of a horror novel. Sweating, I flopped into my desk chair; my back to the door.

This thing at my door was a mobile disease merchant who transmitted her virus through contact via telephone, letters, or in person. Money had to have entered into her existence at some level, I contemplated. Normal wants and pleasures apparently didn't factor into the equation. Of this I felt certain. While she might be out to make a buck, her disease could be defined as "time consumed" so that those who came in contact with her had no time for anything else. This could be the first reported disease transmitted through the mail if she wanted to send letters, without a biological vector being transmitted.

Time would slip away from the victim as life lost to the black hole of time. Entire lives can be wasted in this manner. A person can waste their own time and chastise themselves for doing so. However, one's time wasted by another quickly spins out of control and one's life is now at the behest of the waster.

If the dark creature's motive wasn't money, maybe the thrill of it drove her, a demonic power housed in the shell of a body roosting within her soul. She couldn't touch absolute time, the rotation of the earth or its travels around the sun. No, subjective time, available time and perceived times were her domain.

Perhaps time was its own god, present before, during, and after the Big Bang. Doubtless, it held dominion over all things, living or dead. Even stars and planets aged. As if life didn't go by fast enough, some kind of a tentacle of time had entered Sally Rostovich to do its further bidding: to expend itself, not extend itself.

How would the equation read? I wondered, as I waited for the creature's repeated knocking to cease. Health institutes would have to work advanced math into the equation because every contact she made generated a loss of time for her target and time was also sucked out of his secretary, his administrator and other subsequent contacts they might make in her regard.

I became lost in my own depths until my wife called and wanted to know where I was. I promised to be home soon.

The damned disease is communicable and lasts beyond breaking contact with the woman. How much time had I been hiding in my office? How much time would I spend explaining the situation to my wife? This thing of Rostovich's is definitely spread from person to person at the mention of her name.

At this point, avoidance was the best way to maintain sanity. Thinking about her also counted as a subtraction. How many people had she destroyed and will yet destroy? How many cumulative hours or even years had she removed from the lives of how many people and more importantly, how many more were like her out there; people who demanded and commanded attention; who had contracted the disease.

Somewhere, there is a transition between spending time on the needy and the self-promoted art and craft of time-sucking from anybody who was still alive and within range—a time vacuum cleaner; indeed, a time vampire. In that regard, I gained some satisfaction and humor in knowing with great certainty that she must be kicking Adrian Lawson's ass around the block and around the clock.

Perhaps I needed to contact the Centers for Disease Control in Atlanta. Perhaps an epidemic was emerging. Indeed, I would be a hero for spotting and defining the first reported case. The woman would have to be placed in isolation, which, of course, would require time generously contributed by the authorities and the workers who manned the isolation units.

You couldn't win with the time creature. Even the death penalty would require countless people to incarcerate the troll and to walk her to the death chamber. Also, consider the time the media and witnesses would spend in her behalf while she died, and even after she was gone. She wins, the world loses.

Checking the bathroom mirror, I found some wrinkles I hadn't noticed before and thought my pate had grown in size. I washed my sweating face with cold water in a vain attempt to tighten and add rejuvenation to it, and finally departed for home consumed by thoughts of how to explain to my wife this entire affair Sally Rostovich was having with me.

At last, shortly before obtaining a restraining order against this entity, this apparition, I had an idea, a last ditch move. I went to her residence and knocked on her door, work bag slung over once shoulder, meter in hand.

She opened the door. I stood walked in. "I'm here to monitor your bathroom," I said.

"Okay," she said, softly.

I let her see the readings as I retested the unit, including the bathroom. "Bath looks good," I told her.

"Okay," she replied. "I feel so much better now."

"That's it?" I said.

"Of course," she shrugged.

"I'll send you a report."

"Whatever," she said, as though I were a fly she had flicked off her arm.

A few days later I learned the woman moved elsewhere, ostensibly to find another project. It turns out, she did.

Adrian Lawson dropped the case. To my great amusement, the grapevine had it that the attorney had permitted Rostovich to get too close to his personal life and had actually engaged in sexual activity with her, a thought too frightening to contemplate. This had ruined his already fragile marriage when she claimed pregnancy. He was disbarred. Publicly, Lawson spent all his time fighting his client's own lawsuit against him. Reportedly, she had found a small rental home that took in Section 8 customers and moved within walking distance of his new residence.

As for me, my bones feel achy each morning, like I've added twenty years to my frame. My wife says it's my imagination while I check out the new gray hairs in my head.

TIME ZONE

I

If one were to ask Beaufort Cunningham and his wife, Sally, how old they were, they'd have to say very old by Earth standards. That's what happens when Thuban 5 forcibly exerts its unruly personality on unwary travelers. Surely, the time warp makes it the strangest of all worlds ever found.

Five years her senior, Beau had spent the majority of his career on the shady, if not darker side of life, with little to show for it. He wasn't the long-term investment kind of guy and decided to apply for a job with All-Space Mineral Surveys to fix that problem.

As for Sally, nicknamed Sal, she excelled in the disparate fields of flight navigation, astrophysics, and geology, while Beau doubled as ship mechanic, strong arm, and business negotiator. They both had experience in tangential fields such as gambling, if only because a person has to take chances in the space-flight business and be excellent in their field(s) of specialization, competition being what it is.

They had served on separate ships for a few years and proved themselves to the extent that All-Space made the decision to remove them from their positions in their respective ore-haulers and put them together on a survey ship. The corporation wanted competent, experienced people to explore new worlds, but they also needed people who knew fraud at the negotiating end to oversee the transfer of premium ores into the cargo bays of the big ships. This is not unlike trying to find competent people to run a restaurant when the hired help is trying to steal the food.

After pairing up, the couple traipsed around the galaxy for a year or so until they got hitched in a place called Las Vegas, Nevada. It's an old city on Earth that once had a reputation for bright lights and gambling. As sentimentalists, they decided to travel seven hundred years into the past, so to speak, and hired an Elvis Presley impersonator to conduct the wedding. (He's a singer who used to live in that time period.)

The couple worked hard, made good money for the company, and received solid bonuses. They'd found some great ore pockets on unexplored planets and asteroids and either directed All-Space to the pockets, or did the mining themselves by loading up the small cargo hold of their ship and hauling it home. Occasionally, they purchased an illegal shipment from bootleggers for ten cents on the dollar and sold it to the company for a dollar-ten on the dollar.

According to Beau, his wife even looked like a navigator, brainy and sort of tomboyish, with a page-boy style of fine brunette hair. The part that wasn't navigator was the part that didn't fit in a world of men. Along with her tall lanky frame and inscrutable sparkling blue eyes, she cut an air of mystery. Men fawned over her and, according to her, she had rejected them all. She exhibited brilliance, dedication and drive with no use for inefficiency under any guise, during or after working hours.

Years before at the Academy, she had won a few college medals in the sprint and relay anchor legs while at Tennessee. According to Beau, they still run like hell over there and she still talks a little funny after these many years. If people wore glasses anymore, she would probably wear the big black ones that screamed, "Hey, I am the reserved, silent, unpretentious type," then bust your nose if you tried to take advantage of her.

Sally had an ulterior motive for joining the academy. Her father, Chris Rockwell, had been assigned to investigate Thuban 5 for the possibility that ores might be found and was never heard from again. Several years after his disappearance, Jennifer Rockwell, his daughter and Sally's older sister, was determined to find him. She excelled in flight school and got hired by All-Space as a navigator. After a few years working the job, she asked her supervisor if she could go to the Thuban system to do some exploring, and maybe look for her father while she was there. Her immediate supervisor told her they were tired of losing ships and good crews to that system and the answer was no to her entreaties. That didn't set well with her, so she single-handedly borrowed a company survey ship, headed to Thuban, and like her father, never returned. Two years later, Sally Rockwell was next in line to look for both father and sister.

As for Beau, he looked his part: gruff and square jawed, never quite clean shaven, and sociable to the extent of earning the designation of a classic sociopath. Sal claims to have fallen in love with him because he was easy going. Standing two inches taller than her, he didn't play any sexual or word games when they were shipping together and both stuck to business.

Beau only spent three of the required five years at the academy before quitting and getting hired on as a weapons-toting murdering mercenary and holed up with a sordid group of wanted criminals on a planet off the beaten path. Raiding and looting other worlds and merchant vessels paid very well. The job was initially proposed to him by his Academy roommate. In fact, it was a set-up because the organization he joined was secretly funded by the Academy.

Why would the Academy support such an illicit organization? Because it was rife with educated motivated men with Academy education who could be molded. Because space exploration and the mining of worlds was a dirty, tough and demanding job, rough unscrupulous persons were required for all aspects of the business. In other words, get some training in the field, then we'll talk. Not even the Academy knew of all the filth their trainees became engaged in.

As a businessman, Beau always believed that honesty is the best policy, except, of course, when there is a buck to be made. He fervently believed that if you weren't very rich, then you were very poor. There was no middle ground. Typically, one's growth potential is limited by the constraint of rules that put a person in a box. The most successful were always those who had broken out of the box. If a person is successful and appears to be clean, then somebody is not seeing the feet paddling beneath the dirty water.

Beau could thank his own father for giving him visions of grandeur whose words rang in his head, "The most important thing in this life is to take what you want. The second most important thing is how you take it. That's for you to work out."

Once he and Sal got hitched, Beau's true personality came forth when he revealed to her his past, which he had failed to mention. He also refused to tell her the grisly details, of which he felt great shame—a dark cloud that would always hang over him. To his surprise, she embraced that part of him. She needed to hook up with a man who could take care of business, take care of her and, of course, was willing to go the distance to help her look for her family that had gotten itself lost somewhere over in Thuban.

They knew All-Space wasn't about to send them to you-know-where and that was exactly where Sal wanted to go. In fact, the couple was tired of paying mileage charges for the lease on their company's mobile home and decided to buy their own. They purchased an old survey ship at a reasonable price, although it took virtually every cent they had saved.

Beau privately christened the ship BOB; an anachronism for Bucket of Bolts. He wanted it to be named after him, Beaufort Cunningham, but Sally nixed the deal. It would cost an unreasonable amount of money to paint that on the side of the ship, as federation regulations called for ships to have a name. The word "BOB" required less paint.

Beau thought they needed to quit the company and work on their own as independent contractors. They had talked about this before and now the time seemed right. He wanted All-Space to be considered first in any negotiations they had to offer regarding their finds before they approached any other company. He wanted to remain on good terms with them and gave them a full ninety days' notice before resigning. This permitted the company time to find replacements and also gave the pair three months to put money back into savings, if at all possible. Ship maintenance can be a black hole for expenses, especially one as old as theirs.

Beau wanted to make a deal with the company. He argued that he and his poor innocent bride were striking out on their own with limited contacts and wanted to help the company all they could. At the bargaining table, All-Space wanted 85% of all profits made from ores the couple brought in or had newly staked, but Beau knew the going rates and knew a screw job when he saw one. He'd gotten drunk with more than one pirate and made a lot better deals than they were giving him.

In the end, the Cunninghams signed documents to the effect that All-Space would receive the 15% and the Cunninghams would get the 85%. The agreement would be timeless and in perpetuity. The largest corporation in the galaxy would now be working for them.

Once out in space again Sally declared, "Honey, I want to go to Thuban."

Beau stared hard at her and beamed. "We must think alike, babe. I was going to suggest the same thing. For fun, we should go someplace so we can be like everybody else and never come back."

"You don't have to get sarcastic," Sal rejoined, then proceeded to tell him the tragic story about her lost family.

Beau was torn. He offered, "Tell you what. Let's put some money in the bank first. Then we'll talk."

"No, because I know you and it will never end and we'll never go and I'll die of old age and every day will be torture. So we're going to go now. I can't live like this anymore, I mean, not knowing."

Beau thought furiously for a way out. He wasn't

used to being confronted so directly. He loved his wife, almost more than anything else. In her own way, Sally convinced him and before long, the couple set sail for the Thuban system, but not without serious trepidation. Star-hoppers are an incredibly superstitious bunch, even worse than baseball players. The couple was not immune to such superstitions, which might have been based on actual events born from a trail of tears.

Thuban is in the Draco Constellation, a mere 215 light-years from Earth. Sally had learned all she could about it. Thuban was historically noted as the Pole Star 2800 years BCE, and some say it played a role in the angle of descent of the primary passage of the Khufu Pyramid in Egypt.

Thuban is a binary off the Hertzsprung–Russell main sequence of stars. It had long since burned hydrogen and has turned toward burning helium. The white giant's luminosity is 35 times that of Sol. Its companion is a red dwarf only some 20 million miles distant from it.

The star system has a galaxy-wide reputation for being the definition of bad luck. Nobody of sound mind went anywhere near the binaries. Good people had gotten lost there and a scheduled round-trip turned out to be a one way, especially when a ship went to the fifth planet. Spacers stayed far away, not knowing how far the bad luck extended from the epicenter. Some spacers never mentioned the place; others compared it to the witches of Vega or stated, factually, that a mini-black hole occupied the system, an argument totally disavowed by astronomers. One could go into a space bar anywhere and hear stories about landing and mining and adventures on strange star systems, including those with three and four stars. What was it about Thuban that captured its prey and wouldn't let it go? It was a Venus fly trap of sorts, offering some unknown sweet nectar to attract insects, soon to be enclosed by enfolded leaves and digested. Even the bravest never ventured there anymore. Only the stupidest. Enter Beau and Sal.

The team approached the twin suns, one of them so incredibly bright that it challenged the solar shielding. The planets had been identified from distance long ago, but, like Earth, only one of them had an oxygen-rich atmosphere, possessed free water, a solid ozone layer, and was on the fringe of the habitable zone, a term that needed redefining considering the presence of dual suns.

The binary system did not bother the pair. Most stars are binary or tertiary. It was the planetary system that drew them like an albatross leading shipboard souls toward a promised land, although rocky shoals may be in the offing.

Suddenly, their ship developed engine trouble in the light-drive, a light-day out from the shoals. "Oh, boy, here we go," said Beau, with both of them at the controls.

According to experts, when your ship becomes herky-jerky upon exiting light speed, that's when it needs a tune-up. Fortunately, BOB pulled out of hyper-light into normal space about the time when they needed to slow down anyway, and close enough to the Thuban system to make them only relatively insecure. As a normal precaution, Beau shut off everything that had to do with interstellar travel.

Finally, operating on hydrogen ions alone, Beau and Sally looked for a place to land and found themselves in a temporary pickle. BOB's hyper-light communicator was linked to the hyper-light drive guidance system and no help would be forthcoming until they could tell somebody about the problem. That nixed an SOS. Even if they did send one out, nobody was going to come for them and they'd be laughing stocks, instead of simply being missing, because they had told no one they had gone to Thuban.

They both figured that the guts of the guidance system were probably fried and they would have to pull out the shoe-box-sized guidance system by the roots. Without repairs, they weren't going anywhere. To do that, somebody would have to exit the ship in open space. It's one cost-saving way they built ships back then and it took forever to make repairs if one had to wear a space suit when doing so. That's why landing on a planet that could support human life makes a big difference in terms of making efficient repairs.

Heading toward planet five in the system in order to land, Sal geo-scanned Thuban 4 and found it to a miner's paradise with solid riches from pole to pole, but the display showed the planet to have a bad atmosphere. It lay pristine and virginal in wait for man to live under domes and mine its incredible riches. A star had gone supernova at some point in the past and had created an incredible quantity of gold and platinum and mountains of other heavy metals. Beau salivated at the prospect. They mentally logged the data for a future time and moved on.

Once the ship was repaired, they would be in a no lose situation, or so they believed at the time. Even with their smaller ship, their cargo bay would hold enough valuable ore from Thuban 4 to buy several new ships should they choose to do so, which was not their priority at the time.

"What does the geo-scanner say, Hon?" Beau asked, as Sal slowly circumnavigated Thuban 5, preparing to bring them in at a moment's notice.

"There are some worthless small pockets of copper and iron ore with a large one a little north of the equator and a heck of a concentration of gold about 500 klicks from the South Pole. If there's more, I'll be dipped and lit."

The screen displayed only green. Metals would show up as yellow, blue, red or shades between, depending on what type of metal they represented. Except for a few faint spots that corresponded to the one pocket of gold and another of copper, and small clusters of other elements, that was it. Other than that, the screen remained very green with abundant liquid water. They wondered how one world could be so incredibly solid with ores nearly blinding a person when they were viewed with instrumentation, yet the next door world totally metal poor.

The Book of Standard Procedures dictates that ships should be brought in unseen, if possible, unless communications had been established with that world first. In their case, there was no evidence of radio signals, city lights, or intelligent life. Only a few days on the ground would be needed. After all, how long should it take to fix a burned-out guidance/com system and a mucked up light-drive?

Standard Procedures also advised that coming in on the night side had its inherent dangers: You couldn't see where you were setting down without landing lights and if you came in too fast, you would glow like a meteor and set off sonic booms. They were out of options. The ship had become a real problem.

BOB was the squat-flat Trilobite variety, well-suited for skimming the upper atmosphere of a planet under scrutiny. The entry door to the command portion was located at the front of the ship and could be unlocked from the outside by pressing a series of numerical codes built into the door. Steps were cut into the skin of the ship that would lower when the code had been entered.

A survey ship is not a luxury liner. It's a shell packed with electronics, along with a small cargo hold containing minimal equipment for dredging and hauling. The ship runs about 25 tons dry weight and 50 tons when full of ore. This is compared with a dry weight of 1000 times that weight for a real ore-hauler.

A double air-pressurized hatch was located above

the ceiling in the command portion which could be accessed by a ladder. This led to the top of the ship where one could walk back about a hundred feet to another hatch that led down to the engine room. The hyper-drive had to be accessed in this manner.

A door at the back of the pilot's cabin led to the crew's quarters which, in turn, was separate from the main body of the ship portioned into the cargo hold and propulsive systems.

Like a submariner, a spaceship is an enclosed vessel that spends a lot of time going from one place to another and anybody who desires to do that for a living better not be prone to claustrophobia. BOB was built for a crew of four to six, so a crew of only two had to be pretty smart to understand how to work everything. Unfortunately, the lack of four additional crew members didn't really provide for that much more space, only less people to run into. Although the two of them couldn't occupy more than one cabin with twin bunk beds, they'd removed the two bunk beds from the remaining cabin and converted it to a storage room and work station for tinkering.

Survey ships have multiple functions. Because of their cargo hold, they often carried ores or ferried goods rapidly from one star system to another, or planet to planet, or ores from a planet to a big hauler. Goods can include heavy equipment, furniture, or electronics. They also tend to accumulate junk.

Sal set BOB down gently and Beau climbed out to the ship's hull where he stopped to look around before walking back toward the rear of the ship where the hatch to the engine room was located. Wearing only a Tee-shirt and accustomed to the cooler clime of the ship's interior, he was immediately assaulted by temperatures that had to be in the high-nineties with humidity high enough to make him break out into an instant sweat. He saw that Sal had landed in a stretch of savanna grassland about waist height with grain ready to harvest. The trees of the savanna consisted of tall very feather-leafed palm-like trees festooned with green fruit that glistened in the sunlight, spaced widely enough to allow sufficient sunlight to reach the grass. As he watched, a gust of wind caused one of the fronds to fall to the ground and caused, what looked like a flying ball of feathers settled in the grass, to screech and take to the sky. In every direction lay the same ecosystem, as far as could be seen with binoculars from the top of the ship, except for some low hills beyond a north-to-south running river a couple of klicks to his right. A curious ribbon of red ran long both banks of the watercourse.

Beau made his way back to the hatch and after accessing the toolbox, unhooked the guidance system and brought it back to the pilot's cabin.

"What's it look like out there," Sal inquired.

"Go take a look," Beau offered, handing her the binoculars.

Sal climbed out and returned several minutes later, her soaked shirt sticking to her body. "No sign of animal life, but pretty humid."

Beau suggested, "What do you think about working out a cross-draft? We can run the dehumidifiers along with the fans and leave the top hatch open. That should give us some cooling."

Sal said, moping her forehead and next with a rag, "It's against Standard Procedures to leave any hatch open when first landing on a new planet, but we'll try it. I'm miserable."

Beau knew what they were about to do was definitely against procedure. You just don't do that on an alien world, whether or not it had sentient life, at least not without alarms or guards. Some bugs can kill as fast as humans can.

"We work for ourselves, not All-Space," Sal said, in a tone that might have gotten them suspended had an open mike been present.

Beau had rarely seen his wife in this mood. If anybody could write the book, it would be her. Miss straight and narrow. Something was eating at her, but he let it go for the moment. He didn't want to get into a fight with the navigator when stranded on a planet with no chance of rescue. He guessed that concern for her lost family was taking its toll. If he knew anything about Sal, he knew she played by the rules—all right, bend them a little after teaming up with him. He guessed that she would be willing to break rules, if necessary, to find the sister and father she loved. She had come to terms with the loss of her father. Not so, Jennifer. She had told him that she had always admired her sister's strength of character and her resolve. To lose her was like losing a part of her heart. Beau wondered where he fit into the picture.

Within two hours, they had repaired the drive-link to the communicator, but saw the Clark drive would take longer to repair. They left the casing on the unit and headed for the shower, with no indication they had landed in the center of a time warp. Their actions appeared to them to be of normal speed.

II

Older survey ships like BOB don't normally carry ground-alarm sensors to detect foreign movement, unless a spacer opts to personally pay for them, which is generally not the case, as they are, by and large, a stingy bunch. One might say they are akin to lobster fishermen of old who could blow thousands in earnings almost overnight after spending months on the high seas.

The couple had just completed dressing in the tiny crew's quarters after having taken a delightful cold shower and awakening from an untroubled sleep. Against her better judgment, Sal opened the exit door, which lowered the ramp, and now a warm damp cross-breeze ran through the front portion of the ship with the top hatch open.

She returned to the crew's quarters to discuss matter of the day with her husband, when the error of their ways immediately became evident when a number of weaponized natives of the planet came up the stairway. A black and white animal similar in appearance to a Panda bear, perhaps five feet in height, stood at the doorway to the crew's quarters twirling a spiked stick in each hand. Other bear-like creatures ran past the doorway.

The bear in front of them had evolved into a bi-pedal form with a black face remarkably human-oid. Its body was covered with black fur with white patches seemingly scattered at random. Its black palms and black head were hairless and its eyes were almost closed to slits, presumably, as an adaptation to the brightness of the white giant sun.

The being had five digits on each hand with an opposable thumb. The middle finger was a very slender digit a full inch beyond the next fingers. Its feet were similarly constructed. The ship's two residents could not fathom a guess as to how a long middle finger or toe would enhance one's survival as an evolutionary trait.

"Look, Beau, a goddamn Panda bear," said Sal. Beau loved it when she swore or talked dirty.

"Yeah, babe, and the bear has a couple of weapons, too," he replied, trying to be light in the face of an armed alien who had entered their home uninvited.

"Move real slow," Sal said.

"Been there, done that, honey."

"What does that mean?" she shot, as an accusing barb, whipping her head around to glare at him, suddenly oblivious to the threat of imminent death.

"Some other time," Beau cringed, a little chagrined.

"I presume you speak Universal Galactic or UG,"

said the bear, as a statement rather than a question.

The couple froze. "Apparently, you do, too," said Beau.

"I try," said the bear. "It's not safe here. We need to get you to our place a short walk from here. It's better than staying to take your chances."

"With what?" Sal asked, now piqued at what might spell more delay.

"There are bad people like us who may be on their way," was the response.

"How about if we just fly away?" suggested Beau, grinning, with utmost innocence and sincerity.

"We'd prefer you didn't do that. Please come with us," said the bear, who stood between the couple and a pair of laser blasters in holsters hanging on wall hooks.

The bear's voice was not unpleasant, only curious. To the humans, it sounded as though the creature possessed two sets of vocal cords and could switch from one to the other or combine them for emphasis.

The bear stepped back and motioned them to leave the room, which they did, moving toward the exit door. Numerous Pandas were overrunning the front portion of the ship.

"What are they up to?" Beau whispered.

"Probably just curious," she replied.

"They must be awfully mechanical, since one of the little bastards has our guidance system," Beau retorted, angrily.

"Where?" asked Sally.

"There," he pointed. One of the Pandas carried the Clark Drive/C om system—the heart and soul of the ship that had been lying on the worktable in the next room.

"No," Sally yelled, exasperated. She tried to run after the bear who had carried the box outside, but the first bear held a safe distance while pointing one stick toward each of them. There was no doubt in their minds the alien knew how to use them. But would it?

"You're coming with us, so you might as well grab some extra clothing. You might be gone for a while," the bear said.

Sal said in English, "If it's letting us take some clothes, it doesn't sound like they're going to imprison or torture us."

Beau replied, "The day is still young. You're thinking like a human. These are aliens. Who knows what they have in store for us."

They each changed from sneakers into brown polyprene breathable work-boots weighing only ounces, placing their lightweight sneakers into backpacks. They added changes of underwear, socks, shirts, and an extra pair of pants and a few toiletries. They left on the short cargo pants they were wearing. The contents of the bag comprised virtually all their clothing, with the exception of cold weather gear. A baseball cap completed the ensemble.

Once the task had been completed, Beau indicated they were ready and the bear creature motioned the couple outside. Once there, Beau decided to risk death and lock up the ship. Turning to the keypad on the doorway, he punched in several numbers and the door closed while the stairs rose to secure the vessel.

Heavy clouds had moved in and it began to rain intermittently. Ten bears marched their captives through the grass heading toward the river. An occasional flying ball of feathers took flight from the grass where they had been disturbed.

Relentless insects attacked the couple. The apparent leader of the natives, their captor, produced a clay container from a pouch in a belt at his waist and gestured for the humans to remain still. He demonstrated how to take a tiny amount of gel and spread it over their faces and exposed skin. "Maybe it will make us grow hair and look like them," Sal quipped.

"Beau said, "My guess is it's a bug repellent."

The group hiked through the grass following a narrow path that Beau presumed their captors had forged on their way in to find them, since no trails had been evident when he had surveyed the landscape from atop the ship the evening before. To the couple, the bears were a chatty group, yet spoke softly, although not in Universal Galactic, apparently fearful their voices would carry. "I think we ought to make a run for the ship," Sal suggested, while she examined the numerous welts on her body, having missed a few sensitive spots with the solution that effectively kept the bugs away.

"Go for it," Beau answered. "Personally, I don't feel like getting stabbed, or used as a dart board at the moment. We'll make a move when the time is right. Just take note of geological markers."

"What geological markers?" she asked, with sweat running down her body in rivulets from the wet heat, a legitimate response to a stupid statement. "That said, don't forget to watch out for broken bottles," she added, with dry humor.

At least she's out of her funk and returned to default setting," Beau thought.

"Hey, Beau, where's our guidance system," Sal exclaimed.

"Damn, Hon, you're right. I don't see it anywhere. Hey boss man," he called.

One of the bears turned to them. "You talking to me?"

"Where's that box you stole from us. Why didn't you steal the whole ship, if you're that desperate for metal?" Beau accused.

"It was a mistake," the bear replied. "When I realized one of our people took it, I roundly chastised him. You had already locked up the ship so I couldn't send him back with it, and I didn't want us to be attacked. Because, for whatever the box is, I didn't want it to fall into the wrong hands, so I sent him to run home with it."

"Great, just great," Sal said, sourly.

"Why would we be attacked, anyway?" Beau asked.

"So the bad guys could capture you," the bear responded and walked on ahead.

An hour later, according to Beau's wrist chronometer, the group arrived at the river and followed along its bank downstream. The ribbon of red Beau had initially observed from the ship consisted of plants that lined both banks. The growth stretched for kilometers. The plants stood perhaps three feet in height with rounded dome-like green tops, each with a number of red fruits the size of a fist poking out of the foliage like jewels adorning a half sphere. Curious, Beau stopped to pull away the vegetation on either side of the fruit and saw a tough branch supporting each fruit. The size of a small person's wrist, the branch forked at ninety-degree angles both vertically and horizontally into the interior of the plant. The trunks of the individual plants grew out of a ground-hugging network of thick vines. Beau noticed the similarity between the trunk, the forks and the weapons the bears used.

"Beau, I have got to take off my boots," Sal complained.

"I agree,"" he said. "I wasn't thinking." Running on a mini-weight-treadmill-combo machine aboard ship was a lot different than hiking for hours over mixed terrain in a soaking rain. He informed their barefooted hosts of the need for them to take care of their feet and the request was granted. The couple removed their boots and socks, soaking their feet in the cooling river water for several minutes. Their socks were replaced with fresh dry ones, knowing they would soon be wet, as well. Yet, at least the chaffing would lessen for some time.

Vines protruded from the damp earth to threaten their step, not so the bears who had exhibited

practiced experience in stepping over them. When
the leader had stopped to permit the humans to rest,
Beau looked at him more closely. The creature had a
black marking on its chest surrounded by a patch of
white hair, quite similar to the Ace of Spades. Beau
came up with the name of Ace, a name which he
shared with his captor, who accepted the name without issue.

During the rest period the Pandas picked the fruit
and provided their guests with the avocado-sized
fruits of their own. On the surface, their captors
appeared friendly, but one doesn't visit a score of
worlds, several with intelligent species, without
learning to be wary.

Within their entourage, one bear could be dis-
tinguished from another by their body and facial
features. Their mouths appeared to have human-like
teeth about half-in number; ears were white and
pointed. Broad splotches of short black and white
hair laid out on their bodies almost as wood ships in
appearance.

From a seated position, Sal motioned to the creature whom they had first confronted, the one they
had dubbed Ace, asking to see his weapon, her innate sense of curiosity coming to the fore. Ace conversed with the others and cautiously handed her
one of his stakes.

Sal hefted the piece and handed it to Beau.
"Hardwood," he said, and made a motion as if to
throw it and looked at Ace questioningly, handing it
back to him.

Ace said something to one of the others who walked several feet to pluck a red fruit from the bush and tossed it into the air. Ace threw the stake and speared the fruit. Only the humans were surprised. Another of the bears walked to the speared fruit and returned the stick to Ace who gave it to Beau.

"Why is it sharpened at both ends if it's for throwing?" Sal asked.

"Possibly for thrusting in several directions," Beau answered. He flipped it from hand to hand, spinning it end over end, then gave it back to Ace.

"It could be better balanced by making certain modifications," Beau told the bear. "To me it looks like you made it from those red bushes,"

"That is correct," replied the bear. "We call that the redfruit plant. The rainy season is ending and now the flying and ground insects will come to eat what we don't pick to eat or take to dry out for later. Then we catch and eat the insects."

"Do you have fish in the river?" Beau asked.

"Yes, replied Ace. "But only in the waters that run east-to-west, not north-to-south. Those go to other places and the fish don't live long."

"That's a curious circumstance," said Sal, not at all fathoming the bear's meaning.

"You're wondering how I could know Universal Galactic," stated Ace.

"That thought did cross our minds; among other things," replied Beau.

Ace nodded. "We had a chance to use it most recently with visitors when some guy named Anders and his crew landed about a dozen sleeps out near the border. I was helping the king with something so I wasn't there, but the story I heard was that the patrol had never seen a spaceship or humans before and watched in hiding when men came out. Our captain finally approached and called to the men."

"They must have pulled weapons," Beau said.

"Of course, and neither of us trusted the other, but we continued to talk."

"Hold on," said Beau. "You spoke Universal Galactic with Anders?"

Ace shrugged. "What else? They didn't know our language,"

"I'm confused," Beau admitted.

Sal laughed. "Don't you know history?"

"No," Beau answered, truthfully.

Sally continued, "Back about 800 years at the beginning of star flight, the Universal Galactic language was created by the newly formed UG institute. They got legislation passed to declare that all spacers must know the language and they sent out ships to the worlds that had sentient life to teach it to them so trading and communications in general would be easier. They must have come here as well."

"And somehow left here to tell about it," Beau contributed.

"Not necessarily," Sal said. "History doesn't record that the ship returned."

Ace added, "They must have done a good job teaching because everybody I ever ran into speaks both our native language and UG. Back as a youth when I took my first language classes, they told me there used to be something about a savior and eternal life in the original teachings, but nobody could remember what the main subject was about."

"So what happened when you started talking to these people?" Beau inquired, smiling at Ace's statement.

"Ace answered, "They said they worked for a mining company and their ship didn't have a lot of weapons and could care less about us. They stayed for quite a while and taught us to build a kiln along with a showing us how to make pottery and the making of tiles and grout for our homes. When they got ready to leave, Anders asked us to store a lot of stuff from their junk pile because they needed the ship's hold empty for ore."

Ace scratched his right armpit with the long middle finger of his left hand and added, "See, our problem is that we can copy anything once we're shown how to do it, but according to the men in Anders' party, our sense of curiosity has been dulled and we're not wired for creative thinking. That's a bad combination."

Sal asked, "Did you ever hear of a man or a woman who came here after Anders by the name of Rockwell? That would a couple of years ago."

"Sorry," said Ace.

"Or any spaceship that landed anywhere after Anders?" she prodded.

"No," Ace responded.

Sal told Beau, "Not too many years before my

father went in, I know Galactic Trading lost a ship here and some indie explorers went looking for it, but that ship never came back, either."

Beau said, "There's even a legend among the den of thieves I used to associate with that one of their own got lost on the planet a good fifty years before Anders, and even more before that one. They can't all have crashed like us, so why didn't they return?"

"I'm guessing a lot of them headed directly for one of the ore deposits or wanted to check out the planet to set up a colony," she contributed, scratching at a bug bite on her neck.

Beau knew he was saying the obvious, but needed to review the facts for his own sake. "All-Space didn't send your dad here to reconnoiter the place for colony purposes, that takes a team effort and it's not what they do. They mine. If you want a colony, call Galactic Trading or some other outfit that deals in those matters as a side job. There's no real money in it. There's more to be made by trading with indigenous races, even if the planet isn't habitable for humans, metals or no metals."

Beau felt badly for his wife. Sal was twenty-nine when Jen had disappeared and for a number of years her sister had to work where she was told and certainly didn't have the money to buy her own ship to go adventuring where she wanted. Nobody would voluntarily take her to this star system. According to Sal, her sister had always set the standards for self-motivation. Having gotten over the loss of her father, the only time he had ever seen his wife come to tears was when she lapsed into melancholy thinking about her lost sibling.

"Do you know happened to Anders?" Sal asked.

Ace replied, "He told us there are only a few sources of available ores on this planet. One of them was farther west and north and another was to the far south. As I said, they never came back, even though they promised they would. I'm not surprised, either."

"There you go," Sal threw at Beau.

"Why do you think . . ." Beau started to ask.

Ace interrupted, "What's a year? You said 'a couple of years ago' and I said 'no', but really, I don't know what the word means. We don't have it in our language."

"It's a period of time," said Sal. "You know, the time it takes for a planet to travel around its sun."

"Time?" said the bear.

"You don't know the word?" Sal asked.

"Of course, but I don't understand it," Ace replied.

"You know daytime and nighttime, don't you?" Beau began to explain.

"We know light and dark," said Ace.

"You know birth and death, don't you?" asked Sal.

"Of course," said Ace. "Death lasts longer than life."

"Then death lasts a longer time than does a lifetime," Beau added.

"Whatever," said Ace, with some finality, apparently tiring of the discussion. "Look," he continued, "the king may be waiting for us so we'd better get going."

Seconds after the rain let up, a hoot was heard from behind. Ace stopped suddenly.

"We're being followed," he said, quietly.

Beau heard a yell. He turned to see one his contingent fall with a stake in his chest. Apparently, it had been thrown. Then two more fell. Several of Ace's bears ran into the leafy vegetation after the attackers. The other's hung back, protecting the humans and their leader.

"Stay down," Beau told Sal. She did. He hunched out of his pack and threw it on the ground against a tree. "Ace, get one of your men to watch over my wife," he directed.

The bear did as requested.

"Where are you going?" Sal asked, her voice high pitched.

"To make some new friends," Beau responded. He scrambled to grab the stakes dropped by a fallen bear and disappeared into the tall grass in an effort to circle around.

Long minutes passed. Sal could hear shouts and screams, but none belonged to her husband. She didn't know whether that was good or bad. For the first time in her life, she felt, not concern, deep worry, or anguish, but quaking fear.

When Beau did return, both stakes were covered with red blood at both ends, as were his arms and his clothing. "You all right, baby?" he asked.

Sal jumped up to throw her arms around her husband. "Wow, you sure know how to get me excited," she said, somewhat shakily, trying to piece together an acceptable smile with her lower lip quivering in fear.

Ace and his other bears returned, one by one. The rain had stopped momentarily. Beau walked several yards over to the river, some 100 meters wide at this point, pulled off his shirt and pants, and washed them along with his arms and face. The blood came off the synthetic fabrics easily. He dressed and returned to the others. Ace motioned them forward.

After several minutes of fast walking, Beau slowed, winded. "Why didn't you tell us we might be attacked?" he asked.

Ace responded, as though this were an everyday occurrence. "I told you on your ship there were unsavory characters in the neighborhood."

"How long have you used these sticks as weapons?" Beau asked.

"Since before my time," replied the bear.

Beau was curious. "Why didn't Anders' people make better weapons for you while they were here?"

"For one thing, if we got into any fights during their stay, it would have been when we were out on patrol, where the big ones usually happen. For another, the subject never came up," Ace answered.

"I want to know why we were attacked," Sal asked.

"They wanted to take you hostage," Ace replied.

"Like you did," she accused.

"Correct," said the bear.

Ignoring the banter, Beau said, "I can think of a lot of ways to make better weapons," flipping the sticks end-to-end.

"Good ole' human ingenuity, huh? Talk's cheap," countered Ace.

Fucking bear had an attitude. He must have picked it up from other humans. They did learn fast. "Well, screw this. Maybe we can fix the problem," Beau said to their protector, who also had blood on his hands.

As they conversed during their trek, Sal pondered their previous discussion about time. In Universal Galactic and virtually every language on Earth and among alien races, there are a large number of sayings relating to time such as, "time to go," "time to change," "time on my hands," "in a timely manner," "time out," "at the last minute," "just a second," "out of time," and many more. Few, if any, however, related to other people or places, unless one used the term "time zone," where changes in time were related to rotation of a planet for the convenience of people living on the planet. Her sense was that it had to do with a north to south designation, not east to west. It was not used as a measurement system. Even the fish didn't live in waterways going north or south, only those going east or west. Something here didn't ring right.

As if he were a mind reader, Ace suddenly said, "Maybe you can help us with our problems."

"We all have problems," Beau said. "Why are yours so different?"

"I don't know that they are different," Ace responded.

"Fair enough," Beau countered.

At that point, the bear made it all clear to them, patiently explaining the basic facts of life, facts he conjectured that everybody knew. He described his world as a planet like all others that existed in a nearly perfect Einsteinian concentric-ring fashion, like a target with a bull's-eye and like all others, had an immigration problem.

Sal's mind wandered, as Ace spoke. The genius of the Twentieth Century had described a dozen different scenarios in which time might exist in a form different from the one in which humans were accustomed. Now the bear was describing one of them as factual.

Another concept Einstein made popular was that time lacked absolute linearity. This was not an especially original idea, but it introduced the idea that time folded back on itself, thus introducing the concept of coincidence—a folding of time of two disparate points that landed in the same space and time.

"You were talking earlier about measuring time," Ace stated.

"Yes," the pair replied, almost in unison.

"Well," Ace began his talk. "Then you understand all about time warps and time places."

Beau replied, "Of course," doesn't everybody? But why don't you tell us about yours. I mean, don't time places have time warps, by definition?" He shrugged, matter-of-factly, trying to engage the bear in a subject he knew nothing about.

Sal understood her husband's sarcasm was an insecurity tell, an indicator. Still, she gave him that "Don't be an ass" look out of the corner of her eye, impatient to hear more from this being.

The bear detailed matters in one simple description and told them the answers to their questions. "You see" Ace said, "at the risk of preaching to the choir, our world is loaded with time warps and the center of the warp is situated at the north and south poles of the planet. We call both of them Place 0 at the top and Place 0 at the bottom. Down from the North Pole and up from the South Pole are Places 1 through 4, then us at the equator. We are in Place 5, in the center. So, the closer one gets to the poles, the faster time moves and the faster life ages. The society of our planet is structured so that the poorest natives live in other areas except in Place 5, where we live the longest."

Ace continued his remarkable tale while his guests listened, looking around warily, as they walked. "The only people we ever heard of live in Places 3 through 5, either north or south. If they lived in other zones, they would have to reproduce like crazy to make up for it; either that or sneak into another zone. Everybody wants to come here to the equator. There may have been occasional visitors from outside our world who landed in Places 1, 2, or 3, who grew old and died very quickly. So if you can help us with our problem with unwanted foreigners, we'd love to hear some ideas.

"Understand that I'm presenting a general picture based on what illegal immigrants and my own people here told me. I mean, we don't have what you might call an infrastructure that is rife with travel."

Sal pondered. The whole thing didn't follow any rules. As bizarre as the story sounded, there certainly could not be clear lines of demarcation between the zones or places Ace spoke of, so flows and fluxes would be expected. Not having faced this conundrum before, she yearned for a deeper philosophical discussion with their host, who had just taught her some astrophysics.

For Beau, a light bulb went on. If what Ace had said held even a smattering of truth, their ill-fated landing on the planet might show some profit yet.

"So your people are in the most advantageous position," Sal concluded, astutely.

"Yes, and I represent the king who is the top dog on the planet, as Anders had said. Actually, he called him a bear and then told us that a dog is an intelligent creature that is man's best friend," Ace chuckled, "We were fine with that."

He went on, still assuming their own time-warping problem was similar to that of other worlds. "Warfare is constant as people in locales on either side of us try to invade our territory. For some unexplained reason everybody wants to live longer. Border disputes are common and can be vicious. Many people inhabit each place and we have the most surface area to protect, being at the equator. That was how we found you. We were on routine patrol when we saw you land."

"Why didn't you come aboard at night when we had the top hatch open? You could have climbed up, if you'd tried hard enough." Beau asked.

"Oh, no, don't tease me like that. Anders told us that humans shoot anything that comes to their home at night, even other humans," Ace responded.

Good ole' Anders, hedging his bet, making sure the bears didn't get any funny ideas, both humans thought, nodding at each other in understanding.

Beau decided to change the subject to something more to his liking. "It seems to me there could be a real advantage to places that are different from yours. I mean, wouldn't food grow faster? Just because you live longer right here compared with other places on your world doesn't mean that I will live longer living here. In fact, our lives could still be shorter than normal by living in your place."

"Then I guess you have a problem," Ace said.

Sal broke out into laughter.

Beau held up a hand. "Wait a minute. I mean, hold on. What happens when your people get really sick? Don't they want to go to say, time Places 4 or 3 to get better faster?"

Ace answered, "Why are you asking me that? What do you do on your world? In a word, yes and no. First of all, they may die faster in another time place in that their illness might be life-threatening and its spread may be accelerated to kill them faster."

Sal had never considered the topic seriously

enough to look at it in terms of practical and not in an astrophysical sense. To her, there might be a middle ground. "Didn't you discuss this issue with Anders?" she asked.

"No. Again, the entire subject never came up," answered Ace. "He helped us and we helped him." Then he added, "Believe it or not, there is a downside to living in our region, mostly related to warfare, although I don't discount local anomalies, ignorance, gossip, superstition, and the like."

As he listened to Ace speak, Beau felt as though they were seated in the presence of masters. Masters of what, he could not say. It was the old story of ignorance versus genius, idiot versus savant. His mind immediately became jammed with thoughts of business ventures. It was as though he were a partially blindfolded person in a house of mirrors who had been tasked to come up with an exit plan. He needed more information.

"Please describe the nature of the time warp on your world," Ace requested.

There it was. Sal replied, uncertain as to how to phrase her response. She decided the direct approach might be best. "We have a distortion anomaly you wouldn't believe. On our planet everybody ages at the same rate."

If a carpet were present, Ace's jaw would have gotten carpet burn, it dropped so hard and fast. "Surely you jest," he replied, employing both sets of vocal cords at the same time. "How can this be?" He explained to the remaining five bears what she had told him. Some of them hooted, one of them fell to the ground and rolled around, holding its side.

"In fact," Sal went on, "out of all the worlds my husband and I have visited or even heard of, yours is the only one on which people age at different rates."

Even as she said this, Sal realized the entire story that Ace was presenting could be a fabrication, a superstition that became inculcated within the population for whatever reason. This was a very common occurrence among sentient beings. Certainly, back home, people believed in God or the Devil, or that certain foods would help one live longer, or that there was life after death. There was no way to prove those beliefs one way or the other. Could Ace's assertions be proved?

Ace switched topics, apparently deciding to go with priorities and bypass Sal's surprising statement. "Based on our experiences with humans, I am certainly enthused about the prospect of your staying with us to help. Having better weapons with which to patrol our borders would be nice, because we lose too many of our people to intruders. And that's the gist of our problem."

"There's something I don't get," Sal said. "If you want to do good for your people, why don't you let the others come in?"

Ace explained, "It's not that simple. People from different areas smell differently. A faster or slower metabolism means a different chemistry and people don't like anyone who smells differently. When foreigners slide into one of our cities, fights break out. That's why our city has patrols to keep them away. The exception to this, of course, is that nobody wants to go to another place where their lives become shorter."

"Now you understand," said Sal. "Time is a measurement of age and is a way to measure length of life."

Ace declared, "I get it. When a person lives a short life, time goes faster for that person."

"Um, not exactly, maybe in your case it does, but not on other worlds. It's all relative and it depends on how you look at it." Sal was beginning to get herself confused.

Ace shook his head in a completely human manner suggesting that he didn't have a clue as to what she had said, which tacitly implied that she didn't either. "Look, this isn't complicated. We flat out don't want foreigners stinking up the place."

Beau considered all that Ace had said and it made a lot of sense. It sure would be nice if people could forget their differences, or at least find a way to all smell the same.

III

Ace led the contingent westward for a kilometer until the terrain morphed into solid grassland. Within minutes, they reached a clearing several hundred meters above the river the west of the watercourse. The white giant sun emerged between a break in the clouds turning the gloomy day of blackened thunderheads into glaring brightness in an instant.

Before them stretched a city of single and two-story buildings of varying sizes that lay perhaps two hundred meters away. The view was quite sterile in that along the streets or between the houses there were to trees, shrubs, lawns, or flowers. A stream of bears carried jugs of water from the river up the incline to the city presumably to slake the thirst of a population that must consume copious amounts of liquid. Others collected fruit and still others were pulling up the vines connecting the plants. The city occupied perhaps a four square kilometer area.

"The city looks drab," observed Sal.

Ace inserted, "If you're thinking about adding color, forget it. We're color blind as a species."

"Then how do you know your redfruit is red?" asked Beau, puzzled.

"We don't. They're all gray to us. Red is what Anders called it. We've always used the terms low fruit and high fruit, to separate what he calls red and green."

Beau shook off the revelation and returned to examining the city. A moment later he uttered the word "Cob."

"What?" asked Sal.

"It's a city made of cob. It's the same thing as adobe; a mixture of clay, sand, straw and water. This suggests a lack of timber, or if they do have it, they lack the means to cut it. You normally use wooden frames to contain the mud in order to make adobe block. Cob is mixed the same way as adobe, but is formed into big balls larger than softballs. They're stacked to make walls, ceilings, and even furniture; stairs in some cases."

Sal stared at her husband. "Where did you learn all that?"

"I've seen them on other worlds and they were present on old Earth. I told you my mother was an agri-scientist. Along with that comes the study of the civilizations that create the agriculture. Those cob houses also tell me their climate is basically hot and dry, otherwise the mud wouldn't dry."

No beasts of burden lumbered in the streets, nor were any animals present that could be defined as pets. In addition, no wheeled vehicles of any kind were visible. The grassland had been cut back perhaps a hundred meters from the entire circumference of the city to expose the dark soil.

"Why is the grass gone like that?" asked Sal.

Ace said, "Field mice. We pull the grass because we need a buffer. Otherwise they come into our homes and eat everything."

"Whose idea was it to do that?" asked Beau.

"To eat everything?" asked Ace, with a straight face.

The bear had a sense of humor. "No, to cut back the grass," answered Beau, chuckling.

"That was before my birth," Ace answered, adding, "There's another big reason, too?"

"Which is?"

"Brush fires," Ace said.

Beau nodded, "That makes sense. The smoke and flying ash can be dangerous, but at least you don't have anything flammable in your city, as far as I can see."

"Not true. We are," the bear stated in a serious manner, bi-tonally for emphasis. He ran a hand along the hair of his body, in such a manner as to inform his visitors that many of his people had perished through the ages from conflagrations.

Sal tore her mental eye from the vision the bear had painted depicting a fire completely surrounding a city to inundate the populace with blowing ash and deadly smoke regardless of which direction the wind might be blowing. An image of bears' fur on fire from blazing ash gave her a different perspective of the challenges facing the populace. Like everybody else everywhere, life and struggle were inexorably linked. The king needed more he[p than even he knew.

Deflecting, she said, "See how it's laid out, Beau?" pointing to various structures in the distance. Sixteen sections constituted the city, with three vertical streets and three cross streets. Three large single-story buildings lay at the center of each sector.

Beau checked his chronometer. Seven hours had passed since their capture. He liked to keep it set to Earth hours and, like Earth, the planet rotated almost completely every 24 hours. No problem there. Nothing crazy like only two minutes or two days passing the start of their trek. Also, his sense of time told him some seven hours had passed. What the hell was the bear talking about?

As the visitors were soon to find out, the city

lacked electricity. As they already had found out by geo-scanner, available metal was virtually non-existent and so was technology of any significance.

Thousands of pandas came out to greet the entourage. All pointed their middle fingers at them, chattering. Many rubbed up against each other or rubbed their hands over their neighbor's body.

"What are they doing?" asked Sal. "It makes me itch watching them do that."

Ace grinned. "Our people rub bug oil into their skin and on each other every few days. This is one of those days. We get the oil from those red shiny fruits on the small plants. Sometimes they use too much and it burns the skin."

Beau asked, "Do they have bugs in their hair or is from all the insects that come out after the rain?"

"Both," said Ace, without elaboration, and led the remainder of his contingent through the throngs of curious bears. The rain began to come down again in sheets, but the bears stood their ground.

During their trek to the city, Ace had explained that his people had all the food they needed. The diets included grains from the grasses to make bread, traps to capture insects, which they fried and ate, and abundant fruits. No fish were available in the south-to-north running river and the nearest east-west running river was too far away to return with fish fresh enough to eat. The natives had long ago discovered that old fruit would ferment and always served as a favorite treat. In addition, field mice were captured and eaten. Ace did make one admonishment to always be on the lookout for a poisonous small red spider that occasionally appears among the insects. They're easy to see, so watch out for them.

The king, naked as a bear, stood outside his home awaiting their arrival. Upon their approach, Ace led them to a wash basin for a cleanup while the king went indoors. After Beau had removed most of the remaining blood with Sal's assistance, Ace motioned for them to follow him. The remaining guards stood watch.

The visitors were shocked once more when they entered the home. Neatly grouted tiles of varying sizes covered the walls, tables and chairs. The problem was that all the tiles were off-white to gray which may have something to do with a lack of available along with the inability of the citizens to see color. The ceiling was constructed of rows of dried vines inlaid in mud, vines that once connected the redfruit plant. Yet the floor of the home remained earthen and smooth.

The king bade his guests to sit while Ace patiently explained to the king about the conversations they'd had along the way. The king would occasionally glance at his guests and looked astounded when Ace got to the part about a single time place everywhere else and on other worlds and about Beau's part in the fight.

Ace reported the details of their capture. On occasion, Sally and Beau added little side comments. Understandably, the king was not put off by their clothing. He had seen it before. Apparently, he gave off an air of intelligent innocence, of great naïveté and strength; a curious conglomeration of attributes for a king, whose name Ace explained was so common that it might as well have been Joe Smith.

Joe Smith appeared pleased. He said, "You call him Ace, like others before you did; whatever Ace means. He tells me you want to help us find a better life for our people."

Beau had thought long and hard about what he was about to say and decided that, like Sal, the direct approach would be the best. "How would you like to be the head of the entire planet and be the most important and richest being that ever lived?"

Sal was taken aback at the statement. He hadn't mentioned a thing to her about making the king an offer for a position that he, Beau, wouldn't mind having.

"Yeah, yeah. Save it. Let's cut to the guts of the matter," said the king, causing Beau to halt his prepared narrative.

"We captured you because there are a lot of bad guys out there and like them, we want you for ourselves. Why? Because we're stuck with nothing. The only wood we have in our Place 5 is from the redfruit plant and we have no metal worth a damn. Oh, incidentally, we have no decent roads, no form of transportation, and can't even build anything that requires something called wheels, whatever they are.

"On the good side, we can spark a fire with some rocks and dry grass and we can easily pull the redfruit plants after the rains and dry the wood for stoking our kilns to make our pottery and our weapons. We have good clay for our homes and kitchens and that about wraps it up. It would be nice to help my people better their lives instead of spending half their time lugging water from the river. Now you want me to be the most important being in the galaxy. Do you see any incongruity there?"

Beau and Sal would have laughed from shock after hearing the king's retort, but didn't feel like ending the day with a wooden stake through their hearts. You do not want to piss off an alien, especially in his own home with his bodyguard standing next to him.

Still, Beau didn't like being accused of anything, especially being called out on a scheme of his own making. "You want to help your people? Give me a sense of how many people we're dealing with."

"I don't know exactly," said the king.

"All right, generally then."

"I'm not sure of that," answered the king, nervously.

"How many cities are on your world or even in your Place 5," Beau pressed on. "How far is the nearest one?"

"Well . . ."

"To be clear, you are really talking about helping people right here in this city, " stated Beau.

"I have no other choice," answered the king, truthfully.

Beau didn't want to lose focus. "You see, my friends, you have the most important planet out of all the worlds. If what you say is true, and I'm not saying it is one way or another, we can have humans, and even other races, come here to live a long life. And to help you, of course."

"How do you know that life is longer here because the others' are shorter?" asked Joe Smith. "Maybe we live longer than they do, but shorter than you do on your world."

The king had a valid point, one that Ace had already alluded to. Yet the chronometer didn't lie, did it? They would have to digest what he said. Beau wanted to get off-planet badly, but somebody had their guidance system and Sal's father and sister were still missing. Worse, they were landlocked. He only had one choice at this point: to make it up as he went along and work out an escape plan.

"If you would like us to, we will be happy to show you all the stars in the sky that you have never seen and you can imagine all the people coming here to spend money. Not only that," his mind open and reeling with possibilities, "people will come to Planet . . . Smith, and yours will be the most famous of all the worlds in the universe. We can be your brokers and arrange it. We will give people a reason to stay, while they are living a very long life and you will help not only your own people, you will help people in other worlds." He omitted the part about helping him and his wife in small matters as they earned an occasional credit or two. He was also flying by the seat of his pants, betting a long shot that the time factor was a real one, something they had no way to prove, as things stood.

"What does 'brokers' mean?" asked Ace suspiciously.

"Oh, that's nothing. Brokers means, uh, eight percent . . . " Sally started to say, then backed off. Beau was the businessman of the family and at that moment he provided his own brand of distortion anomaly, the complete reversal.

Beau quickly inserted, "That means you get eight percent of the gross revenue and we get ninety-two percent."

Sally said nothing while the two bears talked over his offer in heated and animated discussion, pulling to the side as they did so. They lapsed into some foreign tongue. At last Ace said, "That is absolutely preposterous. Are you trying to trick us, treat us like children who don't know any better? Shame on you."

Truly chastised with souls bared for all to see, Sally and Beau knelt on the ground before their ruler and master with new-found weakness. Brokers did get eight percent, the standard fee. The fact that the bears were the ones getting the eight was beside the point. A terrible guilt appeared to assail the pair.

"Arise," the future King of the Universe commanded. In his most regal form, His Royalty deepened his bi-tonal voice and said, "You are trying to take advantage of us. You think we are ignorant? We will take no less than fifteen percent of the profits!"

"What!" Beau shot back. "That's like robbing your honored guest." He took a very visible deep breath and looked upward toward some unknown force, then slung his head downward. He pulled Sal aside for their own private conversation. She pretended to put up an argument, then relinquished.

Beau shook his head back and forth, sadly, looking down and finally said, "All right, sir, you have us at a disadvantage. "Let's compromise at twelve/eighty-eight. After all, it is our idea."

"Deal," said both of the Pandas in unison, swollen with pride at having thoroughly beaten the humans at their own game while the humans looked totally upbraided, shamed to the core. The king shook both of their hands, his middle finger and thumb digging into their forearms deeply. The king said. "I have a job for you. Sure, I am concerned about weapons, but you are here for a reason. I want to take advantage of your brains and build a better world. Whatever happens in one time place stays in that place. Let's make ours the best."

"What do you need us to do?" asked Sally, still confused.

"I told you, I need a better world."

"You are the Joe Smith of Smith City," Beau remarked. "Surely you have the power to make changes."

"Yes," he replied. "I have the power, but not the materials. I'm listening, if you want to tell me what you can do."

All-Space had a strict written policy declaring that their employees must not to become involved in the internal strife of other worlds and not to deliver, manufacture or abet in weapons production and distribution. However, as independent contractors,

Beau and Sal no longer worked for the company and could do as they pleased, given that the company didn't find out.

Sal said, "King, if you want us to help you in the way you desire, we are going to need our ship for that job. It's a big responsibility."

She pulled Beau aside for another conference. "Babe, we still have to prove this whole absurd time nonsense thing exists."

"I've got a couple of ideas," he said. "But we're going to need to get to those ore deposits first."

Turning back to their hosts, Beau said, "We can give you a lot more than you have. What do we get out of it?"

The Pandans, at least in this time place, were trapped without metals and a limited amount of hardwood. They could and had survived without abundant wood; not so metal. They can express their intelligence through numerous avenues, but without metals they couldn't take the next step, which placed the earthlings in a number of serious binds.

After the fight and during their walk into the city Sal had asked Ace how he had become Joe's chief aid. He told her that, as a baby, he had been left at the king's doorstep, a normal custom. Pandas commonly left their children at the doorsteps of others because they did not have the means or desire to care for them, or they simply wanted to present a gift to someone who could not have children.

The king rejected virtually all bears left at his

doorstep, but his youngest adopted daughter, as well as his wife, both fell in love with Ace. According to the females, Ace's ears were a little more pointed than those of the average bear and he had this great decoration on this chest. So Ace grew up among a few other adopted children.

Sal had to ask, "To my husband and me, everybody looks alike to us. How do you tell males from females?"

Ace answered, "You don't, until one us starts to smell differently and a few days later lays an egg. That egg is supposed to be fertilized by the mate, but sometimes somebody else comes along and does it instead. Did you ever hear of such an awful thing?"

"That's terrible. It should be a crime," Beau threw in.

"It is. I make them carry river water," the king retorted.

The couple thought about all the bears they had seen who were doing exactly that and considered that those must represent only the ones who got caught.

Ace asked innocently, "We understand that each of you each has features that are different from the other. Can you show them to us?"

Beau was about to comply when Sal said, "Maybe later. Let's stick to the subject at hand."

As a ruler, the king demonstrated unusual qualities in that he was not politically enraptured, hedonistic, narcissistic, or demented. Joe Smith said, "You won't leave us if we take you to your spaceship?"

That was an honest question and called for the two humans to go into another huddle.

Sal whispered, "All right, Beau, what now? We're not going to lie, but I have got to look for my family at some point, so maybe we can stay here for a little while and do what we can for them."

"Sally, let's get out of here and go back to our jobs. It sounds like they're giving us the ship. We can come back later. Aren't you done with this place? Haven't you had enough fun for one day?"

"Yes, I am, and no I haven't. They need help," she replied, but with a lack of conviction. Beau was getting weary of her flip-flopping.

"Okay, if we do stay for a short while, maybe a week, I make the decisions regarding the next generation of weapons. I should be able to do that in nothing flat."

"Agreed," she replied simply.

"And I have an idea about your sister, too," Beau said, almost resignedly.

"You do? What idea?" Sal looked surprised.

"Well, if she's gone, she's gone. If she's in another zone or place, somebody will find her. As a human, she has value, unless she's stuck alone somewhere. Remember that ore deposit inside Zone 4 about a hundred klicks from the border of Zone 5? What if your dad and his crew and even your sister got captured and traded. I mean, didn't Ace tell us everyone wanted to get into this particular place?"

Beau turned to Ace. "Ace, you said people, bears,

smell differently. Do they lose that smell over time in another place?"

Ace replied, "Our people always have a smell about them, but when they go into another place, their metabolism changes, then they smell like everybody else in that place."

"How long does that take?" Beau asked.

"Maybe fifteen sleep periods," Ace responded.

Beau turned back to his wife. "That's what I'm talking about. If they got captured, then their captors have bargaining chips, free passes into Zone 5. If it was me, I'd say, 'I'll trade you our humans, their ingenuity, and all their attributes, for a free pass into your zone; as long as you let us hide out for a couple of weeks. So, if I had my druthers, I'd go straight south from the ore deposit into Zone 4 and start asking around."

Sal turned to the two Pandas and smiled as sweetly as teenager awaiting her first kiss. "You've got a deal."

Ace walked the couple to their new home, located, curiously, immediately next door to the royal household. "You will live here," he said. Then, he turned and walked away.

"Ace," Beau called after the bear. Ace stopped and turned. "I'm confused. Where did all this tile come from?"

"From our kilns; sixteen of them," Ace replied.

Ace saw the look on Beau's face and added, "One of Anders' men was a construction engineer and showed us how to reconstruct our kilns to fire pottery and make tiles. He put the men to work and Anders had to stay until the job was finished. Now we can't make tiles fast enough. This reinforces our notion that humans are inventive and we need you here." Ace turned abruptly and walked out.

The couple stood aghast. Accustomed to the cramped quarters onboard ship, this was a palatial mansion where they didn't have to hold in their elbows when passing one another. "We've two rooms, a wash basin, what looks to be a toilet, and beds made of grass and leaves. And an upstairs—maybe another bedroom. Not too shabby," Beau said, noting a bowl of different fruits, bread, and berries set in the center of a table in the main living area. "I've lived in a lot worse during my college years or even onboard various ships including our own. We can turn one area into a workspace."

"True enough, if we had something to work with. I'm getting pretty hungry. I don't see anything that resembles a kitchen or any cookware either. Guess we'll have to send out for some Chinese."

"We'll eat what they left us here and in the morning we'll ask around," suggested Beau.

The next morning the couple awoke stiff and sore. Neither could remember having walked that many miles at one time, certainly not on a treadmill. Yet, their biorhythm sense of Earth time felt comfortable and matched the reading on Beau's chronometer. No anomalies noted. The time business had been a hoax, or had some meaning they couldn't fathom.

Shortly after arising, Ace took the couple to the local kitchen which was one the three large buildings in the central portion of their sector. According to Ace, it provided two meals a day to the local populace. Virtually all foods were fresh, but the bears discarded leftovers thanks to a lack of refrigeration. Another building next to the kitchen was termed the recreation center and the third large building held manufacturing plant for the making of pottery, tiles, and grout.

The edifice had a central heating unit running its length where bread was baked and foods were cooked. Three-foot-wide by two meter-long ceramic slabs with cooking pots sat atop the lengthy heater. Just as somebody on earth had discovered centuries before that adding boron to glass made it able to withstand the direct flame of a torch, a similar addition must have been introduced here by Anders' men, or perhaps, a visitor before them.

Everybody worked all the time; there were no deadbeats or starving citizens. They either caught or harvested the food, cleaned and cooked it, carried water from the river, baked various flour products, cleaned the kitchen, helped others with their homes, made tiles, or washed the dishes and the cooking vessels. Bears rotated the duties with few complaints, unless workers couldn't get along with one another.

The king and many of his subordinates spent most of their time in consultation regarding matters of family disputes and sundry matters of litigation.

The hot weather soon became a problem for the visitors, especially with no cooling whatsoever available. The bears were adapted to it, not so the humans.

At least large pots of water were always available outside their front entrance each day for drinking and bathing. After spending several nights of sleeping in their own sweat, Beau decided to adopt a plan he had formulated one sleepless night. He asked Ace to get one his people to obtain a number of the large feathered palm leaves that had fallen in the savanna. He thought he might be able to use one to wave around for a cooling effect, but he soon had a better idea after more closely inspecting the stem. He found that it was fibrous and the fine fibers could be peeled off to give strips more than a meter in length. They were surprisingly flexible, enough so that baskets could be made from them, but for his purposes, he needed to braid them into a rope and connect two lengths to give him sufficient length to work with. He took the longest wooden redfruit vine he had on hand and inserted it into the stem which he secured by wrapping the new rope around it. He made a loop out of the other end and inserted the stem-vine combination into a hole he had gouged out in the earthen floor of his residence hooking the loop around his shoe. The length of the entire affair was his height when standing. Now he could tap his foot and get the frond to wave, providing a cooling breeze. Doubtless, adjustments would have to be made and the string reinforced, perhaps with a plant resin he might find, but for now, he had a working prototype.

Sal had inserted herself into the school system and began teaching math. If they stayed, she might want to teach the natives how to make string or rope which might be reinforced a number of ways; and baskets, windbreaks, fire starter material, or roofing material, if she chose to do so off of his mini-discovery. But that would be for somebody else to do, because their week was almost up and Beau was getting antsy to obtain the guidance system and leave for good.

He had spent his time tinkering with the throwing/stabbing stakes trying to come up with something novel and efficient, until, frustrated, he decided to visit his next door neighbor while Sal was in class. Unfortunately, he hadn't thought out a plan and fell into the trap of letting his emotions get the best of him, with every intention of searching for Sal's family.

Beau waited for a lengthy period until the stream of visitors had left the king's consult before showing himself at the door.

"You may come in," said the monarch.

"King, we've been here for the better part of seven sleeps and we'd like to get going to obtain the materials we need to help you," Beau began.

"Anders didn't need his ship to help us. Why do you think you need yours?" retorted the king.

Beau was caught. He didn't want to talk about Sal's family because the king would think they would take off for good, and it had nothing to do with the Pandans whatsoever. The bitter truth was that he would be right in that thinking.

Anticipating Beau's next words, the king added, "And don't tell me it's about getting metals. You

think I don't know we need them? What's more important is your assistance right here and now, not
some future investment fantasy of yours. We made
an agreement and I'm good with that. I'm not good
with letting you leave before you've shown your
worth. Once you do that, then we'll talk. That's it."
At that, the monarch gave Beau a dismissive hand.

Beau returned home. He had to give the bear
credit for not verbally ripping him to shreds, which
is what he deserved. In the absence of a bottle of serious hooch and a bar room fight, he became sullen
and remained so until Sal came home. Without saying hello, she flopped into a chair and foot-peddled
the palm leaf while he waved another one around.

She was polite in not telling her husband "I do
you so," and listened to him vent, feeling deeply
hurt at the news all the same. "Guess we'd better get
to work," she said, pulling up a palm frond from the
pile to begin stripping fibers from it.

Doing their best to resign themselves to their fate
over the months, the couple slowly lost their urgency to escape, spending as much time indoors as possible to avoid the glaring sunlight. Beau spent virtually all his waking hours trying to develop a new
weapon while Sal taught math to children and construction of woven products in after-dinner hours in
the packed recreation hall. Ace had cooperated and
sent out a team to collect as many of the feathery
fronds as they could find.

This, while Beau became increasingly angry with

himself. One day he became an outside observer critical of everything he didn't do. "Good job, Cunningham. You can shoot down intelligent aliens on their own world who are trying to protect their treasures. Is that what this is about, trying to make up for it? You held people hostage for ransom money and stole private space yachts, but you can't even make a weapon to defend yourself, let alone a population you pledged to help. Nice resumé. What did the cavemen use to kill animals? Well, they used clubs made from thigh bones and elsewhere when they killed zebras and large mammals. But there are no large animals here. You can't even make a reusable club from rocks because you don't have a reliable way to attach the rock to the handle; no, not even rawhide. How about a spear. All you have is the short curvilinear sticks from the redfruit vines. And even the natives have to use sharp edges of rock to cut them off and to make points at their ends. When it comes down to it, you're useless in the real world."

Listening to this diatribe, Sal had had enough. She was becoming more and more frustrated with her husband who appeared to be in a deep rut. She wondered if she loved him for the right reasons or only for convenience. For the moment, she needed to take positive action. "Sweetheart, we're stuck here for a little while so I need you to help me teach them how to create. Can you do that?" she asked.

"I thought that's what I am doing," he responded, more angrily than he intended, dropping a stick that he tried to insert a broken tile into for purposes cutting.

"Beau, we didn't land her separately. We landed here together. So let's work together. Here's an idea. You help me with my projects and I'll help you with yours."

Beau stretched and looked at their small home workspace adorned with pottery, broken tiles, red-fruit plants, fresh and dried grasses, palm fronds, and unsharpened sticks. "Nothing but junk and more junk," he declared, in answer to her request, now angry at himself for permitting her to prod him into staying, even if it was to help the bears.

A sudden thought struck him. What did Ace say about Anders wanting to clean out the junk from the ship? "Sal, come with me," he said, and told her his thought.

Ace led the excited pair to the storage room tightly packed with various items from Anders' ship. Open spaces in the walls served as windows. On the north side, the direction from which the storms came, a large down-sloping overhang prevented rain from entering the room, similar to that found in the homes.

Before them lay collections of items from other planets that might be traded, but were voided from the ship in light of the prospect of replacing the free space with gold ore that, according to the geo-scanner, would take a minimum effort to dredge without serious mining efforts.

Tired of looking at tile and wood, Beau's eyes widened at the sight of the loot in front of them. Back on point, he said, "I could still create one single nasty weapon out of this, but we need something that can be made for a lot of people on patrol. Let's look around."

They rummaged through electronics, works of art, statuettes from different worlds, miscellany, large and small. "Look here, Hon. What do you think?" Sal said, after much of the room had been cleared out to reveal a number of meter-square sheets of thin polyrubber, which were rolled and bound.

Beau stopped and stared, then made a quick turn to look behind him. A large coil of wire stood against one wall. His mind reeled. "We have got to get back to the ship to get some tools. Seriously. This could work."

Sal looked at the large stack of electronic items and said, with quiet enthusiasm, "And I have an idea of my own."

Without explanation, Beau picked up the roll of rubber and removed it from the room to place it outside with the coil. With the assistance of Ace, the three repacked the room and hauled the riches to the already crowded work room of their home.

Beau asked, "Ace, how long would it take for you to make this room three times this size? We need space to work. We want the space here in our house, not somewhere else."

"We can do it in thirty sleeps. We should finish before the shorter rainy season starts," responded the bear.

"We also need tools," Beau shot back.

Two days later, after a round trip to the ship

with an armed entourage—partly to protect them and partly to keep them from escaping, Beau surmised—he returned dehydrated, exhausted, and foot worn with the tools both he and Sal would need. One wall of the workroom had already been removed and work had begun on its expansion.

Already familiar with the brick, pottery and tile production facilities, Beau continued working on a gun made of hardened ceramic with a small top-loading magazine that held as many as a score of four centimeter long spear-like tile fragments. The propulsion mechanism would be the wire which he would heat and turn into individual springs. A knob would be pulled and released like a pinball machine to shoot the spears. He would install a rubber buffer between the spring and the gun frame. To make this happen he needed a hardened ceramic tube to serve as a gun barrel.

For recreation, Sal came up with idea of creating ceramic combs to assist the bears in their overall cleanliness. These soon became part of the culture. This led to body-hair-styling with the added perk of scratching an itch. Combing one's own fur and that of another turned into a ritual without end. Despite her entreaties, the king forbid the introduction of hair coloring into the new societal fashion statement.

Sal also went to work on her main idea: making time measurement sensors. "If we can get the king's blessing to use the ship, I think we have enough of our own stuff onboard along with what's in Anders' junk pile to make a hundred or more of these sensors and release them into the lower atmosphere around the planet. We'll log the air currents and the time variations and take some averages. Each will send a signal every fifteen seconds. If it's in a faster zone, then the signal will be less than fifteen. I tag each with its own ID code. In the end, we'll be able to map the various time zones of the planet. Within a couple of days they should all settle out, wind currents being one of the big variables. We can decide what to do after that."

The bears loved to party and in the local central hall of their sector they would put on skits and play music. Many came from distant sectors to see the humans mocked; how they talked, walked and dressed. After Sal had tossed and turned that same evening, her good humor turned sour, thinking of her own plight. Beau had wanted to get out a long time ago. She had insisted on their staying. Now she was done with it. She had long since become attached to the simple and beautiful people and her husband had, too. But there was a reason she was in the Thuban system in the first place and it had nothing to do with socializing with the natives. All this business about time was very interesting, but she had lost sight of her priorities.

The dark mood extended to the thought that she might have loved her husband for the wrong reasons, all of which were selfish, and once she found her family, perhaps it might be best to go their separate ways. Maybe she should tell him everything was her fault. Her head was going to explode. Her body began to shake.

Somebody grabbed her, calling her name, raising her to a seated position, putting drink in her mouth. "Sal, wake up, Get up, it's me, Beau. Sally." She took one sip then another.

"You've been poisoned," Beau said. "Somebody slipped one of the poison spiders into your portion of food. It may have been meant for me. I just came from seeing the king. He told me the symptoms. He said his people are absolutely meticulous about removing them from the insect dishes. Somebody put it in there on purpose. Now drink the entire glass."

Hours later, at first light, they requested an audience with the king to discuss the matter. The king asked Ace, "Who worked the kitchen last meal?"

"A new rotation, sir," answered Ace.

"Take your bears and bring them there," Joe Smith directed.

The king, Beau, and Sal walked with Ace the few hundred meter's distance to wait only a short while when twelve bears appeared along with the guards.

The king walked over to each bear and sniffed around him. No new ones here. "Go to your stations," he ordered.

They did as requested. None seemed to be surprised to see Sal, but one was surprised to see Beau, who said, "Wait, Ace, that one has a limp."

Ace grabbed the bear and spoke with him. The bear gave the equivalent of a shrug and pointed to an area on his thigh.

Ace examined it closely. He turned to the king

and to Beau. "It is a deep dagger wound."

"I'm probably the one who gave it to him," Beau offered, grinning down at the shorter creature, who averted its eyes.

The bear began to argue and gesticulate. The king stated, "He's lying. Take him out and make sure your men get ample practice with their new weapons."

"After that we're going to find my family," Sal said.

"We don't want you to go. We need you here," said the king.

Sal snapped. Angrily, she told the listeners about her lost family and their desire to help the bears as much as they could, but they needed the ship for both and had to have the box one of them took from the ship.

"That box is my fault," said Ace. I was preoccupied with you and didn't notice one of my people had it until much later."

"Did I miss something, Beau," said Sal in English, "or did he offer to give us back our guidance system?"

"If he did, I didn't catch that part," Beau replied. "What I did catch was that the play committee now has terrific new material to draw from. Look, king, we've been here for very many sleep periods and we know what we need to help you most. We've given you a lot already. Now you need metals. We need our ship to get them. We've talked about this before. Let us do our job and take care of that for you."

"How do I know you will return?" asked the

king, leading the couple back to his home while Ace supervised target practice on the errant bear. The three walked in the warm sunshine down the wide dirt streets, not slippery with mud, which was their main boast during the main rainy season.

"So we're prisoners, then, is that it?" asked Sal, beginning to get piqued again, as the king led them indoors.

"Do I have your word of honor you will return?" asked the king again, ignoring the question.

Sal said, forcefully, "Yes, you have it. Now give us some room to move." She neglected to tell him they could travel throughout the solar system and all over his world with their ship now, but didn't have a chance to leave the solar system without the box. She also neglected to tell him that to her, as of this point in time, honor is a relative term.

"Deal," said the king," as he reached into a large urn, pulled out the box. "I will send our best guards for your protection."

The next afternoon, the large well-armed group returned to the ship. It took two more days to repair the guidance system on the Clark Drive in their little tinkering room. Finally, and with great relish, Beau grabbed a handset, climbed to the roof, and carried the unit back to the engine room hatch where he opened the door, climbed down and turned on the lights.

"Holy shit, Sal, get down here," he yelled into the handset.

Moments later she appeared at the hatch, climbed

down and stared. Field mice nests of grass were wedged between cables and machinery. Droppings were everywhere.

"They didn't come through the rocket ports because those close automatically after the ship cools," she said.

"Yep," he said.

"The bastards ate through the heavy insulation of the cable leading from the nuclear power plant to the ignition switch for the rockets."

"Yep," he said.

"We're not going anywhere," she said.

"Nope," he responded. "They did come in from somewhere, though."

Beau began to walk toward the rear of the ship. "Let's look around."

A few moments later he said, "Got it."

Sal heard him rummage around through the tool box and loud banging sounds echoed throughout the ship. She heard more banging followed by a whirring sound followed a few seconds later by a clang.

Beau reappeared, grinning with hammer in hand. "That should take care of the rat problem. One port didn't close and they came up along the fuel line. You have to know where to hit these things sometimes to get them unstuck."

They left the engine room and Beau carried the Clark unit back to the pilot's cabin for safety, then exited the ship to explain to Ace and the other guards what had happened.

"Guys, it's getting late so we're all going to have

to stay here tonight. You can come onboard and find a place to sleep, if you want. We'll close the hatch and it will be safe. In the morning Sal and I will have another look."

"We can't go into a human's house at night. It's forbidden," Ace said. "You know that."

"It's not night, yet. Do you want to sleep inside or outside? Your choice," Sal stated.

In the morning, the ship smelled rank after ten bears had spent the night on-board, with the hatch and door closed, standard procedures being what they are and both humans sorry they didn't let the bears sleep outdoors ,as they always do when on patrol.

The couple went back to the engine room for another inspection. They found a gash in the insulation around the power cable to the nuclear plant— enough so that the sensors would prohibit ignition. Beau measured the gash in the insulation and found it to be roughly one-half centimeter wide by three centimeters deep by four centimeters long. It was all on top. The mice had been working on it for reasons of their own. They might as well have been eating through the fuel line itself. Either way, the ship wouldn't start without danger of fire or explosion.

"Now let's see what we have in our own junk pile." He wended his way to the storage area located behind the power plant.

"See anything you can use to re-insulate the cable?" she asked, looking at some electronics and old instruments.

"No," he declared angrily.

Sal looked at her husband whose emotional swing was all over the place, having accepted her own plight. Beats the hell out of being depressed, she thought. She wondered where her own emotions would take her now that she was free to find her lost family, but couldn't, and there wasn't a thing she could do about it.

Repair of the ship was going to take some deep thought, especially on a planet with minimal resources. Beau needed to relegate that project to the back-burner for now. He didn't enjoy teaching because he wasn't a good teacher and he didn't have the patience for students who didn't want to learn. He did enjoy the challenge of taking the time to create new weapons, and also taking care of the bears. Or was it taking care of himself? He began to wonder which of came first.

Sal still had her physical outlets, but once again, was rocked by the pain of entrapment and helplessness.

After returning home, Beau let Ace tell the king what had happened. He did not want the embarrassment of facing the bear who might be gloating.

"I'm a spaceman and I'm going stir crazy," Beau said, in the privacy of their home.

"Ditto. We've been burying it for a long time."

He said, "I have an idea. We'll have the bears file the edges of the polyrubber so that we have a fine dust."

"And?"

He said, "Poly is a mixture of silicone and rubber, right? We need to dissolve the rubber portion. Water or alcohol won't do it. We need something acidic."

"Redfruit is acidic before it matures," she offered.

"True. That might be worth a try. Trouble is, it's out of season. Grab some of that bug oil and let's find some of that magnesium carbonate lime they use for grout making," he said.

The couple walked over to building three and found a good supply of the white powder in large covered pots. Beau added a few drops of oil to it and the lime immediately began to fizz. "This stuff is acidic. No wonder it can burn the skin," he said.

Back in their office/laboratory, Beau added a small quantity of oil to the polyrubber shavings and watched carefully. He saw no immediate reaction. The next morning he did note a clear indication that some of the blackness of the rubber had transferred to the liquid of the oil.

"We do this again and warm it on a kiln to speed the reaction. We'll neutralize the reaction with lime until we have a paste that will harden," he said. "We'll do this on a kitchen stove or on a kiln to speed up the reactions. "

"This project is going to take a lot of time," Sal said, without thinking.

"And?" Beau quipped, in his turn.

By Beau's chronometer, two years of experimentation passed to create enough slurry using six cubic centimeters of powder and triplicate the results to their satisfaction. One mistake and they would be dead meat. With a contingent of guards armed with spear guns that had been tested in battle, the couple boarded BOB and Beau poured the mixture into the wounded conduit, heating it with Sal's mini hair dryer she recharged on-board. They waited until the next morning and finger-touched the results of their efforts to find the fix was rock hard. Keeping their fingers crossed, both returned to the pilot's cabin where Sal hit the button to open the rocket ports, then held her breath and hit the fuel switch followed by the ignition switch. The signal was received and the rockets fired. She permitted a slow burn for a few moments letting the ship rock in place, as if both were saying to one another, "Thank you, I needed that."

She shut down. The ship still smelled after the bears had spent another night onboard. The couple went back to check on their work. No problem. With their guards as company, they lifted off to slowly fly back to Smith City for purposes of reorganization. Sal landed on a dirt patch near their home well clear of the grass to the amazement of the entire city's populace, virtually none of whom had seen a spaceship. Once parked, Beau ensured the rocket ports were tightly closed and the couple left the vessel to get organized for the next day's project.

At the crack of dawn, the couple prepared to leave but decided it wouldn't be polite to blast off and wake a city full of natives so they waited another hour. At last cruising the planet, Sal released her drone sensors.

Several days later the data were in. Sal tore the sheet from the ship's printer and examined it.

TIME

ZONE NUMBER	UNIVERSAL GALACTIC	RELATIVE TO NORMAL
North		
0	1	unknown
1	1	8.7
2	1	6.2
3	1	1.6
4	1	1.0
Center		
5	1	1
South		
4	1	1.0
3	1	1.4
2	1	5.9
1	1	8.5
0	1	unknown

"Now we know something, finally," Beau said. "It looks like those of us situated in Zone 5 age only one-tenth as fast as normal. For the two plus years we've lived here, we've aged between two and three months. Which suggests that to the rest of the galaxy, that's how long we've been missing."

"And," added Sal, "simply moving from Zones 4 to 5, would mean you would age fifty percent faster than UGT. Beyond that you're a gonner almost as soon as you're born. This means that if my sister is in Zone 4, a good four years has passed for her compared with a couple of months for us. Furthermore, when the sensors were all airborne, they followed UGT. They didn't register time differences until they hit the ground."

"What's this 'unknown' mean at the poles and how far does it extend?" Beau asked.

"It means there are no data," was her simple response.

"There have to be data. Time can only run forward," he scoffed. Bad mistake.

Sal smile at him in a cutesy sarcastic manner, "Let us not forget 'no time at all', which is what is happening at the poles.

"How can you have no time? There has to be time."

"If you say so, dear. Let me know what you come up with," responded the astrophysicist, to leave him hanging.

The two adventurers took off for the primary copper ore pocket on the planet, located in Zone 4, some 3000 kilometers from Smith City and perhaps fifty kilometers outside the border of Zone 5. Beau cruised the circumference of the pocket while Sal looked into the geo-scanner. Most of the pocket was located in a large hillock that measured some ten kilometers in diameter.

"Stop," Sal yelled. He did so. The scanner suddenly glowed with the colors representing a high concentration of titanium and a blend of aluminum and synthetic metals. It had to be another ship.

Excited, he landed in the lush vegetation of the jungle, the ship blowing out a large circumference of vegetation. The entourage exited. Excited to be back in their element, the couple strapped on their side arms and each carried a rifle. Once outside, Sal gave unnecessary orders for the guards to be vigilant.

She approached the closed ship that appeared to be similar to the one Jen was reported to have stolen. On a hunch, she punched in the codes for her sister's birthdate. The door opened. The ship indeed belonged to Jen, replete with her belongings. There was no evidence of any other crew member and no indication of violence. She could locate no weapons or communication handsets. Sal could only hope her sister had taken both with her.

"Looks like we can now have two ships to load ore onto," said Beau, feeling pleased from a number of standpoints.

Now in the mood to hard-laser anyone or anything in her path, Sal said, "There're no satellites here. I'm going to call on the standard frequency once I get airborne and try to reach Jen."

She lightly took the ship to altitude and used the ship's com system to call. "Jennifer, this is Sally. We're nearby. Answer, if you can hear me."

After a number of attempts, rising in height each attempt, she received a response. "Sal, it's Jen, I'm here. Where are you?"

Ebullient, Sal said, "Beau and I were at your ship. Are you all right?"

"Yes, Oh, My God, it's you," came the reply. "I got captured right after I landed and was marched down to this city maybe a hundred klicks south of the ship. Who's Beau?"

"He's my husband. I got married after you disappeared. Did you ever find dad?"

"Rumors spread fast around here. Is it really you? They don't exactly have radio so you don't know what to believe, but word has it he looked over the place where you found my ship and decided to go for the gold way south of here. I stopped to check out the copper deposit when I got grabbed. Had to hard laser a whole bunch of them, before getting grabbed."

"Well, you're safe now, but it sounds like dad went to time place 1 or 2 or thereabouts," Sal said.

"Time place what?" asked Jen.

"You don't know about time zones?" Sal asked.

"No. Should I?"

"We'll come and pick you up," Sal offered.

Jen said, "Let's do it at daybreak tomorrow. I have a lot of goodbyes to say first." Then she added, "About two klicks south of the city you'll see two rivers come together. I'll meet you there on the west side of the fork."

"See you then," Sal signed off.

"There's something we need to do first before we load, Hon," Sal said.

"I'm listening," Beau replied.

"You can begin to load up BOB with ore. After I pick up Jen in her ship in the morning, well, she doesn't know it yet, but we're going to look for our father."

Beau became silent and serious. "I was beginning to wonder when you planned to do that. I'm going, too."

"No, you're not," Sal stated flatly.

"I insist," Beau said. "You're going to need protection and you've talked about him so much I feel I know him."

Sal said emphatically, "Look, we have two ships and ten bears. We need an empty ship to go search because we can't fly around in one loaded with heavy ore and we can't take the bears home and we can't leave them here while we take both ships. The king will be very upset if we did that. So you stay here and load and we'll go look for our father. That's it."

"Can you make sure you're seriously weaponized? Stay in touch, babe, in case I have to come and rescue you."

Sal looked at him and saw a dead serious man. "I'm impressed and it's good to know we have you for our backup," and gave him a kiss on the cheek.

The next morning, after Jen boarded the ship and the sisters hugged, Sal took off for the gold deposit. They held their respective stories for later, concentrating on looking over the terrain beneath them. Sal did explain to her astonished sister what she had learned about the way the differences in time on the planet affected the type of vegetation and the population, showing her the data sheet.

When they reached the area of the designated coordinates, Jen worked the geo-scanner. At last they found the gold deposit along with signatures of two ships, although one was almost completely washed out.

Sal dropped Jen's ship closer, which brought to life the image of a survey vessel with the door open and the stairs gone. Half the ship was buried in sand. It lay in a landscape as barren and bleak as the surface of Mars. A strong crosswind blew the dust in gusts and Sal had to fight the controls to hold her vessel stable. On closer inspection, the skin of the ship on the ground appeared to be heavily pitted. The remains of a second vessel was barely recognizable some distance away with the remains of the front portion still visible.

"Take us down. I'm going in," Jen said.

Sal stated, "Get out as soon as I land. As far as the data, the zones relate to the ground only. So I'm going airborne to be safe and watch. Grab a weapon and a handset."

"Wasn't Anders one of the first to get lost here?" Jen asked.

"Not really, there were others before him, but that could be his old ship. If it is, it's a pile of junk now," Sal contributed.

Jen walked down the four steps to the ground trying to shield herself from the blowing dust and headed for the old vessel, protecting herself from the blasting sand when Sal lifted off. When she reached the relic, she had to climb a small sand dune to reach the entrance, which she found to be open.

She checked the small platinum ID plate attached to the door frame, then pulled out a multi-tool to pry it off. The plate fell into her hand. She placed it in her pocket, took a quick look inside, and decided to move over to the next ship.

"I'm going to drop a sensor," Sal radioed.

Jen climbed another sand hillock to enter the newer ship. Hovering from above, Sal saw her sister inspect the ID tag and remove it, as well.

Minutes went by, then Jen came out the door and went around the rear of the ship to enter the cargo bay where she disappeared inside. With rapt attention, Sal watched her sister's every movement when she remembered to check the readings broadcast by the time-sensor. When she did, she screamed into the com, "Jen, get the fuck out. Now. Run. Don't ask, just do it." She repeated her words until she saw her sister running.

Sal dropped the wind-blown bucking ship on minimum jets and hit the ground hard with the door already open for Jen, who ran onboard. "Strap in and hang on," Sal declared as she went to altitude and shot northward on full power, as if a hive of hornets were chasing her.

"What happened?" Jen asked.

Sal said, "The time sensor fluctuated but hovered around 5000:1, that's what happened. You were gone, what, eight-ten minutes?" She ran a quick mental calculation. "That means you aged a good month. There must be a multiplier effect between the zone and the density of the heavy metal. Was the second one dad's ship?"

"It was," Jen said.

"Well, the first one belongs to Anders and with it missing for 127 years, it must over 600,000 years old by now and anything that came before him is untraceable."

Jen agreed and pulled out the platinum door ID tags, showing them to her sister. "This one belongs to dad and the other is, in fact, Anders. Which explains it. As for dad, the men got old before they knew what hit them. From what you say, one day would equal maybe fifteen years. It takes a week to load when working around the clock. From what I saw, the cargo bay was only partially full.

"I don't want to think about this place anymore."

Suddenly, Sal declared, "Oh, my God! Beau! He's sitting in the middle of a copper deposit, which means there's a multiplier effect for him, as well. She called him.

When he answered the handset, he said, "High, babe, I was about to call and see how you were doing."

"Get out," she yelled. "Now." She quickly told him what they'd found.

"It's going to take some time to get the equipment . . ."

"Leave it. Get out," she ordered. "We'll meet back at the house. I want to know when you're airborne."

"Can you drop another sensor over where he is" asked Jen.

"Fresh out and I don't care right now," Sal declared.

A few minutes later Beau called to confirm he and the bears were airborne.

When the second ship landed outside Smith City, a bearded man named Beau watched in anticipation as the door opened and two women stepped out who were completely different in appearance. Of the two, Jen appeared to be more stout, or perhaps a little more muscular. She stood an inch shorter and wore short dark brown hair. In addition, her face lacked the leanness of Sal's, with a more square-cut jaw line. She presented a no-nonsense look and was quite attractive to him. He guessed that anyone who would permanently borrow a spaceship from All-Space had to have serious nerve and a good reason to do so. She had found her reason.

Before Sal could say anything, Jen came over to Beau and introduced herself.

They learned that during Sal's brief absence, an attack had been made on BOB during their mining operation. The repeater rifles had proven to be vastly superior to native weaponry to the great delight of the bears, who had learned to copy Beau's original design and could make as many as they desired.

Piloting BOB home with his Panda contingent, another idea formed in Beau's mind, which, he thought, definitely warranted discussion with the girls. This would be right up their alley and would make heroes of them all, although perhaps not to the king's liking— a slight setback.

IV

The Earth-born guests reported to the king who looked aghast at two spaceships that had landed in, what was essentially, his front yard. Ace had the honors of introducing Sal's sister and explained all that had happened.

"So, you returned as promised," said Joe Smith. "What riches have you brought us to better our lives?"

Beau had not looked forward to this moment, but on the trip back he was struck with an inspiration that needed development. Hoping the king would be out making the rounds when they returned, so he could talk it over and get organized, he feigned delight upon seeing the monarch. "If it's all right with you, king, we need to get some rest and talk to you later about our great plans for you and all your people."

Mollified for the moment, the king relented and dismissed the three foreigners with a wave of the hand with suspicion clouding his brow.

Remembering to bring instant coffee from her stores, Jen set a small pot of cold water on the table next to the soft chair in their next-door home and began her story.

"After I landed, I took my heavy-laser pistol and my handset, as per standard procedures, and clipped the com into my belt. Same stuff I'd done for years. I locked the ship and wanted to look around at the site from the ground. I couldn't see much from the air with all the vegetation. If dad had landed thereabouts, his ship could have been hidden by growth by this time, but even if that were the case, I saw no indication of ship metal from the air.

"I walked through the jungle for a while and was about to go back to the ship, when a horde of upright bear-like creatures jumped out of the growth at me. I thought they were trying to kill me, but after I shot a few, it turned out they wanted to capture me, but bring me to no harm. They carried bows, but didn't use them."

Beau interrupted. "This group had bows and arrows, not sticks?"

"Correct."

"So they have access to flexible wood for the bow and hardwood for the arrows and can make string or a good substitute. Fletching is easy to get. Different location, different materials," mused Beau out loud.

Jen continued, "I didn't know about that part. Once I got to our destination, all I saw was sharpened sticks for weapons. Anyway, they marched me for miles. My feet hurt and I needed rest. The bears let me sit down and lean up against a tree to sleep for a couple of hours, gave me something to eat, and made me walk again. That said, they weren't cruel about it. It was the opposite. I might have been an honored guest, but we had a lot of ground to cover.

"After a couple days of this, we were encircled by another group of bears and one or two from each band chatted to each other. I got turned over to the second group and the first group came in our direction for a few hours, then disappeared. Eventually, I got to the city where you found me. The new group took me to a house and gave me food and water and showed me a bucket and large water basin and a shower area, then left me. My gun was gone, but I still had my com hooked to my belt.

"That's where I lived. I had a vague idea of where the ship was located, but couldn't have gotten to it if I'd wanted to. When I heard from you, Sal, I was at home getting ready to teach and then help in the kitchen."

Sal declared, "Beau, you were right. She was traded up. Now that I think of it, we found her in Zone 5, the same zone as ours. It's obvious she hasn't aged 20 or 30 years."

"Did your city have a king?" asked Beau.

"No, it had a supreme ruler. I was under his protection at all times. He said there is only one king of the planet and he's in the city where we are now. I called my guy the Super.

"One of the many problems that beset Super City, as I call it, was illegal immigrants. They'd come from afar, hang out in the jungle for a couple of weeks until they smelled the same as everybody else, and then saunter into the city. The population was growing too fast and the Super didn't know how to stop it.

"I came up with a plan. I figured that if these bears can build two story buildings, they can build a six story tower. Because their city was surrounded by a field of medium height grass and palm-like trees maybe a kilometer in either direction, they could now have an observation tower to search for other bears who might be sneaking in. It was easy from then on to develop a semaphore flag system where hostiles were not only observed, but patrols could look back and follow the semaphore, which would guide them to the invaders in terms of distance, direction, numbers, and other variables."

Jen mixed a spoon of coffee into a cup of cold water and took a satisfying sip. "From the fibrous meshes of grass fibers, we made sheets of paper for writing and drawing. I also made flower paste and rolled the sheets into tubes which could serve as flutes or slides that would go in and out for other musical instruments. Also, once we had the sheets, I taught them to write and use numerals. Invention was without end. Once they learned, they were terrific at copying, but seriously lacking in original thought. Once I showed them how to make water filters, it became a simple matter to show them how to make flying colored spinners. Now everybody has several. How about you two?"

Sal began the lengthy story which Beau ended with a demonstration of his repeating rifle. He concluded by saying, "It appears we are out of luck in getting them metals. I'm thinking there's another way to give them what they need and, as an aside, we can become very wealthy. But first, I would like you two to help me with an idea I have. My mom was an agriculturist and one thing I learned from her was that an extremely dilute solution of copper sulfate in water can be used to spray plants to keep off bugs. I sometimes think of that when the word copper comes up. Apparently, the bears have bugs or fleas that always live in their hair. What if we could rid them of this scourge by treating them with a solution of this? I mean, seriously, you wouldn't need much to do it. All we'd have to do is to dissolve some of this copper mineral in water, figure out the concentration and . . . "

"And put it in their bug oil," exclaimed Jen.

"Beau, what an idea," said Sal.

"Where are you going to get the copper?" Jen asked.

"It only takes a trace amount and I still have a couple of loads of the ore in the hold of the ship. Hell, man, there's enough copper there to last a thousand years for this little project."

"How are we supposed to make money off of that?" Sal asked.

"We're not. There's something else, though." Beau explained his other idea in some detail. The women were astonished at the breadth of it and the three were soon in agreement.

Sal presented the copper experiment to the king who required reassurance that none of his people would be harmed. Sal gave that assurance, as she tried to hide her own reservations. Both women took it upon themselves to enter the UG library onboard ship to research the topic.

Before Beau called Earth, there were a couple of things he needed to do regarding his second idea.

V

Beau's Grand Plan called for Thuban 5 to be officially renamed Planet Joe Smith and to be turned into a galactic tourist haven; to use the other zones for the rapid growth of crops which would be robotically controlled with no loss of human years. Whether the faster time zones could be used for the rapid healing of ailments would take further investigation. Nevertheless, the construction of a small metropolis to start, to be named King Smith City, would be the focal point of the plan directed toward those who were willing to pay a king's ransom to live a very long time. More cities could be constructed after that.

"There's a little wrinkle in our plan," Beau said. "Until we know more about what we're dealing with, the city can't be built out of metal."

Jen said, "Obviously. So how do we build it," Jen asked.

"We don't. The Pandas do. We'll have to ship in plumbing, wiring, glass, and electronics. The buildings will be re-bar reinforced adobe mixed with added petroleum for waterproofing. We'll need a single small nuclear power plant and along with a couple of very large kilns for brick making. We can get them a water wheel, solar power, wind turbines and drill the water table so they don't have to lug water up the hill anymore. That will release the water carriers into the workforce for other purposes such as creating tile-lined drainage ditches for water runoff. No problem once we get our hands on a few billion credits."

"Oh, is that all. Whose ship are we going to take to Earth?" Jen asked.

Beau said, thoughtfully, "You need to return the ship you borrowed so we'd better take both. I don't want to be stuck there penniless and right now, I'm a little short of cash. We're going to see if All-Space will drop any charges against you as part of the negotiations."

"I can't argue with that," said Sal, ready to quit her past life of teaching math and basket weaving. "I'll go with you, Jen, and Beau can take Ace and the king with him. We'll rendezvous in Lunar City and then proceed to Earth for a meeting."

Jen said, "I don't think those two will be too pleased about leaving their world for a time that is faster to them."

"Faster for us, too," added Sal. "Let's see the list you put together, Beau."

He handed Sal a sheet of reed-paper. She read, "PRELIMINARY WANT LIST: Roads, air conditioning units, signage, casinos, hotels, security, sewage disposal, fresh water, foods, tourist items, watercraft, protection against bugs during rainy season, sales offices . . . nothing too big," she said facetiously.

Beau added, "The Pandas will have more than their share of troubles, once the galaxy learns of the time anomalies and immigration by the wealthy starts. At that point, debauchery will begin in earnest. They'll need a police force with some good weapons. Finding defense contractors willing to do the job should be the easy part."

Beau came up with the idea of using a bear hand with a large middle finger as a symbol for invitation to the planet. Sal thought that idea might have to be test marketed on a small scale, since that particular human motion and accusatory involvement had found its way down through the ages and into all planetary systems where the human race had settled; nay, had even visited.

Several sleep periods later, the three poured over the time warp numbers again. Jen pointed to the areas on the printout. "See how the rate of decent of each probe corresponds to the zone that it is in."

Beau looked at his wife, "I thought you said . . . "

"I said that the time influence did not extend into the atmosphere, but this is gravitation," Sal replied. "And yes, if you want to split hairs, gravitation is part of the atmosphere."

"Which suggests the core of the core of the planet might be striated," offered Beau, trying to grasp another new concept, presented by experts who could shame him in their everyday conversation about what he pretended to understand. *Shut up, Beau. You're getting caught in foot-in-mouth disease.*

"So are we heavier or lighter?" he asked.

"Beau, what are you talking about? Are you even listening to me?" Sal complained.

"Jen, please explain it to him," Sal implored. "His slow grasp of the language is making my brain hurt."

Jen began, patiently and calmly. "Beau, the sensors all register the same time until they hit the ground. However, they fall at different rates. There is no constant here because of the introduction of time into the equation. The amount of gravity varies, depending on where you are standing on the planet. Besides gravity, we've known from the early Twentieth Century that time is also inextricably bound with mass and light speed. The entire electromagnetic spectrum has to be affected here. Throw communications into the mix. And how about the rate of anything. Since rate means speed over time, the rate of radioactive decay has to be altered. There might even be new elements out there. Physicists are going to have a field day. Our understanding of the entire universe will soon change."

Beau dared not ask further questions. Knowing the girls, they had already begun writing scientific papers on the subject. All he could do was to fake an understanding. Worst case scenario: admit to their superior intelligence, and that wasn't going to happen. Instead, he offered, "Let's head over to BOB and make the call. It should go through. If it doesn't, we'll call from space."

Beau sent a supra-light instantaneous contact signal to All-Space Mineral Surveys, their old company, hoping the frequency of nearly three years ago still worked.

Shortly, a return message was received that they had been acknowledged. Please present your identification numbers. Where had they been for the past four months? Jennifer Rockwell was with them? Did she find Chris Rockwell? Where's the ship she took?

After Beau requested a meeting of the Executive Council of All-Space, they prepared their ships for the journey. Jen asked her sister, "Do you ever feel guilty about possibly living longer than any other people, aside from those in biblical years?"

"No. Do you?"

"Sometimes, yes," Jen replied.

"Why? Are you still the same old sentimental-ist?"

"Maybe I am. I can't decide whether it's fair or it's right or wrong," Jen confessed.

Sal wasn't going to let her sister get away with feeling guilty. "Look, Jen, we didn't invent a potion to keep exclusively for the bears to keep for them-selves, or for ourselves. We discovered a totally nat-ural potion and we want to share it with those who can afford it. Tens of billions of sentient beings can't fit here so we sell it. A couple of years ago, if some-body asked you if you would pay for those years, would you do it? You're damn right you would. Well, you got them for free. Now, think about so many others willing and able to pay?" On the other side, Sal had every right to be concerned about the unknown mysteries the planet still held. Was it too good to be true?

A single sleep period later, All-Space granted permission for the meeting.

VI

The two Panda guests plastered their faces to the portholes of the ship on the way out of the solar system until things went gray. Beau showed them their quarters and the galley, gave them a crash course in astronomy, showed them holograms of Man's expansion through the galaxy, where the alien races were located and their characteristics, fed them, and then left them to their own devices. The bears absorbed, learned, asked questions, and exhibited a great thirst for more knowledge.

A few days out, Beau called All-Space Mineral Surveys and gave a very general description of where they had been. He waited a considerable period of time for a response and eventually received a communiqué from one of the business partners, who authenticated their existence, fraudulent claims notwithstanding. All-Space acknowledged that the initial contact signal received they had received had not been a robotic voice. It had been presented by a human calling from the coordinates of the Thuban system.

The two ships rendezvoused at Lunar City before coming together on Earth. Jen worried about a meeting with a committee of humans waiting to bite her head off. Sal worried about trying to borrow a lot of money from hard-core businessmen, which was slightly different than singing with fun-loving aliens while teaching them how to comb their own hair. Beau had his own game plan.

The Executive Committee of the largest space

fleet in the known galaxy consisted of eighteen members. Only twelve could be present on short notice. Most were monthly or quarterly warriors, living off-planet. A few saw a great hoax in the making, refusing to attend or were too far away to make it. Those who did wanted to meet the miracle trio who had returned from having been eaten by the devil Thuban system. The word got out and the galaxy watched.

Billy "Mad Dog" Bryne served as the current CEO of All-Space and possessed a rough appearance similar to that of Beau. After graduating from the academy decades before, he joined the space police and chased pirates in his sector for a number of years, destroying their nests and confiscating their ships. His promotion to captain did not diminish his enthusiasm for action, especially when his daughter, Alistair, who now sat at his right, was his copilot for several of those years. Finally, All-Space hired him on as their CEO because of his no quit attitude and his leadership abilities.

Alistair was slated to become CEO when her father retired within the year. Nobody else on the board wanted the thankless position. They all knew Bryne saved their company years before with the destruction of one arm of the pirate league, so he appeared to be the logical choice to receive an invitation. Military in appearance and bearing, he surprised himself by accepting.

When the guests described their situation, he was more curious about the negotiations and the security of the operation than about the trio or the Pandas themselves. He'd seen plenty of aliens in his day. The others seated at the large oval table owned their own airline companies; sharp tough men and women whom Billy respected, although disliked in some cases.

Sally and Beau had disagreed in one major regard. She wanted to bring Joe Smith and Ace to the meeting. She wanted the committee to speak with them to see how open and gracious they could be. Beau did not want the committee to see them as simplistic, or as aliens who might be taken advantage of. A compromise brought the bears into the conference room, where they said "hello" in Pandan by showing their middle finger and took a seat.

Beau wanted a lot of things from All-Space, which included financing for the advertising. For collateral, they offered another planet full of heavy metals without mentioning its name.

The committee dismissed the story about the metal planet as a fabrication. This left the guests with themselves and the Pandas as proof of their tale. Beau saw an opportunity. "Before we go any further, a few of you are you telling us this metal planet doesn't exist, is that right? If that's the case, then I want a signed waver saying it belongs solely to us and All-Space relinquishes all rights to this planet. Please draw up such as agreement for us to sign before we leave here today."

Bryne smiled as he saw through Beau's apparent bluff and nodded to one of the board members who arose and stepped aside. He pulled out a slate and began to dictate into it.

Beau continued, "That's the first order of business. Now to the second." They told their stories and left out factors that would have cast a negative light on the Pandas or themselves. Beau related about the housing and food, the kitchens, the lack of technology and especially about the time zones. He then explained what they had in mind in terms of tourist trade and the potential benefits to All-Space as far as providing startup capital, ships, security and other measures that would help this budding enterprise.

In addition to natives from the regions to the immediate north and south of Zone 5, one heck of a lot of off-worlders would be moving to planet Smith. That was part of what they wanted in their contract with All-Space. The company would be the sole carrier with the three of them as part owners.

Beau summarized, "In a ship shell, it comes down to this. All-Space can be part of this venture, or I can contact a few old friends on the fringe of behavioral integrity who would welcome the offer." Beau named several, which caused Bryne's eyebrows to raise. He was still looking for them.

The CEO responded, addressing Jennifer, "Intriguing. First, Ms. Rockwell isn't it?" He seemed fixated on her and kept glancing her way, even while Beau spoke. "As for that old relic you purportedly stole or borrowed, you could have done better. However, Mister Cunningham tells us you discovered both your own father's vessel, as well as that of the one belonging to the Anders' crew. Is that right?"

"Yes, sir, it is," Jen replied, standing.

Bryne displayed a bemused look, as he looked side-to-side at the council members, "You wouldn't happen to have proof of that, would you?"

"Actually, sir, I do." Without lifting her eyes from the CEO, she reached into a pouch at her side and pulled out the two thin platinum ID plates she had retrieved from the door frames of the dead space-ships. She walked over to Bryne and handed them to him. He inspected the medallions and his smile vanished in an instant. He spend a full two minutes looking at them and passed one in each direction to the council members. He let another minute pass as the plaques were examined.

Bryne visibly relaxed and, with compassion, said, "Miss Rockwell, we accept your findings with our profound regrets. All-Space sent both Anders and your father to explore this world without under-standing what it beheld and we must accept respon-sibility. You will receive appropriate compensation for the loss of your father. Furthermore, you may keep the ship you . . . borrowed?" At that, Bryne looked left and right and saw no objections.

"As for the rest of it, what I do care about is not investing the funds of this company in this well thought out scheme you are presenting. Who is to say that you have this great planet of metals you want to use as collateral."

Beau stood up. "You're the one to say because I have a lengthy legal document signed by yourself as the CEO and all board members and attendant attorneys and bankers belonging to All-Space. This document states that we have eight-five percent of that planet and you get fifteen. Signed, sealed and delivered. In a word, you're stuck. We deliver the planet, you can mine it, and you can pay."

"You wouldn't have copy of that document, would you?" Bryne asked somewhat tentatively, re-calling that he had signed it only months before and was now wary of these visitors whom he had never met in person.

"Actually, I do," said Beau, who reached into a satchel to pull out a lengthy document. He walked forward and handed it to Bryne who took sever-al moments to look through it and passed it to his daughter.

Bryne asked, "Where is this planet?"

"It's Thuban 4," Beau replied.

"Come on, Mister Cunningham," Bryne grinned, "we've known for centuries the planet is dense due to its large iron core. We don't need iron. So you can mine it yourself all you want, but don't expect to use it as collateral for your Thuban 5 enterprise.

"Okay, will do. Glad that's settled. Everybody heard him," Beau stated flatly.

Bryne became serious, "Mister Cunningham, I believe our business is concluded. I suggest we call these proceedings to a halt and let you get back to outer space with your little teddy bears."

Ace made a move to stand, but the king laid a hand on his arm, who stood instead. His Universal

Galactic Language had been refreshed with the presence of Beau and his wife, and, as a Pandan, once learned, never forgotten. Furthermore, he had no problem speaking in front of groups.

"Excuse me, Mr. Bryne. I'm certain you're not an ignorant man, only one who pretends to be."

The king turned to Ace and said a couple of sentences in Pandan, which were overheard by Beau, Sal and Jen, who began laughing. By this time, while they could never be able to mimic the incredibly complex system of tonal qualities expressed by two sets of vocal cords owned by the bears, they had at least been able to gain a fair understanding of the vocabulary. When the three forcibly controlled themselves, the king turned back to the committee. "It is obvious that you are so backward you don't understand the basics of inverted time fluxes, coincidental occurrences of time loops, instantaneous time, zero time, moving time spirals, and other fundamentals basic to universal constants as pertains to life. In fact, all you know about, or fundamentally care about, is to live year-to-year and look forward to death in a plain old boring straight timeline fashion. I feel sorry for you.

"What do you know about wanting to help your own people better the quality of their lives, which doesn't mean getting somewhere faster?"

Beau, Sal and Jen were surprised to see the king so confrontational. Clearly he had qualities they had yet to discern.

"Here's my suggestion to you, sir," said the king.

"Come to Thuban . . . Planet Joe Smith, the planet named after me . . . by the way, how many do you have named after you? . . . and see what it is that we do, and run your own experiments on our time zones."

The king turned to his human companions and said in Pandan, "We can put him in Time Place 3 for a month and see how he likes it."

Sal replied to the king in UG. "I think a week should serve to age him ten years, which will help him understand your planet better." Her great exaggeration was meant for the council's ears. A week would multiply to some four months in that particular zone.

The king turned back to Bryne, "Matter of fact, if you do not want to help us insignificant little teddy bears, well, I feel quite certain my people can work with our human friends to acquire investors. Some people might call them very nasty, extremely wealthy, highly motivated pirates. We prefer to call them opportunists. Feel free to get cut out of the loop. And friend, it is my damn planet and I can damn well do what I damn well please with it."

Beau had done his homework and had coached the king on the ship. The king could not and would not lie, so Beau told him the truth—that he personally knew these pirates and had once belonged to their group.

Before they left the Thuban system for Earth, Beau and the girls time-probed Thuban 4 and found that it lay out of the time warp and could be mined without danger. Bryne had now given his consent for them to mine the planet. They would soon be wealthy beyond their dreams and he would rue the day he turned down their offer.

The pirate statement made by the king hit Bryne hard. He grimaced.

The king nodded to Ace and the pair stood again, gave the middle finger to Bryne as a final greeting, and prepared to depart.

The council shrank back in disgust. Beau laughed and decided against explaining about their digits and what they were used for. He would do that once the negotiations had concluded, if they hadn't already.

Bryne suppressed a grin. He hadn't been treated this badly since boot camp. His curiosity aroused, he said to the king and Ace, "Before we talk further, we would like to give you a tour of our planet. That includes our three human guests. Mister Cunningham tells me one of you is a king. Is that correct?"

Joe Smith answered, "I am king of my city and king of my planet. Can you say the same?"

"Have these three people helped your people?" Bryne asked.

"Yes, in immeasurable ways," answered Joe Smith.

"Thank you," said Bryne. "If you'll be so kind as to wait a few moments, I'll have arrangements made for your accommodations."

The meeting adjourned and Bryne walked over to the trio and shook their hands. "Quite entertaining," he said. "By the way, what did the king say to his assistant that made you laugh?"

Jen grinned and said, "First he called you an even fingered idiot. Then he said that you're so stupid you probably couldn't scratch your ass with both hands."

Bryne laughed out loud. His mind spun. He had heard presentations from alien races over the years. He had too much experience to harbor preconceived ideas regarding guilt or innocence when it came to initial meetings with them. This one was quite different.

"Well, thank you. Jennifer, isn't it?" He reached out to shake her hand and held it longer than necessary.

VII

There came the day ten Earth years later, when Joe Smith, the omnipresent king, Ace, Jen, Sal, and Beau met in the lobby of Hotel Smith in King City. The sound of slot machines sent musical chimes through the airways as beings from light years distant spent their scrip, and human and non-human waitresses plied them with free drinks.

"Mister Cunningham and wife, these tourists are stinking up my city," the king complained.

"And?" Beau replied, confused as to the significance of the complaint.

Ace, their best student of debauchery, spoke for his master. "The king would like to know if we can cut down on the number of killings and muggings."

Jen had been learning a business. After the All-Space meeting, she had decided to develop a new persona. She shaved off her hair and oiled her head in keeping with the new fashion she had seen recently on Earth. "King, with all due respect, we ask you to think of the money you are taking in," she replied. "Things could be a whole lot worse if Mister Bryne wasn't coordinating security on this planet and hadn't married me."

After Billy Bryne had toured the planet and dropped another hundred sensors, he became convinced of what he'd been told: The time zones were ground-based only and did not project upward. He requested employment. His reasoning was simple: He wanted to live a long time and do so under conditions of great wealth. His wife had left him years before for a more stable life and his daughter now served as CEO of All-Space.

The team was pleased to have him in the family. The man was ruthless—the kind of man they needed. He held the crime rate extremely low, despite the king's perception. To him, one crime was one too many.

"You mean the money *you* are taking in," the king threw back at her.

Beau suspected that the monarch would have a problem with certain aspects of advanced civilization. As such, he had prepared himself for this meeting. Sometimes, in business as in life, pushing forward can provide less angst than retreat. Isn't it more practical to seek forgiveness than to ask for permission?

Beau said, "King, look, this is only the beginning and it's too early to draw conclusions. We have been working out some things and we would like to present you with other plans for the planet, which of course, is now the most famous in the galaxy. People are paying extraordinary prices to live a long time in Zone 5, are they not?"

The king nodded warily and wearily, probably regretting for the nth time having ever met them. Everything had been under control—well, most things—until the humans showed up to add new problems to his life.

"With your permission," Beau continued, glancing at Sally who nodded her encouragement, "we can open up virtually the entire planet."

"And our indigenous population of Pandas can run the robotics to reap the profits from the high-yield agricultural areas," said Ace, getting into the flow.

"A certain percentage of the profits are theirs." Beau agreed. "In addition, your new kitchens are operating around the clock with foods from every world. We are also finding that certain non-life-threatening diseases can be cured overnight, such as the common cold. Aside from the money, that's what we call doing a lot of good for people. Forget the money, you are feeding a lot of hungry people."

"No doubt, yourself included among the starving," inserted the king.

Beau tried philosophy. "Sir, there is always a trade-off. You are providing longer life to people and that's a good thing. The trade-off is that you have to give up your old way of life. I understand your entire world is upside down. Nothing will ever be the same. And that's all right. Because that's what time does. It changes things."

"You are preaching to the preacher," responded the ruler with a trace of bitterness in his once calm voice. "Perhaps I have everything I could ever want right now. What will another few more billions of credits do for me except stink up my planet more? Next, you'll want to do something to my world to try and stop the rainfall."

"No sir, we don't want to do that and won't let anybody else do it for a lot of reasons. For one, we don't like messing with ecosystems unless we are terraforming a barren world; we don't know what the relationship is between the time zones and the rainfall and general ecological balance of your world, and like you say, how much money can a person make, anyway?"

Beau's answers came so fast and smooth that the king must have known Beau had given previous thought to the matter.

The rainy season of Planet of Joe Smith was built into the advertising campaign that had launched when granted the loan from All-Space. All involved had already received a return on investment many times over. One ad ran: "Looking to buy time? This is the place." Another: "Planet Smith: The only place in the universe where life keeps on giving." Still another: "Injuries too slow to heal? Lose a few years and gain hundreds."

What worked best was the time spent in Zone 5 when compared with time on other planets. That is, the depiction of the average family living decades, looking the same, and going back to their home world to find their relatives hadn't aged much at all. Even their bills wouldn't be too far overdue, given that any remained after their move to Thuban. The king was the only one who could screw up the entire enterprise.

In their luxury top floor condo, Beau said, "The fees we charge are incredible and we raise them every year, do we not?"

Joe Smith, Ace and Sal bobbed their heads up and down very slowly, watching Beau's every move, obviously confounded as to the dimensions of this new scheme.

To mark the moment, a spaceship could be heard landing somewhere in the ten thousand acres that had been cleared south of the city. Trams came and went from the capital city to the spaceport. Super City, Jen's old home, was a short shuttle flight away. In both communities, violence was met with instant retribution by banishment from the planet for life, another one of Bryne's' ideas. The thought of banishment served as the single most important deterrent the security force possessed for the maintenance of law and order.

"Despite this, we still have a thousand times more applicants than we can handle. Right?" More nodding. Sally splayed her hands outward in a "get-to-the-point" gesture.

At that moment, Beau wanted to say there was no point to be made. Initially, he had great uncertainty as to whether Joe and Ace would want to rule the galaxy. It is, after all, an undertaking that could keep one overly occupied.

Beau plowed onward. "Friends, Planet Smith, needs good people like you to concentrate their efforts here. If we go out into space you will age. We will, too, but that is our destiny. Why don't you govern here and we'll assist you? At the same time we will sacrifice our lives to traveling and helping others to get here and we'll take care of the business of ruling. How does that sound?"

"You mean we don't have to rule the galaxy?" asked the monarch. The two Pandas looked so relieved Beau thought they were going to give him the finger. Instead, they all embraced in a great big bear hug.

Beau had used the word "rule" the galaxy since "own" was a word foreign to the vocabulary of the Pandas, similar to the American Indians who couldn't conceive of owning land, something the Great Spirit had given to everyone. And a discussion of the concept of *time share* would fall on the deaf ears of the same Indian.

But own they did. They just didn't want to rule. In fact, years after Beau had presented his grand plan, he and Sal, the two bears, Jen and Bryne, owned a large number of planets and star systems and could do what they wanted with them.

A simple computer check had shown that only a

handful of the top rulers of their planet had even visited Planet Joe Smith since commercial operations
began. In most cases, in turns out that the benefits
had not reached their ears. This pointed to a flaw in
the advertising campaign.

The group's bank accounts weren't doing too
shabbily, either; never mind that they owned the
banks. They did quite well mining gold, silver and
platinum on Thuban 4 and selling it to All-Space.

Beau's offer to the large number of single rulers
of their planets and star systems went something like
this: Turn over control of your planet to the BeauSal
Corporation. Once you do that, you, and members
of the ruling class, can live virtually forever in complete luxury on Planet Joe Smith for free.

The thought of a very long life that smacks of
eternity always had a certain appeal. Eventually the
BeauSal Corporation came to own scores of planetary systems.

At Beau's insistence, the Capellans were to be
allowed free residency, no money wanted. "But why
that one alien group? What's your thinking?" Bryne
inquired, mystified.

"Because there aren't too many of them left and
we go back a ways," Beau answered, trying to make
amends for what he had done to them in another life
not that many years ago, no matter how it is measured.

There was only one thing better than living in
Time Zone 5 and being the wealthiest people in the
galaxy while doing so.

The monitors dropped by Jen, and later by Bryne, found that the time zones were not perfectly concentric. Beau and his wife were not completely satisfied with the original findings, so she asked the Pandas to make another thousand, which she launched.

Of a sudden, another area glared out of the data. Located in the middle of Zone 2 South, there existed an oval patch of dirt measuring two hundred by three hundred kilometers surrounded by a sea of short ground cover. The four had seen this seen this type of thing before on other worlds and it usually represented an area of toxicity unsuitable for life. That toxicity might be natural or man-made. Neither was the case here where time should be some sixty times faster than in Zone 5.

The three family members were sitting in the warm spa of one of their penthouses overlooking the comings and goings of spaceships, trams, aliens, and of course, money. Sally walked in holding a sheaf of papers, sat at the edge of the spa and put her feet into the warm water. "Guys, I got back the data from the newest batch of monitors. Look here."

"That's screwy," Bryne said, first grabbing the sheet of paper Sal proffered and reading it. "Bad units."

"That's what I thought at first," Sal said. "So I went back and dropped several more there and at the poles. The data are consistent. As far as the dirt patch, the entire thing got mapped, as well as the area outside of it. Look," she turned to the next page and passed it around.

"They're all in unison," Jen said, sitting up straight. "This is astounding."

The three climbed out of the tub, put on robes and stood in a circle, pouring over rows of numbers. A chill went up three sets of spines.

"You realize what we have here, don't you?" said Beau.

"I'm not that stupid, dear. After all, I did marry you," she grinned.

Beau stroked his chin. "Time running backward would explain the lack of vegetation. Probably a lack of bugs, too. See, the other areas outside the oval are running typically fast."

"Yeah, I see it as back-running *inside the oval*," Jen said. "The whole thing measures around a couple thousand square kilometers and now it comes to mind what the king had said way back when about time spirals."

"We gots us a freaking time-reversal zone," was all Bryne could say, his voice rasping with incredulity. "If Universal Galactic is 1, then that one little patch is minus 4.2. For every week there, we lose more than a month of age. Ten years there means we lose forty. We don't age much slower, we become younger!"

"Might you call that prime real estate, my dears?" Sal grinned.

"We better not tie one on and oversleep there, or we might not wake up at all," Jen quipped.

"This one we have to treat with great respect,"

said Bryne, who had let his beard grow in keeping with the fashion.

"Here's something else I've been working on," Sal said. She pulled up a hologram of the planet. Instead of showing land masses, mountains, oceans, and other geographical features, the rotating multi-colored sphere depicted time zone variations with a single bright red oval in Zone 2 to the south. Numerous ebbs and fluctuations were still-captured as they existed when the data from the thousand sensors had returned and processed.

Pointing at the floating sphere, Sal said, "See how that central yellow portion is fairly stable. That's us. Things get more warped and convoluted the closer you get to the poles."

"What are those little black dots?" Jen asked.

"They're ore deposits near the south pole where the time flux is enhanced where you were, when you checked out the two dead ships," Sal replied, lapsing for an instant sadly recollecting that one of them belonged to their father, "and a gray one where Beau was mining the copper."

"What is that rainbow colored perfect circle in Zone 5 on the other side of the planet?" Beau asked.

"It's a time whirlpool," Jen said.

"You mean like a black hole?" Beau inquired, scratching his head.

"More like a sloshing of time," Sal summarized.

"That's crazy." Beau looked over at Bryne for help.

The head of security shrugged and said, grinning.

"She's your wife."

"Maybe we should situate 10,000 permanent sensors around the planet and update this map on a regular basis," Beau suggested, trying to climb out of the hole he had dug for himself.

"Already ordered," Sal said.

Beau wondered if that bright red time reversal area might be the same thing as going back in time. Probably no more than getting older was traveling into the future. He mused that there may actually be spots or lines of time warps where such a thing might actually happen on this crazy world. Might there even be time tunnels? He'd have to ask the king about that.

"Can you colorize each of the zones," Beau asked.

Sal made some adjustments with her hand-held controller and different yellows, greens and browns appeared, some of them overlapping in place.

Beau said, "I'll bet you anything those are vegetation types were looking at also correspond to the time zones. Vegetation type is a function of rainfall, elevation, slope, soil conditions, available sunlight, and so forth. Here, we can add time to the equation. Something will reproduce faster, grow faster, and die faster in a fast-moving time frame so we can expect the plants should be shorter and more densely packed. If we look at the vegetation and correlate that with sensor readings, we should enhance our understanding of this phenomenon, excluding the fact that half the planet is oceans, lakes, and watercourses, which we know nothing about. Sal, overlay the two, if you will," he requested.

She did so. The images closely matched.

"Good call, Beau," complimented Jen. "It's interesting in that we have variations, probably because of ebbs and flows of the time variable which will cause changes in the plant growth rate. I'd hate to be a bear population living in one of those areas trying to figure out life. I'm having enough trouble as it is."

The group remained silent for a moment after that statement, each in their own thoughts.

Bryne said, "Except for the King Smith City and Super City where you guys lived, we don't even know how many cities there are on the planet, or if there are other intelligent life forms."

Beau responded, "It's a planet definitely worth extensive exploration. Regarding the oceans and lakes, if any sensors got blown into them, we have no data. Maybe something ate them. But as far as Sal's red zone, we need to keep that location quiet until we find out more." Beau's mind spun with possibilities. This little tidbit had nothing to do with money or power, it had to do with the nature and the meaning of life itself.

He added, "If it works out for us, I'd like to tell the king and Ace and see if they want to be a part of it." He knew his wife thought about the occurrence in terms of four dimensional Euclidean Geometry and space-time mechanics. It wasn't only that she was smart, it had to do with her ability to see things others didn't and her speed of mental data processing.

Beau reverted to scheming mode. "Once we start living in BeauSal Zone, people are going to notice us as time goes on. We'll need to think and talk before we tell and invite."

"Excuse me? Where did that name come from?" Sal said, in an accusatory tone?

"Call it a spontaneous reaction. I was trying to think of a name for our new home," Beau responded, defensively.

"It's going to be called Sally's," she declared.

"Sally's what?" he asked, looking at her a little squinty eyed.

"Not Sally's 'what'." The lines on her forehead furrowed. "Just plain 'Sally's'. Sally found it, described it, defined it, researched it, and named it."

The others gave thought to what she said before Beau brought them back on point. "We can bring prefab building supplies via ships, if we decide we're in a big hurry to construct our dream homes. One trip does it all. And any baby would have to be conceived and grow up elsewhere because it couldn't be conceived there."

"No worries there dear," Sal smiled, broadly.

"What? You mean that you, we . . . "

Sal froze her grin in place.

"Well, it's about time," Beau exclaimed. They all broke out in laughter.

Despite living many years in the equatorial region, the earthlings were beginning to show age-lines. A number of them had occurred during time spent off-planet, but Beau noticed that Sally had begun to examine herself in the mirror more frequent-ly. It's fair to say that a controlled amount of time spent in an area with time reversal would give them a different perspective on life.

"This means we can traipse around the galaxy all we want, as long as we come back here occasional-ly," they said, almost in unison.

Eventually, the foursome bought out All-Space. Even the board of directors didn't mind living in Zone 5 for a little trade-off. As Beau would say, "Hey, a man has a right to earn a living to support his growing family."

ARENA GAMES
(From Dying to Read)

Jeff expected to get a call from the senator any time in the near future. He leaned back in his desk chair in Lab No. 1 of his new institute and closed his eyes. Damn he was tired.

He couldn't stop thinking about what Carmen had told him about how his divorce was eating at him and how it had changed him. It made him give serious thought about what other people thought about him and the thoughts weren't pleasant.

The deep thoughts of Carmen that he shared only with himself; where would they lead? Would they lead him into more fantasies or would they lead him into an entirely new life that he could share with her.

The phone rang, and Carmen picked up. She looked over at her boss, head slumped.

"The president wants to talk with you."

"The president of what?" Jeff mumbled.

"The president of the United States of America.

Should I tell him you're too busy to talk and to call back later?"

Jeff bolted upright. The funk was gone. He stored it for later usage, something he was accustomed to doing. In his own view of himself, his mental storage locker was getting pretty full, and he needed to delete a lot of files. How he could do that posed another problem. He reentered reality. "Sorry. Of course, put him through."

Senator Evans was supposed to call again to see if Jeff wanted to take on the project. The last person he expected to hear from was the president. Somehow Evans must have convinced the man who now called him personally.

Jeff heard a couple of clicks on the phone line while a distant female voice confirmed his presence. Then there was a moment of silence.

"Dr. Shenero, how good of you to take my call. I hate to interrupt you during a busy workday," said the president, with amusement in his tone.

Jeff had to laugh at the man's ongoing sense of humor. "Sir, it's an honor to accept your interruptions."

Jeff's dark mood, his frustration—all vanished in an instant. It was as if a drain plug had been pulled and the foulness flowed away from him like so much detritus.

"Doctor, Senator Evans told me he spoke with you a yesterday about our problem."

Without waiting for a response, the president went on, "Remember Ochenko, the Russian, and Albert, your old friend?"

"No friend of mine," Jeff replied.

The president said, "Politics and world-class bad guys have occupied my time more than I like, and now the issue has recycled. From what I'm told, our people couldn't account for the entire amount of mold toxin the men produced.

"Thanks to your girl there, Marilyn, I believe, we now know that whatever is going on, it will occur either in Tucson or Phoenix. One of those cities is in imminent danger and the attack would involve a large number of people. He thinks it might happen on his father's birthday, which is coming up on August thirty-first.

"How soon can you get organized and leave for the Southwest?"

Jeff thought furiously. August thirty-first was two days away, and he wasn't given the opportunity to say no or to ask him his opinion. Basically Jeff had received an order from the president.

"Give me twelve hours," he said into the phone.

"Good. I'll have a Department of Defense agent meet up with you. Which city are you going to?" the president asked.

Jeff said, "Let's start with Tucson. I have a feel for the place and I was there recently."

"All right. The man you meet will be from my personal team, so we can pull heavy strings if we have to. Call the following number in an hour. We'll have your itinerary for you." The president provided the number and the extension.

"If there are no further questions, I'll wish you Godspeed."

The phone line went dead.

Jeff wanted to tell the president what he believed would happen and how it would happen and with what weapon. What if he was wrong? Besides, he didn't need to take up the man's time with scientific technicalities. With Paul now in England he'd have to go it alone.

Jeff walked over to Carmen's desk. He pulled up a chair next to her and gave her a summary of his conversation.

Then he added, "Why either of those cities?"

Carmen contributed, "Maybe Tucson because they owned the paper there and may have some connections."

Carmen put her hand on Jeff's arm. "I don't want anything to happen to you. I'm scared for you. And you know what? I'm always scared for you. I need to take good care of myself so I can stay healthy and take better care of you. You're my doctor."

Jeff needed to man up and tell her that it was their time to be together as partners. Was he too busy to do that or was he afraid of another relationship?

Once back at his home, Carmen helped Jeff pack. It would be very hot and the eight percent humidity of the desert summer could and would rapidly suck the moisture from a person.

After packing Jeff called the number he had been given and saw that there was time for a couple of hours of sleep.

At that point Carmen kissed him deeply and excused herself.

On Thursday morning, at 6:10, the Delta jet that left from Oklahoma City touched down at Tucson International.

Upon entering the concourse, Jeff was met by a neatly groomed, well-dressed, fit man in a blue suit. He was of middle age with a youthful face and short light brown hair. He was a man who radiated poise and confidence and who must have shown credentials to get through security. Jeff took him to be about forty-five. He stood at five-foot-ten, an inch shorter than the scientist.

Jeff's face was no secret, certainly not to the professional who greeted him and stuck out his hand.

"Dr. Shenero, I'm Brett Overton. I believe the president mentioned to you that I would be here."

"Nothing personal, sir, but I need to see some proof of that statement." Jeff was never in a mood to play games with imposters. He did mind impersonators, which included a wide swath of humanity.

"As you please, sir." His visitor produced FBI credentials, Secret Service credentials, a presidential envoy card, a badge on his belt, and a sidearm, which he revealed with discretion.

"My pleasure to make your acquaintance, Mr. Overton. You can call me Jeff."

"And you can call me Brett."

"It's a long flight from Washington," stated Jeff as the men descended to the lower level to the baggage carousel.

"I took a faster plane than you did and actually got here an hour ago. I did manage to get a little sleep on the flight," responded the agent.

Jeff made a quick call to Carmen to let her know of his safe arrival and with carry-on in tow, Jeff went with Brett to baggage claim and picked up a suit-case.

"Got mine earlier," said Brett in response to Jeff's unasked question.

Jeff followed the agent to the car parked in the lot and said, "Why don't you let me drive. I know my way around a little."

Jeff paid the parking fee as they exited the lot. Then he asked, "How's your mycology, Brett?"

Brett said, "A police science major in college takes basic biology and not much more than core courses after the first two years. However, I am up on my terrorist plots, which includes following your adventures."

Jeff laughed at his new friend's statement. The man was what he expected: trim, sharp, and witty. He gave off good vibes. The man could use a lit-tle outdoor time to get some color, though. He was about as far from Brewer as one could get.

What a difference there was between the two men with Brewer destined to spend eternity in pris-on without any of the money he thought well hidden.

Jeff said, "I've made reservations at the Sher-aton Four Points. It's fairly centrally located for our needs."

"Which are?" Brett inquired.

"Not much driving and great Mexican food," was the response.

"Next question. How's your knowledge of aerosols?" asked Jeff,

"Hairspray or otherwise?"

"Otherwise."

"Not much," replied Brett.

Jeff explained, "When mold grows on something, it sends runners called mycelium into the food source for nutrition like any plant does. Some molds produce antibiotics and some fungal toxins, we call them mycotoxins.

"If it's grown a certain way, say in vats, you can produce a lot of mycelium. The liquid and the mycelium will both have the poison.

"Now, if you freeze dry the pounds of mycelium you might collect over time, you can reduce it to a powder. You now have an aerosol. There would be only one reason to do that in my view.

"If it was me, I'd grind the stuff down to a certain size to keep the particles from clumping. Therefore, a trillion particles of pure poison will remain a trillion particles."

"I'm impressed," said Brett. Deep concern and fear was evident in the agent's face. "That's some nasty business."

"It gets worse, my friend," said Jeff.

"How so?" asked Brett, now staring intently at the scientist.

Jeff saw the fear in Brett's eyes and his inability

to comprehend that things could be worse than what Jeff had presented.

Each time Jeff's mind led him to his conclusions, the more certain he was that they were right on, and it gave him the cold sweats. He couldn't be certain that the terrorists even considered this angle.

"When you look at a pipe it looks flat, right?" Jeff asked.

"Right."

"And when you look at it end on you see it's actually a tube, right?"

"Right."

"Well, mold mycelium looks like that. If you see it under the microscope, it's a thread. If you look at it end on, it's actually tubular and it has segments. Each segment has DNA inside of it. This means that if you mince up the mold and plant it on agar, each of the segments will grow."

"I'm sort of with you. You mean it will grow on something like fruit or bread?" said Brett, not grasping what Jeff was getting at.

"Not just on something, in something," answered Jeff.

"Such as growing into the fruit or bread?"

"No, I mean like grow on human skin and inside lungs," answered Jeff.

"So if I drank it, I'm in trouble?" Brett continued.

"Or if enough of it is sprayed into the air to land on your skin or enter your lungs or both," was the answer.

Jeff paused in his narrative, then asked, "Did you bring a laptop?"

"Sure," said Brett.

"So did I. We're going to park ourselves in our room for a while, and we're going to do a little work. Then we'll go to the city waterworks to find out what we can."

"Like any employees they've let go recently, that sort of thing?" responded Brett.

"Right. FYI, no major food manufacturing plants are in Tucson, and the newspaper here got shut down and may never restart. Cosmetics are out because there is no plant here that distributes only locally. Same with food. I'm thinking that ink is out now, which leaves water and air for anything really big. What do you think?"

"Any sports stadiums?" asked Brett.

"Two that I know of. One is McKale Center, where the basketball team plays, and the other is the football stadium. Both of them are within a half mile of our hotel.

"Anything going on from your end?" Jeff asked.

"Yes, plenty. When I got my directive, I made a couple of calls and found out a lot about the air force base and the defense contractor here separate from the base. The defense facility makes guidance systems for missiles and satellites and half a hundred military items for both incoming and outgoing. You knock down either of those, and this nation will take a big hit.

"You don't simply go online to pull up technicals on either of them, so I asked our own people to pull out the specs. As far as both were concerned, we have a number of people in place so we don't have to do that legwork.

"Now that I know more about what to look for, I'll make more contacts when we get to our room," Brett added.

Jeff maintained serious doubts about people already in place. Brewer and Whitaker were well placed, and so were the senators and congressmen who were paid off in the newspaper scam.

At that moment Jeff pulled into the hotel lot and each man took his luggage to check-in and then to their room where they unpacked and changed into comfortable clothing. They ate a quick breakfast at the hotel restaurant and returned to the room.

Jeff opened up his computer and did some research on Tucson Water while Brett made his calls.

Having finished their work, Jeff said, "Let's see." He punched some numbers into his laptop. "The arena holds about thirteen thousand, and the stadium about fifty thousand."

"The problem with those is that this isn't football or basketball season," said Brett.

"Besides, what can you do in a football stadium with the stuff?" Jeff mumbled.

"A low-flying private plane could drop the powder during a game."

"That isn't our case here," said Jeff. "I suppose you could powder the place when it's unoccupied and wait for the people to come in. That sounds too chancy for these guys. They like a nice clean mass-poisoning job."

Then Jeff said, "Tell you what, in a couple of hours I'll call the city and get us an appointment with the director of water. He should be able to help with some of these issues."

At 11:00 a.m. the two men drove downtown to Tucson Water and met the director. A jovial and portly man, Rich Nordstrom's white baldness was natural compared with Jeff's slightly browned, shaved head. Nordstrom had held the directorship for twenty years and looked forward to helping the men as much as he could. They soon found that he also knew how to run a tight ship.

"Since your call, gentlemen, I asked our people to check the records. In the past year we've lost thirty-seven people—by attrition mostly—and we haven't replaced them, thanks to the economy, which leaves us with around four hundred. By the way, I also asked them to print out data on those persons you might want to look at."

Nordstrom continued, "We consider that number a skeleton crew for all the jobs we need to perform to serve the better portion of a million people."

"Such as?" asked Brett. They might have to do background checks on thirty-seven former employees, not to mention the possibility of checking on all of the existing ones.

"Such as ensuring that the water has no coliform bacteria and that it is properly chlorinated, making up tens of thousands of bottles of drinking water for various promotions and sporting events." Nordstrom went on for several minutes listing a score of duties that were necessary to operate a large water supply system for a city.

"Should I go on? How about billings and water meter readings?" Nordstrom was obviously proud of his work.

"What can you tell us about the people who left the last year?" asked Brett.

Nordstrom looked at some papers on his desk. "Well, some retired, others found better jobs, a couple were fired, a few moved out of state, took maternity leave, that sort of thing. And some we don't have information on their whereabouts."

"How do you have all that information about former employees?" Jeff was fascinated with the man's efficiency.

"Because we make an effort to keep up with them. Sometimes we need to gear up in a certain area and have the money to do so. While it's always convenient to transfer somebody over, that takes training and training takes money. Why do that when we can rehire somebody who is local and knows the field? That's worked well over the years."

"Let's talk about your present employees. I mean, do any of them desperately need money?" Brett asked sheepishly.

Nordstrom checked his fingernails. "We all need money, Mr. Overton. And desperation is a relative term."

Brett grinned. "I'll give you that. Here's what I'm getting at. Do any of them need money enough to sell their soul for a very large amount?"

"If they do, it doesn't show on their faces or their actions, as far as I know. They must hide it well," Nordstrom said.

"Those kind usually do," retorted Jeff, now out of his comfort zone. Something about Nordstrom's overbearing presence and sense of security irritated him. He tried to ascribe the feeling to his own problems of insecurity regarding real terrorists who had infiltrated his life. For a moment he felt as though he was trying to blame Nordstrom for his own weaknesses.

"Tell us about those reservoirs and also about the water bottles," said Jeff.

Nordstrom said, "You mentioned over the phone you were expecting somebody might try to poison the water, and frankly, I don't figure how or where that could happen. See, a good portion of our water supply comes from the CAP, or the Central Arizona Project. We get water from the Colorado River that runs here down a concrete viaduct. Along the way, it picks up a lot of minerals. Those minerals corrode our home pipes. We found that out the hard way. So now we blend CAP water with water from our aquifers. There are millions, if not tens of millions of gallons to deal with and frankly, where somebody might poison the water is beyond me.

"I suppose it might be at the point where we chlorinate the water supply or bottle it. As far as the reservoirs, the water flows in, and it flows out. Theoretically, I guess it's doable. And it is because of that potential problem that we keep tight reins on all those horses."

Neither man listening was impressed with tight reins where terrorism was involved. Their experiences dictated that the bad guys always managed to find a chink, and Nordstrom was playing the innocent role.

Jeff looked up from the notes he was taking. This was important, yet he couldn't get captivated by Nordstrom's enthusiasm or the prospect of checking out the possible areas where contamination of the city's water system might be initiated. Finally, to display a semblance of interest, he asked, "How many reservoirs are there?"

"We have six, and there are only a half dozen keys to the fenced yards that house them." Nordstrom stood and pointed to the wall behind him at a laminated map of the greater Tucson metropolitan area. He encircled the areas with the reservoirs using an erasable marker.

"Could you get us a guide who would take us to one or two of them?" Brett requested.

"How about tomorrow morning for that?" agreed Nordstrom. Brett nodded his agreement.

"Also can you give us a list of the employees you let go in the past two years?" asked Jeff.

"Right here." The director handed numerous pages of documents to Overton, who reached out to receive them. "I'm ahead of you," he said.

"Okay, now let's talk about the bottles of water you give out, if you don't mind," said Jeff.

Nordstrom detailed the process of bottling the water from its source distribution to the countless bottles that were supplied to various city-sponsored events.

At last, the two guests stood and prepared to leave.

Jeff suddenly said, "Oh, Mr. Nordstrom, would you know who to contact to get into McKale Center if we want to inspect it?"

"McKale? Sure. But why? The place is under complete renovation beginning last month and it'll be another month 'till it's finished," replied Nordstrom.

"Thanks," said Jeff. He didn't know whether to have a sinking feeling or to feel relieved.

The two men left the office secure in that they were purview to a lot of new information. Whether it was useful or not was another story.

Once outdoors, Brett asked, "I was told you were here recently. You didn't know about the arena being renovated?"

Jeff felt chagrined and quickly recovered. "Excuse me, sir. My mission statement at that time was to track down a national terrorist plot, not to keep track of sports venues in the city."

"Apology accepted," returned Brett, smiling.

Jeff laughed. Tragedy and impending doom aside, he was actually beginning to enjoy himself. At home he would be dragging. Now he was charged.

He wanted to get in a run. Unfortunately, time was critical. He checked his watch. "It's pushing twelve thirty. Let's go out for Mexican and reorganize. How does that sound?"

"Lead on," said Brett enthusiastically. "I'm also thinking that six million gallons per reservoir is equivalent to six hundred backyard swimming pools each. That's a lot of water and too iffy to me. Terrorists don't like 'iffys.'"

"Rumor is, they like to blow things up," said Jeff.

"I heard your sense of humor can be rather droll," said Brett.

Jeff started the car and turned on the air conditioning. Even though they were in a covered parking lot, the temperature was over ninety degrees.

Jeff pulled up the calculator on his cell phone. "Hang on a sec, Brett. I want to run some conversions. Let's see, fifty pounds is how many micrograms in six million gallons?"

A minute later he looked up and said, "Given that it's evenly mixed, all you need to drink is a half a glass or half a bottle of water to be dead five times over. Aflatoxin is one of the most toxic naturally occurring chemicals known to man."

"Can you test for that little?" asked the agent.

Jeff paused, the said, "Something doesn't feel right and I can't tell you why and yes, I can test for that little.

"Let's look around tomorrow morning anyway. Tonight we can check on the employees."

"Let me make our lives easier," said Brett. "I've

got a secure wireless fax with my laptop. Let me fax these documents to my people and have them take care of it. By the time we get back from lunch we'll check and see what they've got."

After Brett faxed the information Nordstrom had given them, Jeff drove the rental car and took them to a restaurant on south Sixth Avenue, laced with Mexican restaurants. He picked one and parked in the lot.

The men were seated and moments later were brought chips and salsa, which Jeff tore into. Brett followed suit and was quickly breathing fire. He gulped water.

"Considered yourself initiated," laughed Jeff. "Try salt, not water to neutralize the oils in the peppers. I call that the Chernobyl hot stuff that glows in the dark. Then there's the lighter Fukushima salsa and the mild type I call the Three Mile Island. Let's order you some light salsa, unless you want me to ask the waiter to bring you some plain ketchup."

"Moderate will be fine, thank you," responded the agent, a bit defensively, as the top of his head began to sweat.

Jeff called over the waiter and ordered moderate salsa in Spanish.

"Can you tell me more about your last visit here?" Brett prompted, trying to deflect attention from the sweat dripping from his pores.

Jeff took several minutes filling Brett in on most of the details of the MaHoud plots. Then Jeff began to chuckle.

"What's so funny?" asked Brett.

"I don't think I ever told this story to anybody. The short version is that I ran into a woman who owned and operated a fishing fleet in Nome, Alaska, where women out-drink the men. She said she was visiting friends here and got three DUIs in two weeks. Now she was headed to see the judge.

"I told her to get ready to check into the courthouse; just don't plan on checking out. Either that or to take off and go back to Alaska and don't make plans to come back to Arizona in this lifetime."

"What did she do?" asked an intrigued and curious federal agent.

"She offered to buy me a drink if I ever got to Nome. Then she turned around and went back the way she came. One of these days I want to go up to Alaska and see what happened to her.

"What do you think she should have done?"

"Can't say. It's not my area," said Brett.

After lunch, Brett received information on former water company employees. Jeff looked over his shoulder as the agent scrolled through the data.

"What's that, shorthand? I can't understand most of it."

"Right," responded Brett. "We get in a lot of information in a small space. None of the people we checked on so far has displayed an unusual amount of money or has any overseas connections or long stays in the Middle East."

"If somebody got paid a lot of cash, they might

have hidden it from the government for a rainy day," contributed Jeff, not quite willing to let it go.

"You mean hide it from the IRS?" asked Brett in all apparent seriousness.

Jeff narrowed his eyes, dropped his head to a forty-five-degree angle, and raised his eyes to stare at the agent from beneath dark eyebrows as if to say, "You're kidding." Then he broke out in laughter which caused Brett to begin laughing in turn as if it were a surprise that people actually hid money from the IRS.

After a moment, Brett sobered up and said, "Let's get back to our Tucson problem. We'll call Nordstrom and tell him we'd like to check out one or two of the water storage units and also the water bottling plant and see what turns up."

Jeff slipped off his shoes and lay down on the bed, hands behind his head.

"Today's the thirtieth," Brett offered.

Then Jeff looked at his watch and said, "It's two thirty now." He checked his computer. "That makes it twelve thirty in the morning on the thirty-first in Saudi Arabia. They're ten hours ahead."

"Which means that it could be happening here right now," responded the agent with a note of urgency in his voice.

Jeff remained silent.

Brett looked long and hard at the man on the bed with the deep scar on his forehead. "It's your call."

Jeff told him his thoughts and Brett made a call. He gave some authentication codes, waited a moment, listened, and then spoke for several minutes.

He made a second call to book a room in downtown Phoenix, satisfied that his instructions to local FBI personnel were clearly understood.

When he phoned the hotel in Phoenix, he received a less than courteous reply by a gum-chewing secretary with apparent nasal congestion. That is, until he identified himself as an FBI agent and a member of the Department of Homeland Security personally assigned by the president, and he would appreciate some assistance as well as her name. She stopped chewing gum, apparently having bitten her tongue, and graciously presented her name. Within seconds she made Brett's reservation for later that same evening.

At least that was how Brett reported it to Jeff.

Jeff could envision the poor woman on the other end of the line. He didn't care how cool Mr. FBI Man appeared on the surface, it must have felt nice to have that much power.

Within the hour the two men were aboard a Southwest Airlines flight to Phoenix. Both were busy working their laptops, scouring locales where an attack might take place. When they finally landed, they had a fair idea of where to start.

Once in their downtown hotel, Brett removed his tie and his shoes and lit up his laptop. He went to his favorites. "We've got a full dozen places where concerts are held, but most of them are outdoors. Even the new football stadium has a roof that opens and closes. Here in the Southwest it's almost always open, I would imagine."

"That leaves the Copper State Arena about two blocks from here. We passed it coming in from the airport. It's got a huge seating capacity at something short of 19,000.

Jeff's mind was calculating, spinning. "If you want to mess with an enclosed sports arena, you don't have to worry about wind currents blowing away and diluting your powder. Instead you've got a place where air is recirculated.

"Now, you get your phony repair crew to check the air conditioners when the game or whatever is getting started, and you load the fresh-air intakes with powder. While the event is in progress, you have a full three hours to saturate the crowd with your mycotoxin. I would call that a captive audience.

"I'll leave the rest to your imagination because, in all honesty, a part of me doesn't want to know. I will say this: this ain't no anthrax scare. You can get vaccinated for that. You can even get vaccinated for rabies and the bubonic plague and smallpox and diphtheria. You can't get vaccinated for this, either before or afterward. Even though you work for our government, you should understand what I am saying."

Brett Overton's review of Jeff's profile included the fact that when he mockingly belittled a person, that person should appreciate him. He should consider that as a compliment. Through his own experience, he also understood that his charge would be an impossible man to interrogate, should it come to that, and that the man was totally trustworthy and a patriot in the truest sense.

Jeff stretched and yawned. "My friend, it's been a long day. Let's set it up for the morning, do some more research, have a good dinner and get some sleep. In the morning we'll get over to the arena to see if that one holds any possibility."

At eight thirty the next morning, the two investigators parked in a slot marked "Staff Only" at the venue, climbed up a ramp, and knocked on a set of double doors. In a moment one door opened and two persons wearing hard hats greeted them. Each wore gray work clothes and brown work boots.

Jeff wore his usual brown loafers and khaki slacks with a polo shirt. A sports watch was on his left wrist and he carried a small briefcase. Brett chose a short-sleeve shirt and lightweight tan suit for an August desert day that would prove to be very warm.

"I'm Brett Overton, and this is Doctor Shenero. I'm the one who called," said Brett to the larger of the two. The other was a woman.

"I'm Bob Hinton, facilities manager here at Copper State, and this is Janey Swan, my first in command." The group shook hands all around.

Hinton looked fairly fit, although his face was craggy which suggested years spent on the hard side of life. Curiously, the man's hands were not as calloused as Jeff might have suspected. He noticed that the man also spoke with the slightest of accents that did not suggest a Southern drawl or an East Coast R depletion. If anything, his Rs were slightly rolled.

This suggested a foreign language influence at some point in the man's life, for whatever that was worth.

Hinton's partner was a fit woman about fiftyish, whose brunette hair spilled out of her hat. She possessed an all-business set to her jaw yet carried a friendly sparkle in her dark eyes.

Hinton said, "I was told that you suggested we might have a problem that we need to know about. Do you mind if I see some ID? Sorry. Rules are rules."

Without a word, Brett pulled out several credentials, showed them the badge at his belt, and let his sidearm be seen without being obvious. "I'll vouch for him," he nodded toward Jeff.

Hinton looked over the credentials as if could recognize a fake presidential seal from a real one "Okay with me."

"Who does the scheduling?" asked Brett.

"Let's go into my office," offered Hinton. "We can be more comfortable talking there. After that I'll give you the tour."

The four walked about a quarter of the way around the upper concourse to an inconspicuous door that Hinton unlocked. He turned on the light.

The office consisted of file cabinets, two desks, and several adjustable desk chairs. A whiteboard hung on one wall, and a detailed colored map of the exterior and interior of the facility hung on another.

Hinton motioned for everyone to be seated while Swan went to one of the file cabinets and pulled a manila folder from a slotted file holder on top of one of the cabinets that held a number of other folders.

She brought the folder to Brett and said, "This is a record of the concerts and various events we've held here for the past couple of months. The upcoming schedules are there, too. They're also listed on the whiteboard."

"How far in advance do you schedule these events?" Brett asked, looking from one to another.

"Sometimes weeks, sometimes months," replied Hinton. "They're either cast in stone because of a contract arrangement, or we pencil them in depending on a lot of factors.

"Last month we had a couple of exhibition basketball games between Russia and the United States even though it's not the season. There was also a rock concert, two political lectures, and a tech seminar with some great video."

"The real question is, what's coming up?" Jeff asked.

Hinton pointed to the whiteboard and read the red lettering. "Let's see. Today is Friday, so we've got Branch Hoag tonight, a rock concert tomorrow, and nothing till next weekend when we have a car show."

"Branch Hoag!" exclaimed Jeff, a little more intensely than he intended.

"Yeah, he sure packed 'em in about four months ago during that terrorist thing. Took home better than a half million even after paying arena rental fees.

"You remember that terrorist thing, the one run by the Hood brothers? If I remember right, some art dealer guy caught on to them."

Jeff glanced at Brett who smiled.

"What's so funny?" asked Hinton, glancing at Swan and back at Jeff. "You didn't know Hoag was coming here? Don't you read the papers?"

"No," said Jeff.

"And I'm stuck back East with limited exposure," said Brett.

Stuck, as in a member of the president's personal team stationed in the White House.

"Wait, hey, I know you," Hinton declared, looking at Jeff. "You're the guy, aren't you? I thought your name was familiar."

Hinton stuck out his hand and Jeff took it. To Jeff, the hand seemed a little clammy.

Swan ignored the banter and returned to business. "Well, we had a full house last time he was here although we didn't have enough security then. Tonight we'll be packed again, this time with a dozen uniformed police, and our entire staff will be working," as though she was the one who might have dropped the ball on deciding how much security was necessary and wasn't going to let it happen again.

"I thought Hoag was tied to racist rants," said Jeff.

"He is. He's added Muslim stuff to his repertoire." replied Hinton.

Hinton continued, "Don't worry, we have it covered. And, say, if you gentlemen are in town, why don't you be our guests?"

Hinton turned to Swan. "Janey, see what we've

got for VIPs left over down front, would you?"

Swan went back to the file, pulled out a drawer, and flipped through wads of tickets.

Brett said, "We'll take you up on your offer. Can you find us seats, say midway up, if it's all right."

"Got it," she said a moment later as she pulled out a pair of tickets. She walked over to the wall map, where she pointed to the seats they would have. "How about halfway around and midway up?

"That'll be section twelve, seats seventeen and eighteen on the end. That'll give you aisle seats, and you'll be close to the concourse, bathrooms, and concessions."

"Perfect," said Brett. "Now, I take it your physical plant is in the basement," said Brett.

"Yes and no," Hinton quickly responded. "In the basement we have electrical, water, sewage, some fire, cold storage for food, a couple of battery-powered golf carts for hauling, storage for extra chairs, general storage, a couple of forklifts, and a medical office.

"Up here, we have a half dozen food concession stands, another medical office, our office, a meeting room, and more fire control equipment.

"On the roof we have the air conditioners and connections to the air ducts. They go on every afternoon and go off an hour after the concert or the game, depending on our setting for the day.

"Janey, let's take these gentlemen where they need to go," Hinton said to his partner.

"Roof," said Brett.

Hinton walked to the door. "Okay, follow me. There're three ways to get up there, two access ladders and an elevator, unless you want to come in by helicopter, and it hasn't happened yet. The elevator holds only two at a time, and it gets stuck once in a while."

He walked them to where the elevator stood and then led the group past one ladder to a second one.

"This one will be fine," said Brett.

Hinton began the climb followed by Swan, then Brett, and then Jeff.

The roof was home to ten air conditioning units. When they opened the trap door and pushed it back, they stepped out onto the warmth of white reflected heat.

"When was the last time you serviced these?" asked Brett, squinting somewhat as they headed toward the nearest one. He reached in his pocket and pulled out dark sunglasses. An occasional gust of hot wind caught the four.

Hinton said, "Serviced them? How? The coils are cleaned as needed and the filters are changed every three months according to specs. We get ample fresh air through these louvers, and the air passes into a mixer of recycled air. Then it's all run through a series of steps, which includes pre-filtration, molecular filtration, and HEPA filtration. We're talking surgical room air filtration before the air enters the arena. This facility is state-of-the-art."

Swan added, "Basically, we slow down the cycle when the place is unoccupied, then speed things up before the crowds come in."

They reached the first unit, and Jeff squatted down to look at the intake. "When did you physically open any of these and look inside?"

Swan scratched her head behind her hardhat. "Oh, a couple of months ago when we cleaned the coils.

"We need to look inside them," said Jeff.

"All of them?" asked Hinton.

"Yes, every single one," responded Jeff.

"Okay. This is going to take some time," said Hinton with a twinge of frustration in his voice.

Hinton and Swan consulted their all-purpose tool kits hung on their waists and began to open the units.

Jeff and Brett visited each one of them together. Neither man saw any powder.

"It would help if you told us what you're looking for," said Hinton somewhat impatiently.

Brett stared hard at Hinton. "We're looking for something foreign, anything unusual. Is there any way to introduce, say, perfume into the air conditioning system?"

"Perfume?" Hinton repeated.

"Just an example," said Jeff.

"No," said Hinton definitively. "That is, not unless you do it from the fresh-air intake here."

Swan remained silent.

"We're going to need to secure this roof for the next couple of days and nights," stated Brett in such a manner that it put him in authority over everyone.

"And I'm going to need a copy of the files on each of your employees, including yourself, sir."

Hinton shrugged. "Come on down, and I'll give you the files to copy. As for security, we can padlock the hatches and pull the key on the elevator. If you want, we can get campus police to watch the ladders and the elevator. I don't have any more ideas."

Brett said, "We'll cover both days and hit it heavy tonight. We'll have plainclothes people in the audience along with your local police. Let's have a couple of police stand by the two ladders and the elevator to be sure nobody gets to the roof without our knowledge."

"Okay, I'll set it up," said Hinton. "If we're finished with the air conditioners, we'll put them back together again."

Thirty minutes later, with file copies in hand, Brett and Jeff walked the arena by themselves, trying to get a feel for the place.

Finally, by mutual consent, they left the building, and Brett pulled out of the parking slot, having removed a parking ticket from his windshield, to Jeff's great delight.

"I need to fax these off to Washington away from prying eyes, so let's get back to the hotel," suggested Brett.

"Good. I need to think," answered Jeff. The hour was nearing eleven o'clock.

After Brett completed his work in the room and Jeff made a few calls of his own, the men seated themselves in the hotel dining room and ordered a pot of coffee.

Brett said, "I'm starting to get fixated on this arena thing. Fixation and gut feelings are two separate entities; right now I'm trying to tell the two apart. I can't. They keep merging."

At that, Brett pulled out his phone and made a call. After a short conversation he hung up.

"The consensus is that water's out. Video camera around the storage units shows no activity except for a maintenance person who only carries a clipboard. Besides, it's not solid enough for me. Water flows in, and it flows out. And they're bottled up for their next couple of activities. To me water is a long shot.

"That leaves out Tucson," said Jeff, "unless your guys come up with something at the base or at the defense contractor."

"Guess we're stuck with Hinton and company," concluded Brett. As if to reinforce his beliefs, they could learn little about the former employees of Tucson Water and nothing from that avenue appeared to offer any leads.

The men spent the remainder of the morning, each in his own world. Brett spent most of his time on the phone, while Jeff made must-do lists for if and when the mycotoxin would be found.

Hoag's program was slated to begin at eight that evening.

By two o'clock Jeff changed into blue jeans, polo shirt, and sneakers. He brought a small briefcase. Brett wore a clean white shirt and a casual, smart, lightweight tan suit.

"Better leave your weapon here, Brett. I don't think they allow guns in the arena," Jeff chided.

"Guess I'll have to take my chances." The agent said and retained firearm.

Brett insisted on driving to the sports arena despite its close proximity. He wanted to have a vehicle ready at hand in case he needed to drive somewhere in a hurry. Once more he parked in a staff-only slot directly in front of the arena. This time he posted a government tag in the windshield that he pulled from a pocket.

"Forgot to use it last time," he confessed.

The men found their seats in the deathly quiet of the empty arena.

Jeff looked hard around him, scanning. "Something is bothering me, something I saw earlier and I can't figure out what it is."

An instant later, he exclaimed, "I know. Look up there, Brett. What do you see?"

Brett answered, "You mean those large slits?"

"Yes. They're air registers and they're part of the air return system that houses the duct-work. That should be in the mezzanine. Why didn't Hinton tell us where the filters are located? Asking that simple question escaped me when we were looking for the powder on the roof."

"That's the problem with simple things," philosophized Brett.

Jeff said, "Well, let's take a look. Swan should be around here somewhere."

The men got up from their seats and took the

broad stairway down to the lower concourse.

Swan was on the phone when they got to Hinton's office. She saw them and hastily hung up the receiver.

"Ticket sales," she said defensively. "What's up?"

The men could see her curly brunette hair was gray at the roots. Jeff wouldn't hold that against her. He was impressed with her personal strength in her position where she worked in a world of men. No rings adorned her fingers.

Brett asked her about the mezzanine.

"No big deal," said Swan. "Let's go."

Fifty feet from the office she opened a steel door with a key on her belt key chain, and they ascended a short stairway until they were standing in an area that encircled the arena. Every fifty to seventy-five yards, galvanized steel duct-work could be seen descending from an air conditioner in the roof. These transitioned to horizontal flex duct as they branched into separate ducts and air registers.

Brett inspected an area where a branch began. A fitting connected the vertical to the horizontal shaft. "Open that," he said. He wasn't polite.

"That's where the filters are located," she said. She reached into a case on her belt and pulled out her multipurpose tool. She opened it to a position and used the tool to remove the connecting portion of the duct-work.

"Slowly and very carefully, please," said Jeff.

She removed the two-foot portion of connecting

duct. Brett pulled a very small powerful penlight from his pants pocket. He peered into the curved duct-work where it ran horizontally from the vertical down shaft to the main horizontal feed.

"My God!" he said and crossed himself.

Jeff looked into the shaft. The filters were gone, and what he saw was not God, but the devil: a two-inch-high and four-inch-wide strip of tan-hued powder.

"It looks like somebody poured the powder from wide*-mouth bottles. How seriously demented is this?" Jeff tried to visualize the action.

Swan forced her way next to Jeff and looked at the mound of dust. "What is it?" she asked.

"Where's Bob?" asked Brett.

Hinton? I don't know," she replied.

"Let's open another one," ordered Brett.

One by one the ducts were opened, inspected, and closed. The filters were gone from each of them, and in their place was powder.

"Janey, I need you to listen to me," said Brett.

Swan's instincts told her they were looking at big trouble. "Yes, sir."

"The program is off tonight. We have a terrorist scare. We don't know if it's real or not so we need to take precautions. You are not to say anything about what we have seen to anybody, not now and not tomorrow and not to Hinton if he returns. However, I am asking you for assistance to do exactly what I tell you to do. Can you do that?"

"Yes, sir. I have the campus police and city police on speed dial at my office." Her lower lip began to tremble with fear.

"Hold on until I make a few calls of my own. We'll meet back here in a little while."

"One more thing, Janey," added Jeff, trying for a little personal touch. "When are the air handlers supposed to turn on?"

Swan checked her watch. "It'll be several hours yet."

"Okay. You must make sure they stay turned off. Can you do that too?"

"Will do," she said.

The woman meekly walked to the stairway like a whipped dog.

"I'll be right back," said Brett. He walked outdoors into the heat of the desert air.

"And I'll go with Swan and watch her turn off the equipment," returned Jeff.

Several minutes later Brett returned to find Jeff sitting at a desk making notations. "What now, Jeff?"

"Let's go back to the mezzanine so I can run some tests," said the mycologist.

The men returned to the ducts, where Jeff explained, "My guess is they poured this garbage in here with large-mouth bottles, something like fruit punch or sports drink bottles you buy anywhere. The bottles were probably filled from a master container which we may find if we look hard enough. That is what I would do if I was stupid and ignorant. Quite frankly, I don't think whoever did this was advised enough as to procedures and may have inhaled some of it and gotten it on their skin."

Jeff looked around. He placed his briefcase on an electrical box. From it he unzipped a leather pouch and pulled out a small test tube rack with miniature test tubes. Into each test tube he added a little of the powder he collected with a miniature spatula, holding his breath as he did so.

Then he took out a vial labeled sulfuric acid and added a few drops to the first test tube. To the second he added a few drops from a vial labeled methyl alcohol. He carefully tapped the tubes at the bottom to ensure the ingredients mixed thoroughly. He pulled out a small clamp and held the first test tube and passed a tiny butane torch back and forth across the bottom. Within seconds the mixture turned bright red.

He repeated the process with the second test tube and dipped a test strip into it, which also turned red.

"How does that work?" asked Brett, honestly curious.

"They're basic chemical tests for aflatoxin. They are very specific thanks to technology.

"And yes, it is definitely aflatoxin—B1, the worst of the worst. We have double proof."

He capped the test tubes and put the case back together again.

"What now?" asked Brett. "How's hazmat going to remove the stuff? I can't picture any way for them to do that."

Jeff's mind was whirling. "Unfortunately, you can't inactivate it with bleach or at five-hundred-degree temperatures. I might have another idea.

"They're not going to remove it. They're going to open the ducts and cover the ends with several layers of heavy gauge polyethylene sheeting, the same kind that's used to set up containment barriers during mold and asbestos removal. Then they're going to secure it with duct tape. After that they're going to cut the duct back about four feet and cap the other end the same way. Then all the duct pieces get hauled out to storage for later analysis and weighing. We'll worry about repairs later.

"So why don't you put me in touch with someone over at hazmat, and I'll tell them what to bring," said Jeff.

Brett did so, and Jeff gave the directives.

"Let's see if there are any more places where they've seeded the toxin," Brett added.

"There's another problem," Jeff continued.

He quit looking at the powder and backed off. If he was going to die, he wanted it to be from basic health problems, which to him would mean a heart attack as a result of running too far or eating too many hamburgers. He made a call back to his lab and spoke with his graduate students and gave them some dimensions of the pile. While he waited he took out his phone and worked the calculator on it.

A return call came within ten minutes. Jeff listened and hung up. "We've got a wide variation in our calculations for a lot of reasons. Our rough guess is that we're missing another five to ten pounds. That's huge. Not counting what we're missing, what

I'm seeing right here is a hundred to a thousand-fold overkill."

Brett pulled out a small digital camera from his left front pocket and began photographing a closed and an open duct system and the powder inside. "I'm going to stay here a few minutes and, like, make some calls. Why don't you get together with Swan and I'll meet you in her office."

Jeff was caught by surprise. Brett had let slip the word "like" in a manner similar to that of a teenager. His guess was that it was a daughter at home.

Swan was waiting nervously for the men to arrive.

"What stuff is it?" she said, seated upright in a well-worn rollaway chair when Jeff walked in.

"It's a powder-like substance that somebody purposefully put into the duct system. It may be harmful." He certainly didn't want to talk about mycotoxins or anthrax when the initial press release might use the term "bomb scare," at Brett's directive.

"What can I do?" she asked.

"Janey, I'm sure Brett is going to ask you a lot of questions, either that or one of his people will be here shortly to ask them."

"I didn't do anything," the woman pleaded, tears welling.

Jeff felt compliant and totally on her side, yet he understood the magnitude of the situation. He wanted to aid her in any way he could, yet the circumstance dictated otherwise. His experience with these situations was jammed into his hard drive to the extent that anybody might be culpable of wrong-doing or murder. He paused to wonder if that included himself.

Jeff forced himself to respond calmly. "Nobody is saying you did anything. If you can help us find out who did, you'd be a hero in my eyes. How about that?"

Jeff was making it up as he went along. He was definitely out of his comfort zone. Interrogating people was not within his purview. That element belonged to other people; research and investigative procedures were his domain.

Sirens sounded as fire trucks and police cordoned off the neighborhood around the sports arena and re-routed traffic.

"Hazmat is on the way," said Brett. "Janey, I need you to relax. What time did you get here today?" asked Brett.

"About eight this morning."

"Were you here all day?"

"No. Right after you guys left, Bob asked me to pick up some valves for a water flow problem we started having a few days ago. The leak happened out of the blue. It took me a good three hours or so to find the right parts. I guess I was back here before noon.

"Wait a minute." She pulled out a drawer and retrieved receipt for the parts she had purchased and handed them to Brett.

He looked at the receipt and had no further questions as he handed it back to her.

"And Bob stayed here with how many men?"

"He was here alone, as far as I know."

"How long have you known Hinton?" Brett continued.

Swan was starting to relax a bit. This questioning wasn't about her.

"He started here about six months ago, she said.

"What do you know about him?" Brett continued. "I mean, who hired him, if you know?"

"Somebody in the city council got him in, I think," she said. "He's a pretty quiet guy when he's not talking shop."

Brett made a call and checked about anything his people could tell him about Hinton. It turned out that the man was high on the wanted list. He relayed this fact to the other two.

"Check the airports and bus station. Hold on a second," said Brett into the phone.

Brett asked Swan to provide a description of a vehicle Hinton might be driving. She did so, and Brett passed on that information.

Then he told the pair, "We're going to have a lot of company pretty soon."

Jeff said, "Janey, there's a lot of this dust that is missing. Where do you think somebody would put it here if they wanted to hurt people?"

"I don't know. I can't think," she said.

"Is Hinton here all day every day?" Brett asked.

"We all come and go. It's the nature of the job," she replied.

Brett worked at trying to get the most information from the woman. "We suspect him but we're not accusing him. Now, you're saying that you've had recent activities here in the arena and everything was fine. Then he sends you for new valves and you're gone for some time. Then we find the stuff in the ducts. "Is that correct?"

Swan simply answered "Yep."

"The air handlers are run every day you have a performance, is that correct?" Brett asked.

"Yep."

"And obviously you both have the keys to come and go if you need to. Is that right?" asked Jeff, kicking himself for letting it come out as an accusation.

Swan became defensive. "I told you, sir, we all come and go. "I probably do more than he does."

"What do you do when you're not here?" asked the agent.

"I do have a life, you know," she replied.

"Which means what," persisted Brett relentlessly.

"Which means reading and working out."

"What about Hinton. What does he do when he's not here?"

"He has another job," Swan said.

"Which is?"

"He works maintenance at the airport. He's in charge of filtration systems for the airplanes and for the terminal itself," she continued. "He always comes back before the program starts."

Jeff ignored her statement. Hinton wouldn't be back. "Checking them over for what?"

"Preparing for insertion into the air-handling systems of jet liners and for the entire airport. He likes to inspect them to make sure they're up to his specifications," she said.

Jeff and Brett looked at each other. Brett pulled out his phone and motioned for Jeff to come with him outside the office. Brett closed the door.

The phone rang even before the agent could make his call. He answered and listened for a moment, then provided his own information to the caller. After he hung up he said to Jeff, "We ran Hinton's prints. His real name is Gregory Polterak, a Russian. He may be the intermediate man whom the MaHouds contacted to obtain Ochenko, and it was Ochenko who hired Stanley Albert to help him make the mycotoxin in the first place. We've been after him since even before then. The man reads, writes, and speaks Arabic fluently. Along with his Russian and English skills, he is very dangerous, as we've seen. Obviously, the man gets around and fits in well. He's the worst kind of sociopath."

Four men from the fire department hazardous materials division arrived, dressed for duty. Accompanied by Swan, Jeff and Brett led the group to the areas that required their attention. Jeff briefed them on what they needed to do to remove the threat.

Brett's phone rang as he and Jeff were returning to the office. "They picked up Hinton at the airport just as he was checking in with his supervisor. He was carrying a satchel."

"Tell them to confiscate any boxes that look like they have filters, large or small, and not to open the boxes or the satchel under any circumstances," Jeff said. "My gut tells me that a lot of the missing aflatoxin is in the satchel he brought with him. I'm also thinking that there's more of it here."

The men were conversing inside one of the main entry doors to the arena. Flashing lights from fire engines and police cars filled the streets and the early evening sky, while news helicopters circled like vultures riding the edges of rising hot-air bubbles.

Jeff stuck up his finger as a point to be made. "What Hinton showed us was the air conditioning system. What we also needed to look at was the forced-air heating system. I mean, if you were rigged to run A/C and the weather switched from hot-to-cold with a thirty to forty-degree temperature drop, you'd have to make sure your heater was brought into play. Even if that doesn't happen for a few months, it *will* happen when winter rolls around."

Jeff wasn't finished. "Man, in addition to the human tragedy, if it did happen, there would be absolutely no way to clean it up. Even if you blew up the building or blew it down, you'd release a cloud of poison. I wouldn't know what to do if we had to face that scenario."

Calmly, Brett called Swan, who was on the mezzanine with the work crew, and asked her to come down to the office.

"Why didn't you tell us about the heating sys-

tem when we asked about your air handlers, Janey?"
asked Brett the moment she entered the room.

"I'm not in the habit of correcting my boss anymore," she responded, crossing her arms defensively. "Every time I used to say or add something, I
got fired or demoted, so I learned how to stay out of
trouble. Job security is better that way."

"Where is your heating system?" Jeff asked.

"In the basement." She jerked her head in the
direction of a stairwell. "It connects with the other
ducts from underneath."

Without saying another word, she got up and led
the men downstairs to a large unit that was one of
the two heaters for the complex.

"It's set to go on when the outdoor temperature
drops below sixty degrees, and that won't be for a
few months from now."

"Disconnect the entire heating system," directed
Jeff.

Brett gave another order and watched her turn off
the timer to the unit, and he followed her to ensure
that she did the same to the second unit.

"Now let's open it up," said Jeff.

Hinton never mentioned the heating system.

Once again, Swan unscrewed the front panel of
the heater. She pulled it off and pulled out the flashlight. They all peered inside.

No powder was visible, and no filter was present.

"Damn, Jeff, nothing here," exclaimed Brett with
great frustration.

"Where's your return air?" asked Jeff.

Swan stooped down at the rear duct of the unit and unscrewed it to reveal a flat area that permitted air to return from the arena into the unit, to be reheated and sent out again through a vertical duct that led into the main ducting system. In that flat area, large mounds of powder stood like a line of foothills.

Jeff took off at a sprint to alert the hazardous materials team of their find. When he returned he found that Brett had opened a door to a storage locker and found all the missing air filters.

The three of them discussed and devised a method of disconnecting the ducts that led from the heaters to the primary ducting system and encapsulating the return air system. Then they would overlay the return air with polyethylene, cut a slit into it, and insert a closely controlled vacuum hose to remove the majority of the toxin. Detailing the area would have to wait for another day. So would buying another vacuum.

In four hours the work was completed. Jeff couldn't wait to return to the relative calm of his lab and the welcoming arms of Carmen. Brett would remain behind to brief other state and federal agents who would soon be arriving.

Jeff thanked his friend and his agency and said he was going to take a slow walk back to the hotel in the late-afternoon sunlight to pack for the trip home.

"Oh, one last thing, Brett. Could you do me a favor?"

"If I can," Brett answered.

"If you see old man MaHoud, tell him that his life is over, and it was completely wasted. One of his sons is dead, and the other one turned him in and helped us guide him to death row. Tell him his empire is finished, and so is he. After you tell him that, tell him that if there are any investors in his enterprise, they will be looking for a way get compensated for their loss. Then tell him to have a nice day."

"Should I mention your name?" asked Brett, smiling. "If you could be so kind," was Jeff's response.

The weather was clear and warm in Phoenix when Jeff's plane departed from Phoenix to Oklahoma City after arriving in Tucson only the morning before. He would have to return soon to oversee the destruction of the toxin and to ensure that all the toxin was gone. For now he could get back to the old lovable workload.

"Any comments on your adventure?" Carmen asked with her arms wrapped around her man's neck as she met him at baggage claim.

To Carmen's surprise Jeff kissed her deeply and then said, "Now, hon, I'm ready for some Chinese."

Jeff walked through four of the six laboratories that were now in use in the building.

He spoke with each student and professional high-end scientists, giving encouragement and guidance to each person he met. And learning from them.

Jeff knew their strengths and weaknesses, perhaps better than they did. *Researchers attach to their inner strength when encouraged by those whom they have high regard for*, Jeff knew.

Lab 5 had been reserved for foreign medical scientists who strove to better humanity and the final lab was reserved for the unexpected.

The phone rang.

"Jeff, it's a Mr. Brett Overton on your secure line." Jeff took his mind from research to focus on the caller.

"Brett, what a pleasant surprise."

"Jeff," Brett began with sincerity, "it is my duty to inform you that on the street you are considered bad luck."

Jeff's stomach sank. He paled. Was there more powder, more mycotoxin, something he missed? How did he screw up? What would be the public's retribution against him? Against his company? Against Carmen?

"Brett, where did I screw up?" Jeff almost stuttered.

Brett gave a hearty laugh. "Not you, Jeff. The word among the terrorists is that you are big trouble. They have superstitions too. Not only did you get the MaHouds and their cronies, we're recovering tens of billions of their dollars. How does it feel to be unappreciated?"

Jeff laughed, permitting oxygen to enter his lungs. "Brett, I couldn't have been a loser without your help."

"The president told me that you'd probably try to transfer the blame to someone else," retorted the agent.

There was a pause then Brett continued. "Here's what we've got so far. The short version is that Hinton's an Al Qaeda player of the worst sort. World class bad guy. We followed his footsteps back to Saudi Arabia, Syria, Russia, and Yemen. He operates—correction—operated his own network of terrorists that intermeshed closely with old man Ma-Houd. As far as MaHoud's sons, their role was as described; to pass on the poisons that were created by Albert and Ochenko.

"And while we're talking about Hinton, we might as well talk about Janey Swan, sister to Hinton; first name Afizah. Her specialty is explosives; blowing up buses filled with school children. They were both hired at the same time. Included in their hiring were city council members, state representatives and on up, people who were embedded for years in some cases.

"I hate to admit it, but Swan had me totally fooled. We caught up with her at the airport later that evening heading for Paris."

Brett paused in his narrative.

Jeff remained speechless.

"I know you're thinking of something. Want to share it with me?" the agent asked.

"I just came face-to-face with two the lowest scum on the planet with Hinton . . . I don't even want to know his real name, and his sister, and I spoke with them and shook hands and saw them in action and right now I feel very dirty. How do I deal with it, Brett? How do I scrub off the filth?"

"For me it's a little different because I have to deal with it head on so I have to train myself to be objective or I'd never remain sane. For you, you might try training your mind to flip to another subject when the thought of those two comes up. It takes a little practice, but it's doable. The simplest thing is to think of it as the world getting purged of a whole lot of filth."

Brett continued. "For what it's worth, Hinton has started having the shakes and is seeing visions every few hours. He even beats and tears at himself, as if trying to remove all-too-real creatures that cover his body. I'm told the attacks seem to be more frequent as time goes on. Also, he has developed rashes on his face and arms that he scratches incessantly. The strange part is that he has a heavy growth of white-brown threads coming out of all of his body openings. Our people say it's mold mycelium. Is that possible?"

"I'm happy to say it is," said Jeff with more than a fleck of sadism.

Then he grew deadly serious. He seemed to be doing that a lot lately. "Brett, that mycelium is highly contagious in its present form. He needs to be in total isolation and anybody who examined him in his present state needs to go on antifungal medication as soon as possible."

Brett contacted the necessary people to give them

Jeff's directives.

Thousands of people had escaped the horror of inhaling the countless fragments, each of which could reproduce into mold colonies within the body while the entire body was poisoned at the same time.

"Expect his medical problems to get worse," Jeff threw in for good measure.

He added, "I guess we made our own luck because we were diligent . . . and I'm

thinking you have a daughter. I hope to see you soon. And by the way, next time you're down here I know a great little Mexican restaurant that serves the best Chernobyl salsa."

"How did you know I had a daughter?" Brett was truly surprised. "Brett, have a wonderful day. Feel free to call anytime."

Clearly puzzled, Brett became almost flippant, "I almost forgot a small detail. The president asked me to thank you for your work in this case. He said to tell you to expect a present. He wants me to send you some tickets to come to Washington for a visit. How many would you like?"

"Would two work?" Jeff asked.

"You got it. Oh, last comment. The president is talking about awarding you the Medal of Freedom. See you." Brett hung up, having gotten in the last word.

Jeff turned to Carmen. It was her turn to receive a favor from him. "Excuse me, ma'am, are you ready to take a flight and pay a visit to someone?"

"To where?" she asked. "Visit who?" Carmen

said absently as she focused on pulling up files of accounts receivable.

"One guess," replied Jeff. "He lives in Washington, DC. And like it or not, you're going to get one hell of a pay raise," Jeff said, as he put his arms around her.

THE FLOOZY

My boxing skills had gotten good enough to where my manager offered me serious dough to take a dive, and being a stupid jock, I did just that. When I met him in his office to collect, he told me he felt obliged to keep ninety percent of the money and called it 'management fees'. I slugged him so hard that he and his dentist became best friends for years, which ate up his bank account and also brought my fighting career to an end.

After I did time for assault with intent to do great bodily harm and having contemplated my state of affairs, I returned to society directionless.

Out of luck and out of work, I heard that old man Dave, who owned one of the local pubs, and who actually raised me during my teen years, was looking for a new bouncer and a barman. I told Dave I needed a job and got hired to work full time. Apparently, I had become a local hero for busting up the shyster boxing promoter and had earned my badge of courage by doing time in the slammer.

One night she just appeared. Her short blond hair and delicate features were a perfect balance with the lightness of her step and the slim blue jeans that must have been painted on. Add the white sneakers that muffled the delicate steps of her small feet and you couldn't keep your eyes off her. She walk's into Dave's—a seedy, gnarly, little back alley bar in the same neighborhood where I grew up. Call her a floozy, bimbo, vixen, moll, or trollop, she was definitely not a dime a dozen ho. When she woke me the next morning, she thanked me for calling her nice names. It had been a long time since that happened, she said. Then she dressed and left.

I didn't see her again for nearly a year. Nothing much had changed in my life except for the passage of time. I was still a barkeep. For pay I got less than minimum wage plus tips along with a bed and toilet in the room above the establishment. Compared with jail, it was paradise. I worked the bar six evenings a week, closed it, and cleaned it. Then I locked it and climbed the stairs to my room. I got no discount on drinks—Dave was no dummy—and I managed a couple of hours each morning to clean up a bowling alley. I never stole from the register and actually made good tip money on weekends and holidays. Frankly, I prefer cleaning the bar over the bowling alley. In this neighborhood, bowling alley folks can be real slobs; people in bars have certain standards.

Then Floozy Suzi shows up again. I named her that in my fantasies because I couldn't remember

her name, if she had even told it to me, and besides,
I was pissed at her for just taking off. I must have
felt something for her. She was maybe eight inches
shorter than my six foot one when I straighten my
rounded and muscular shoulders. Some called her
good looking. I called her perfection. I had been a
part of perfection for a night way back when.

This time she had a black eye as slick as the ones
I used to hand out to others in my old boxing days.
She ordered a double Scotch, no rocks. I just stared.
"I remember you."

"Yeah, I'll bet you say that to every girl who
comes in here," she replied, teasingly, downing the
double in a single tilt of her head.

I'm taking a quick look around and see a lot of
heads turned in our direction. If I had to hazard a
guess, I'd say they're not looking at me. The place
was full. A while back I suggested to Dave that his
business would probably increase if he invested in
a nice flat screen TV (we had no TV up till then) so
folks could come in early to watch ball games or the
news or whatever, and while he was at it, he might
as well add another three tables. He did it and after
that, business boomed, especially on game nights
and my tips increased proportionately. Dave backed
off coming in to work except to help me out on those
big nights, leaving the bulk of operations up to me.
I had no problem with the responsibility and I kept
good records.

"True, enough," I tell her. "So where have you
been for the past year? I really missed you." If any-

thing, I'm an honest cheat. In truth, I never missed anybody or anything, except for missing a good fight, and this girl, who was maybe in her late twenties. I wanted desperately to reconnect with her, but had the skill level of a bumbling amateur.

"I've been out of town," she replied, ordering another drink.

Her intellectual response didn't give me a lot of information. Obviously, I found myself chasing ghosts and was about to throw in the towel on this babe—just another one night stand down memory lane.

Then she floored me as if I'd been sucker punched. "I missed you, too. You're Damien, the boxer. I'm Barb."

I'm a not a too bad looking square cut guy with a few facial scars and an okay mid-section. For an instant I felt like a man again, until reality set in. In my drunken stupor a year earlier, I must have told her my name along with some other stuff. I'm a pretty private guy and who knows what I might have said, but what they hey, there's nothing I have that anybody would want to steal.

When she said her name was Barb, I immediately thought of barbed wire, but let it go. She decided to pay up front, but hung around. We talked off and on for a long time until I closed the bar, cleaned up and invited her up to my penthouse for the second time. This was an eight-by-eight room with a single bed and a commode room with a shower you'd find in a mobile home. A four-drawer dresser stood against a side wall with half the knobs missing. A window opened onto an alley where the garbage truck came by each morning and the walls bounced off echoes of sirens to wake me at all hours.

Apparently, my boxing trophies situated atop the dresser still impressed her. She stayed until morning and neither of us had any serious booze. It was better than the first time, at least for me. I took her for breakfast at a greasy spoon down the street that I'd been going to as long as I can remember. She ate as if she were trying to fill some empty void. I found her charming with lots of colorful stories about her travels and with a great deal potential for success. Potential for what I couldn't define at the time. She seemed lonely. Maybe we both were.

You know how something is going wrong and you ask yourself what could be worse than this until something worse happens? Just like that I asked Barb if she wanted to marry me. I watched her process the information. The instant I decided to do a fast back pedal and retract the question, she consented.

Three days later we became husband and wife. For the moment, we renovated my upstairs apartment so we could both live there. She moved in all three dresses that she owned and a couple of pairs of jeans. She picked up a hotplate from some thrift store and we were as happy as two animals in a cage could be.

On our wedding night, I finally told Barb my story. After my dad left my mom, she killed herself with drugs and I bounced around a number of foster homes for years until my early teens when Dave picked me up and raised me. I got paid for helping out at the Dive and he paid for my boxing lessons. "You need them in this neighborhood, in case you haven't noticed," he declared. It nearly broke his heart to hear that I had taken a bribe in trade for a fall and I swore to him that I would stick to the straight and narrow from then on. He believed me and I believed me and he saw that I meant it.

"Dave's Dive" did even better once I hired Barb to help out. Guys used to come in just to get waited on. She knew how to flirt and earn the tips even when everybody knew we were married. I quit the bowling alley job. We raised prices for everything by five percent to cover the cost of the cable TV service and were filled to capacity most nights. Dave's gross income more than doubled.

There was rarely any trouble, unless newbees came to town. I kept one eye on them and one on the .45 beneath the counter. Generally, people steered clear of trouble in the Dive because of my reputation. I didn't stand for any rough stuff unless I could finish it.

After a while, Dave gave me a raise. I was a man of simple means, although between Barb and I, we brought in serious money. Dave never found a flaw in our finances because there was none to be found. Dave insisted I take the raise.

Dave was one of these big fat guys who had had a family a long time ago but they all moved away. He never took care of himself and one day he declared that he wanted to go away on a long vacation. Would I be interested in buying the business from him? Except for meeting Barb, that was the first time in a number of years that somebody ever floored me. She and I talked it over. We knew Dave had me on the ropes and there was no going back. I had no place else to go. I enjoyed pulling my own weight and becoming a street bum was not an option.

We bought Dave's Dive, kept the name the same, and moved into a real apartment located only a couple of blocks away. The neighborhood was still seedy, so we fit right in. Despite that, Barb claimed it was the best place she had ever lived in, having grown up with a dozen siblings in a literal shack and both parents abusive and alcoholic. I was her hero and she continually thanked me in the best way she knew how.

As a barkeep I know a lot of people and hear a lot of stories. I also make a lot of friends. One of our regulars named Ernie, a disbarred attorney who had served as a financial advisor, helped us to reorganize our own finances. His wife filed for divorce, threw him out and took what money they had saved. He still had to pay child support. So I made him an offer to clean the place because he didn't know diddly about bartending. He could live in the flop house on the top floor. He took me up on it. That gave me (us) hours more free time.

Barb and I went into our meager savings and bought Ernie's old '58 Chevy six cylinder stick shift. The thing ran on four baloney skins for tires, but after I changed the plugs, it got us around and made life a lot easier for us.

As a new purchasing owner, I had a responsibility to ensure the money was right and the place was tight. I had to clean out the cash drawer and count it to compute what I would need to order to load it up again before the next day started. I had to keep the cigarette and soda machines full and clean out the money from them each week. We made good money out of our vending machines. Thousands of coins add up. A lot of bars don't like to dilute their sales by having machines. All I know is, it worked for us.

It was quite an operation to be responsible for a business and Dave taught me to pay attention to details. I translated what I had learned in the ring into business. I became a detail freak.

Each day I had the responsibility of getting daily cash home and then to the bank the next day. I couldn't stash it at the Dive, and Dave trusted himself more than a safe, so when he showed up, he took the cash with him. The rest was up to me.

Barb loved to roll the coins and I'd take several pounds of coinage along with bills to the bank nearly every day because there was nowhere safe to keep it. One time, when we were on our out way out just locking the door, wouldn't you know it but two big guys pushed us up against the front of the store and wanted any money we had. One of them had something hard against my gut. Before I could say a word, Barb freaked and raked her long rock-hard fingernails down the side of the other guys face from start to finish. He ran, never to hide—evermore. I'm telling you ladies, this is perfect. The guy will never outlive this and make him easy for the cops to find. Barb's move distracted my assailant. I took care of him real good. Man, it felt great to loosen up the old ham hocks. The best part was that I became a hero all over again in my wife's eyes.

Barb is the brains of the outfit. I'm just the grunt, the man, the protector. When I get dealt a hand, I play that hand until the end. Yeah, I know enough to clean the toilets and collect and count the money. Now Barb, she trades in some cards for some others. Sometimes she'll trade in three out of the five, whatever they allow. She is always looking ahead, strategizing, planning. When she hooked up with me, her life changed, not because I'm some killer deal, but because the deck in her life got reshuffled and she got dealt a new hand, one that had a couple of bucks in it, maybe with a potential for a lot more.

Back to Dave. He didn't have any family that he cared about or cared about him, unless you can claim your bar as your family. The last time I saw him a few months ago when he stopped by to BS, he looked like he'd lost some weight. Right after that I heard from his lawyer that Dave's heart gave out. I figured I might have to get back into fighting in the old man division to make ends meet. Then, in the next breath, the lawyer told me to come down to his office. I set a time when Barb and I could get there. This couldn't be good, I thought.

Not having seen the inside of a lawyer's office

before, I didn't know if his was very nice or very average and figured that if we had to drive across town and not just walk down the street, it must be pretty nice. He asked me for ID which I showed him sufficient and he told me as follows: "My time is valuable as I'm sure yours is. Now, we don't need to talk about Dave's debts or his family. Suffice it to say that he trusted you more than any person he ever trusted and left you personally the bar and forgave all your debt to him. In short, you own the business and the building free and clear. All you need to do is sign a few documents. If you don't sign them, then the state will take over the establishment."

I can't speak for my wife, but for me I don't know where the turnaround time occurred. It might have been when I met her, but Dave still would have died and still left me the bar. On the other hand, he knew I had married and he'd met Barb and that could have sealed the deal. Or maybe it was just a fresh roll of the dice. You know, you try to get your fingers into as many pies as you can and eventually pull out a plum from one of them.

We were rich beyond either of our practical dreams. All the money that was in Dave's account went to me (us), the bar and its net profits went to us. I cut Ernie in on the deal because by then he'd learned how to pour a drink. So I gave him a raise.

We planned every single night. My wife was a delight and flowered. I gave her money to buy new clothes and yes, we moved into a middle-class neighborhood and got a newer car. With my blessing, Barb had applied for a job at a restaurant in a good section of town that paid a lot better than what she earned at the bar. Sure enough she got hired immediately as an assistant manager, partly because she was good with numbers, along with her looks, new dress, gift of gab, and well-kept mannerisms.

I can't understand why she began to drink heavily. I believe she couldn't stand success and didn't think she deserved it. She had returned to her roots. I would find cocaine in the home and became infuriated after I first attempted to become delicate. Aside from an occasional binge, I was never an alcohol abuser and never a drug user. Okay, I smoked. So what?

In the end, it hurt me to throw her out and file for divorce. But the bar was mine free and clear and maybe that was where I belonged. At least I could live in a nice neighborhood and drive a nice car and meet nice people.

I owe my better life to Dave and to Barb as I continue my upward climb bringing home six figures a year. I did that for a few short years, then got offered a half-million dollars for the business. I asked Ernie about it and hired him to be my financial advisor on the deal. Once the negotiations closed, I gave Ernie a hefty amount of money to make his life easier.

When that happened, again with Ernie's help, I invested some of the money into real estate. I bought some vacant acreage in a better area of town and sold it for a good profit when shopping center people approached me.

He also told me about this new company called Amazon. He said that if he had the money he'd buy into it. When I bought 1000 shares for me, I loaned Ernie enough for another 1000. Back then, shares went for $18 each. Nothing ventured nothing gained. The company sounded like it might go places. The next thing we knew the stock split 2:1 then 3:1 and each of us owns six shares for each one purchased. Some 25 years later the shares are worth over $3000 each. Once in a while I sell off a few at a discounted price if I need a spare million or two.

Gruff as I am, I found a good woman from a good family, quit smoking, and became a father. I traded my .45 for golf clubs and once in a while, when I get the urge, I'll go back to the place where I grew up, watch some sports on TV, and look around to see if there's anybody in particular who might show up unexpectedly.

WHEN THE DEVIL WENT TO COLLEGE

At 7:00 p.m., Jeff Shenero knocked on the rear door of the "High Life" CBD store. A moment later, Jerry Hughes opened it. Jeff saw that his old college friend had not changed much since the last time he had visited him and his family at their home some three years before. He wore the same genuine smile, slender, but fit physique, and cheerful dark brown eyes. The men exchanged pleasantries, both declaring that it had been too long since their last visit. Jerry motioned for the scientist to come in and take a seat in one of two leather swivel-armchairs that faced a desk. Jerry took the desk chair. The office was the size of large bedroom, simply kept. A single picture 11" x 14" of the Manoa waterfalls on the big Island of Hawaii hung on one wall, and a large window Jeff took to be one-way opened onto the next room where sales were conducted. A five-foot tall, *Cannabis* plant, stood proudly in one corner maintained under high intensity UV lighting above it.

Numerous books on marijuana farming and health benefits of CBD oil occupied three layers of book-shelves behind the desk.

Jerry began, "You told me on the phone you wanted to talk about the psychosis going around. I'd love to have you onboard, Jeff. It's killing our industry."

Jeff responded, "You know me. Normally, I don't get involved with things outside my field, but this one hit home when two of my best students had to drop out. One may need serious care. I know only what everybody else knows: that smoking marijuana is involved. I need information because I make a habit of not watching the news or reading the papers. Keeps me from getting depressed."

Jerry laughed. "I hear that."

Jeff turned serious. "Smoking weed has been around for a thousand years so why the sudden rash of psychotic episodes? They seem to follow the trend of states when they legalize the stuff. People commit crimes, are unable to be subdued, they take off their clothes and run around in public, a few have died from liver involvement, or get angry to the point where police have to be called in . . . it's almost like they're being poisoned. It's not just college students, is it?"

Jerry said, "Primarily, yes, it is. Used to be just hippies walked in, but the press reports it's happening occasionally among middle-age personnel. These days we get business men and women coming through the door and once in a while even they end up getting loopy, too. Experts tell us that a high percentage of those who do get affected also have students in college. You don't know what to believe. I'm starting to think it's higher education that people are allergic to."

"We're both in trouble, then," Jeff declared. "Fill me in. Tell me about the business."

Jerry responded, "This is medium-size outfit, but we'll gross $1000-$5000 a day. I own two stores. The tax revenue the state gets from the bunch of us sellers goes toward schools and roads, or so they say. They probably received a good $100 million last year. From my end, the problem becomes what to do with my profits because the sale of any cannabanoid that has over 0.3 % THC, or tetrahydrocannabinol, is still not legal on the federal level. CBD oil is supposed to have less than that so it's been okayed for sale under the Farm Bill. The federal law against the sale of THC a good thing because it keeps the feds from spending revenue received from the sale of our products on crucial needs, such as giving themselves pay raises. It's a bad thing because a new administration could shut down all the stores nationwide overnight.

"Our biggest issue right now is that the clinical problems occurring have become a federal issue because more than one state is involved; more like a couple of dozen states. I had agents come in last week to collect samples of everything for analysis. They're not ruling out terrorist involvement."

Jerry let out a breath. "That said, let's go into the shop."

Jeff followed him through another door that led to a room the size of a large family room. Jerry flipped a switch and light reflected off the gleaming white tile floor, not glaring, though. Shelving adorned three walls with glass cases on those three sides containing a wide variety of products. No visible fingerprints stood out on the surface of the case nearest him. A can is disinfectant spray and another can of wipes stood at the end of each counter.

"Whatever you want is here," Jerry swung his arm around. "We've got chocolate bars, fruit loops, suckers, CBD oil, drinks, gummy bears—new items come in all the time. What sells stays. This is probably what you're most interest in."

Jerry pulled a glass jar from a shelf lined with glass jars. All were filled with marijuana. "We've got different strains, grades, varieties, you name it. There are hundreds, if you want to get really specialized." He pulled the lid from one of the jars and gave it to Jeff to smell. "Recognize that smell?"

"Takes me back a few years," Jeff admitted, grinning.

"Take a close look at this." Jerry pulled a pair of tweezers from a drawer, lifted out a flower bud and put it the palm of Jeff's hand. "This is seedless, not the kind you and I used to smoke when it was hard to roll a joint and hot seeds would pop out to put a hole in our clothes. This bud probably has 10-20 times the potency of the stuff we smoked 20 years ago. And I'm not saying that's a good thing, because it's not."

Jerry pulled out a magnifying glass from the same drawer and handed it to Jeff. "Take a close look. Each of those little globules is secreted resin which has the highest concentration of THC compared with leaves. Roots are a different story. If left out in the air, the THC will oxidize and the potency will be lost. That's why you handle the buds with kid gloves and store your stash in the freezer."

"Keep going, the truth has to be in here someplace," Jeff offered, listening, absorbing.

"THC quantity and quality depends on a lot of factors: strain, species, intensity of UV light, whether the plants are grown in soil, hydroponically or aeroponically, methods of harvesting and handling, and so forth.

"Along with the THC, the plant also produces hundreds of side products, such as terpenes, similar to when you grow mold to get an antibiotic or fungal toxin, like you used to explain to me. We can filter those out by smoking a water pipe using white wine instead of water—white so you can see the impurities build up and know when to change the wine; alcohol, because THC and the byproducts are more soluble in alcohol than in water; and wine because it's relatively inexpensive."

Jeff said, "I don't understand. You said that the alcohol also filters out the THC. Why would anybody want to do that?"

"Because it's a matter of ratio. It's the byproducts that lead to flashbacks, headaches, sleeplessness, and a host of unwanted effects. Filtration will remove some THC, yes, but will remove a higher percentage of byproducts, thus providing a cleaner high and smoother come down."

Jeff put the bud back in the jar, which Jerry closed, and placed back on the shelf. "Are you saying we have a bad strain that is being sold nationwide?" Jeff asked.

"I wish it were that simple. The distribution of the varieties will vary depending on location, but not enough to make that difference. Believe me, this topic is the first thing we discuss during owners' meetings. You said you wanted to know about the business, so I'm tell you."

"Guess I need to go back to college, if I want to find out," Jeff shrugged, resignedly.

Jerry held up a finger and pulled out his cell phone. "Maybe not. You know my son, Andy. He's a junior now and belongs to a fraternity. He works part time here at the store for a couple of hours each day. He's very popular at school. I like to think it's because of his charming personality, but more likely it's because I'm his father and own the store. Maybe he can shed a little light on the subject with you here, because I couldn't find out anything from him."

Jeff chided, "So he gets volume discounts for purchases?"

"Not from me. Maybe from other dealers, but there are a lot of ways to make money in this business without selling dope to kids," Jerry responded, tartly.

Jerry made the call to his son, who promised to be

over within 30 minutes. Andy had always admired Jeff for his commitment to help people in need, not to mention the numerous awards he had received locally and nationally.

On time as promised, Andy knocked, then let himself into the back door of the office. Like his father, Andy was of medium height, somewhat bland in appearance, but with dark eyes and an honest smile. Unlike his father, he still had all his hair. Jeff stood to greet him, Jerry remained seated.

"Doctor Shenero, how can I be of service?" Andy asked, politely, extending his hand. The men shook and Jeff returned to the chair. Jerry motioned for his son to take the vacant seat.

Jeff told Andy what he and his father had discussed. Andy said, "Doctor, I don't smoke the stuff. I hate to go from zero to sixty in nothing flat. I'd rather eat a cookie and an hour later say to myself, "Gee, I think I've had a buzz on for a while. I'm probably the only guy you'll see in the business school library on a Sunday wearing a smile. Besides, my father will fire anybody who comes to work stoned. Although, now that I think of it, I did have a scary experience a month back when I took a hit one evening from a fraternity brother's joint, a guy I share a room with."

"What happened?" Jeff asked.

"Nothing happened to me. I just took a small drag out of courtesy. But my friend finished the whole thing, got sick as a dog, threw up, and had a terrible headache. We thought he caught the flu and had to put cold compresses on his head all night. It took him a couple of days to recover. We never thought it had anything to do with this psychosis problem we're talking about, we still don't."

"What happened to the weed you guys smoked," Jerry asked.

"Never touched it again. As far as I know, it's still in our room. stashed in the back of one of his drawers."

"Where did he get the smoke from? Did he buy it here?" Jerry asked, deeply concerned. "Think it was laced with something?"

Andy scratched his chin. "I don't know where he bought it. Could be from any one of a hundred places or people. I do know that before we smoked it, he pulled it out of the ground." Seeing the confused faces of the other men, he added, "The fad is to bury your baggie in the ground for a couple of weeks before smoking it, especially when your stash is fresh and still moist. Supposed to get you higher with less. It won't work if it's dried out."

"And you never noticed this before," Jeff inquired, puzzled by the practice. A crawl began to move up his spine.

"I told you, doctor, that's not my thing. Definitely not, after that happened," Andy responded, truthfully.

"What's the idea behind sticking it in the ground, anyway, to smoke bugs?" Jeff gave a half-laugh, suddenly feeling like he was either missing something, or on the hot trail of something.

"Beats me. I didn't seen any bugs in there, but the stuff was all fuzzy," Andy said.

Jeff froze. "Oh, shit." Could this be it? He had the sinking feeling that it didn't matter who the supplier had been.

"What does that mean?" Jerry asked, suddenly concerned.

"Andy, can you get me his stash or some that looks like it?" Jeff asked.

"Probably. What do you want me to do with it?"

"Can you bring it here and leave it with your father tomorrow when you come to work?" Jeff requested, looking at Jerry, who nodded in agreement.

"No problem. Glad to help," Andy replied, and left.

ASSOCIATED PRESS:

Famed scientist, Dr. Jeffrey Shenero, believes he has found the cause of the paranoia that has gripped many weed smokers. In his news conference, he said that there is a spreading practice of burying a baggie with pot in the ground for some time before smoking it. He discovered a mold growing on the pot. It is the same mold that produces aflatoxin, a deadly toxin known to kill animals and humans alike when it grows on foodstuffs. According to Dr. Shenero, when smoked, this mold can cause the clinical effects reported by the public. Those who smoke marijuana are advised to cease the use of this practice.

Complete Stories in less than 50 Words

THE PIRATE

Having one good eye was the least of his problems

The pirate captain lay on the poop deck, exhausted after the battle. He sported a peg leg, patched eye and hook hand.

Gulls circled overhead. He screamed.

"Dammit," he cursed. "Gull bombs me square in me good eye and I goes and wipes it off with me wrong hand."

THE PESSIMISTS

Two Men Share Views on the World

Two old friends sat on a park bench feeding pigeons.

"Vell," began the philosophy professor, "Vot giffs today?"

"Nothin'," shrugged his friend, "just killink time, vaiting to die."

The professor deliberated, nodded, then confessed, "Better dan me; at least you haff sometink to look forward to.

THE AFTER-PARTY

Another blond

Half-dressed and driving home from the party at dawn she gets pulled over for various traffic infractions.

Feeling embarrassed and defensive, she decides to pull rank

"Do you have any idea who I am or who my parents are?"

"Afraid not," groused the officer.

"Oh, darn it," she slurs.

THE JOCK

Love Thyself First

"Yo, I'm John." He hands out cards to three gym babes,

"And?" replies one.

"Here to assist you with your needs," he grins broadly, looking them up and down, then leaves.

"What an ass." another declares.

Overhearing, John thinks, *"They noticed my great derriere; can't wait till tomorrow.*

THE REWARDS OF EFFORT

Two Winos Converse

The old wino asked, "How much did you find to-day?"

The second held out his hand and pigeons flew.

"Wow, three pennies," declared the first.

The second replied, "My mother said I never was worth two cents.

I sure showed her."

THE VACATION

Stepping up as a Man

"How was the long drive to your vacation spot?" asked the friend.

The man answered, "The usual. Going out, she drove while I slept."

"Oh, then you switched off coming back?" asked the friend.

"Right. Then I slept while she drove," replied the man.

MICROBIOLOGY VS. ASTRONOMY

There is nothing new about a simple observation: The rules of nature repeat themselves from the smallest scale to the largest scale. Therefore, as a microbiologist, I found great interest in the article entitled *Why do Galaxies Align?* by Michael West. (Astronomy magazine, October 2020 Cosmos: Origin and Fate of the Universe.) To me, the similarities between a small universe dominated by bacteria and the universe at large are more significant than their differences.

When one wishes to count an unknown number of bacteria, nutrient agar is autoclaved in a flask. When the agar cools sufficiently, the bacteria are added to it along with a magnetic pebble and the flask is placed on a magnetic stirrer in order to "randomize" the mixture. Then the agar is poured into Petri plates. However, micro-eddies occur within the agar during the cooling process, the results of which are the formation of an almost infinite number of unseen microfissures, similar to what may have occurred in outer space.

Why can we extrapolate this from one to the other? Because when the bacteria begin to multiply, where the cooling is even on all sides, the colonies become globular to semi-globular in appearace, similar to globular galaxies, while those colonies (galaxies) that grow within the fracture lines themselves are flattened or slightly bulging on one side, the latter because of unequal pressure. This is similar to *galactic alignments* that present similarly shaped galaxies. Is that due to gravitational influence or perhaps due to unequal cooling. Indeed, some bacterial colonies are much larger than others and may be of different hues and colors such as white, cream colored, yellow and red; the latter two are radiation-related.

These are the readily visible colonies. On the other hand, some are so dim that they require a magnifying glass. I wouldn't be surprised that more would appear if the Petri plate was subjected to wavelengths ranging from infrared to ultraviolet. Some are close enough to merge, others keep their distance, but all reach a maximum size, based on available growth material (hydrogen vs. nutrients.) Let us not discount the presence of older vs. younger bacteria within the colonies. Some species exude agents that permeate the agar to prevent others from coming too near. Is that yet to be discovered in the greater universe where everything appears to be bound by gravitation, dark matter, and perhaps other factors?

In our smaller universe, clusters and superclusters of colonies are also evident, as "long filamentous strands of galaxies woven together into a vast cosmic web,"—so aptly noted by Michael West as regards the greater universe.

Eventually the bacteria within the colonies will die to undergo lysis on an individual, then on a grand scale. There are likely numerous other similarities. For example, forgetting preconceived notions, we can ask: What other influence might the growth medium between the colonies have on the development of the colonies; indeed, upon their survival? Finally, the surface of the agar offers a completely different environment where colonies appear as domes, fried-eggs or "swarming," because they are free from the constraints of the medium. Are there also radically different environments in the greater universe as demarked by clusters of very odd-shaped galaxies?

Perhaps it would serve us well to institute an in-depth study of the characteristics of the microcosm to better understand the macrocosm. Aside from the fact that stars don't self-replicate or that bacterial colonies don't rotate, our universe may not be filled with the living cultures found in a Petri dish, but it sure acts like it does.

www.ingramcontent.com/pod-product-compliance
Lightning Source LLC
Chambersburg PA
CBHW060259100726
47907CB00002B/206